THE BROKEN STATUE

THE BROKEN STATUE

A Novel

Bob Perry

iUniverse, Inc.
New York Lincoln Shanghai

The Broken Statue

Copyright © 2006 by William Robert Perry

iUniverse books may be ordered through booksellers or by contacting:

iUniverse
2021 Pine Lake Road, Suite 100
Lincoln, NE 68512
www.iuniverse.com
1-800-Authors (1-800-288-4677)

While some characters and events in this piece may be historically accurate, this is a work of fiction. Characters, names, incidents, organizations and dialogue in this novel are either the products of the author's imagination or are used fictitiously.

ISBN-13: 978-0-595-41090-3 (pbk)
ISBN-13: 978-0-595-85449-3 (ebk)
ISBN-10: 0-595-41090-1 (pbk)
ISBN-10: 0-595-85449-4 (ebk)

Printed in the United States of America

PART I

CHAPTER 1

▼

Clank…. Clank. Clank.

"I've hit something!" exclaimed a sturdy young man as he leaned on his shovel.

"Be careful," I said. "Let me have a look."

I must have been a sight on that blazing hot day, waddling on my old bowlegs to get a look at a piece of history many thought lost.

The hole was about three foot long, two foot wide, and angled down into the earth almost two more feet. The reddish-brown dirt barely covered the creamy-white treasure trapped in this earthen tomb.

With a grunt, then a groan, I knelt down for a closer look. "Could it be?" I gasped almost talking to myself.

Looking a little closer, I excitedly cried out, "This really could be it!"

Our sporadic searching the past two years had produced many small holes in Kay County in northern Oklahoma. During that time, our amateur expeditions had unearthed rocks, roots, and even a bone, although it turned out to be just a cow bone. This, however, could be the prize for which we had been looking.

The two young men doing the digging on this search should have been accustomed to my eccentric behavior by now, but when I dropped to the ground to lie flat on my stomach, they must have thought I finally was having the heart attack that my beloved daughter had warned about all summer.

"Charlie…you all right?" asked the concerned young man who had uncovered the find.

"As fit as a worn-out fiddle," I replied with a broad grin, "but don't tell my daughter I'm rolling around down here, will ya."

I am too old to lie on the ground and dig in the dirt. It takes me ten minutes to get the courage to climb out of bed every morning with all the aches and pains the years have brought me. However, it is rare a man my age gets passionate about a project and I had been obsessed with finding what we had been searching for—a lost and hidden statue. I could not wait to see if this was really it.

Brushing the dirt away, I reached down to feel the smooth, cool texture of polished stone. I worked a little longer until my shoulder cramped in rebellion, then I laid there just staring at the treasure.

"What is it?" one of the boys asked.

"A knee," I replied.

"Ya'ell", they both shrieked. You would have thought they had found an outlaw's buried gold or brought in one of those gushers from days gone by when all they had really done was help an old man find a bit of the past and in a way, a little of their past too.

For the next two hours, the boys labored to get a glimpse of what they had only seen in black and white photos. I had seen the statue many times in its glory days, when it stood majestically on the edge of a picturesque garden, carefully framed in a scenic vista highlighting its prominence. More importantly, to me anyway, I knew the story behind the statue and I longed to see it one more time. The statue had a story to tell. A story about what was and what could have been.

There was no doubt about it now. We had found it. The boy's labor had uncovered a woman's leg from the thigh to the toe, clothed in a long skirt and high-heel shoes.

My name is Charlie McDonagh by the way. I probably should have introduced myself by now, but my name and my story are not really important. I was simply a witness and bystander to extraordinary events and even more extraordinary people. I was born in Ponca City in 1900. Not many people my age can make that claim. Oklahoma is a young state, having been a territory until 1907. At eighty-nine years old, I am older than the state itself. My parents came to the territory shortly after the great land run, to stake their claim to new land and a promise of fortunes to come. Oklahoma was a wild land, a land of opportunity, and a land of opportunity lost.

"She's a looker Charlie," one of the boys said as he looked at the large portion of the statue still lying in the ground.

"She was beautiful, but she was more than that," I replied as my forehead wrinkled in thought. "She had troubles and tragedies, but she had her own kind of strength. You know that grit you need to get through life."

The two boys nodded politely, but they had no interest in the philosophies of an old man. By the end of the day, the lower half of the statue had been unearthed. We were somewhat disappointed to find the statue broken into so many pieces, but even in our wearied state, there was a feeling of euphoria and of great accomplishment.

Over the next several weeks, there was genuine excitement in Ponca City as people came to help our little expedition. In the end, people rescued over seven hundred pieces of the once alluring statue from the earth.

Each piece was carefully cataloged, photographed, and examined to determine its place in this shattered puzzle. At a local monument company, plans were made to reconstruct this memorial to a life past and a way of life long gone.

On a warm Saturday evening, my daughter Lizzy and her daughter Mary drove me downtown to have what would become my nightly look at the statue. Lizzy lives with me...or more correctly, I live with her. I hate to admit I need anything at my age, but children have been my great blessing. Mary, my granddaughter, is gracious enough to drive me on these nightly trips. For some reason the girls do not like me driving in the evenings.

Walking across Grand Avenue to the monument company gave me an uneasy feeling. I had avoided the place in the past, not anxious to imagine what my tombstone would look like. Now, however, in the display window sat the broken statue.

The figure was still beautiful even in its shattered state. The store lights glimmered on the polished, white stone. Bigger sections were easy to identify. The biggest piece showed a life-size, young woman from the waist down. Other pieces looked like an assortment of crushed rock...shattered pieces, representing a shattered life.

"Why do you come here every evening grandpa?" Mary sweetly inquired. "What's so special about this piece of rock?"

I gave her the standard answer about wanting to preserve the history of the town and leaving a legacy for future generations. It was the same story I had been telling ever since I heard the statue might still exist. It was the kind of tired and repetitive story an old man would passionately tell to polite, but apathetic younger listeners.

Mary was a twenty-eight year old beauty and I could not help but notice she was the same age as the woman carved in the statue. The woman's image captured in this piece of stone represented a young woman at her peak of charm; complete with youth, poise, attractiveness, and hope for the future.

My granddaughter and I were close, cut from the same fabric. Mary knew me well enough to know there was more to the story. Her cocked head, slight smile, and folded-arms told me I was going to have to reveal more.

"I knew her," I finally confessed.

"What!" Mary exclaimed, a little taken back. "You knew the woman in the statue?"

I sheepishly nodded.

"Why didn't you say so?" she questioned. "Why haven't you told everyone?"

I just looked at the ground and contemplated the real reason the statue had been my obsession.

After a brief silence, indicating I was not going to tell the story willingly, she asked, "Did you know her well?"

"Go ahead and tell her," my daughter Lizzy encouraged.

"Yes," I finally confessed. "In fact, I knew her quite well at one time."

"Did you know her 'quite well' before you met grandma?" Mary quizzed teasingly.

"Oh yes," I instinctively revealed, "but it was nothing like that, we were young and her life was…complicated."

"So, you know the story of the statue," Mary added.

"I do," I stated reflectively. "But the story of this statue is not really about the woman it's about the times and the place. She was only a character in this tragedy."

"A tragedy?" Mary quizzed.

"Yes," I spoke quickly as if I had just had an epiphany. "It *was* like a Greek tragedy and I saw it happening like a spectator in a theatre. The characters were noble yet flawed and eventually they were crushed by forces outside of their control."

"Poor girl," I continued. "She had so much and wanted so little."

"Sounds interesting," Mary said. "Let's get you home and have a cup of coffee. This sounds like a story I want to hear. How does it begin?"

Looking at Mary, I realized her generation was more or less unaware about the exceptional events and people that shaped her hometown. Reflecting on those times of hope and promise as well as the corresponding disappointment and heartbreak, I felt compelled to share my point of view about this unique time in history. I wanted her to know how greed, ambition, and treachery could ruin lives. I wanted Mary and her generation to know the secrets held in the stones of the shattered rock. As we walked toward the car, I began to tell the story of the broken statue. The events had been untold and trapped in my mind for many years.

"The story of the statue," I began, "is really the story of Oklahoma. It's about opportunities and opportunities lost. It begins with Ernest Whitworth Marland or as the folks around here called him, E.W.."

CHAPTER 2

▼

Ernest Whitworth Marland stepped off the train in Ponca City in 1908 with two good suits of clothes, an air of success, and not a nickel to his name. By age 19, he had earned a law degree from the University of Michigan and a reputation as a fearless card player. Poker games lasting until dawn were common and E.W. seemed to have tireless energy and stamina.

His law practice in Pittsburg, Pennsylvania thrived with a combination of competence, charisma, and driving ambition. Although a popular young man, he escaped matrimony until Virginia Collins captured his heart in 1903 when he was twenty-nine.

Virginia was a couple of years younger and was a woman of striking intelligence, beauty, and quiet strength. She was slender with flowing dark hair. Her calm demeanor and sensibility was the perfect match for E.W. Marland's risk-taking nature. He had been infatuated with her from their first meeting, but he also realized the practicality of a lifelong partnership with a woman of such superior charm and stability.

The match worked well and E.W. became a millionaire by age thirty-three, turning his law degree and an instinctive knowledge of geology into black gold from the oil fields of West Virginia. Through aggressive speculation, he had acquired significant holdings, all of which were lost in the Panic of 1907.

Many men would have quit, been discouraged, and tried a more ordinary livelihood, but E.W. Marland was no ordinary man. He would have been within his rights to blame the eastern bankers for his demise, since they profited from his early labors, but he was rarely a bitter or vindictive person. E.W. was determined to rebuild what was lost and learn from the experience.

A relative stationed at Fort Sill in southwest Oklahoma had told him about oil discoveries in the new state. Although friends and family encouraged E.W. to rebuild his financial security by reestablishing his law practice, the lure of finding oil was in his blood.

What I noticed as a dusty eight-year-old boy hanging around the train station was his shiny boots, a broad smile, and a look that said he was totally in charge of everything around him.

"Young man," he commanded, as he looked me square in the eye having just stepped off the train. "Do you know this town?"

"Sure enough sir," I replied.

He seemed to study me for a moment then asked in a comfortable demeanor, "Then maybe you could tell me the location of a good hotel."

"Yes sir. Are you here to see the 101?" He looked like many other travelers who came to visit the 101 Ranch a few miles south of town. The ranch sprawled over 110,000 acres of leased Ponca Indian land. It was a cattle ranch when founded in 1879, but by 1908, the ranch was a strange collection of cowboys, entertainers, and other characters. The popularity of the Wild West Show had made the 101 Ranch famous. Many tourists made the trip west to visit the 101 Ranch and to stay in one of the guest houses.

Mr. Marland looked kindly at me and said, "I definitely want to see the ranch, but I'm here on business and prefer a place in town."

"We have a couple of hotels, but the best one is the Arcade down the street."

"That sounds fine, thank-you," replied Mr. Marland.

"I can show ya' the way," I offered. "It's only a couple of blocks."

"That would be outstanding," he said with an amused smile.

I grabbed one of his smaller bags and headed down the street. The boys around the train station were used to giving directions and helping with the bags of visitors in town to see the 101 Ranch. This hospitality often resulted in a gift of a penny and sometimes even a nickel. Mr. Marland seemed to be taking in the town as I talked almost constantly on the short walk telling him all the history and benefits of the only town I had known.

The Arcade Hotel was a three-story building sitting in the middle of town. A porch below and a balcony above surrounded the whole structure. The white stucco exterior looked like a Spanish mission. The hotel had a dining room with nine servers and three cooks. I had never eaten there, but had often smelled the fresh baked bread from the kitchen. Ponca City was a small town, but the train station and the Arcade Hotel hummed with activity. The hustle and bustle of the hotel was in stark contrast to the quiet pace evident in the rest of the town.

As we entered the lobby of the hotel, Mr. Wiker the manager gave me a stern look. Mr. Wiker was a stocky man with a round face and spectacles on his nose. He did not like the local boys inside the hotel, but I tried my best to show the bag I was carrying belonged to a potential guest.

"Hello," greeted Mr. Marland. "I'm looking for a room for a few weeks."

"Well you've come to the best hotel in Ponca City sir," replied the proud manager.

"I'm here on business," Mr. Marland explained, "looking for oil."

"Oil!" exclaimed Mr. Wiker. "I think you are a little too far west. Frank Phillips and his brother are finding oil on the other side of the Arkansas River in the Osage Reservation, but nobody's finding oil here."

"Nobody yet," clarified a confident Marland.

Mr. Wiker carefully looked over this stranger before him and soon sensed the calm and calculating self-confidence of E.W. Marland. "Well good luck to you. Rooms are a dollar a day or five dollars by the week. Meals are available in the dining room."

As Mr. Wiker handed E.W. the sign-in register, E.W. reached into his pocket and handed the manager a letter. "Currently I'm a little short on cash, but I have a letter of credit from the First National Bank of Pittsburg that will vouch for my character and ability to fulfill my obligations."

Mr. Wiker's faced looked less than pleased as he reluctantly took the letter from Mr. Marland's hand. He studied it for a few moments. The letter stated in some detail the financial plight that had afflicted E.W. Marland because of the recent bank panic. It told little of Marland's lost fortune or the role the eastern bankers played in his losses. The letter did tell of his extraordinary efforts to pay all liens and fulfill all obligations although the result was his personal financial demise. The letter also vouched for E.W.'s personal integrity.

The letter had its desired effect and shortly, Mr. Wiker looked up and said, "I don't generally give credit, but it seems that this bank has a level of confidence in you and you seem to be an upright fellow."

Mr. Marland completed the transaction and received his room assignment. He then turned to me and took the bag I had been toting from the train station. Mr. Marland knelt down to look me in the eye and say, "What's your name young man?"

"Charlie," I replied.

"Well Charles, I don't have a nickel for you today, but I will give you a tip," he whispered and he knelt closer, "never miss an opportunity to make a new friend."

I must have looked confused because I did not comprehend what he had just said. He gave me a big grin, patted me on the head, and said, "Don't worry Charles, I will make it up to you later. You are, after all, my first friend in Ponca City."

CHAPTER 3

▼

The next several weeks, found E.W. Marland on a rented horse surveying the surrounding countryside. He had worked many wells in the oil fields back east and was looking for promising rock formations in the small hills and prairie of Kay County.

After returning from these expeditions, he would often walk about town exploring its streets and its people. E.W. was a curiosity to the people of Ponca City. The area was accustomed to a wide variety of characters from real cowboys and Indians to various performers working the 101 Ranch, including a group of Arabian horsemen. Many visitors migrated to the 101 Ranch to get a taste of the west they had read about in the dime novels. None of these visitors, however, had the commanding presence of E.W. Marland.

His dress, manners, and general appearance gave him the air of an English gentleman viewing his estate. He wore knee high boots with a suit coat, necktie, and vest no matter how hot the weather. His most unusual feature was his hat. The cowboys all wore broad-rimmed, well-worn Stetson hats and even the tourists sported their renditions of these cowboy hats to look the part. E.W. Marland, however, wore a distinctive fedora hat.

In an area famed for expert horsemanship, E.W. seemed capable on his mount. People immediately detected his intelligence and sensibility. Beyond formal education, he had a common sense allowing him to relate to the diversity of characters making up this former frontier land.

On one of his walks through town, he spotted me doing chores in my yard. E.W. walked across the dirt road to say, "Charles my good friend, how are you doing this fine evening?"

Somewhat shocked at such a cheerful greeting from an adult, I replied with a confused, "Fine sir."

E.W. made a few polite comments about my work and the neighborhood then asked if my mother or father were around. Dad was hard at work as a butcher's helper in the market downtown, but I went directly to fetch mother.

The McDonagh house was a poor looking place by most standards.

The three-room house featured a plank floor as the only luxury and always seemed to need a coat of paint. To an eight-year-old boy, however, the house did not matter. The three-room shack, a back-yard garden, a bed shared with two younger brothers, and shabby clothes were all I had known. Our surroundings were not much different from many in Ponca City. Some folks did better, others worse. As a young boy, economic prosperity did not matter much. With a father working in a market, we always had meat on the table and our family was content with what we had.

My mother had thick, dark hair and a smooth, tanned complexion. She was extremely shy by nature, but playful with her children. Her enthusiasm to meet my new friend did not match mine, but Mr. Marland was gracious and polite as he carried the conversation. My mother had a wonderful singing voice, but few outside of the McDonagh household ever heard her speak.

After five minutes, E.W. actually had her engaged in conversation. As an active and fidgety boy, this adult conversation did not interest me until I heard Mr. Marland say, "The 101 Ranch."

"I've ridden around most of the land around town and everyone insists, including your Charles, that I need to see the ranch," continued E.W. Marland.

"It is a nice place," replied my mother in one of her longer sentences.

"I was hoping to drive out tomorrow and wondered if young Charles could be my guide?" he asked.

I could hardly believe my ears! We had been to the Fourth of July rodeo once, but the 101 Ranch was a mystical place for any young boy.

"He was quite helpful my first day here and I haven't been able to properly repay him," Mr. Marland continued.

Mother never had a chance. E.W. Marland was persuasive, if he was anything. He could sell a raincoat to a fish. The arrangements were soon made and I was to meet Mr. Marland in the lobby of the Arcade Hotel seven o'clock tomorrow morning. He also asked if I could bring a bed role in case we needed to camp for the evening.

The excitement of tomorrow's adventures made sleep difficult. At dawn, I fed the chickens, quickly ate a cold biscuit, grabbed my bed role, and headed to town.

It was a cool morning and the fire inside the hotel lobby felt good. Mr. Marland was waiting. He invited me to eat breakfast. It was the first time I ever ate at the Arcade Hotel; in fact, it was my first time ever to eat at a restaurant. It cost twenty cents and I had never tasted bacon and eggs so good. The bacon and eggs, however, seemed somewhat average after tasting the buttermilk biscuits. I ate four biscuits, one with apple jelly, two with gravy, and one with sorghum and molasses.

Mr. Marland seemed amused and said, "I've never seen such a big appetite from such a small boy."

Mr. Marland and Mr. Wiker were engaged in an animated discussion after breakfast. These conversations would become routine and I later discovered they all involved Mr. Marland's hotel bill. Mr. Marland had borrowed a buckboard wagon pulled by his rented horse for our trip. The sun was higher in the sky now and its warmth made for a comfortable spring day.

Mr. Marland and I engaged in a typical conversation between a man and a young boy. He asked questions and I gave brief answers that were probably non-sensical to him. In retrospect, he was doing much more than passing the time. Mr. Marland wanted to know about the people living in this prairie land. Who lived where? Who owned what land? Who was related to whom? He knew the value of information and understood the objectivity of an eight-year-old boy in providing an innocent and honest perspective.

Mr. Marland was easy to talk to, not like most adults. He was playful and cheerful in his tone of voice and sometimes seemed like a kid himself. After awhile, I was comfortable enough to ask him a question.

"What's you doin' out here Mr. Marland?" I inquired, understanding even as a child that he did not really seem like other people I had known.

"Well Charles, I am looking for oil," was his factual response.

"What for?"

"I'm going to find it, bring it out of the ground and sell it."

"What for?"

"People need it. You can make a lot of money selling oil," he explained.

"Like a hundred dollars?"

He laughed a little then with a grin quizzed, "Is a hundred dollars a lot of money?"

"I guess that would be more money than a feller could spend!" I exclaimed.

"What would you do with a hundred dollars Charles?"

"I'd buy me a horse. I'd buy one for daddy too and momma, I would git her a new dress…from a store and buy my brothers and me all the candy we could eat."

"That's a lot," Marland agreed showing a broad grin.

I nodded and allowed myself to daydream about the fantasy fortune I had been describing.

"If you found oil Charles, you would have all that and more."

I listened with interest and disbelief.

Marland then used this interest to teach a little finance. "If you had ten one hundred dollars that would be a thousand dollars. Can you count to a hundred?"

I nodded…. although I am not sure, I could.

"Imagine counting to one hundred ten times, that would be a thousand."

I stared in disbelief and bewilderment.

"If you could count to one thousand, then count to one thousand one thousand times you would count to a million."

I feigned understanding though I did not fathom the concept by saying, "That'd be a bunch."

"Yes it would," Marland said with a little laugh and some satisfaction.

"What'd you buy with a mill'un dollars Mr. Marland?"

He grinned then said, "You can buy anything. Houses, carriages, land…more oil wells. When you have a million dollars they call you a millionaire."

His energy and charisma were captivating, although I did not really understand this conversation.

He hesitated then said, "A millionaire can buy better lives for lots of people. He can create jobs and wealth. A million dollars will buy you the power to make a difference, Charlie."

It was the first time Mr. Marland had ever called me Charlie.

After a few seconds of hesitation, he said with a wry grin, "I was a millionaire once."

"I thought you was rich Mr. Marland."

"'Was rich' is right," his countenance never changed dramatically as he continued. "I made a fortune, but lost a fortune too."

"Where'd you lose it at?"

"Well, it was really taken from me."

"Was you robbed?" I exclaimed conjuring up visions of bandits and desperados robbing Mr. Marland by gunpoint.

He laughed, "Yes…robbed. The bankers robbed me actually." He seemed on the verge of saying something else then stopped. "You have got to be careful with bankers Charles, they want their money back at the most inopportune times."

I did not always understand E.W. Marland, but I could not keep from listening to him.

"Money is fine but there is nothing like bringing in a well. It makes you feel…complete," Mr. Marland said as he looked away from me and into the horizon.

We continued and soon came to the bridge crossing the Salt Fork River. A makeshift tent city was strung out on the north bank of the river. These tent cities were common as people struggled to build towns out of the prairie, hoping to find an economic reason for their new town's existence. Mr. Marland stopped briefly to talk to a tall man named Bill McFadden before continuing our journey.

Although we had entered the 101 Ranch several miles back, the first sign of the ranch structures appeared on the south side of the Salt Fork River at the River Camp. The camp was a new enterprise of the 101 Ranch catering to tourists who wanted access to the Ranch attractions with more of the conveniences of town.

A group of about twenty, three-room cottages sat in a shady elm grove near the banks of the river. A water-well featured in the middle of the cottages, gave the place a sense of quaintness and order. The camp operated from May to November so a small group of workers busily prepared for the upcoming season. Everything was neat and freshly painted.

The headquarters of the 101 Ranch were located another three or four miles south of the camp close to the town of Bliss. The town featured a Santa Fe rail station, which connected it to Ponca City, a newspaper, and several small stores. The surrounding ranch buildings, however, dwarfed the town of Bliss.

The ranch enterprise was more like a small city. As many as 2,000 cowboys, performers, and supporting personnel called the ranch home. Blacksmith shops, stables, leather shops, and barns were clustered together. A large rodeo arena was prominently featured with surrounding grounds and booths resembling a county fair midway. The ranch had a café, a hotel, and a general store. There was bustling activity everywhere we looked.

Mr. Marland stopped the horse in front of a large adobe structure that looked like a Mexican castle. He invited me to explore the surroundings, while he headed into the main building. I was glad to oblige. The headquarters looked foreboding, but Mr. Marland strode in with a confidence that he belonged.

While Mr. Marland was inside, I ran from building to building trying my best to see the entire ranch all at once. It was nearly an hour before Mr. Marland reappeared with a man matching his air of authority. They spoke briefly and then enthusiastically shook hands. I would later learn the tall stranger was Joe Miller, the patriarch of the famous Miller brothers. The Miller brothers included Joe, George, and Zack. Together the brothers owned the 101 Ranch. Mr. Marland had made another new friend in Joe Miller, one who would forever help shape his future in Kay County.

Mr. Marland waved for me to come over. I ran across the yard from the corral that held the large reddish-brown stallion I had been admiring. He quickly introduced me to the distinguished man. Mr. Marland then put his hand on my shoulder as we walked away.

"Charles, we have been invited to a barbeque," Mr. Marland stated in a satisfactory tone as if he had just accomplished a mission.

"When we gonna eat," I replied. It was a little after noon and my four biscuits had about worn off.

"Are you hungry?" he questioned with a mock look of disbelief.

I nodded.

"The cookout is not till tonight, but I think we can find some sandwiches at that store down the way."

We had lunch and spent the rest of the afternoon touring the ranch. The Wild West Show was preparing for the upcoming season so we saw riders and ropers as well as people preparing props and costumes. The cowboys were playful and simply amazing in their ability with horses and ropes.

We trampled around the grounds the rest of the afternoon and I think Mr. Marland was as excited as I to see all the action happening at the 101 Ranch.

E. W. Marland had been looking for a change of scenery, something to take his mind off the failed business and conniving financiers of the east. As he looked across the open expanse of prairie crowned with a brilliant blue sky and felt the warm wind in his face, one could tell E. W. felt a freedom and optimism that had been missing for many months.

About six o'clock, we headed back to the ranch headquarters. There was a party of about 30 individuals at the back veranda for the barbeque. A variety of smoked meats, potatoes, canned pears, yams, and baked pies filled the air. An older woman called Miss Molly seemed to be in charge and was most hospitable. I was the only child in the group and stood silently by the side of Mr. Marland during the whole affair.

Mr. Marland took special care to be seated by Joe Miller. I found out years later that the jovial Miss Molly was the mother of the Miller boys. They served plenty of beer and I had the sweetest tea I had ever tasted.

During the course of the evening, it became apparent Mr. Marland's meeting with the Millers had not been an accident. His nephew stationed at Fort Sill had been friends with George Miller. The nephew had written his uncle before the financial setbacks in West Virginia saying he should come west and drill for oil. Frank Philips and others had found oil east of the Arkansas River on the Osage Reservation. As some of the largest landowners in northern Oklahoma, the Miller's ranch seemed a prudent business acquaintance for E. W. Marland.

CHAPTER 4

▼

It is said, "Iron sharpens iron, and one man sharpens another." This described the relationship between E.W. Marland and Joe Miller perfectly. Both were smart and intelligent men, but when interacting with each other they became brilliant, each building on the ideas of the other. By the end of the evening, E. W., Joe Miller, and his brother George separated themselves from the rest of the party and engaged in conversation about a variety of subjects as they attempted to get a feel for each other.

"What about the Indians, Joe? Do they cause the ranch operations much trouble?" asked Marland.

"The Ponca? No," Joe replied. "There wouldn't be a 101 Ranch without 'em."

Mr. Marland listened intently as Joe Miller continued.

"Poor devils, the government never gave 'em a chance. Sent 'em here with no food or horses just what they could carry from Nebraska."

"Except for old Standing Bear," added George Miller.

"That's right," agreed Joe. "Old Standing Bear took 'em to court."

"Who's Standing Bear?" asked E. W.

"Standing Bear was the last Chief of the Ponca in their home land on the Niobrara River. The government force-marched 'em down here after the Indian agent messed up their treaty giving their land to the Sioux! Hundreds of 'em died…including Standing Bear's son." Joe explained respectfully.

George added, "Yeah, Old Standing Bear got him a lawyer and took the government to their own court."

Joe nodded, "Standing Bear won the case. It was the first time the government ever said that Indians were people too. Standing Bear got to bury his son and return to his home, but the Ponca had to stay here in Indian Territory."

"Good land, but the people had no resources, no way to make a go of it here," George added.

"Daddy helped 'em though. Of course they helped daddy too," Joe laughed.

"What do you mean?" asked E.W.

"Tell him the story of the run, Joe," George suggested.

"Not much to tell," Joe started. "We rode in and staked a claim on the south bank of the Salt Fork River. Daddy had always admired this grass land while driving cattle through it from Texas."

"There's more than that E.W.," George hastily added. "Joe here rode a Kentucky thoroughbred racing horse that day. Fastest horse in the Cherokee Strip land run. Joe rode that stallion till it dropped dead right where the land claim was! Horse dropped dead on the spot, he was rode so hard. Joe put a marker in the land to claim it and later we put a marker there for the horse."

Joe sheepishly grinned, too embarrassed to tell the enhanced version of the story himself. "Daddy started with 700 acres, a few head of cattle, some horses, and some know-how about runnin' a ranch," explained Joe. "The Ponca had all this land west of the Arkansas River but couldn't feed their kids. Daddy traded 'em know-how for land."

"A hundred thousand acres of land," quipped George.

"Sounds like your father got the best of that deal," stated E.W.

"Maybe," admitted Joe. "But daddy respected the Ponca and their ways. Anything he could give 'em or get for 'em he did. These people don't want nothing but to be left be and eat. We've let 'em be and made sure they didn't starve."

George excitedly added, "Joe here's a Chief!"

"A Chief, very interesting," E.W. quipped. "You don't really look Indian."

Joe grinned, "Well I'm kind of a sub-chief…an honorary title so to speak."

"He's being humble," George interjected. "Chief Little Standing Buffalo requested on his death bed that the Ponca adopt Joe as one of their own."

"I'm impressed," said E.W. as he made a mock bow.

Joe Miller blushed at his brother's teasing and revelation of his relationship with the Ponca Indians. "Well, they're a good people. As much as I can, I try to do for 'em. It's respect. I respect them and they've respected me a little. I tell you one thing, no government Indian agent is going to mess with 'em on the 101 as long as I'm here."

"To the 101," George lifted his mug up in a mock toast. "Besides, half these cowboys couldn't ride if these Indian boys didn't teach 'em how."

Joe added, "Most of the cowboys got Indian in 'em if they didn't disguise their genealogy."

"Whose genealogy are you boys disputing now!" interjected a loud voice from the dark, as Zack Miller the third of the Miller brothers emerged from the evening shadows.

"Look who's draggin' in," observed George. "We was just tellin' Mr. Marland here about the Ponca."

"Good to see you again, Zack," Mr. Marland stated as he shook the young man's hand.

"These two been talkin' bad about me?" Zack playfully asked.

"How'd you git away from the Mrs. is what I'd like to know," asked Joe.

George grinned, "Zack here's a newlywed. Been married fifteen months and got a one-year-old kid. Do the math."

Zack grimaced, as Joe said, "Well there's no such thing as a full gestation period on that first child."

"I'm impressed with all the brotherly love," E.W. noted.

"We were talking about the Ponca," Joe interjected tactfully changing the conversation.

"The Ponca, most of 'em are all right. They don't steal…much," said Zack.

"You know they don't steal Zack. Daddy just gave 'em permission to borrow within reason," clarified Joe.

"You know I don't have no real problem with 'em Joe," Zack conceded.

"They're just like the rest of this state," added George. "Everybody here was run out of everyplace good. The Indians were marched here, then when the whites decided the land was too good for 'em we let any white man that had nothin' line up and stake a claim!"

"Don't forget the outlaws," quipped Zack.

"That's right, the outlaws," corrected George. "That makes my point. Every person in this state was either marched here, running away from the law, came for free land, or was run out of anyplace better."

"Are you ready to leave town now? It sounds like quite a place, don't it E.W.," joked Joe Miller.

E. W. did not miss the fact that Joe had addressed him in such a casual manner and replied, "No not at all. In fact, a place without pretensions is quite appealing. Everyone back east is interested in *who* you are or *who* your grandparents are rather that what you are. They would much prefer you to have a good pedigree than good character. I find the people here refreshing."

"Refreshing," mused Joe. "What a way to describe the characters around here."

"Speakin' of characters, I hear the Cherokee Kid got hitched this spring," announced Zack.

"When's his kid due?" chided George.

Zack pretended to throw something at him then Joe said, "Come on guys, there are some respectable people in the world. I'm sure the Kid was in love."

"Who's the Cherokee Kid?" asked E.W.

"He's this cowboy performer from the northeast part of the territory, I mean the state," answered Joe.

"A roper," added George.

"Darn good roper," added Zack.

"Can't keep his mouth shut though. I've never seen someone talk as much as that fella," said George.

"He does talk a lot, but a great roper. You see that trick he did with two lariats, when he spun the one inside the other?" Zack asked.

The other boys nodded.

George said, "He woulda' been good in the Wild West Show…but he talked all the time."

"Couldn't ride all that good either," noted Zack.

"Don't worry, he'll do fine," assured Joe. "I hear he's back from Argentina and on stage now back east."

"Is he Cherokee?" asked E.W.

The brothers all laughed.

"No, not really," said Joe.

"As white as you and me," said George.

"There ain't really a lot of difference between the whites and some Indians around here," Zack clarified. "You see if you want anything round here you'd better be white. Most of these smart Indians figured this out."

"They've inter-married and pretend to be white so long who knows? Look at that kid's mom," Zack concluded as he casually pointed towards me.

I had been so engrossed in their conversation of the evening I had almost forgotten I was part of the group. I did not dare speak and now felt uncomfortable as Zack had made me the center of attention.

"You're old Will McDonagh's kid aren't ya?" Zack Miller inquired.

I nodded, not really sure what I was agreeing to.

"Yeah his mother is Willie Cries-For-War's second cousin or something," Zack informed.

I felt like their eyes were stinging me as all four men gazed my way. Mr. Marland came to my defense. "I think you may be mistaken, I've met Mrs. McDonagh and I don't think she was an Indian."

"That's what I mean," exclaimed Zack. "She looks white, acts white, but her mother was an Indian who raised her white. Nobody would know."

Mr. Marland was silent.

"She don't get out in the sun much does she boy," Zack Miller asked.

I cannot remember answering though I must have nodded as I shook inside from all the sudden attention.

"And when she does, she's always covered up with long sleeves and a bonnet. It could be a hundred degrees out and she's covered up…It ain't just modesty."

Joe Miller finally put a stop to the interrogation. "It doesn't really matter Zack. If she's part of Willie Cry's clan, she's good people. Maybe she *is* just modest."

"I'm just saying…" Zack was cut off before he could finish.

"I'm just saying that this boy is a guest of the ranch and he doesn't want to talk about his mother when there is more interesting conversation," said Joe with some authority.

Thankfully, the conversation changed to more talk about the land, the cattle business, and politics. One of the housemaids soon escorted me to a room in the big white house where the Miller brothers lived and entertained guests of the ranch. Miss Molly was still up and greeted me warmly as she directed me upstairs. I fell into the softest feather bed I had ever laid on and thought about the day's events. The ranch had been exciting, but I could not help but think about the conversation this evening. I knew my mother was part Ponca Indian. It was not a big secret to anybody, yet Mr. Marland seemed to be taken by surprise. Could it be that he did not know he was the guardian of an Indian, although part Indian, boy? More importantly, would it matter? The day, however, had been wonderful fun and I soon fell asleep to dream of even more adventures at the 101 Ranch.

By the time I woke the next morning, Mr. Marland had gone. Miss Molly explained that he and her oldest son Joe had ridden to the Bar L Ranch about a day's ride away to check on some cattle. She went on to explain that Mr. Marland had decided to spend a few extra days on the ranch, but had made arrangements for Joe's wife to escort me back to town.

I was a little disappointed, but Miss Molly made me feel welcome, like I belonged at the ranch by feeding me breakfast and getting me ready for the trip home. Joe's wife Pearl was a beautiful and pleasant woman who let me ride one of the ranch's ponies back while she followed in a fancy surrey pulled by a pair of handsome animals. I was home in time for supper. It would be several weeks before I would see Mr. Marland again.

CHAPTER 5

▼

Summer came to Ponca City and I had almost forgotten about my outing with Mr. Marland. School was out and the weather was already hot. There was plenty of work to do. Chores around the house and odd jobs around town like picking blackberries kept a boy like me busy. The days were long, however, leaving plenty of time for summer adventures.

Walt Johnson was my best friend, and we were always on the verge of mischief during these months. Walt, it seemed, was on the edge of trouble most times. He was a year older than me, but in the same grade. My family was pretty well off compared to Walt's. His father was gone most of the time. In fact, I had never really seen Walt's dad. Walt and his mom lived down the street from the train station in a one-room apartment above a small café in a more rundown part of town. He spent most of his time, however, at my house and we were inseparable.

Although our town had ample activities to entertain a pair of young boys, many of our favorite pastimes required more than two. Walt and I developed our own little network of rag-tag boys that became our gang. We wrestled each other in a game resembling football and after dark would play hide-and-go-seek. There was fishing in the Arkansas River and where there was fishing, there would be swimming. If the water in the river was too high for swimming, there was a pond nearby. When we were not with the gang, Walt and I spent time hanging around the train station. We watched the tourists come to town and picked up an occasional tip for carrying bags.

Walt used to say, "The train station is the gateway to the world."

The train station provided a constant change of scenery as people came and went everyday. It offered a good source of entertainment for two boys looking for adventure. On one of these hot summer days, Walt and I were sitting under the shade of a big oak tree adjacent to the train station.

"Train's a comin'," observed Walt.

"Yep," I casually replied.

"Think I could stay the night?" asked Walt.

"Guess so, I'll have to asked mom," I said. Asking mom's permission and thinking of different excuses for why Walt should stay the night was a full time job for me since Walt stayed over most nights.

Walt was a tall blonde headed kid, with big front teeth and blue eyes. He had little guidance from adults, but was actually fairly well mannered…most of the time. He had learned adults were naturally suspicious of him so he had a way of putting on a polite persona that frankly made most adults even more leery of him.

We watched the train come to a complete stop. Familiar faces exited the train as well as the usual tourists. One of the last passengers to exit the first class Pullman car was an obviously wealthy woman wearing a nicely tailored yellow dress. The woman was petite, with dark hair pulled up making her features look like a china doll.

Walt said, "She looks like a good tip. Let's see if she needs help."

We combed our hair with our unwashed fingers, trying our best to be respectable.

"Ma'am, could we help you with your bags?" asked a superficially polite Walt.

The woman looked kindly at the two rag-a-muffin boys and said in a pleasant and soft voice, "That's very kind of you, but my husband should be here to meet me. I have quite a lot of baggage to be delivered to the hotel."

A hand clutched my shoulder quickly disturbing my momentary disappointment. At that same moment I heard Mr. Marland's voice say, "Charles, you aren't trying to court my wife are you?"

I was somewhat stunned to see Mr. Marland. I felt as if I had been caught red handed running the same elaborate scheme I had used on him months earlier.

Mrs. Marland seemed embarrassed by her husband's familiarity with us and scolded, "Ernest, you shouldn't tease these nice boys. They were only trying to help. They might think you're mean spirited making such an allegation."

Mr. Marland laughed, which made me feel instantly better once I knew he was only teasing us. "Virginia, this is my good friend Charles. He knows I was just playing."

I had wondered what Mr. Marland thought of me after that night at the 101 Ranch, especially after he had left so abruptly. It felt comforting to hear him call me his friend. His demeanor and tone of voice left no doubt that he held no ill feeling toward me. It was also evident he was excited to see his wife as he lifted her up with a big bear hug.

"Ernest, you're embarrassing me," she exclaimed.

"Don't worry dear, you're not back east you know. You will find people here much more relaxed and informal," Mr. Marland assured.

You could tell Mrs. Marland was uncomfortable with the public affection as she hastened to straighten herself.

"Virginia, I would like to introduce you to Mr. Charles McDonagh," Mr. Marland said as he gestured my way with an exaggerated hand sweep.

Mrs. Marland, having regained her composure, playfully gave me a curtsey and said, "How do you do, Mr. McDonagh?"

I was speechless until Mr. Marland asked, "And who's your friend, young Charles?"

"This is Walt," I replied.

"He and me were just seein' if folks needed any help," I added still trying to cover up the fact that we were hustling tips.

"Good to meet you Walt," Mr. Marland replied.

"Virginia, I have a porter from the hotel to move our things, but we surely have a bag for these two boys to carry."

Mrs. Marland smiled and nodded. She walked away and then quickly returned with a bag not much bigger than a purse and a small box. Walt and I took our cargo and began following the Marland's toward the Arcade Hotel.

Mrs. Marland rested her arm on Mr. Marland's as they strolled toward the Arcade Hotel followed by their two baggage handlers.

"What do you think of Ponca City?" Mr. Marland enthusiastically asked.

Mrs. Marland looked around the train platform deliberately and then said, "It is…provincial."

"Provincial?" Mr. Marland questioned with a smile. "Would have thought charming, quaint, or picturesque would have been more appropriate."

"There's nothing wrong with this place," Virginia Marland affirmed while looking devotedly into her husband's eyes. "It's just not our place. I appreciate your needing to come here for a visit Ernest, but seriously when are we going home?"

"This may be home for us. I've been riding around the Miller's ranch and have found some very promising formations," Mr. Marland argued.

"Mr. Marland," she addressed him in a mockingly formal tone, "when I met you…when I married you…"

"For better or worse," Mr. Marland interrupted.

"You were a promising, almost successful attorney in Pittsburg," she continued. "You left your wife alone entirely too often looking for oil."

"And I found it and bought you a deserving lifestyle," he added.

"That you did, and then you lost it." Mrs. Marland regretted making this last statement seeing the hurt in Mr. Marland's eyes. She quickly added, "Which was great with me, because then I got to see my husband more often."

This turned out to be an extraordinary conversation between the Marland couple. Not because of the content, but because Mrs. Marland, I would later discover, never talked so casually in front of anyone but Mr. Marland. She was always a very respectful wife and would have never questioned him in public. It was also the first time and one of the only times I could remember anyone, calling E. W. Marland, Ernest.

Mr. Marland walked a few steps in reflection then said, "I know it must be hard to understand, but I feel alive when I'm looking for something valuable. I feel that I'm producing something of value."

"Lawyers make a nice living," she added.

"It's not about money. Don't get me wrong I want to spoil you and make more money than you can spend, but practicing law is working on other people's accomplishments more than mine. It's…hard to explain."

"No need to explain. Like you said, I'm here now for better or for worse," she said with a sly smile.

Mr. Marland smiled and said, "Yes you are…and speaking of being here, welcome to the Arcade Hotel."

Our foursome had arrived at the front steps of what was to become the Marland's first home in Ponca City. The couple thanked us for our efforts as we clumsily set the small bags down in the lobby. Mr. Marland gave us both a piece of hard candy. Mrs. Marland took special care to thank us and invited us to come and visit her. We ran out the front door of the Arcade Hotel with our wages in hand to see what other events the day might have in store.

The Marlands settled into a three-room suite on the top floor. Mrs. Marland would become the standard for sophistication in Ponca City. She was surely the most educated, intelligent, and cultured woman the young city had ever seen. Virginia would become much more visible to the citizens of the town than her husband would in these early years. Mr. Marland was prospecting for oil while Mrs. Marland was managing their affairs in town, including the job of pacifying the many creditors E. W. Marland was accumulating.

Virginia Marland was the perfect balance for E. W. Marland. She had the pragmatism to control his passion and ambition. She was a private person who liked to keep to herself, although she was involved in many community causes. People had the sense she had influence over E. W., although he had the outgoing personality and charisma. She also loved children, especially ornery little boys. In a painful irony, she and Mr. Marland had none, which is one reason the children of Ponca City were to become so familiar with Virginia Marland.

The Marland's were official residents of Ponca City. Hopes were high and optimism surrounded the both of them. The sculptor's chisel, however, was already forming their destiny. The day Virginia Marland arrived in town was a bright and cheerful beginning to the fateful tragedy destined to haunt this charmed couple.

CHAPTER 6

▼

E.W. Marland secured the rights to drill his first well on the 101 Ranch and busily made preparations to set up the rig. He had wanted to drill further east on the Ponca reservation, but found it easier to get permission from the Miller brothers than the Ponca Indians. We did not see much of him during this time. Walt and I, however, became friends with Mrs. Marland while he was away looking for oil. She read to us several times a week and always seemed to enjoy our tales of adventure. Mrs. Marland was especially fond of Walt. Since he lived closer to downtown, he spent time with her most days.

By the end of summer, Walt and I felt we had done everything there was to do in our town. We had swam, played ball, gone on hikes, and played pirates. On a mid-week afternoon on a late summer day, I found myself aimlessly sitting under the big oak tree next to the train station with Walt.

"Ya' want'a see something?" Walt asked with a twisted smirk.

I stopped scratching the dirt with a stick as Walt leaned over to show me what appeared to be a small brown brick he was carrying in his pocket.

"Look what I got," he whispered.

I looked at it with some interest.

"What is it?" I asked.

"It's tobacco," Walt stated smugly.

"Where'd you git it?" I inquired.

"Found it," Walt replied. Walt had a knack of finding all kinds of contraband.

"What'cha gonna do with it?" I asked already knowing the probable answer.

"We're goin' to try it." Walt declared. "Come on," He directed as we headed away from downtown and the train station.

"Where we going?" I quizzed.

"We need to get away from here. I don't want anyone but us using this," he replied.

We walked quickly and sometimes ran about a mile out of town to a place called Red Bud Creek. The creek was little more than a dry ditch this time of year, but it was secluded in a shady area and had a nice wooden bridge to sit on. Walt took the brick of tobacco out of his overalls pocket and carefully examined it again.

"Do you know how?" I asked warily. "It looks kind'a hard."

"Sure, you just take a bite and chew," Walt instructed as he bit into the corner of the brown square. He grimaced as his taste buds experienced the new sensation. "It's smooth," Walt assured, somewhat unconvincingly.

Walt handed me the remains. I looked intently at it before finally giving it a sniff.

"Ain't you goin' to try some?" Walt chided.

I did not reply. I had seen the old men around town chew tobacco many times, but seeing them spit never made me think it was something I wanted to do.

"Well, come on," Walt badgered impatiently, "are ya chicken?"

"No," I replied defensively.

For some reason, all sensibility leaves a boy when someone suggests he might be "chicken" or a coward. It is a primary reason for many of a young man's troubles. My father used to ask, "If everyone else jumped of the cliff would you?" I guess the answer was probably, "Yes," as I bit into the course brown stick.

Walt grinned as I almost gagged.

Walt encouraged, "Taste good don't it?"

I nodded as if in agreement, but the taste was far from good. Having never chewed before, I held the brown wad in my mouth. I knew the old men spit occasionally, but really did not know much more about the art of chewing than that. We both sat calmly dangling our feet off the bridge as if we were enjoying our new found vice.

It was difficult to talk with a mouthful of chew, so Walt and I just chewed. I cannot remember how long I chewed, but none of it was pleasant. Both of us kept the brown paste in our mouths longer than we would have, if we were alone. Camaraderie breeds such strange courage. Neither of us wanted to be the first to fail, so we just sat in silence.

It takes an amazingly small amount of tobacco juice to ruin your day. With no experienced tutor, we had made many fundamental chewing errors. The most devastating was the failure to spit often enough. After a while, I began to feel a cold, sweating sensation all over my body that started in the pit of my stomach and permeated to my head. The sights and sounds began to swim together in an uneasy mix of strange new feelings.

I was the first to spit out my wad. I gagged as the brown ooze dropped to the dry creek bed below. I began to feel more dizzy, then weak, and then sick. It took all my effort to move from a sitting position with my feet hanging off the bridge to lying on my stomach with my head hanging over the bridge.

Somehow, Walt had been able to accomplish this maneuver quicker than I. The sound of him throwing up caused my system to purge everything I had ever eaten. I do not remember how long we lay on the bridge suffering, but I can honestly say it was the first time in my life that I did not care if I lived or died. After a while, I was uncomfortable enough with my head hanging over the bridge that I rolled over and sprawled flat on my back on the edge of the wooden bridge.

Walt was still "enjoying" his chewing experience as he continued to spit and spew the remains of his tobacco down the dry creek bed. Lying flat on my back, I felt woozy and uncomfortable. My head was spinning and sweat poured from my pores. Soon Walt joined me in this laid-back position. I still felt queasy and nauseous in the pit of my stomach, but at least no longer desired death.

We lay speechless on the bridge for a long time until Walt said, "That wasn't too bad."

I could not even muster a response.

"It kind 'a tasted better on the way out," he quipped.

I smirked a little at this comment. After a while, I was able to admit that I did not really care for chewing tobacco. Walt held to the notion that it was a fine product worthy of another try. I could not see myself ever chewing again, but I did not have the strength to argue with him.

We rested almost an hour before starting back toward town. Mother would be cooking supper soon, although food sounded about as tempting as another mouth full of chewing tobacco.

The walk back to town was taking considerably longer than the walk out to the bridge. My legs still felt wobbly and Walt did not seem to have much more spirit than I had. The sun glistened off the gravel road as the hot, stagnate air made us even more miserable.

Back down the road behind us, I heard a strange sound. It was a distant popping sound, almost like a gun shot but more muffled. The sound also was moving and moving quickly. The strangeness of the noise combined with my weakened state made for an uneasy feeling.

The sound continued and it was definitely moving toward us. A cloud of dust billowed from the road behind us like a herd of cattle being driven. The noise was more distinct now and was clearly more of a roar than a pop. About a half mile down the road, you could see a glint of glass and soon you could see the commotion was coming from an automobile.

I had seen automobiles a time or two, but never on the open road. This vehicle was bigger and shinier than any auto I had seen in town. It was black with two rows of seats and moving very fast.

Walt waved with all his might at the big black automobile approaching us at a speed faster than a galloping horse. As it approached, you could see a man wearing a cap and goggles driving the automobile. I joined Walt in waving, envisioning a ride in the shiny car. Any chance to ride in an automobile was a big event, but the way I felt, a lift into town would be more than a fun ride. It would be a lifesaver.

The vehicle approached making more noise and creating more dust as it approached. At about forty yards, it was apparent the driver had no intentions of slowing down much less stopping. Not only was he accelerating as he approached, he did not seem to care if he missed hitting us. The car passed within a few feet of Walt and me as we dove into the ditch by the side of the road, dodging gravel and flying rocks. Covered in dust and dirt, Walt jumped up and instinctively grabbed a rock, hurling it toward the passing car.

Walt was always more impetuous than I dared to be, but I had to agree with his sentiments on this occasion. The rock landed harmlessly behind the speeding vehicle. For a moment, it seemed the incident was over when suddenly the car slid to an abrupt stop. The sickening feeling was returning as a tall man with dark black hair jumped out to inspect the rear of his vehicle.

After a brief look, he turned toward us with a sharp look in his dark eyes and an angry grimace. I felt completely helpless. I was too sick to run and besides the angry stranger stood between us and the town.

Walt turned to run, when a powerful voice shouted, "Stop!"

His instinct to run could not overpower the authority in the stranger's voice to stand still. The dark stranger walked toward us, deliberately and sternly. At about twenty yards, the profanity started and with each step, he became more foreboding and intimidating.

"Which of you little tramps threw that rock!" he shouted.

We both froze in silence too afraid to talk.

"Tell me now or you will both get a beating!" he exclaimed still moving steadily toward us.

"We…what rock," Walt muttered, "We didn't throw no rock."

"Little liars," the stranger accused.

"We was just trying to hit a bird over there," Walt pleaded.

The man was within several steps of us now. There was no escape. He slowly removed his driving gloves. I did not know if he would slap us with the gloves or if he did not want them bloodied, but he meant to be threatening with this deliberate gesture.

"Please mister, you don't have to…" Walt's voice faded to unintelligible as he pleaded. I had to admire Walt's efforts to talk us out of this mess, though I think it was the first time I had seen him really afraid.

"Little white-trash liar," the stranger said clenching his teeth. He never broke eye contact or stride as he walked to Walt and slapped him so hard that the young boy tumbled to the ground in a pile.

Without hesitation, the angry man turned to me and with a wicked grin said, "Since neither of you were man enough to take responsibility, you'll get worse."

I braced for the blows, too dumbfounded, too scared, and too sick to run.

"Take responsibility for what, Craigan?" shouted the unmistakable voice of E.W. Marland.

We had been unaware of Mr. Marland's approach on horseback.

The stranger seemed startled and bewildered to hear his name shouted, seemingly out of nowhere. He squinted into the afternoon sun to see the cavalier figure stopping his horse not ten yards from him. The surprised demeanor of the stranger turned quickly to concern when he finally recognized his questioner.

"E.W. Marland?" the stranger asked perplexingly.

Mr. Marland ignored his question and continued in a stern voice, "Do we have a problem?"

Walt was sitting up and wiping some blood from his busted lip. Mr. Marland dismounted and placed himself between the stranger and us.

"Are you all right son?" Mr. Marland asked with a tone of genuine concern.

Walt nodded without really making any eye contact.

"What are you doing out in this God forsaken country Marland?" the stranger asked.

"I've been watching a snake in the grass slap a kid most recently," Marland sternly replied.

Mr. Marland had obviously seen the whole event. From the sweat and heavy breathing of his horse, he had come to the rescue at a full gallop from a ways off.

"The kid…the kid threw a rock at me," the stranger answered still confused at the appearance of Mr. Marland.

"I doubt he did anything. Knowing you, he should've hit you in the head," Marland emphasized.

The stranger, who we were to learn, was Daniel Craigan, now seemed totally disinterested in Walt and me. He turned his attention to the appearance of E. W. Marland instead. The two obviously knew each other and from the tone of voice and posturing did not like each other.

"I can't believe you're out here," Craigan sneered. "I heard you had gone back to Pittsburg to practice law."

"You heard wrong," came the curt reply.

Craigan was more composed now and laughed a little as he said, "I heard you lost everything during the panic. I tried to tell you that you were getting too full of yourself."

Mr. Marland listened in silence with his jaw set in contempt for the conversation and the man making it.

"You should've gotten on board with that Morgan deal," Craigan chided.

"Morgan and the other bankers are thieves," Marland retorted.

"It wasn't thievery, it was timing. If you hadn't been so bent on proving how much smarter you were than the whole finance industry, they might have given you a heads-up about what was really happening."

Marland was defensive now, "I didn't need any favors, just the financing to expand."

"Well you got the financing," Craigan proclaimed in a mocking tone.

"They called my note," Marland defended.

"That they did. J.P. Morgan made a fortune off that panic. Those on board with Morgan made a fortune too," bragged Craigan.

Mr. Marland did not respond for a moment then said, "Well they say the cream eventually rises to the top. I'm doing fine."

Craigan replied with a cynical tone, "Doing what, rustling cattle? You look like a cowboy except your wearing that fedora."

Mr. Marland did not say a word.

"You had better smarten up Marland," Craigan taunted. "You may be able to fool the hicks out here, but you and I know the money people back east make the real deals."

"Things are different here."

"They might be different, but some people like you are destined to show the rest of us what not to do," replied Craigan. "I bought that 'Mary Gin' oil well you drilled for 30 cents on the dollar by the way. It's still pumping 20 barrels a day for me."

Mr. Marland stiffened and slowly walked toward Daniel Craigan. The two came face to face. Craigan was a bit taller than Mr. Marland but Marland was clearly the more confident and dominant of the two men.

"Maybe I need to show you something right now," Marland threatened. "Maybe you would like to hit someone closer to your own size."

Craigan swallowed hard and took a step back, then another. "I don't have any problems here," he said as he began back peddling toward his car. "I don't have any problems with you Marland, just trying to give you a little guidance."

Mr. Marland let him have the last word as Craigan walked more quickly toward his escape. Soon the automobile vanished in a cloud of dust as Daniel Craigan drove toward town.

"You sure you're all right son?" Mr. Marland asked Walt as he helped him to his feet and dusted him off.

"Yes sir," Walt replied.

"What's your name again?" Mr. Marland asked.

"Walt. Walt Johnson. I read books with your wife."

"We're sure glad to see you Mr. Marland," I interjected.

Mr. Marland smiled then looked back at Walt, "Thought I had seen you around. You almost hit him, didn't you?"

Walt sheepishly nodded.

"I admire your spunk kid, but you've got to be careful who you pick your fights with," Mr. Marland admonished.

"Who was that guy?" Walt asked.

"That's Daniel Craigan," answered Mr. Marland.

I inquisitively asked, "Do you know him Mr. Marland?"

"Yes, we were competitors back in the oil fields of West Virginia."

Walt and I just listened. All we knew is that Daniel Craigan had a temper and we never wanted to cross paths with him again.

"Craigan is smart. He's ruthless, but smart. You boys need to stay away from him."

We nodded in agreement.

Mr. Marland's voice turned less serious as he asked, "What are you boys doing out here?"

"Nothin'," I said.

"Fishin'," Walt said almost at the same time.

"Nothing and fishing," Mr. Marland observed with a smile. "Looks like maybe you're fishing with nothing."

Walt had not thought through his lie very well since we had no poles, tackle, or even water around.

"Boys, you need to learn to tell the truth," Mr. Marland coached. "Every time you tell a lie it's like pulling a thread on a piece of fabric…pretty soon it just all comes unraveled."

"We was chewing tobacco," Walt admitted. Mr. Marland's speech must have made a profound impact on Walt, since I had rarely heard him recant a lie no matter how outrageous the circumstances. I squirmed uncomfortably at the idea of Mr. Marland telling my parents or even Mrs. Marland. Walt had picked a great time to pick up honesty. His parents would never know.

Mr. Marland grinned, "Let me see it."

Walt produced the tobacco and handed it to Mr. Marland. He looked it over then asked, "How about I trade you boys this tobacco for some candy when we get back to town."

We nodded in agreement.

E.W. Marland then bent down on his knee to look Walt eye to eye and said, "Son you got courage. You stick with the truth and that courage will take you far."

He then stood up and rubbed Walt's unkempt hair and said to both of us, "Would you boys like to ride back into town?"

Again, we nodded. Mr. Marland helped us up on to his mount and led the animal toward town by the reins. He continued to volunteer little bits of information about Mr. Craigan on the ride into town. Craigan had been drilling wells with less success than Mr. Marland back in West Virginia. Mr. Marland was actually working on a deal to buy Mr. Craigan's interest in several wells when people made a run on the banks forcing many to close. Mr. Marland was heavily in debt when the price of oil dipped. The bank called for him to pay his loans and he had to sell everything. Mr. Craigan did not have the same debt problems and was able to buy much of Mr. Marland's former oil holdings.

"One thing's for sure," Mr. Marland concluded with a tone of seriousness, "I'm not the only one in Kay County looking for oil now."

You could tell this was a concern to Mr. Marland.

"Walt, you stay away from chewing tobacco and Mr. Craigan," Mr. Marland warned. He then turned to look me square in the eye, "Charles, you watch out for Mr. Craigan too, especially if he comes around your mother. Would you boys stop by and tell Mrs. Marland to have supper without me? I need to go see Joe Miller."

This surprised me. It was understandable to stay clear of Mr. Craigan, but what did my mother have to do with this new stranger in town? It would be a long time before I learned the significance of this statement. It would be even longer before I learned that E. W. Marland left little to chance. I would discover in time that E.W. Marland did almost everything with a calculating purpose.

This day, however, seemed to have a profound influence on Walt Johnson. It not only foreshadowed future interactions with Daniel Craigan, but it was also the last time I ever remember Walt Johnson telling a lie.

CHAPTER 7

▼

As fall arrived and school started, I saw much more of Mrs. Marland than I did her husband. Mr. Marland was often out of town, traveling back east to find investors or out at the well on the 101 Ranch.

The respect Mrs. Marland commanded in the community continued to grow. Virginia Marland looked like she belonged in one of the fancy cities back east in a fashionable, upper-class neighborhood, but she had the intelligence and good character to adapt to her circumstances. She was gracious to everyone and generous with her time, particularly with the local children. She had taken a particular liking to Walt and she continued to spend time with him almost every day. Walt had never had the kind of attention Mrs. Marland showed him and he became more trusting of all people under her kind influence.

Walt was an enigma to those who took the time to know him. He had no family to speak of except a mother of questionable reputation. He did no better than average in school, but still there was something about Walt, even in these early years that made him different. With Mrs. Marland's encouragement, Walt developed more self-assurance. Even though few others believed in him, Walt's optimism was contagious and he drew others to him like a light draws moths. Walt was a born leader with big plans and dreams. Virginia Marland often laughed at his tireless enthusiasm and called him "Little E.W." because Walt always looked at any problem as an enjoyable challenge and opportunity.

Although Mrs. Marland was well respected around town, the local people were less sure of Mr. Marland. He was gone often and always had to explain why bills were piling up and debts were unpaid. Mr. Marland was doing much of the drilling work himself and spent many nights camped at the well site.

Daniel Craigan was not having much luck either. He was rarely in the field, but his big black car was often seen at the Arcade Hotel. He had a crew of five hired men and was drilling a well on the Ponca reservation. Rumor around town said he had gotten Jim Big Thunder drunk and bought the mineral rights on the Indian's 160 acres of land for a case of whiskey.

Mr. Marland's demeanor changed during this period. He was much more serious and solemn. It was easy to tell that his finances and lack of success finding oil weighed heavily on him. Mr. Marland had secured a true friend, however, in Joe Miller. Miller's reputation and faith in E.W. seemed to be all that the oilman had going for him.

Matters came to a head on a chilly October afternoon when Mr. Marland and Craigan ran into each other in the lobby of the Arcade Hotel.

"Marland, how are you doing?" asked Daniel Craigan as the conversation began civilly.

"Fine Craigan," was the formal answer.

The two exchanged the customary conversation about the weather, news, and other non-personal events when Mr. Craigan asked, "How deep have you gone on that well?"

Mr. Marland's eyes shifted left to right as he looked away from Mr. Craigan and said, "We're making progress."

"Hmm," Mr. Craigan acknowledged. "We've gone 900 feet. I don't think there's oil on this side of the river."

"Oh there's oil," Mr. Marland defended. "I'm seeing good formations and several promising domes."

"That a fact," Craigan noted. "Don't guess you would share where?"

Mr. Marland smiled, both men knowing that would never happen.

Craigan continued by saying, "I think I'm going to try my luck over on the Osage reservation. Phillips is hitting wells all over that place."

"That might be smart," Mr. Marland admitted.

"But you don't think so do you Marland?"

"That land is pretty leased up."

"Well these Indians are less than sophisticated," Craigan said with a smirk. "You give them enough social lubricant and they're fairly agreeable."

"You'll do anything for a buck," Marland scolded.

"Almost anything…there's a difference," Craigan defended.

Mr. Marland gave a skeptical look and began to leave when Craigan asked, "How deep have you drilled?"

Mr. Marland stopped, but refused to answer.

"A thousand feet? Twelve Hundred?" Craigan asked.

E.W. just looked at him silently.

Craigan moved closer to him and said in a low tone, "If you've gone twelve hundred feet, we both know you got a dry well."

E.W. Marland's body language betrayed him. He had past 1,200 feet three weeks ago. Daniel Craigan gloated in quiet satisfaction at the failure of E.W. Marland.

"Why don't you get smart?" asked Craigan with a little smirk. "Come to work for me. You know oil, but I have financing. This doesn't have to be a competition."

Mr. Marland thought for a minute then walked face to face with Craigan and said in a hushed but stern tone, "I'll be doing dishes at this hotel before I become partners with you."

"Does the wife know?" Craigan asked taking the opportunity to mock his adversary. "Does Wiker know?"

Mr. Marland worriedly looked over at Mr. Wiker the hotel manager at the counter, but did not respond to the question. Craigan let it go. There was no reason to keep knocking E. W. Marland down. He was all but finished.

E. W. Marland went to tell Virginia the news about the dry well. By the time he was able to tell his wife, all Ponca City knew E.W. Marland had drilled a dry hole.

CHAPTER 8

▼

Another year came and went with 1909. They built a new bank in Newkirk twenty miles away. The 101 Ranch was growing into the biggest Wild West Show in the country and E.W. Marland stubbornly searched for oil.

Time is different when you are young. For Walt and me one year seemed a lifetime, but for Mr. Marland time was running out. He traveled tirelessly, back east to find investors and then out in the field to look for oil. Investors, so far, had been easier to find.

Mr. Marland was still pleasant the rare times we would see him. Mrs. Marland did not see him much more than we did. He was good to write and she would often update us on his travels. She seemed more like his office manager sometimes, than a wife. She still found time to volunteer around town and help children with everything from reading lessons to scraped knees. The Marlands still had no children of their own.

It was hard to hear some of the things people where saying about Mr. Marland. He had drilled four wells in 1909 and found nothing but gas. One of the low characters in town called him the "bean man", then explained that all Marland could find was gas. Gas wells were thought worthless at the time. Three more dry wells in 1910 were making E.W. Marland a desperate man.

Walt and I endured no such desperation. We were old enough to be more courageous in our adventures, but still maintained the carefree independence of youth. Mrs. Marland encouraged Walt to read *The Adventure of Tom Sawyer*, and he fantasized about the grand deeds we would do. We built a raft to float the Arkansas River to New Orleans, but it sunk more than it floated and was completely ruined on a sand bar a quarter mile after launching. I also ran away from home for about three hours one time that summer, but no one but Walt noticed. We even searched for buried treasure hidden by the Jesse James gang who frequently had hideouts in the old Indian Territory.

We were a part of a pack of young boys that roamed about town in between chores and odd jobs. Sometimes our gang had as many as eight to ten boys from our part of town. Walt Johnson was our designated leader. Walt did not have a lot going for him from a grownup's perspective. He had little guidance at home and school was sometimes a struggle. Mrs. Marland's tutoring, however, had helped him become a good reader.

From a kid's point of view, however, Walt was a natural leader. He did not have as many chores to do as the rest of us and no parents asking troublesome questions, which made him available for any adventure. Walt was muscular, blonde, and pleasant looking with a broad smile. He was also fearless. Walt had a belief in himself that people could just sense. Walt was like Mr. Marland in many ways, which may be why he always seemed to be Mrs. Marland's favorite.

Late one afternoon, our gang scampered across town to hunt frogs in Red Bud Creek. Floyd Wills, one of our group, was whistling loudly when an Indian man slumped over by an alleyway shouted sternly, "Don't whistle or the dead spirits will take your soul."

We looked at him in startled disbelief. Not so much at what he said, but that an Indian would actually take the initiative to speak to us. As we continued to stare at him waiting for more details, he quickly looked away and muttered, "That's what the Kickapoo say, not me."

He was obviously embarrassed at making such a bold statement, especially to a group of white boys. We laughed apprehensively at the strange comment then continued on our quest to capture every frog in Kay County. After several hours of throwing rocks at frogs, we stopped at the bridge to make new plans.

"Floyd," Walt asked, "what song were you whistling back in town in front of that Indian?"

"I don't know," Floyd answered.

"Come on Floyd, you had to be whistling something," I added to the inquiry, although I had no idea why Walt had asked.

"Probably some church song, I really don't know, I whistle all the time," Floyd replied.

Walt thought on this information for a moment then said, "Ya'll know them Indian people know a lot about spirits and stuff." We nodded as Walt continued, "They have these things called vision quests where the young braves go out to seek visions of their future and stuff."

The Indian cultures were always a mystery to the people who lived in town. We rarely saw their daily lives, just the ceremonies and rituals they wanted us to see at public Pow Wows. Some of the Indians even preformed versions of these rituals for the Wild West Show at the 101 Ranch.

"It makes you wonder," Walt proposed, "if we need to go on a vision quest."

Our group had about run out of ideas for new escapades to keep ourselves entertained. Leave it to Walt to come up with something new.

"Let's do it," I was quick to endorse.

The rest of the group followed right in line with this new scheme.

"We'll have to plan it out," Walt stated.

For us, "planning it out" was most of the fun. In fact, very few of our conceived adventures ever actually took place. Typically, after weeks of careful scheming and detailed planning the idea would eventually be forgotten as we were either distracted by more appealing adventures or found the idea involved too much work.

Like the time we were going to build a hot air balloon. We spent days gathering any scrap of fabric we could find and firewood to heat the air. I even stole some thread from my mother to sew the thing together, but after a few stitches, it was apparent that the grand plot to build a balloon far out stripped our abilities. In such cases, we generally just abandoned the idea with a silent groupthink and endeavored on another task that we thought even more grandiose. Most of our true adventures happened in the playful imagination of these planning exercises.

The rest of the evening and most of the next day were spent preparing every detail of our vision quest. One of the things we learned in our group planning was the existence of a Ponca Indian burial grounds on a hill south of town. Floyd Wills' father worked as a county assessor and had knowledge of the area including the Indian reservation. Floyd was able to discreetly question his father and found the exact location of the burial grounds. According to Floyd, we would need to go five miles south on the Arkansas River until it made a sharp turn to the east. At that point, Bodark Creek drained into the Arkansas River. You walked another half mile up Bodark Creek to a long, isolated hill where you would find the "sacred" burial grounds.

Our excitement grew with every detail over the next few days. Walt even drew a map on the back of some packing paper he had found downtown. I did not know what the map said and I am sure it contained no accurate information, but we studied it nonetheless. The plan called for us to ask for permission to camp out by Red Bud Creek. Walt would not have to ask, but the rest of us felt sure we could get permission with various levels of the truth. We would leave in the morning and camp at the bend of the river where Bodark Creek entered. Of course, we would never tell our parents we were camping so far away from town. After making camp, we would scout out the area then wait for dark. Close to midnight, we would climb the hill to the top of the burial ground to complete our quest and discover any ancient Indian secrets hidden there.

We collected three old lanterns, some jerky, and various other items we somehow imagined would be useful. Ten boys started on the trip. By the time we reached the river two had changed their minds about this bold quest and turned back home. We swore them to secrecy and continued. This trip was only for the committed. By the time we got to the Salt Fork River crossing, two more were tired and turned for home. Those that made it to Bodark Creek included Walt, Floyd Wills, a short kid named Perry McGee we called Cricket, Bobby Williams, Raeford Dutton who we called Raef, and myself.

A quick survey of the area was encouraging. The surrounding area was fairly level terrain with trees at the base of the hill. The hill was impossible to miss since it was the only high place in sight. We were all tired from the trip, so after beans, biscuits, and jerky the group rested determined to leave about an hour after dark to make our rendezvous with the spirits. Raef was the keeper of the fire and before long I had fallen into a deep sleep.

I awoke to Walt tugging on my shoulder and saying, "Wake up, it's past ten o'clock. I jumped up with a start. The other three were still sound asleep. Floyd and Cricket refused to wake up and go, either too fatigued or too frightened to continue. Raef argued that he needed to tend the fire in camp.

After ridicule and some cursing of the others by Walt, it was apparent he and I were the only two making this quest. If not for Walt's determination and my fear of letting him down, the count would have been one. Going out into the dark to an Indian burial ground suddenly seemed as bad an idea as building a balloon. Staying in camp with Raef to watch the fire and sleep seemed a sensible plan to me. The howl of a distant coyote added to my lack of enthusiasm about the midnight trip.

To Walt, it was never a discussion. He intended to go and just assumed I would go along. We lit two small lanterns and headed up the trail next to Bodark Creek.

There was a decent moon out and we navigated the trail fairly well with the help of our lanterns. I tripped over a gofer hole once and Walt got tangled up in a briar patch we did not see until too late, but within an hour we were close to the base of the hill. We started up what we first thought was an old cow trail, then discovered there were two tracks, which meant some type of wagon used the road.

We were now making steady tracks and my fears had evaporated somewhat. Everything seemed to be going to plan when Walt suddenly stopped and said in an excited whisper, "Listen! Did you hear that?"

My heart stopped. After a moment of hearing nothing, I figured Walt was just trying to scare me. "Don't do that," I scolded, "you about made me jump out'ta my skin."

"Shut up and listen," he scolded.

I knew Walt well enough to know when he was kidding and this was not one of those times. I had not experienced him being frightened often, but felt this must be what it was like. After listening a moment, I whispered, "I don't hear anything."

"Isn't that kinda' strange?" he asked.

"I don't know," I replied. Immediately it occurred to me that it was strange. There were no tree frogs, no crickets chirping, no owls hooting, no coyotes just silence.

"I thought I heard footsteps," Walt explained.

"Maybe we better head back."

Walt listened a minute more then said, "No it's nothing, just our nerves. This is probably part of the experience. Let's go."

With that, Walt headed up the trail again, at first timidly, but then with a more steady pace as he regained his confidence. Suddenly he stopped again, turned and grabbed me by the mouth. I was stunned at his sudden behavior and caught by surprise when he put his hand over my mouth, but I could clearly hear footsteps marching several steps after we had stopped! They were clearly not our own…and they were coming from behind us. There was a noise from the direction of the footsteps that sounded like a birdcall or some other wild animal, but there was something that told us the stalker was no animal or bird…it was a human.

I had been prepared to face whatever supernatural horrors awaited us on top of the burial grounds, but I had not been expecting to run into a real person, which I found a much more terrifying prospect. For a moment, my mind conjured up all kinds of bad men that might be lurking in the dark from outlaws to angry Indians. No one out at this time of night could be up to any good. I then thought it might be one of our own group out to scare us. The steps, after all, were coming from behind us toward the direction of the camp. After more thorough thought however, it seemed inconceivable any of our group would dare venture out of camp.

"We gotta' get out of here," I gasped.

"How?" Walt replied, "They're between us and the camp. Let me think."

My heart was racing now. I felt like a trapped rat. There was nothing to do, but rely on the cool judgments of one Walt Johnson.

"What are we gonna' do?" I asked in a panic.

Walt was quick and decisive, "We got to continue up this road until we can find a spot to circle back around."

We headed on up the trail. A path that was completely foreign to both of us. We did not run, but were walking much quicker now. We would have liked to run, but did not know where to go and did not want to tip off the person or persons behind us to our panic. In the distance, you could vaguely see a strange shadowy space in the road ahead. It was very strange, like a dark place in the night. It did not really look like a shadow and it was too regularly shaped to be a tree, bush, or animal. It kind of looked like a tunnel, but not exactly. One of the many tales the Indian people tell was of large mysterious creatures that could appear and disappear in the darkness. Fearsome creatures that looked like a man and bear combined into one horrifying monster. In a few more steps, we could tell the dark space was no bush, or tunnel, or hair-raising beast, it was much worse.

CHAPTER 9

▼

Walt and I walked quickly up the unfamiliar trail. The noises behind us were getting closer and we were trapped. Every step took us further away from the relative safety of our camp and our feeling of panic was about to intensify.

Walt stopped suddenly and I plowed into his back. "Oh no," he sighed.

Setting in front of us was our worst nightmare, a shining black car...Daniel Craigan's car. Fear rushed through my entire body. We had not told anyone where we were going. Two bodies floating down the Arkansas River would take weeks to find. I could not help but remember our first frightening encounter with Mr. Craigan.

"Let's go this way," Walt directed decisively as he took a ninety-degree angle from the trail through brush and shoulder high grass. Suddenly you could hear the steps behind us more clearly as they picked up the pace and closed in on us. The steps behind us were no longer trying to conceal their presence, but were now just interested in closing the gap. Simultaneously, Walt and I broke into a run. After only a few steps, we both crashed into a big presence of a man and screamed like little girls at Halloween. The man was terrifying. His face was darkened with some kind of grease or dirt and his eyes were shining wildly in the moon light. His custom-made knickers with shining boots, tailored coat, and fedora hat soon revealed that we had not seen a monster of the night or strange spirits. Standing before us in the middle of the night at an Indian cemetery was E.W. Marland!

"What the devil are you boys doing out here?" asked a stern E.W. Marland.

"Running from Craigan!" I exclaimed.

"Craigan," Mr. Marland asked, obviously concerned. "Where did you see him?"

"We didn't sir," I said nearly out of breath, "but his car is parked back on the trail."

"Oh," Mr. Marland said with a little sigh.

"I don't think Craigan is out here tonight."

Walt hurriedly informed, "But Mr. Marland there is someone after us."

"Let's see who it is," Mr. Marland coolly replied. "Willie, is that you?"

"Yip," came the reply from a mild voice about thirty yards from us.

Mr. Marland waved the stranger toward us and said, "Boys, I want you to meet Willie Cries-For-War."

A young Indian man appeared from the tall grass. He looked to be barely twenty and dark skinned. Other than his tanned complexion, you would not have thought him an Indian. He wore overalls with a flannel shirt and had short cut hair just like you would get in town.

"Call me Willie Cry," he requested.

"This is Willie's land," Mr. Marland explained.

After a brief silence I had to ask, "What's you doing out here Mr. Marland?"

"That's a good question, but I would rather know what you're doing here?" he questioned.

Walt and I began a garbled assortment of incoherent statements and thin reasoning to cover the true mission. Walt would not lie to Mr. Marland, but we did not reveal the whole truth either. With Willie Cry in our midst, we were even more ashamed to be trespassing on Indian burial grounds.

"Sounds like quite a story," Mr. Marland consoled finally putting us out of our misery. "Willie and I were just checking some formations out. I found some rainbows in the water of Bodark creek which might indicate oil deposits under this rock formation."

What Mr. Marland did not tell us is that he was there at that hour to keep anyone, including the Ponca Indian Chief White Eagle, from knowing he was surveying this sacred spot for a potential drilling site.

"What's Mr. Craigan doing out here?" I asked still a little weary of his whereabouts.

Mr. Marland grinned and said, "Mr. Craigan is in town and I believe he is engaged for the evening."

Mr. Marland's eyes shifted briefly at Walt then he continued, "I'm...borrowing his car."

Mr. Marland was not exactly lying, but he was also not telling the complete truth. He did "borrow the car" in that he intended to return it before morning, but he failed to tell us that he did not have Craigan's permission to utilize it.

Any further explanation was cut off by Walt excitedly shouting, "What's that?" as he pointed back toward camp.

A faint glow glimmered in the sky toward our river camp. It was more than Raef's campfire. The glowing reflection in the sky was a real fire!

Mr. Marland was quick and decisive as he ordered, "Willie, you head down there. I'll see if I can get this car started."

Willie Cry disappeared quickly into the night as Mr. Marland, Walt, and myself headed to Mr. Craigan's car. Automobiles were rarely as useful as a horse on Kay County roads, but they did have one distinct advantage. The electric running lights made night travel more feasible. The reliability of starting, however, made it a poor choice in an emergency. Mr. Marland, however, was composed as he went through the routine of bringing the vehicle to life flawlessly. Within minutes, we were rolling back toward camp.

If we had done better reconnaissance work, Walt and I would have discovered the road we were walking on followed level terrain away from Bodark creek and led to within 100 yards of our camp. We quickly jumped out and ran with reckless abandon to the spot of the fire. Raef, Floyd, Cricket, Bobby, and Willie Cry had about beat out the last of the potentially dangerous prairie fire. Fortunately the south breeze was light this evening and blew the fire toward the river's edge. Willie Cry had arrived in a nick of time to help the boys beat out the flames.

Walt and I surveyed the damage. About a fifty yard oval of charred grass was all that remained of our camp and our pieced together camp equipment. We spent a few moments kicking around the remains while Mr. Marland and Willie Cry made sure the fire was indeed out. Raef it seems was more of a firebug than keeper of the fire. While playing in the fire with a stick, he had flipped an ember onto the dry grass. Fifteen more minutes and the whole county would have known about our misadventure.

Mr. Marland offered to take us back to town in Mr. Craigan's car. We agreed to ride back to the Red Bud Creek Bridge. We knew we could not go to our houses at such an early hour without raising suspicion. He agreed and we loaded the few remains of the camp into the car. Mr. Marland shook hands with Willie Cry and the two had a conversation in private. We drove to the Red Bud Creek Bridge with little conversation or incident.

When we unloaded at the bridge for the rest of our night's sleep, Mr. Marland knelt on one knee to talk to all of us. "You boys know tonight could have been a disaster."

We all sheepishly nodded.

"You could've been hurt or destroyed a lot of land out there tonight," he scolded.

We all looked at out feet expecting this lecture to last awhile when he stopped.

"But, there wasn't any real harm done," he continued. "How about we make a deal? You guys don't tell anyone you saw me tonight and I won't tell anyone I saw you."

We eagerly agreed and assured Mr. Marland that this would never be mentioned again. He made us shake hands on it then mutter something about getting the car back before daybreak.

Exhausted we found the soft ground next to the creek a good bed and soon fell asleep.

We kept our secret pact with Mr. Marland. Not all boys were so faithful. By morning, the part of our gang that turned back to town had forgotten their pledge not to tell anyone about the burial grounds. By daybreak, a group of concerned and angry parents were looking for us, including my father.

It turned out to be a stroke of luck that Mr. Marland had transported us to the Red Bud Creek Bridge. When the group of parents found us by the creek instead of miles away, it was the three traitors who had told their parents about our quest to the burial grounds who were scolded for alarming everyone. The promise to Mr. Marland, the fire, and misadventures of the evening were enough to keep us silent about the true events of the night for years to come. It would be many more years before I learned the real significance of this night.

CHAPTER 10

▼

No one mentioned the burial ground incident outside of our little group for many years. Those who had told their parents were punished by being ignorant of the true events of Bodark Creek. They had to endure our much exaggerated and ever changing accounts about the daring acts of that night. Walt had sworn the rest of us to secrecy. Mr. Marland was also the epitome of discretion in the matter. We continued our boyhood exploits and Mr. Marland continued his quest for oil.

Mr. Marland was having regular conversations with Mr. Wiker about his hotel bill and other creditors around town were running out of patience. Mrs. Marland was always by his side and at his defense making excuses and tempering Mr. Marland's occasional brusque manner. Although E.W. Marland's financial woes alienated some and tested Mrs. Marland's superb abilities in tact and affability, he did have his supporters.

E.W. Marland was no respecter of persons and made friends easily with all types of people. Bill McFadden was an acquaintance he had met on our first trip to the 101 Ranch. McFadden lived in a tent city on the north bank of the Salt Fork River across from the 101 Ranch's Riverside camp. He seemed to be like many other struggling settlers in the new state. McFadden, however, had managed a steel foundry back east before coming to Oklahoma and was a man of some means. Toxic vapors from the acid utilized in the galvanizing compound in the steel mill had irritated his lungs to a near fatal point. He had come to Oklahoma for the fresh air, thinking he was going to die.

The fresh air did wonders for Bill McFadden who soon made a full recovery. McFadden had bought life insurance as a young man and cashed it in to come to

Oklahoma. He had one commodity that was in scarce supply, cash. McFadden carried close to $100,000 dollars in cash with him. No one would have thought there would be anyone with financial capital in one of the tent cities in this new state, but E.W. Marland could smell opportunity. The two men became friends and Marland had gotten McFadden excited about the oil business. E.W. Marland had found a financial investor, but he also needed leasing rights.

Mr. Marland may have been the object of ridicule to some in Kay County, but he had made a sure friend in Joe Miller from the 101 Ranch. I spotted them coming off the train on an early fall day in 1910. They both happened to be on the train from Tulsa by coincidence and decided to share a compartment for the trip home. The tone of their conversation on the platform of the train station was more serious than any I had witnessed from Mr. Marland before. His forehead was tense with stress.

"There's oil in those formations Joe," Mr. Marland preached. "The pressure from the petroleum and natural gas causes the rock to rise. You can see it all over the Ponca reservation. Trust me, when you see a raised rock formation, a dome, with no erosion factors, there's something under it."

"I don't doubt you, but you've been drilling for over a year with nothing to show for it but angry investors and growing bills," observed Joe Miller.

"I know Joe," Mr. Marland admitted with an exasperated tone, "but we're hitting gas and that means we're close."

Joe Miller listened with no reaction.

"I've got to drill on the Ponca reservation," Mr. Marland pleaded, "and on their land, not what they've leased to you."

Joe Miller hesitated then timidly suggested, "Maybe you need to come to work for the 101 Ranch. Business is booming and we could use a smart fellow like you that's experienced with the law."

Mr. Marland rubbed his forehead and turned away slightly as he pondered the offer. After thinking a moment E.W. said, "Joe, you're the greatest rancher, and showman, and friend I've ever known. You're great at all these things because you have passion. I appreciate your offer, but I don't want to do something I'm not passionate about. It wouldn't be fair to you and it wouldn't be right for me."

Joe Miller could say nothing to comfort his friend so he listened in silence.

Mr. Marland had the tone of a desperate man, a man running out of options and time. "Joe you know these people. The Ponca respect you. I need your help to get permission to drill."

Joe Miller stared at his boots a moment, and then stretched his back and neck before looking E.W. Marland straight in the eye to say, "The Ponca respect me because I respect them. I will try to help you, but only because I trust you'll be fair."

Mr. Marland tilted his head in agreement.

"This Craigan fellow hasn't made it easy. The Ponca don't like him. He treats them like Indians not people," Joe added.

Mr. Marland listened in silence. He was a shrewd enough card player to know when to push for an answer and when to let the other person talk.

After this brief silence Joe Miller asked, "If you had one shot, what's the best looking spot to drill on?"

"There's an elongated and isolated hill near Bodark Creek that's a geological as well as a topographical high. We drill there WE WILL FIND OIL," Mr. Marland emphasized.

Joe Miller gave a sigh then a slight grimace. "Well, you can sure pick 'em."

"You asked for the best spot."

"That's a burial ground for the Ponca," Joe Miller explained. "The Ponca think the earth is sacred, holy you might say. They call it 'wina mina', it means 'under one sun.'"

Mr. Marland listened with a look of anxious curiosity as if he had no idea about the burial ground. He and I knew better, but neither one of us was talking.

"Is there any place else?" Joe asked.

"That's the best spot. There is a strong anticline beneath that hill that's caused by the petroleum," Mr. Marland explained.

Joe Miller thought for a moment then asked, "How close do you need to be?"

"The closer the better…there's a spot off the crest of the hill near the creek that would be best," informed Mr. Marland.

"That would be better, that's Willie Cry's place," Joe pondered.

Mr. Marland showed an air of optimism in his demeanor.

Joe Miller began to devise a strategy, "White Eagle is the chief of the Ponca. We'll have to talk to him of course. I think I can help you with Willie Cry, but there may be someone in town that can help us with White Eagle. Let's get some coffee and develop a plan."

The two men sounded like our gang of boys planning their next big adventure, but Joe Miller and E.W. Marland would be playing for high stakes. The two men took their bags and walked toward the Arcade Hotel. Joe Miller would risk his reputation. E.W. Marland was risking everything on this plan. I would soon learn Mr. E.W. Marland was always prepared and that he did few things without an underlying purpose.

CHAPTER 11

▼

Dad had been promoted assistant to the manager at the local market. The extra pay and careful saving by mother allowed us to move a few blocks up town. Our new house was a small two-story home with a parlor down stairs, running water, electric lights, and two bedrooms upstairs.

To a boy my age, the neighborhood and house did not mean too much. All I knew is that I had to walk six extra blocks to the train station and two fewer blocks to school. I was in the fifth grade and gaining seniority at the elementary school. On a blustery autumn day, I went to play with Walt downtown. It felt cold outside and the wind blew as if it was determined to knock us off our feet. I would have come home earlier, but Walt rarely wanted to head to his house any sooner than absolutely necessary.

It was dusk as I opened the gate to the front yard of our house. There was a horse tied up to the front fence and from the shadows in the window, it was obvious the McDonaghs had company. A local preacher or door-to-door peddler was the best guess, but I was not prepared to see E.W. Marland sitting in my front room.

Panic overwhelmed me. Had Mr. Marland broken our promise? Had he for some reason decided he could not bear the guilt of that night at the burial grounds when we nearly burnt down the county? My mind raced and rapidly developed escape strategies and clever excuses for the accusations that were sure to come. My young mind rationalized that it was not me at all; it was Floyd, Cricket, Bobby, and Raeford. As quickly as the tide of panic swept over me, it vanished as it became quickly apparent that the conversation did not involve me at all. My mother was the focus of this deep discussion.

"Mrs. McDonagh is it all right if I call you Myrtle?" Mr. Marland asked.

Mom nodded slightly. It was rare to hear anyone use my mother's first name, but Mr. Marland was accustomed to addressing most people by their first name, especially when he wished to be persuasive. This was somewhat ironic since almost everyone addressed E. W. Marland by Mr. Marland. It was obvious the conversation had just begun. I slid to the side of the room to be as invisible as possible, but still within earshot. Dad was in the room sitting by mother but it was clear she was the center of the conversation.

"Myrtle, I need your help to convince the Ponca elders to consider leasing some of their land for oil exploration," Mr. Marland stated in a matter of fact tone.

"I...I don't see how I can help," Mother softly replied.

"Really Mr. Marland, my wife hasn't spoken to anyone out there for years," Dad added.

"That may be true," Mr. Marland said with an emphasis on the word may, "but I think your wife might have more influence in the matter than you or I may know."

Mother sat in silence.

"Myrtle, wasn't your mother's name Min Wau?" asked Mr. Marland.

My mother straightened in her chair somewhat surprised to hear that name.

"That name means something to you doesn't it. It means 'One Moon' in Ponca."

Mother stared at the floor and answered, "Yes. My mother's real name was Min Wau, but most people called her Minnie."

"Minnie Tremain, right?"

Mother nodded in agreement.

"But she didn't have a last name until she was married, did she?" Mr. Marland continued.

"Mr. Marland it is no secret that Myrtle is part Indian. We've not tried to keep that a secret," Dad interjected. He was only telling part of the truth. We never denied mother's heritage, but it was one of those topics the family did not discuss or feel comfortable having discussed.

"What I'm getting at," Mr. Marland continued sensing he was too close to conducting a cross examination, "is that your wife is the direct relative of a very important Ponca Indian."

Dad seemed surprised and quickly responded in disbelief, "Minnie Tremain?"

There was a brief silence as Dad tried to make sense of his wife being someone that Mr. Marland would think was important.

"He doesn't know, does he?" Mr. Marland tactfully asked looking straight at my mother.

Mother sighed, "No."

She sat silent for just a second and then began a story I had never heard, but somehow Mr. Marland had pieced together.

"My grandmother was white but her family moved to the frontier during the War Between the States. Some kind of sickness passed through the family killing everyone but Grandmother. She was a baby. The only people around were the Ponca and they adopted her, she lived as a Ponca, and she married a great Ponca warrior. My mother was born Ponca, albeit half Ponca, but to the Ponca it didn't matter. She was one of them. She was forced to Oklahoma in the march from Nebraska. Many died that winter. Mother was pretty I am told. I don't really remember…she died when I was young and we have no pictures. When she came here they had no food, no money, no seed, just land. She met my father who was white. Daddy had some money and food, but he had no land.

I had heard vague references to this story but never in such detail and at one time. Generally, mother would guard these facts about her past as if they were tightly held secrets. I knew my mother was part Indian, but that was about the extent of the family history revealed to me.

Mother continued the tale, "When mother fell in love with daddy, their marriage was a good arrangement. Some did not like that, including my grandfather. Her brother died and her father was determined to go back to their lands, but she had a life here now with a husband and child on the way. Many Indian people choose to live as the whites, but some don't think that is the way. For mother it was difficult because her father was Chief Standing Bear leader of the Ponca Nation."

Mother had never talked so much about her family even to my father. Chief Standing Bear had made the trip to Oklahoma during the Ponca Indian's Trail of Tears. When his son died because of the march, he was determined to bring his family back to the ancestral lands by the Niobrara River in Nebraska. Chief Standing Bear won a lawsuit with the United States government that allowed him to remain in Nebraska but most of his people were forced to Indian Territory. *I could not believe what my mother was saying.* Chief Standing Bear was a legend and according to mother, my great Grandfather! I was one eighth Ponca Indian and great grandson of the famous chief.

"Mother was invited back to their land in Nebraska, but she had a different life here. My father told me it was a very bad time. After mother died, father remarried. He didn't tell me about my real mother until I was about Charlie's age. The mother I knew was white so I was raised white," mother concluded in a matter of fact way.

"You see Mr. McDonagh, your wife is the granddaughter of Chief Standing Bear and great niece to Chief White Eagle, chief to the Ponca nation," Mr. Marland summarized.

Dad sat in stunned silence at the revelation.

After a moment mother said, "I still don't see how you think I could help. I haven't been a Ponca my whole life and I doubt they think of me as one of them."

"That's true, but Joe Miller seems to think you would have some influence with White Eagle and frankly so do I," Mr. Marland replied.

"I still find it hard to believe that anyone would listen to me, but I guess what I'm wondering is why would I want to have a say?" mother asked.

Mr. Marland, who was always prepared for every objection replied, "First it would be good for you and your family if oil was found…financially I mean. Generally, there's a half penny a barrel override on the first 2,000 barrels produced for people who help secure leases. That's one hundred dollars to you if we find oil."

One hundred dollars was a lot of money to the McDonagh family in those days. Mother did not say a word but she fidgeted in her seat. She knew what one hundred dollars would mean to the family, but she was a very ethical woman. One of her favorite sayings was, "Doing the right thing is not always easy, but it's always the right thing to do." Something did not seem quite right to her about making money off someone else's property.

Mr. Marland sensed the hesitation and continued, "Finding an oil field would be good for a lot of people. It would mean good jobs and better lives."

He remained silent for a brief moment to let the last point sink in then said, "It would also be good for the Ponca people."

Mother straightened ever so slightly and looked at Mr. Marland's face after the last statement. Mr. Marland caught this slight body language suggesting her interest. In a softer, more sober tone he added, "These people have been mistreated and taken advantage of for a long time. There are plenty of people now that will mislead them. Daniel Craigan has already signed some leases that are worth much less than fair to their owners. There are bad things happening in the Osage Nation right now. I don't want to see that kind of thing happen to the Ponca Indians."

Mr. Marland could tell he was making progress and went for the close, "My business philosophy is that the only good deal is a good deal for all concerned. If I do well, I'll guarantee the people I deal with will also do well."

There was another moment of silence as mother pondered all the information. She then asked, "When do you need to know Mr. Marland?"

"The decision is yours Myrtle," Mr. Marland confided, "but as for me, I'm running out of time. I've been in this town over a year now. I think you know me and my wife enough to know we are honorable people."

Mother again nodded in agreement.

"Joe Miller has set up a meeting with White Eagle and a young Indian man named Willie Cry at the 101 Ranch this Saturday. I believe Willie is your second cousin."

Mother again looked surprised at the scope of Mr. Marland's knowledge of her family history, but nodded in agreement. I remembered the name Willie Cry. His name was mentioned that evening at the 101 Ranch when Zack Miller had made me feel so uncomfortable. He was also the young man who helped us avoid disaster with the fire that night at the burial grounds. Mr. Marland really was paying attention to the people and their connections in Kay County.

Mr. Marland continued his pitch by saying, "I'm taking a surrey out about nine o'clock Saturday morning. I would love for you and your family to join me. If nothing else it would be a great day for your family. The Ponca are going to do the Sun Dance. It should be quite a show," Mr. Marland concluded as he looked at each family member. I think he may have even given me a little wink.

Mother smiled politely and assured Mr. Marland that she would give the matter serious thought and prayer.

Mr. Marland left with a pleasant good-bye and a smile on his face. He was no fool and knew when a deal had been made. Mr. Marland felt he had made a compelling argument to Myrtle McDonagh. He was also confident she could not resist three sons eager for a trip to the 101 Ranch.

CHAPTER 12

▼

Mr. Marland had accomplished his goal of getting my mother to the 101 Ranch. Myrtle McDonagh had no real choice. Two younger brothers and myself were determined to make the trip to the ranch. Even Dad took a rare day off from work to come. The whole McDonagh family met Mr. and Mrs. Marland in front of the Arcade Hotel Saturday morning.

The McDonagh family was dressed in various shades of brown and beige except for mother who wore a grey flannel dress. The Marland's, by contrast were colorful. Mr. Marland wore a green plaid jacket with coordinating tailored slacks. Mrs. Marland wore a stylish and sporty blue dress with large white buttons. She also wore a large brimmed hat trimmed in matching blue ribbon, which made her look like one of the Gibson Girls from a magazine.

Mr. Marland, as always, was talkative and in control. He invited Dad to sit up front with him. The two women occupied the second seat and we three boys literally wrestled for position in the small back seat. Being the oldest, I was able to secure one end seat while James, my brother two years younger, scrambled for the other. Poor Allen, the youngest, was stuck in the middle. Allen became a human battering ram as we battled to secure more territory and to irritate each other.

Except for the occasional scolding from Mother about the commotion we were causing from the rear seat, the trip was uneventful. Dad and Mr. Marland talked politics, baseball, and business. Mr. Marland's ability to make people feel important was not lost on Dad, who seemed to enjoy the dialogue. E.W. Marland knew being interested in the other people made them more interested in you. It was one of his unique gifts.

Mrs. Marland had her work cut out getting Myrtle McDonagh engaged in much conversation. Mrs. Marland was always gracious, considerate, and kind, but the two women had little in common. Mother sewed simple dresses, mended overalls, cooked, and worked around the house. Virginia Marland embroidered fancy clothes, shopped, ate at the hotel, and supported Mr. Marland's business dealings. The Marland's were Catholic and the McDonagh's were occasionally Presbyterian. Mrs. Marland was charged with maintaining most of the conversation, which was not her typical personality. The one thing the two women had in common was their love of children. To avoid awkward silences, Mrs. Marland would turn around and question Myrtle McDonagh's three sons about a variety of topics. She even told us about nieces and nephews she had back east. Two relatives, George and Lydie Roberts were actually planning to visit her next summer. Lydie was my age and George was three years older, but I was not that interested. My attention and eyes focused on the 101 Ranch House in the distance.

Upon arriving at the big white ranch house, we three boys scampered out of the surrey like ants on a hot plate. I took charge and showed the other two brothers around as if I was an old hand although I had only been to the ranch house that one time. My brothers tried to see everything at once, just like I had on the previous visit.

We were soon met by Miss Molly and Joe Miller. There was plenty of activity this day from wild horse riding and steer wrestling to shooting and rope tricks. About mid afternoon, we all headed down to an open field about a half mile away and just out of sight of the ranch house. A large group of Indians were there wearing colorful ceremonial costumes.

The large group, which wandered around with no particular order became silent, as our group approached. The crowd parted like the Red Sea as Mr. Miller, Mr. Marland, and Myrtle McDonagh moved toward a small group surrounding Chief White Eagle. Dad and my two brothers were close behind mother with Mrs. Marland and Miss Molly behind us. Surrounded by so many people quietly staring at you was an intimidating and somewhat frightening experience.

Chief White Eagle stood silently and regally. Like an eagle in the sky or a wolf at the head of a pack, the chief was majestic before his people. His advanced age was only evident in the crevices of his face. These deep wrinkles on his dark face were carved by a combination of sun, wind, and time, which gave him a haggard and tough appearance. His lean body was covered in buckskin clothing. His eyes were dark and sharp as he surveyed the people following Joe Miller.

Mr. Marland stopped a few feet from the chief and guided my mother by the arm to where she was standing directly in front of White Eagle. Joe Miller said a few words of greeting in the Ponca language and the chief responded with words of his own.

Joe Miller then said, "Chief White Eagle I would like to introduce you to Myrtle McDonagh, granddaughter to Chief Standing Bear of the Ponca people and your great niece."

The whole gathering waited tensely as the chief stood stoically looking at my mother while she stood there uncomfortably looking only at her shoes. Just seconds after this awkward pause an older woman who seemed to be White Eagle's wife cried out as she stepped forward to give mother a warm embrace.

This hug seemed to break the tension and the many people watching the reunion began to talk among themselves causing a slight roar. White Eagle's wife whose name was Evening Star, guided mother to the side of White Eagle and the two women embraced.

From then it became a genuine family reunion as people lined up to give mother a hug. Soon my brothers and I were the center of attention as numerous strangers came to pat us on the head and the old women hugged us. The adults sat down in a semi-circle to visit while we were led away to play with the children. All the children our age spoke English and we were soon involved in the games kids play.

It seems mother had more contact with the Ponca tribe than she had led us to believe. Her father had brought her several times to see various relatives from her deceased mother's side of the family. She had not been back since I was born and it turned out to be a wonderful day for her to be reintroduced to family and show off her offspring.

Later in the afternoon, mother even introduced us to her second cousin Willie Cry, the young man I had met the night of the fire. I had a hard time looking Willie in the eye for fear he would betray me, but for now he kept my secret safe from my mother's knowledge. I do not know if Willie was being kind to me, did not want to spoil the day, or just did not care about my misadventure as much as I did. For me, it was just a relief to not have to explain things to my mother.

As evening approached, a large group of Ponca Indians performed the Sun Dance, a ritual that predated memory for them. The men were dressed in colorful beads, turquoise colored cloth, and buckskin. There was drumming, chanting, and dancing as the young men performed many acrobatic maneuvers. This day's ritual was mostly a show. The actual Sun Dance would sometimes last days, involving animal costumes, and heavy symbolism. Willie Cry told me years later that he had actually seen a real Sun Dance as a child, but this performance was more than impressive to this young boy nonetheless.

More hugs and promises to come back accented our departure back to Ponca City. Chief White Eagle was not part of this group, however. The Chief, Willie Cry, Joe Miller, and Mr. Marland had separated themselves for part of the afternoon to smoke and discuss the mineral rights of the Ponca reservation.

You could easily tell from Mr. Marland's demeanor that the meeting had gone well. He was in exceptionally good spirits and talkative on our return to Ponca City. Mrs. Marland sat up front with him on the way back to town and the contrast between the two was evident. Mr. Marland would sometimes be boisterous and loud when excited while Mrs. Marland tended to always have the same benign manner. His passion was tempered by her pragmatism, his assertiveness balanced by her tactfulness, his risk taking moderated by her conservative nature, and his tremendous creativity complemented by her contentment with any situation. They were clearly a well-matched pair of individuals.

The McDonagh family was a tired but happy group at the end of the day. Mother was smiling more than usual and dad seemed to enjoy his visit with Mr. Marland. E. W. Marland, however, was the happiest of all. He had secured the rights to drill for oil on Willie Cry's section of land.

CHAPTER 13

▼

"Marland, are you putting another hole in the ground?" Daniel Craigan asked in a sarcastic tone of voice from the lobby of the Arcade Hotel.

"I'm drilling for oil if that's what you mean," was E.W.'s curt reply.

"Does Wiker know you have enough money to drill?" Craigan prodded. "He's probably wondering how far your line of credit will stretch."

E.W. Marland made a quick survey of the lobby to see if Mr. Wiker was around. He did not mind Mr. Wiker asking about the large bill he had accumulated at the hotel, but he had important things to do today and did not want to expend the energy to explain the nature of the oil business again.

"Don't worry about my bills or my character Craigan," Mr. Marland assured. "Unlike some in this world, I'm not out to profit at the expense of everyone else."

"Well, you won't have to worry about my company much longer," Craigan confided. "I'm taking what's left of my fortune and heading out of this berg. Train leaves this afternoon."

Mr. Marland smiled ever so slightly and with feigned sincerity said, "That's too bad."

Daniel Craigan did not respond to that reply and continued to adjust and count his bags that were sitting in the lobby. Mr. Marland was not anxious to continue the conversation and headed out to his well number nine on Willie Cry's land. It brought him brief comfort to think that Daniel Craigan was leaving on the afternoon train, but he had plenty of problems of his own.

The well E.W. Marland currently drilled was perhaps his final hope. Bill McFadden represented the last investor Mr. Marland could possibly find. The tension in E.W. Marland's face showed the pressure of drilling on a friend's dollar. Not that he had enjoyed any of the dry holes, but those were business deals. He had been upfront with investors and they knew the risk. Wealthy investors from the banking houses back east could afford a loss. Besides, they had secured plenty of his money in the last financial panic. Bill McFadden was different. E.W. had a sense of dread when he thought of having to explain another dry hole with Bill's money.

It was a typical hot June day in 1911 when E.W. Marland headed out to the field with a sense of satisfaction at having outlasted Craigan but also a sense of dread about letting down his friends like Joe Miller, Bill McFadden, and Willie Cry.

That day Walt and I were once again at our hangout near the train station. It was our sanctuary most days, but today we kept a low profile because Daniel Craigan had been around hassling the porters and asking them to take special care of his baggage. We were not generally prejudiced about who we got our tips from, but Daniel Craigan was still on the list of people from which we wished to stay away.

We were older now and spent more time working than playing. I was eleven and old enough to work most afternoons at dad's market stacking boxes or doing clean up chores. Walt was not as lucky. He usually ended up with the hard and dirty jobs no one else would do. Walt was a good worker though and we still enjoyed our occasional afternoons at the train station.

"What the…" somebody down the street yelled. Everyone's attention was focused down the street where a large commotion was taking place. It was apparent something was happening and immediately people on the street began to migrate to see the source of the uproar. As everyone, including Walt and myself, moved with the flow of the crowd we were nearly run over by a brutish man moving against the flow. My heart stopped to realize it was Daniel Craigan, but it was apparent he had no interest in us this day but instead bullied himself against the flow of the crowd. The noise and congestion grew. Walt grabbed my arm as we forced our way through the legs of the crowd to get a better look.

When we had arrived at the curb of the street, we discovered that the commotion was none other than E.W. Marland. He had just dismounted his horse covered from head to toe in oil!

Mr. Marland was always impeccably dressed even when he was working in the field, and was considered by many a fancy man compared to the cowboys and other ruffians of the town. However, Mr. Marland's dapper appearance masked a toughness and determination many failed to see until this point. He had slept in the derrick of many of a discovery well, gone for a week at a time without even taking his boots off. E.W. had been wet to the skin in freezing weather, ate meals out of a dinner pail and loved the excitement and satisfaction that came to him from looking for the underground treasure house of nature filled with black gold.

E.W. Marland was now clothed in that black gold. Willie Cry's number nine hole had hit a gusher at 700 feet. He walked into the hotel with a broad grin and straight-ahead look. He did not talk to anyone and did not acknowledge anybody's questions. E.W. Marland was going to share the news first with his main business partner, Virginia Marland.

When faced with a lack of information, people will make up their own news. Rumors were rampant that afternoon about what the find would mean. Mr. Marland had instantly transformed from a character of curiosity and suspicion to one of genuine celebrity. The only bad news for E.W. Marland this day was that Daniel Craigan unpacked his bags and secured a long-term lease at the Arcade Hotel.

Days later, the details of the find were circulating throughout the whole county. The well was pumping 60 barrels a day. Mr. Marland had already secured contracts to refine and sell the production. He had predicted the automobile would make oil the hottest commodity in the history of mankind and E.W. Marland was now positioned to take full advantage of this new opportunity.

E.W. Marland was true to his word when he had told my mother that an oil find would be good for many people. Willie Cry had become the richest Ponca Indian overnight receiving a $1,000 per year lease for the surface rights and 12.5 cents per barrel royalty. Bill McFadden's investment in E.W. made him an oil tycoon and he later declared, "There are four essentials to life: air, water, food, and oil."

Joe Miller's reputation and wealth also grew because that day in June of 1911 would mark the beginning of the 101 Oil Company. William McDonagh, my father, became the third person hired by Mr. Marland's company to be foreman of a pumping crew.

The day after Mr. Marland's first well came in, he walked into the kitchen where Mr. Wiker was going over the menus and asked him about his tab. The bill came to $850. Mr. Marland wrote him a check for the full amount and then gave a generous tip to all the hotel employees. He also secured a long-term lease on the finest suite in the hotel.

When E.W. Marland came to Ponca City in 1908, he was broke and had nothing but a letter of credit and a belief in himself. He had told Mr. Wiker he knew there was oil, and if Mr. Wiker would trust him for his money, he would pay him when he hit oil. E.W. Marland was true to his word. His life was about to change in the most dramatic fashion. One thing was sure; things in Ponca City would never be the same.

PART II

▼

CHAPTER 14

▼

Most men would have celebrated success, enjoyed the satisfaction of being right, and took life a little more leisurely. E.W. Marland, however, was no ordinary man. If anything, he worked longer and harder after the Willie Cry well hit oil. He quickly drilled two more producing wells and the oil rush was officially on in Kay County.

Besides Daniel Craigan, there were other men from all over the country coming to Ponca City to try their luck. Lewis Wentz came to Ponca City with less than Marland. Mrs. Rhoades, the owner of the Arcade Hotel, took a liking to Wentz and furnished him a grub steak. Wentz would turn that favor into millions over the next few years.

Men came to speculate, open stores, work in the fields, or even run scams, but E.W. Marland clearly had the gift for finding oil and walked around town like a monarch. The Marlands lived in the front three-room apartment located next to the hotel dining room. The apartment provided plenty of room for Virginia Marland since E.W. was generally out in the field or traveling to promote the new business. The dining room and lobby of the Arcade Hotel became the unofficial oil capital of Kay County. To some, it was the oil capital of the world.

Many new people and many new businesses were coming to Ponca City that year. My gang was particularly thrilled to have a Coca Cola bottler open in the area. Mr. Marland loved Coca Cola and would occasionally treat the whole gang to a round of the soda. He said, "Even King Solomon never drank anything as good as a Coca Cola."

Mrs. Marland had befriended Jackie McFarlin, a young girl who was sometimes a trick rider for the 101 Wild West Show, but most of the time was a cook at the Arcade Hotel. She was always cooking something special for Mrs. Marland and her friends. Mrs. Marland would give Jackie advice and make fancy dresses on her new sewing machine for her. Jackie caused quite a stir one afternoon when Mr. Wiker had asked her to try some new recipes out of a cookbook he had purchased. A lady friend of Mrs. Marland's shrieked and demanded Jackie take the muffins back because some kind of bug had gotten mixed into the flour. It was no bug. That is how blueberry muffins were introduced in Ponca City.

In the summer of 1912, two other visitors inconspicuously entered the social fabric of Ponca City. George and Lydie Roberts, the nephew and niece of Virginia Marland, came to visit for the summer. The first time I saw the two, I was struck by how pale they looked. They were shy and well mannered, but not well prepared to be the center of attention that the Marland's commanded in Ponca City in those days.

George was a lanky boy with legs longer than his proportion. He was three years older than his sister and very protective of her. George had an easy grin and a laid-back personality that made him easy to like. Lydie appeared somewhat more reserved and unsure of herself. She was a lean, athletic girl with no distinctive feminine shape and like me was twelve-years-old. Lydie had shoulder length, brown hair and inquisitive brown eyes. Though shy, she had a warm smile and dimpled cheeks.

The Arcade Hotel was probably a great place for adults and businessmen, but to a kid it held no real entertainment. After George and Lydie had been in town a few days, Mrs. Marland arranged for me to come by and officially meet the two. After the customary awkward introductions, we were excused to go about town.

Getting to know a stranger at age twelve is a graceless and self-conscious endeavor. There is never much to discuss with a person you know nothing about and most adolescents are clumsy at investigating the other person's point of view. I struggled to think of questions to ask the two and my only real plan was introducing them to the gang.

The city had constructed Pecan Park close to the train station. It had huge pecan trees that gave plenty of shade for our new hangout. Floyd Wills, Bobby Williams, Cricket, and Raeford Dutton, our infamous fire starter, along with Walt and several other boys were sitting around a stone fire pit in the middle of the park. It did not occur to me until later that Lydie was the only girl and might feel uncomfortable, but this was the group I knew.

After small talk on the way to the park and introductions to the gang, Walt began the interrogation. "What kind of name is Roberts?" he asked looking George square in the face.

"I don't know, it's just my family name," George replied sheepishly.

"I mean is it Irish or German or is it some made up name?" Walt continued.

"I don't really know, does it matter?" George countered.

"Guess not," Walt admitted.

"What kind of name is Walt Johnson?" George asked taking a more proactive approach to the questioning.

"I think its Scottish?" was Walt's curt reply. Walt decided he did not really want to discuss ancestry with anyone and quickly changed the topic.

"How old are you?" Walt asked in a sneering tone as he sized up George's height.

"Fifteen," George answered as he pulled his shoulders back to appear a little taller. George Roberts was older than anyone in our group. He was not only taller than the rest of us but very thin. His overall appearance was certainly less than intimidating. In fact, his timidity gave him an initial appearance of weakness.

Walt was definitely sizing up any competition that might challenge his authority in the group and asked, "You guys know how to ride or rope or do anything like that?"

George looked to his sister quickly then said, "No, I mean I've been on a horse before but not one I could ride all the time."

Raeford could be depended on to cut to the chase and ask the direct questions everyone else was too polite to ask.

"I guess you're one of those rich fellas from up north," Raeford challenged.

George kind of half laughed as his sister sat in uncomfortable silence at the male posturing.

"Did I say something funny?" Raeford said taking a step forward. Raeford was the least likely to win a fight of anyone in our group. I doubt he could have whipped Lydie much less George, but with the backing of the group, he was the most cocky and likely to get the rest of us into a fracas.

Walt quickly stepped in to defuse the situation realizing that George Roberts possessed no real threat to his dominance.

"Shut up Raeford," Walt scolded.

"That's all right," George interjected, "I'm not a rich kid form back east. That's why I laughed."

We all looked at the tall gangly kid that had been subtly bullied and began to feel empathy for his plight as a stranger.

George took the opportunity to tell us a little more about himself. "We're not really that poor but my family back in Flourtown are not what you would call 'well to do' people."

"Where's Flourtown?" Cricket asked.

"Pennsylvania," George replied. "It's a suburb of Philly. My dad works most days as a push peddler and we live in a small three room flat."

The ice was broken and the conversation blossomed from there. We learned a lot about the Roberts family, Flourtown, and their unique ways of doing the same things we did in Ponca City. We quickly determined George was like one of us and an all right guy. One of the great things about kids is that arch rivals of one moment can be the best of friends the next. That is how George Roberts and Walt Johnson became friends that summer and how George became part of our gang.

Lydie on the other hand was in social no man's land. The only person in the state of Oklahoma she really knew was her brother George. We did not expressly forbid girls in our group but the issue had never come up before. We did not like girls and girls did not like us. They did not seem to like any of the things we found interesting. Nevertheless, Lydie was part of the package deal with George. She was stuck with us and we were stuck with her.

It is remarkable how quickly kids can make connections with one another. By that afternoon, George was completely integrated into our group. Being the new guy, he was getting special attention from Walt and the other boys. I did not mind. Walt and I were good enough friends for me not to worry about being second fiddle to anyone. It did mean, however, that I was stuck entertaining Lydie for the afternoon.

As the day wore on, I found talking to Lydie was not as bad as I thought it would be. In fact, I began enjoying our conversation. Her initial shyness soon wore away and I found she was spirited and competitive. We discovered she could run nearly as fast as George could and quite a bit faster than Raeford. Lydie was not like talking to any of the girls at school. She liked doing the things we liked to do so we soon forgot about her being a girl and she too was adopted into our little circle.

By evening, we made plans to meet again the next day. The Roberts had a fairly good tour of the interesting parts of Ponca City, but the next day we would show them our special hideouts and places.

The next day we picked up where we left off the day before. We walked to the bridge by Red Bud Creek, went to the banks of the Arkansas River, and even walked far enough to see the ruins of the Sacred Heart cemetery. We talked about sports, fishing, hunting, and all of our past adventures, including the Indian burial grounds excursion.

We saw George and Lydie almost every day that summer. They liked to come to my mother's kitchen for dinner. They loved the okra and tomatoes mom cooked with fresh roast beef, baked bread, and cinnamon rolls. Myrtle McDonagh was a fantastic cook and could fix almost anything. Her one weakness was making jelly. Mom was always frustrated because her jelly was runny which gave it the texture of grape syrup. George and Lydie, however, loved what they called her "thin jelly".

Mr. Marland arranged for us to ride on the "Doodle Bug" several times that summer to ride horses at the 101 Ranch. The Doodle Bug was a short train comprised of an engine and a car together that served as a trolley for local traffic between Ponca City and the 101 Ranch. It was Lydie's first experience on horseback and George's first time to ride extensively. I had always dreamed of being a cowboy and a great horseman, but somehow was never that comfortable on a horse. In about a month, George and Lydie had far surpassed my riding abilities.

We went swimming almost every day. Lydie was a great swimmer although she forced us to dress for swimming which was something we were not accustomed. When Mrs. Marland found out that Lydie had been swimming with the boys, she was horrified for some reason. She prohibited Lydie from swimming with us, which meant much of our summer, was spent finding ways to sneak off and swim without Lydie being caught.

George and Lydie were particularly interested in the Indians. They asked ridiculous questions like if they scalped people or went on the warpath. It was information they could only get from those paper back stories they sold back east.

We were quick to capitalize on their interest in the local Indians, however, by telling and embellishing our local experiences. We talked about Jim Thorpe, a Sac and Fox Indian from around Shawnee who had stunned the world that summer in Stockholm, Sweden by winning the decathlon in the Olympic Games. We talked about him as if we were personal friends. The King of Sweden himself declared Thorpe the "greatest athlete ever" to which Thorpe replied, "Thanks King." We talked about how Jim Thorpe learned to run down horses on the banks of the Arkansas River, although I think he actually lived by the Canadian River down south in Pottawatomie County.

A strange thing happened to the gang that summer. Lydie had transformed from a person we had to tolerate, to one who was becoming more and more the center of attention. Taking advantage of her interest in our local Indians, I even exaggerated to everyone that I was blood relative to the Ponca Chief and probably would become an important chief myself someday. The guys all mocked me, but Lydie seemed to be impressed.

It was turning into a great summer and all of us seemed to be competing more and more for Lydie's attentions. She was the perfect girl. Not ugly, athletic, interested in sports, and easy to talk to once you got to know her. Lydie and I became great friends that summer. Even though Walt had teased and tormented her most of the summer, she seemed to always have her eye on him.

Walt had always been as much a brother to me as a friend. This was the first time we had actually competed with each other and we began making more and more snide remarks towards each other to gain the attention of Lydie. For all the posturing and great conversation I utilized to win Lydie's affections, her attention focused on Walt. It did not really matter if Walt won or lost, he just had that something that drew people to him. This summer he was drawing Lydie like the night attracted fire flies.

George turned out to be very affable and became one of Walt's close friends. As fall approached, Lydie and George were preparing to head back home. Our gang needed one last adventure to celebrate the end of this summer.

Cricket, of all people, came up with our next scheme…to spend the night at Sacred Heart Cemetery. Sacred Heart cemetery was part of an old Catholic mission dating back to the Indian Territory days before statehood. It was located a few miles west of town in a remote location about a mile off the road. All that was left of the mission were three walls of the old church building, the foundation of a burnt schoolhouse, and a few tombstones in the cemetery. The church operations had long since moved into Ponca City to St. Mary's and the place was mostly forgotten except by the schoolboys of the town.

Cricket was a small wiry boy who generally kept to himself. I do not know exactly how he received his nickname but he had been Cricket for as long as I could remember. Only his mother called him Perry. Cricket's plan was simple. We would hide our bed rolls in the park, sneak out of the house after dark, get to the graveyard before midnight, spend the night, and head home at dawn.

The stories and legends about the strange occurrences at Sacred Heart were well documented although no one we knew had in reality witnessed anything. Our scheme had some similarity to our burial grounds expedition, but Sacred Heart would be a much shorter trip. Since Walt and I had been the only two who actually went to the Indian burial grounds, our renditions of the story had caused a bit of jealousy with others in the gang.

The biggest hang-up to the Sacred Heart trip was Lydie. She was determined to go, but we knew she was the one Mrs. Marland kept the closest eye on. Sneaking out of the Arcade hotel without getting caught would be a challenge. George assured us that it would not be a problem since Mr. Marland was on business back east. Mrs. Marland typically went to bed early in the evening so the only real danger was being seen by one of the hotel staff.

Walt devised a plan where he would cause a distraction about nine o'clock so George and Lydie could sneak out the back door. Walt's distraction was pure genius and required no damage to the hotel's property. Walt entered the lobby to ask if the Marland's were in. George conveniently happened to be within earshot of the lobby to take the call with Lydie hiding near the cloakroom. Walt then screamed, "Snake!" while pointing at a huge Bull Snake he had carried into the hotel in a paper sack hidden in his baggy overalls. Bull snakes were completely harmless to anybody, but the appearance of the large black snake created the desired chaos. Walt, George, and Lydie met up with the rest of the gang ten minutes later by the train station.

The moon was full and illuminated the countryside with an eerie glow for our walk. The trip to the cemetery would generally take about an hour in the daylight, but would take about two hours in the moonlight. The conversation was jovial and relaxed until we ventured off the road and toward the cemetery that was wedged between two small hills.

Bobby Williams began a spine-chilling story about a crazed ax murderer who was never caught. The sinister fiend roamed the countryside stalking those who dared to come out of the city after dark. The story was implausible and unbelievable, but the surroundings were perfect for a fright. As we approached the old church building, the group was quiet and Lydie was clenching my arm! Her fingers dug in as she pulled close to me imagining that somehow I could provide some protection. Every sound and strange shadow kept her close to my side. There was definitely nothing supernatural going on but the overall ambiance made it an uncomfortable place to be in the middle of the night.

In the dark of the night, a wild wind suddenly blew across the surrounding prairie stirring up dust and making the guys cling to their hats. Distant lightening flashed in the western sky, which was enough to make us decide staying the night was a bad idea. We still had time to get back to town before midnight and get back to the places we were supposed to be.

With Lydie clinging to my arm, I was the only one with any desire to stay longer. Overriding my objections, the group quickly walked away from the spooky Sacred Heart cemetery and back toward town. Lydie had regained her composure and soon separated herself from my arm and my side.

We made the trip back with more purpose and more speed. The lightening was nearing and intensifying. The rumblings of thunder soon accompanied the furious-looking lightening. Storms here could come quickly and fiercely. Even I was glad to be back to town as a few sprinkles of rain began to fall. The rest of the gang went to the north part of town leaving Walt, George, Lydie, and myself to get to the Arcade Hotel. Walt and I would then sleep at my house.

As we walked down Main Street, we could see a strange man standing in front of one of the local establishments. We discreetly moved to the other side, but the stranger crossed the street blocking our path. He was obviously drunk and as we came closer, we were horrified to see Daniel Craigan between us and the Arcade Hotel. He obviously recognized our group and looked determined to have a midnight meeting. It was beginning to rain lightly as the thunder and lightening became more imminent. There was no turning back for us. We had to cross Daniel Craigan.

I was surprised and temporarily relieved that Craigan had no interest in Walt or me. The relief was brief as it became evident he was focused on confronting George and Lydie.

"You!" shouted Craigan angrily, as he looked toward George Roberts. George looked around trying to determine whom the drunken man was addressing.

"Yeah, you," he continued now pointing at the tall youth. "You're that kid staying with Marland."

George politely said, "Yes sir."

"Your uncle's trying to ruin me," Craigan accused with some slurred speech.

George listened in silence.

"He's got every good lease from those stinking Indians and libeled me to where they won't even talk to me," Craigan charged. By this time, Craigan had moved face to face with George and without warning pushed him hard enough to send George sprawling onto the damp ground.

I was stunned at what was happening on this empty street. Craigan, however, did not hesitate and grabbed Lydie hard by the arm.

Craigan began to say, "And you little…" Before Craigan could get the obscenity out of his drunken mouth, Walt Johnson plowed him to the ground! I had been paralyzed with fear, but Walt responded instinctively. Although Daniel Craigan was nearly twice Walt's size, the tall man groaned as he hit the ground with Walt landing on top of him. It was a tackle Jim Thorpe would have been proud of and as soon as Walt hit Craigan he bounced up to help his friend George to his feet. We ran away from a stunned Craigan as quickly as Walt had dropped him.

Out of breath and wet, we stopped in front of the Arcade Hotel.

"Who was that guy?" George asked.

"That's Craigan," Walt responded.

"We've had run-ins with him before," I added quickly trying desperately to be part of Walt's rescue.

"You leveled him good!" George enthusiastically noted.

"I guess so," Walt sheepishly admitted.

"I mean I thought we were in real trouble back there," George continued.

"Are you okay?" Walt asked suddenly turning to Lydie.

She nodded blushingly without really saying anything.

"Thanks Walt," George said.

"You would have done the same for me," Walt said.

I do not to this day know if Walt really believed that any of the rest of us would have taken on Daniel Craigan. If I had been able to respond, I feel sure I would have run away for help. Walt Johnson did not run away and did not cower to bullies. He had taken the challenge head on and put Craigan flat on his back.

Walt and I said good-by to George and Lydie as they proceeded to sneak into their empty beds without Mrs. Marland or any of the staff stopping them. We ran to my front porch. I was still shaking. Neither of us discussed Walt's action again that night. We were both tired and ready for a dry bed. The thunderstorm turned into an easy excuse for coming home before the campout was over. Mother was up and worried about us. She had no idea where we had been, but could tell by our wet clothes that we had been in the weather.

Walt and I quickly fell asleep that night. George and Lydie Roberts would be gone in two more days.

CHAPTER 15

▼

Mr. Marland promised my mother that finding oil would be good for many people. He had been good to his word. Willie Cry was making a fortune for owning a hundred and sixty acres of hilly grassland. Bill McFadden was on his way to becoming a millionaire. Joe Miller had added oil tycoon to his title as successful rancher, farmer, and showman. Lewis Wentz had made his millions and had the distinction of being America's most eligible bachelor. My father was also riding the wave of Marland success as he moved from drilling foreman to production manager for the new company. Even Daniel Craigan was in the game after finding oil, although outside the boundaries of the Ponca Nation.

My father proved to be an enterprising employee and Mr. Marland treated his employees very well. The McDonagh's were doing great. I was starting high school and dad even talked about a college fund for me even though no McDonagh had ever spent a day on a college campus. Businesses grew, employees were in demand, and almost everyone was benefiting from Marland's boom. E.W. Marland continued to find oil almost every place he looked and soon was hiring the smartest engineers and geologists he could find. People from across the state and even the nation were calling Ponca City home.

George and Lydie became frequent visitors to Ponca City, even managing a winter trip close to Christmas when the Marland's were able to lavish many gifts on the two. George was still part of our gang, but he was older and began developing a group of friends more equal to the Marland's social status.

In 1913, Francis Ouimet won the United States Open Golf Championship beating two of the best professional players from England, although he was just a twenty-year-old amateur. Mr. Marland loved the egalitarian aspects of this story and determined that Ponca City needed a golf club. He proceeded to plan and fund the construction on some land he had purchased.

E.W. Marland was a man of great contrast and paradox. He seemed to fancy himself as an English nobleman wearing sporting clothes instead of western wear common to our area. This gave him the appearance of being soft, but those that knew him could vouch for his toughness, determination, and stamina. He loved the formality of the European lifestyle and the arts, but also saw himself as the champion of the common man. He hated the snobbery and elitism of the east he had left, yet continued to travel back there for pleasure and to finance his growing business. One thing was for sure, E.W. Marland could do no wrong in Ponca City.

In that year, Chief White Eagle died. Some said he was over 100 years old. He was certainly the oldest Ponca Indian and may well have been the oldest person in Oklahoma. No one really knew for sure. Hundreds in the community, including the Marlands, attended his funeral. Mother cried at the great chief's passing.

E.W. Marland was making more money than even he could spend. He dreamed of a day when he controlled the distribution of oil from the ground until it was pumped at one of his Marland gasoline stations. He had a logo designed that had a red triangle with Marland printed in the middle. The gasoline stations Mr. Marland built looked like little English cottages and they were uniquely different from any other architecture seen on the growing American roads.

The Great War in Europe only fueled the demand and need for the oil that E.W. seemed to have a genius to find. In fact, E.W. was spending less and less time prospecting for oil and more time building his empire. He was hiring the smartest people in the country. E.W. Marland had a knack for leadership and was able to develop employees that truly believed in his vision. He even went back east to hire a college friend of his, Randle Haman, to act as Chief Financial Officer for the corporation now called Marland Oil.

Randle Haman was a handsome and affable man who had been a roommate of E.W. Marland while they were in law school in Michigan. He was always nicely dressed and seemed to be one of Mr. Marland's closest confidants. Mr. Marland was even able to overlook Haman's past employer, the hated J.P. Morgan Bank.

The Arcade Hotel brought in stately leather furnishings for the lobby where many of the biggest oil deals took place. Of the 100 rooms at the Arcade Hotel, 22 were rented to millionaires. E.W. Marland, however, over shadowed all the other millionaires as he closed in on being one of the nation's elite billionaires.

By 1914, the Arcade Hotel could not hold E.W. Marland and he broke ground on a house on Grand Avenue across from the golf course that was finished in the spring of 1915. The mansion was to have 22 rooms, including a large ballroom and almost eight acres of sculptured gardens. It would be known as the Grand Mansion. Opulence was coming to Kay County.

I got a job as a caddie at Mr. Marland's golf course, but frankly spent nearly as much time playing as caddying. Almost all the caddies were sons of Marland Oil employees and executives.

Walt was not as lucky. He needed real money to try to pay the rent. Mrs. Marland helped him secure a landscaping job for the magnificent gardens at the Marland's Grand Mansion. It was hard work, but the Marlands paid well. The labor tanned his skin and built his muscles to where he vaguely resembled the little boy that used to loiter around the train station.

George and Lydie were nearly full-time residents. They seemed happy in Ponca City and took full advantage of all the leisure and recreational activities the oil boom had brought. Besides the golf course, Lou Wentz was building a large swimming pool for anyone in the city to use. Mr. Marland helped establish a Polo association and built three polo fields as well as horse stables. George became one of the best polo players around and had become an expert equestrian.

Lydie developed and blossomed into a beautiful young woman during these years. Her playful spirit and athleticism were still evident, but she had developed a much more womanly shape. The Marland's wealth gave Lydie many opportunities to socialize. She went to the finest schools and ran around with her own group of stylish girls.

The mansion on Grand Avenue was finished by 1916 and it was indeed grand. The lavish twenty-two room house was located on a slight hill next to the golf course. Eight acres of manicured gardens encircled the property with open-air splendor and beauty. The gardens featured many walkways and fountains with a variety of hedges, shrubberies, flowering plants, and ornamental trees. The house featured a large terrace overlooking the magnificent garden. The inside of the house was modern in every way, including a built-in vacuuming system, a grandiose hanging staircase, a large ballroom, and even an indoor swimming pool. Mr. Marland had hired 12 men, including Walt Johnson just to mow and maintain the grounds.

Before E.W. and Virginia Marland moved from the Arcade Hotel, they took a vacation back east. The Marlands had everything they could want in life except children. Virginia might not have been able to have children, but E.W. found a way to manufacture a family. He negotiated with the parents of George and

Lydie Roberts to adopt the two children that had spent so much time with their wealthy aunt and uncle. When the Marlands returned form Pennsylvania to move into the Grand Mansion they were four…E.W., Virginia, George, and Lydie Marland.

CHAPTER 16

▼

Our old gang was changing forever. Each had developed separate interests. Lydie was involved in social refinements. George was always off playing polo or some other sport like football. Raeford Dutton took an interest in musical instruments. Robert Williams had grown up into a fine high school athlete specializing in baseball. Cricket spent a lot of time with me caddying and playing on the golf course. Floyd Wills moved south to Potawatomie County in central Oklahoma. Walt had become a handsome young man, but had dropped out of school to make his way in the world. Although he was barely 16, Walt had little time for our former boyhood adventures.

Walt and I continued to be close friends. He came by the house for frequent meals and slept over some nights. We still talked of adventures and about life, but we spent more time talking about our hopes, dreams, and aspirations for the future. Although Walt's future did not seem bright to many, he had determination and ambition few could imagine. I continued to enjoy our talks together, but Walt spent much of his time caring for his ailing mother. Walt was not able to stay in school, but Mrs. Marland had instilled a love of reading in him. He carried a book around with him most of the time and was determined to better himself even without school.

The people from the gang were for the most part still friends but our lives and interests had stretched our relationships and moved us down different paths. The exception was George and Walt. The two former friends had grown apart to the point they rarely spoke without it becoming a verbal duel.

Part of the conflict involved their changing social positions. George was now living the life of a pampered nephew to one the richest men in the country, while

Walt struggled to provide for himself and his mother. The real cause, however, was Lydie. Like a magnet to steel, Walt and Lydie were drawn to each other. It was easy to see their natural attraction. George, however, did not approve of this relationship and was determined to protect his younger sister.

Lydie did not go to the public high school. She attended a private Catholic school supplemented by the finest tutors and private lessons money could buy. With Lydie attending school across town and Walt out of school, I had no better amusements than heading to the golf course in the afternoon. I typically did not waste much time making my escape after the last bell and today was no different. After securing my books in a bag, I mounted my bicycle to go play nine holes.

After a half a block, I had built up a good head of steam. My mind was already on the golf course when I heard a familiar voice shout, "Charlie."

I turned to see Lydie waving at the corner across the street. I peddled to her, and then said, "How's it going Miss Marland?"

Lydie blushed a little, and then replied with a smile, "Just Lydie to you."

Lydie was still not completely comfortable with her new last name and I enjoyed teasing her about it.

"What are you doing on this side of town?" I asked.

"I came to see you."

"Really, I'm flattered," I said in a flirty tone.

"I came to see if you've seen Walt today," Lydie asked.

I was only slightly deflated. My flirtations with Lydie were always innocent. Her attraction to Walt had been obvious for a long time.

"No, I haven't seen him in a couple of days," I answered in a more serious tone. "Is anything the matter?"

"I don't think so, but he hasn't been at work since Monday. I snuck off to ask the head gardener about him this morning and he said he had come by early to say he was sick," Lydie related.

"That's odd."

"I'm worried. Why would he come by if he were sick?" she asked.

"I don't know."

"Anyway," Lydie continued, "I've never been to Walt's house and I'm embarrassed to say that after all these years I don't even know where he lives."

I knew where Walt lived, but I had only been to his home once when I was much younger. Walt lived in a one-room apartment with his mother. The place was shabby looking even to a young boy. Walt and I had been close friends for as long as I could remember, but we had an unspoken rule that we never went to

Walt's place. Something about the whole atmosphere gave me an uneasy feeling and I had not been to his apartment in years.

Lydie was becoming impatience with my stone silence and she asked again, "Charlie, do you know where Walt lives or not?"

Hesitantly I said, "Yes."

Pushing my bicycle along, Lydie and I began the long walk across town to the other side of the tracks.

CHAPTER 17

▼

The Norwood Hotel was the antithesis of the Arcade Hotel. The Norwood catered to those who had nowhere else to go…a sleazy hotel on the wrong side of town surrounded by the wrong kind of people. It had been Walt Johnson's home for most of his life.

Ponca City was prosperous and upscale during the early days of the oil boom, but every town has its hidden underbelly, places where people go to be forgotten and do things in obscurity. The Norwood was the center of this oasis of darkness. It was the kind of place I could imagine Daniel Craigan frequenting. The overall environment always made me feel anxious.

The Norwood was a three-story structure with a bar and grill that was more bar than grill occupying the first floor. Rumor around town said the Norwood's back room was the place to go for gambling, cock-fighting, and other diversions. The whole place looked old and cheap. The old was understandable, but the place looked as if it had never seen better days. The only respectable looking place was a corner grocery store called the Sunshine Market, which seemed safe…at least in the light of day.

"Lydie," I commanded, "stay here. I'll go see about Walt."

I did not give her the opportunity to argue as I left the bicycle with her and headed across the street. The apprehension of walking into a place where I did not feel I belonged was strong. Lydie watching me from the corner made it difficult to back out now and besides, I was genuinely concerned about my friend Walt who had missed two days of work.

Fortunately, a back staircase went directly to the second floor, which meant I did not have to endure the stale smoke and unpleasant smells of the bar and grill.

The hallway was long and dark with six non-descript apartments on each side of the hall. A staircase to the first and third floors stood at the other end of the hall.

To the best of my memory, Walt's door was the second from this end. I was disappointed to find no markings on the door to confirm this was the Johnson residence. It made me nervous to think what I might be disturbing if my memory was faulty. I tentatively knocked on the door and heard the distinctive voice of Walt Johnson answer, "Who is it?"

I was relieved to hear Walt's voice and I said in a loud whisper, "It's Charlie."

Rustling noises could be heard inside. In a few moments, the door opened wide enough for Walt's head to protrude through the opening.

"What are you doing here?" Walt asked with a raised eyebrow and some terseness in his voice.

"Lydie said you have been sick the past two days," I responded.

Although Walt was doing his best to block the door, I could see Mrs. Johnson lying in a bed by the window. It was obvious Walt was not ill, but Mrs. Johnson looked like death warmed over. She was curled up into a ball lying on her side. Red blotchy spots covered her face. She was awake but her eyes had a faraway look as if she was not aware of anything happening in the room.

"I'm fine," Walt assured in a curt tone of voice. "It's mom….she's not been well."

"Is there anything I can do?" I asked.

Walt seemed to be over his irritation about having an uninvited guest and smiled slightly as he said, "No, but thanks for asking."

He did not invite me in, but he smiled a little more and asked, "How's Lydie?"

"She's fine. I left her downstairs."

Walt's countenance immediately changed. His smile vanished in an instant and he said asked with grave concern, "You brought Lydie here!"

I had been so intent on seeing Walt and so seduced by Lydie's request to take her to him that I had forgotten how sensitive he was about his family life. As I stammered for a moment trying to find an answer, Walt's face became pale and ashen before turning a pinkish red. Without a word, Walt slammed the door in my face!

CHAPTER 18

▼

It only took an instant to discover why Walt had rudely slammed the apartment door. Lydie Marland stood at the far end of the hall.

"Lydie!" I exclaimed trying to cover my own mistake in bringing her to this part of town, "What are you doing here? I told you to stay across the street!"

She did not respond. Lydie just started walking methodically towards the door. I could think of nothing to do but walk toward her and block her from Walt's door. *Maybe if I am not standing by the door she will not know which one is his,* I rationalized. I stepped quickly towards her and we stopped face to face, two doors down from Walt's. Neither of us spoke. Lydie's attention focused on the dire surroundings of the Norwood Hotel.

I could not have felt worse. Taking Lydie to this place was possibly the most offensive thing I could have done to Walt. The awkward silence needed to be broken and all I could think to suggest was to leave.

"Lydie…" I began.

Before I could say another word, Walt bolted through the door. Without saying a word, he shot an angry glance at me, and then walked quickly away from us toward the back steps. Lydie and I looked at each other for a second, then in unison walked after him.

We did not get within earshot of him until he hit the bottom of the steps.

Lydie yelled, "Walt!"

He never broke stride.

"Walt," I joined in as he still ignored us.

As he crossed the street toward the corner market, Lydie broke into a non-ladylike run, caught up with him, and grabbed him by the arm. I joined them a few seconds later.

"Walt, what's wrong?" Lydie pleaded.

Still no answer, but at least Walt had stopped walking. I knew Walt well enough to know I needed to say nothing until he cooled off.

"Walt?" Lydie continued, desperate to get some response.

A few more seconds of silence then Walt unloaded on us, "You two have no right coming here. No right to invade my privacy."

Lydie and I looked at him in stone silence. I could not help but think the "invade my privacy" argument was pretty weak for a guy who lived at my house more then he did in his own home.

"I…" Walt began to say more, then just bent his head down and remained silent.

Walt was not angry with us, I soon realized. He was embarrassed.

I was clueless as to what to say. Fortunately, Lydie knew just what to say. She stepped from his side and came face to face with Walt. Lydie positioned herself to force eye-contact then said with a soft smile, "It's all right Walt."

He looked at her. Walt appeared as if he might well-up in tears. It was hard to imagine that fearless Walt Johnson had been most afraid of someone finding out about his sad family life.

Lydie reached up and touched his cheek and said, "It's okay…It doesn't matter…It doesn't matter to me."

Lydie seemed instinctively to understand Walt's humiliation. He looked away a moment and bit his lower lip before looking back at Lydie and saying, "I know, but I didn't want you to see this place. It's…"

Lydie cut him off by saying, "It's just a neighborhood Walt. It's just four walls where you live. It's not what you are. Trust me, I've seen worse."

Walt grinned slightly as he took a deep breath to regain his composure. He looked up into the sky for a moment before saying, "Mom…she's not well. The doctor came by and gave her some medicine, but all it does is make her stare at the wall."

"I'm sorry," Lydie sympathized. "Is there…"

Before she could ask if she could help, Walt said, "Yeah. Let's get out of here for a while and walk to the train station."

Walt suddenly remembered that I was standing in the background and said to me, "You can come too."

"Thanks," I replied sensing that Walt did not need me to make him feel better, "but I've got some things to do."

I always enjoyed spending time with Walt or Lydie, but I was tactful and observant enough to know they were a couple now. Walt and Lydie had an unspoken understanding of each other. Lydie might have been the daughter of a wealthy oil tycoon, but she understood growing up in poverty. She could empathize with Walt and more importantly could see his potential. I gathered up my bicycle as Walt and Lydie walked toward the train station…hand in hand.

CHAPTER 19

▼

Prosperity appeared to embrace the whole of Ponca City with the exception of Walt Johnson and his mother. Lydie let Mrs. Marland know about Mrs. Johnson's illness. Mrs. Marland had discreetly arranged for her doctor to go and care for Walt's mother. Not even Walt knew about this kindness from Mrs. Marland. The doctor told Walt that he was part of a county program to help those who could not afford medical services.

Walt's mother was chronically ill, however, and her health continued to decline. With no father around, Walt became the primary source of income. If not for the charity of Mrs. Marland and other benevolent souls in town, Walt and his mother's situation would have been much worse. Nothing seemed to get Walt down, however, and he dutifully provided for his ailing mother as best he could.

Walt and Lydie had begun to spend more and more time with each other. Most activities the past couple of years had involved all the gang. During these group gatherings, however, Walt and Lydie paired off with each other more often as time passed. Walt even held Lydie's hand at the Forth of July picnic, which did not sit well with George.

Lydie had developed a crush on Walt from that very first summer. Walt's swashbuckling tackle of Daniel Craigan had probably fanned the infatuation. As time went on, Walt began to notice Lydie as more than a friend. Lydie developed into a beautiful young lady, with personality, spirit, and intelligence. George, forever protective of his kid sister, did not like this new interest from Walt Johnson. He did all in his power to dissuade and discourage their innocent courtship. Walt was not one to be easily deterred and so the two former friends found themselves more and more in conflict.

Things got worse for Walt Johnson during the winter. Despite the help from Mrs. Marland's doctor, his mother passed away. Like many others, Walt's mother had led an unexceptional life and there had even been rumors about a dubious past. The funeral was small with only a few friends of Walt to help him through his grief. The McDonagh family, Virginia and Lydie Marland, and a few others were there. The only apparent mark Mrs. Johnson had made in the world had been her son. Walt moved into a room in the back of the maintenance barn by the golf course.

Walt was too old to be an orphan and really too young to be on his own, but those were the cards dealt him. Everything in Walt Johnson's life seemed hopeless and still he was able to maintain an optimistic outlook about his life. For all of his challenges, Walt Johnson had a persistent and unrelenting belief in himself.

CHAPTER 20

▼

The transformation of Lydie Marland had been dramatic. The shy, skinny, twelve year old girl that first came to Ponca City was now a shapely and alluring young woman. She had silky brown hair, warm brown eyes, and distinctive dimples on her cheeks that radiated pure joy when she smiled. Lydie loved to dance, swim, and ride horses. Mr. Marland gave her access to the finest schools in the country and Virginia's influence was evident in Lydie's style and grace. Added to all of Lydie's natural charm was the fact that she was now the only daughter to one of the nation's wealthiest men. She was the object of attention for gentleman from literally all over the world.

For a while, it seemed as many young men were coming through the train station to court Lydie as there were coming to drill for oil. There were aspiring businessmen from New York City, sons of the nouveau rich oil tycoons, a host of young men of noble birth from Europe hiding out from the Great War, and even a Count from some European country coming to the lavish balls hosted by the Marlands. They came to see if they could win the grand prize, which would have been the fortune, prestige, and company of Lydie Marland.

The grandeur of the parties at the Marland's home was something the people of Ponca City had never seen. Invitations were coveted and special trains from Tulsa delivered the many out-of-town visitors. Lydie and I had remained close friends throughout the years. I was invited to most of the parties because of this relationship and my father's rising stature in Marland Oil. One of the grandest parties celebrated the completion of the new home on Grand Avenue and Lydie's seventeenth birthday.

Raeford was part of the band providing the music that night and I was glad to see a familiar face. Few locals were actually a part of these social gathering and I knew few people at this party. Walt, of course, was never invited to one of these formal gatherings. George made sure as many barriers as possible were put between Walt and Lydie. Since Lydie had no romantic interest in me, my relationship was non-threatening to George. The Marland men always had a watchful eye on the youngest Marland. I was often chosen by George to be Lydie's dance partner to relieve her from any overly ambitious suitors.

This evening Lydie wore a stunning blue satin dress that flowed off her shoulders into a kind of ruffle that then draped down to the floor. It was hard to imagine this was the gangly girl that had clung to my arm so tightly that night at Sacred Heart cemetery. She had her entourage of girlfriends about her and as lovely as Lydie looked, I was more enthralled with one of her friends that evening.

I found myself transfixed on Elizabeth Cassidy that night whose father was a local dentist. She was a short, petite girl with sandy blonde hair and sparkling blue eyes. Elizabeth was surrounded by a group of Lydie's friends including Carol Thompson who was enduring some social instructions from her mother and Tara Kelly. Elizabeth's features were delicate and she seemed to get absorbed in the smallest of details. I had just worked up the courage to break through the circle of women surrounding Elizabeth when a hand landed on my shoulder, gently turning me around. It was George Marland.

"Do you see that guy?" George asked with a tone of disgust as he directed my attention to a young man talking to Lydie.

"The guy in the black suit with the pipe?" I asked.

"This is not good," George concluded.

Lydie was engaged in conversation with a stylish man wearing a black tuxedo and holding an expensive pipe in this right hand. He appeared to be in his late twenties. Lydie was laughing and seemed to be well entertained.

"Who is it?" I asked.

"It's a friend of Haman's," answered George.

Randle Haman was a college friend and roommate of E.W. Marland. He had bright and commanding eyes and a look of aristocracy. Few people in town had much interaction with Mr. Haman, but he had unquestionably established himself as E.W. Marland's second in command at Marland Oil. Mr. Haman was serving as Chief Financial Officer and had brought many bright young men from schools back east to help with the financial management of the fast growing Marland Oil.

"Mr. Marland will not approve of Lydie socializing with employees," George stated.

In truth, Mr. Marland and George did not seem to approve of any young man who might have a romantic interest in Lydie. They were infamous for their interrogations of any gentlemen expressing too much attention toward Lydie. The fact that this young man was an employee of Marland Oil was just one of many excuses they used to protect her. Virginia Marland would have been able to make the two Marland men behave, but she was not feeling well and had retired to her room before the party even started.

"If you'll go ask Lydie to dance, I'll have the band play a waltz," George instructed.

I shrugged and went on my mission. Who was I to complain? Going over to ask one of the prettiest girls at the ball to dance knowing she would say yes was not a burdensome task. Even if she said no, Lydie would think none the less of me; it would just mean she wanted to continue her flirting. It is what Mr. Marland would call a win-win situation. Lydie was an easy girl to talk to and I could always make her laugh. She seemed to like my company and never really declined one of my invitations. Part of her willingness to accommodate me was, I am sure, a fear of a more direct and intrusive interruption from her brother.

Walking over to her, I asked in a formal tone, "Lydie, could I have this dance?"

"I did promise you this dance, didn't I Mr. McDonagh," she stated in an equally formal tone. She had not previously promised to dance with me, but this was a sure signal that she was ready for a change in company.

"Mr. McDonagh I would like to introduce you to Mr. Whittier," she continued.

We exchanged handshakes and greetings.

"Mr. Whittier is a friend of Mr. Haman's. He is coming to work as a bookkeeper or something," Lydie informed.

"Actually I'm going to work for Mr. Haman as a chief accountant," Mr. Whittier quickly corrected.

"Actually if you're working at Marland Oil, you'll be working for Mr. Marland," Lydie added with a slight smirk.

"Of course, that's what I mean," Mr. Whittier quickly admitted.

"Mr. Whittier played football at Yale," Lydie added as the young man postured at the compliment.

"Mr. McDonagh, they're starting our waltz," she concluded.

Lydie excused herself from Mr. Whittier, took me by the hand, and we began to dance.

After a few steps she asked, "Who sent you, George or Mr. Marland?"

"George," I admitted. "Hope you don't mind."

"I wonder why you are willing to continually do the Marland men's dirty work?" she scolded mockingly.

"So you did mind?"

"Not at all," she said as we continued our waltz. "He was a tremendous bore, worse than most. All he could talk about was himself and all he asked me about was money."

"You were putting on a good act."

"Thank-you," she said with a smile. "I know Mr. Marland trusts Mr. Haman, but I don't like any of these people he brings in. They're arrogant, know-it-alls."

"Oh, I hate those guys," I said with a grin. I had developed a bit of a reputation as a know-it-all myself.

"You know what I mean," she scolded in jest. "You're not arrogant, just irritating."

"You know," I retorted, "people that think they know everything are a real irritant to those of us that do know everything."

Lydie laughed. Although I had long gotten over the fact that she would never think of me romantically, I still loved to hear her laugh.

"Well, I'm glad George trusts you to do his dirty work, I do need someone around who can still make me laugh," she sighed.

Her tone turned slightly more serious as she asked, "How's Walt?"

"It's been tough," I confided. "I actually think he's better now that he doesn't have to worry about his mom, but he works all the time."

In many ways, I was still a boy, childish, immature, with the luxury of still being playful. Walt, on the other hand, had transformed into a man. His shoulders and arms had broadened with hard work while his blonde hair had darkened to more of a sandy brown. His broad grin and high cheekbones were highlighted by his dark tan. Walt's overall appearance made him look more serious and more mature.

Lydie had a look of concern as she said wistfully, "I wish he could be here tonight."

"Me too," I replied feeling somewhat guilty when I was able to come to an event where my friend was denied access.

"George is impossible with him and Mr. Marland's not much better. They throw these big bashes for me then brow-beat any boy that shows any interest," Lydie lamented.

"It looks like you're showing a lot of interest tonight," I said.

Lydie smiled, "It's just an act…mainly to keep those two off track."

I looked over to see that Mr. Whittier was involved in an "interview" with the two Marland men. It was certain he would be under close surveillance for the rest of the evening.

Lydie continued, "I love living here in Ponca City. I could have never dreamed I could live like this, but sometimes it's so inconvenient. Don't you wish sometimes it could be like that first summer when we did what we wanted and didn't have all this staged entertainment?"

"That was a great summer," I had to admit as I reminisced about our childhood escapades.

"I wish I could go swimming in the river or just sit on the bridge with Walt and talk without all these distractions," Lydie said while looking around the room at all the guests and activities.

"I guess you're still kind 'a hung up on Walt?" I asked already knowing the answer.

Her face seemed to illuminate at the mere mention of his name.

"Of course…He's not like any of these pretentious, pampered gentlemen," she replied with no shame and a tone of cynicism. "Walt is genuine. He's my knight in shining armor."

I could not help but smile at her tone and candor.

"You still see him don't you Charlie? Does he ever mention me?" she asked in a pleading tone.

When Walt would come by the house, he would talk of little else than Lydie. I was probably the only person besides Lydie to know they had been secretly seeing each other for months. She had to know that, but Lydie just wanted to be reassured.

"Only every other word," I assured her.

Lydie could not help but smile glowingly and then asked, "And how about you…are there any young ladies you're telling him about?"

I blushed enough that Lydie knew to interrogate further.

"There is!" she exclaimed excitingly. "Who is it?"

I looked around and hesitated for a moment then said, "I was on my way to ask Elizabeth Cassidy if she would like to dance before George collared me."

"Elizabeth!" Lydie shrieked almost loud enough to be heard over the music. She giggled under her breath a little and said, "She would be perfect for you. You should definitely ask her to dance."

Her tone of voice made me a little suspicious so I asked, "You're mocking me, right."

"Oh no," she assured. "Elizabeth is a sweet, dear girl. She would be perfect for you. In fact, I'll introduce you."

The waltz was ending and Lydie escorted me directly to Elizabeth Cassidy for the introduction she had promised. Lydie was right. Elizabeth was charming, sweet, and witty. We visited for a long-time as I worked up the nerve to ask her to dance. I learned that her father liked to play golf. She was the oldest child, like me, with two younger brothers named David and Shawn.

When an appropriate song was announced, I calmly asked if she would like to dance, to which she replied "no." After a few more moments of awkward conversation, I excused myself and immediately began to search for Lydie, who was surely making sport of me. Lydie was not to be found, however. She had already slipped off to meet Walt.

CHAPTER 21

▼

After about an hour more at the party, I had enough entertainment for the evening. I had not seen Lydie since she disappeared after introducing me to Elizabeth. George was still stalking Mr. Whittier, but I feared it was only a matter of time before he interrogated me about Lydie's whereabouts.

I left a party that still had plenty of energy to stroll down the walkway of the Marland gardens toward the street. The gardens were always a peaceful place even during these parties. Although not as colorful as they were in the daylight, they still provided ample beauty in the soft moonlight.

The flowering plants were not on my mind this night, however. I was still licking my wounds from Elizabeth Cassidy's rejection. I kept going over the conversation in my mind trying to analyze my errors. Things seemed to be going well, then suddenly rejection.

As I left the garden and stepped onto the city street for home, I picked up my pace. I was tired and ready to get to bed when a sudden sound startled me from behind. It was Walt Johnson running up to me.

"Charlie," he said in between a whisper and shout, "wait up."

I turned around and nonchalantly said, "What's going on?"

"Not much," Walt said with a grin. "I was in the garden with Lydie when Mr. Marland came out for a smoke."

"Did he see you?" I asked in a genuinely concerned tone.

"Naw," Walt answered, "but we had to hide in the shadows about fifteen minutes until he left."

"You two are going to get caught and then there'll be heck to pay," I warned.

"You're probably right, but it was nice to just hold her there in the dark," he shared.

I kept walking, not really interested in knowing more about their escapades.

"Lydie was telling me you met someone tonight," Walt noted.

I let out a slight groan then said, "I bet Lydie had a good laugh about that."

"You mean about the dance, don't let that bother you," he said with a little laugh as if he had some secret insight.

We were within a couple of blocks of home so I offered, "Do you want to stay over tonight?"

"Sure," Walt answered as he threw his arm around my neck. "I've been needing to talk to you anyway."

"What about?"

"Lydie."

"What about Lydie?" I asked.

Walt hesitated for a few seconds then exclaimed, "We're promised to each other."

"What?!" I exclaimed in surprise.

"We've promised each other not to see anyone else," Walt proudly stated.

"I understand what 'promised' means, but I don't see how either of you think this is going to work," I tried to reason.

My lack of enthusiasm deflated Walt for a moment, but then he explained, "We've been seeing each other for a long-time now and you know we've liked each other for longer than that. She understands me Charlie."

"I know that, but I also know that George and Mr. Marland will not approve," I tried to tactfully explain.

"Fortunately it's not their decision, it's Lydie's," Walt reminded.

"You're only eighteen and she's only seventeen Walt. Don't you think you're rushing things?"

Walt grimaced a little then became more serious and said, "I know she's young, but sometimes you just know when a person's right and I...we think we're right for each other. You don't know how she looks at me Charlie. You don't know how she makes me feel. I mean you're my best friend and all, but sometimes I think Lydie is all that makes the world right."

I was silent as I thought about his words. I might not know how Lydie made Walt feel, but I certainly had known for a long time that Lydie looked at Walt as she did for no other. I would like to have been caught up in romance like Walt and Lydie but I tended to be more practical. I knew first hand how protective

George was of his little sister. I also feared being put in the middle between the Marlands and Walt.

"How about George?" I asked.

"That's a problem for sure," Walt admitted. "I like George, but he's gotten a little too full of himself since that adoption. It don't mean anything except they're living here fulltime now. Give me time and I'll win George back over. It'll take some time, but it's not like we're getting married next year or anything. I'll get Mr. Marland on my side too. He always kind of liked me anyway. Never give up on anyone Charlie. Miracles happen all the time."

I was less confident than Walt about his prospects of ever convincing the Marland men that he would be a good match for Lydie, but I admired his consistent optimism. We arrived at my house and Walt had a snack from mom's leftovers. We talked until late in the night. I was tired, but Walt was the sort of guy that had contagious enthusiasm and I always found myself staying up late whenever he came over. All he could really get excited about this night, however, was talking about Lydie.

CHAPTER 22

▼

Lavish parties became routine at the Marland's Grand Mansion. Besides entertainment for George and Lydie, they provided the perfect opportunity for E.W. Marland to conduct business and show off the trimmings of his growing empire. Many thought E.W. Marland would make his millions then build a big house back east to live with other people of his own class. E.W. Marland, however, had fallen in love with the spirit, people, and opportunities of this new land.

Each new party brought a fresh host of eligible admirers for Lydie. George, however, was as diligent as ever in protecting his debutante sister from all suitors. George had also gained a powerful ally in putting up this line of defense, E.W. Marland.

Although Mr. Marland's association with Lydie during her early trips to Ponca City was limited, he took the role of protective father seriously. One of Mr. Marland's many contrasts in personality was his ability to be so persuasive and interested in other people while being so suspicious and guarded about their motives. Possibly, because of his bad experiences in losing his first fortune, he had developed a genuine paranoia about strangers. He was faced with the paradox of thinking no one in Kay County was good enough for his Lydie and no one from outside could be trusted.

Unbeknownst to E.W. and George, they were wasting their time protecting Lydie from all the gentlemen callers coming to the Grand Mansion. The only man Lydie was interested in was never at the great parties. While the Marland men were vigilant partners in keeping any gold digging suitor from sweeping Lydie off her feet, she had already been swept. Lydie and Walt had learned the value of stealth and secrecy as they grew in their devotion for one another. Walt's living across the road was perfect for their seemingly innocent rendezvous in the garden on Lydie's many evening walks.

The relationship between Walt and George, however, became even more contentious. George observed the two talking several times in the garden. One day, Lydie demonstrated a little too much delight in her dialogue with Walt. George came storming down from the veranda overlooking the garden grounds and scolded his sister while reminding Walt he was to work, not entertain Lydie.

Walt felt discretion was better than an argument for Lydie's sake. To continue seeing Lydie, he employed caution and secrecy. Lydie and Walt continued meeting each other regularly without anyone knowing. Lydie was as good at maintaining the deception as Walt. Many nights she would dance away the evening flirting with boys possessing acceptable pedigrees only to disappear in the night to meet her Walt.

E.W. Marland was not used to being naïve. He was accustom to knowing the current reality in situations before anyone else and found himself bewildered on the rare occasions when he had misjudged circumstances. He was completely shocked the evening he discovered Walt and Lydie kissing in a secluded portion of his grand garden.

"What the…" E.W. exclaimed in bewilderment.

Lydie and Walt were as surprised to see Mr. Marland as he was to see Lydie in the arms of a man. E.W. had been so confident in his monitoring of Lydie that it never occurred to him that she might have this secret life. It only took him a second to recognize Walt as the culprit.

"You?" he bellowed in an increasingly aggravated tone realizing Lydie was embraced by one of his hired men instead of one of the noble gentleman he had been guarding so much against.

"Good evening sir…" was all Walt was able to get out.

"You be quiet," Mr. Marland commanded pointing a threatening finger at Walt. "Lydie, have you lost your mind? Your reputation could be ruined if someone saw you here rubbing up against one of the hired servants."

E.W. was usually sensitive to working people but he had chosen the word "servant" for emphasis.

"Mr. Marland, I was just out for a walk," she tried to explain.

"A walk! Is that what they call it now?" Mr. Marland accused.

"But…" Lydie began to defend.

"But nothing," Mr. Marland interrupted. "There is no discussion here. You go to the house now."

Lydie looked painfully at Walt then dutifully began the long walk back to the house. Walt began to leave too when Mr. Marland commanded, "Stop, we have some things to talk about."

Walt stopped in his tracks and the two men waited while Lydie walked out of earshot.

"I've never seen such behavior young man," Mr. Marland began to scold. "She's only seventeen and you're…"

"Eighteen sir," Walt injected.

"And you're a hired hand working at this house. You have to understand that this is not acceptable. What if one of the guests had been here instead of me to see this behavior?" Marland scolded. "I have nothing against you personally son, but you will never be worthy of Lydie. I'm glad to help you out and give you a job but this is unacceptable."

Walt listened in silence.

"Your family…you have no family and that's an improvement over the reputation of what family you did have," Mr. Marland added. "Lydie is being prepared for a life that you cannot possibly imagine. You will cripple her ability to find the kind of family that will generate a legacy…a family heritage."

Walt's teeth bit hard together making his jaw clench.

Mr. Marland, sensing he had gone too far concluded, "I just want you to know that you can't have close contact with Lydie. I think it best if you don't even see or speak to her. Just walk away whenever you see her. If you're working and have to leave the grounds, I'll fix it with the ground foreman." Mr. Marland was feeling relieved having resolved this indiscretion with such diplomacy and charity.

"I can't do that," Walt finally stated. He slowly looked E.W. Marland in the eye and said, "Lydie and I are in love."

"What?" E.W. exploded having never expected the young man in front of him to do anything but acknowledge his orders.

"Lydie and I are in love. We have been for a while and we will be married after I save some money."

E.W. Marland laughed a little in disgust and disbelief, "That's not possible. I would never allow it. Lydie would be completely disowned. Trust me son you will never marry Lydie Marland. You don't even know what love is."

"No, I'll be marrying Lydie Roberts. We've talked it over. We won't need your money. I'll make it on my own."

A flabbergasted E. W. Marland stood in stunned disbelief as Walt Johnson dared to inform him of plans and conversations involving Lydie.

Walt took advantage of this hesitation by Mr. Marland to vent some of the frustration he had felt the past months while keeping his relationship a secret and said, "If you knew Lydie....If you ever listened to her, you would see that she doesn't care about the money, the prestige, or even a heritage. She's a good person, with a kind heart, and that's good enough for her. You're the one trying to cripple her ability to be happy."

A vein popped out in Mr. Marland's forehead, a forehead that was now turning red with anger. His nostrils flared and Mr. Marland looked sternly at Walt as if he might explode. In E. W. Marland's most intimidating matter he stated, "First, you're fired. You get whatever things you keep in the shack and leave tonight. Secondly, you are to never set foot on this property or any Marland property again. If you do I'll have you shot."

Walt never flinched, but E.W. Marland was in no mood for further debate. With those explicit instructions, E. W. Marland walked away leaving a defiant Walt in the secluded garden spot. Mr. Marland would meet with Lydie later that night and explain the circumstances to her also. Walt gathered his things and came to the only place he knew he could lay his head, Charlie McDonagh's house.

CHAPTER 23

▼

A few days after Mr. Marland discovered Walt and Lydie in the garden, Lydie came by the golf course to play a few holes. She requested I caddy, which meant I played while toting her golf clubs. Lydie enjoyed many outdoor activities, but golf was not one of her favorites. She would generally let me hit any difficult shot for her. When she did play, it was either to entertain someone or to talk. She was alone this afternoon. Our game only lasted two holes until we were far away from the mansion grounds and in an isolated spot where she could talk.

"It was terrible," she related. I had never seen Lydie cry or even lose her composure, but I felt tears were imminent. "I've never seen Mr. Marland so angry."

"Walt told me," I replied. "He said Mr. Marland was going to have him shot if he came back on the grounds."

"It's worse than that; he told me that if I ever saw Walt again he would ship me back to Flourtown as far away from 'that boy' as possible."

I listened with concern.

"Besides that," she continued, "he said he was going to hire men to watch Walt and me to make sure we didn't try anything stupid."

This was a new twist that I was sure Walt did not know.

Lydie stepped close to me and said, "Charlie, I need you. You're the only link I have to Walt."

"I think both of you are swell," was all I was able to get out as I thought how precarious my situation had become being the liaison between a forbidden love, especially one forbidden by E.W. Marland.

"We'll have to be very careful," she said in whispered, frightened tones. "He could have people anywhere."

"What are you going to do?" I questioned.

"I don't know," she answered in dismay. "I honestly don't think I can live without him, but I don't want to disappoint Mr. Marland either. Mr. Marland was so disappointed last night. I tried to reason with him and talk about Walt's good qualities. They're both just alike you know, but Mr. Marland would only talk about the future and being practical. I don't know what to do. I'm a mess."

Lydie looked off in the distance lost momentarily in her own thoughts. She trembled slightly as she tried to collect her thoughts and her eyes were constantly scanning her surroundings.

"I wish sometimes that I had never come here as part of the Marland family. I wish Walt and I could have met and just been a regular couple somewhere else. Charlie you know him. Walt can do anything he wants in life. He has a truly great character within him. I just don't understand why Mr. Marland can't see it."

Lydie spoke fearlessly and with determination. I assured her that I would do anything I could to help. We then cut across to the seventh hole so that it would appear we had played the entire nine holes.

After the last hole, Lydie asked me to carry her bag across the road to the house. As we walked through the garden grounds, her mood became slightly more cheerful as she asked, "How did the dance go with Elizabeth?"

I had not seen Elizabeth since the time I had asked her to dance. There had been several functions at the mansion since then, but Elizabeth had not been there.

"You set me up," I replied. "She turned me down."

Lydie laughed a little and said, "She turned you down because her church doesn't dance. They don't believe in it or something. I had to talk for hours just to get her to come to the party."

"Thanks for the warning," I said in a sarcastic tone.

Lydie was quick to interject, "Don't worry, I talked to her just last week and she really does like you. She asked me to see if you would invite her out sometime or maybe go to a church meeting. I think you should, you would be a cute couple."

"I'll think about it," I assured her, feeling somewhat justified knowing that I was not completely repulsive to Elizabeth Cassidy,

Suddenly Lydie froze in her tracks. She stood still for a second looking down at the ground.

I had walked a few steps up the path and had to turn back around to ask, "What's the matter?"

Lydie stood still, looking at the ground. She slowly bent down and picked up the butt of a cigarette.

"Don't you have gardeners to pick up?" I joked.

Lydie was very somber and said, "They do."

She then looked up at the house and had an ashen look as she said, "That's my window."

I turned around to look at the house and noticed an upstairs window that Lydie pointed to as hers. You could not see into the room from this vantage point, but Lydie was obviously distressed about something.

"For the last several nights…since Mr. Marland caught me with Walt, I've noticed a strange glow coming from this part of the garden. I hadn't known what it was till now…," she said as her voice drifted into a kind of strange awareness.

I remained silent for a moment, but her voice and overall demeanor were unsettling.

"Known what?" I finally asked.

She answered very softly, as if someone were listening, "Someone has been watching me. That strange glow is someone standing right here smoking a cigarette and watching me…They've been standing right here."

I felt a chill and could sense Lydie's alarm and anxiety. It was a strange, almost eerie feeling to know someone had been on this very spot spying on Lydie. They could not see into her room and she had only noticed the strange light by walking to the window to overlook the garden. Still it was discomforting to know someone had been watching from that spot.

Lydie did her best to dismiss the find as a coincidence, but she grew nervous and fidgety as she looked about as if some one was still watching. I knew without her saying a word that any midnight meetings with Walt in the garden would be impossible.

"Don't tell Walt," she pleaded in an uncharacteristically panicked tone. "I don't want him to worry."

I felt this was good advice even though I did not understand Lydie's intense trepidation. I knew Walt would have surely come to investigate this stranger.

"I won't," I replied.

"Thanks Charlie, thanks for listening," Lydie said with a smile as she regained her composure almost as quickly as she had lost it.

As Lydie walked away, I felt uneasy. I could see no good coming from this secret romance between her and Walt. Walt, George, and probably Mr. Marland were in mortal conflict with each other and I felt squeezed in the middle. Little did I know circumstances outside anyone's control were about to change everything.

CHAPTER 24

▼

The social and economic growth of the area was booming, primarily as the result of Marland Oil. Other things were also happening to change this small city. The 101 Ranch was still expanding with infusions of oil money. The ranch had added such exotic attractions as an ostrich herd and a resident bear to entertain the tourists that still came for a getaway. While the 101 Ranch appealed to the notion outsiders had about the Wild West in Oklahoma, E.W. Marland was doing much to upgrade the culture of Kay County.

Mr. Marland had brought opera to the city, built a golf course, and financed a polo club that traveled all over the country to play. He had generously contributed to almost any worthy charity. Virginia Marland's tireless volunteering had diminished somewhat with her health struggles and she was seldom seen away from the Grand Mansion. Mr. Marland had commissioned various art projects and sculptures for the community and was regarded as one of the great patrons of the arts nationally. His European gardens surrounding the Grand Mansion were regarded as the finest west of the Mississippi and were envied by some of the wealthiest individuals in the country.

Mr. Marland fancied himself as an English gentleman and strove to bring as much English refinement to north central Oklahoma as possible. One of the most popular and unique traditions he introduced was foxhunting. A Marland foxhunt was a spectacular event and a coveted invitation. Mr. Marland even hired a "Master of the Hounds" to teach hunters the proper etiquette during a hunt. These foxhunts became the elite thing to do, and everyone aspired to be part of the "Horsey Set" that was invited to these events.

Mr. Marland owned a fine stable of horses for polo and the hunts. He kept a kennel of the best bloodhounds money could buy, and had even imported several European foxes that were caged and well fed until let loose for the hunt. Not all the foxes were caught, however, and unto this day, the countryside sports a few "Marland" foxes.

The hunting parties would sometimes number as many as one hundred hunters and Mr. Marland insisted all the party dress in traditional garb complete with knee high boots and red hunting jackets. I was surprised and honored the day I received an invitation to go on a hunt. Lydie, I was sure, initiated the invitation. Although I was an average rider at best, I was looking forward to it.

Lydie and Walt had stayed in touch by messages usually delivered by me. They sometimes found secret meeting places, but this was difficult in a small town. Walt did not challenge Mr. Marland's warning about staying away from the Grand Mansion and the gardens. This not only made it more difficult for him to see Lydie, but also segregated Walt from Mrs. Marland who seldom left the Grand Mansion because of her declining health. I never told Walt about the spy watching Lydie's room. I wandered by the gardens a couple of times to see if I could detect the stranger to no avail. I had run into George and Mr. Marland a couple of times and determined I needed to be more invisible in this secret relationship.

Walt had been acting and talking strangely lately. I did not really know what to make of him. Being on Mr. Marland's bad list was not a good thing in Kay County. He had tried to get work in Newkirk, but that did not work out. He moved to Arkansas City, Kansas for a few months.

Lydie was actually able to visit him there a few times until she was nearly caught. She would drive to Arkansas City with her group of friends then slip away to spend an hour or two with Walt. Although these trips were risky, her girlfriends were loyal and never betrayed her secret. A Kansas state trooper nearly exposed Lydie, however, when he pulled the girls over and arrested them after finding a bottle of wine under the seat. Mr. Marland had to drive up and straighten the mess out. The wine turned out to be sacraments for the Catholic Church that one of Mrs. Marland's friends had left behind. The girls did not even know it was in the car. Soon after, Walt drifted back to Ponca City doing whatever odd jobs he could find.

Lydie found me at the golf course a few days before the foxhunt. The last note I smuggled for Walt was troubling her. The note said he was desperate to see her, but the message did not reveal any reasons. She quizzed me about the content, but I was honestly ignorant. After much prodding, she was convinced I did not know. She told me the foxhunt would be the best opportunity for her to see him. Lydie asked me to have Walt meet her at the Red Bud Creek Bridge shortly after the hunt started and gave me a note for him. I was to stay as close to George and Mr. Marland as possible. If they headed toward the bridge, I was to warn Lydie and Walt. If the Marlands started asking questions about Lydie's location, I could come and get her.

The plan was less than perfect, but it was the best we had. It would be risky. In my first and probably last foxhunt, I would need to be at least as clever as the fox.

The day of the hunt was grey and overcast with a drizzling fog. Mr. Marland probably thought it the perfect English weather for a hunt. The splendor and ceremony of the hunt was a spectacle to see with red jackets and handsome horses everywhere. The fox was darting around its cage and the hounds were barking. Mr. Marland made a brief speech about the history of foxhunting and related that to some long-winded point. Celebrities and powerful people could be seen everywhere. I was aware of at least two United States Senators and several more state lawmakers.

A brass horn blew and the fox was let loose. The dog keepers struggled to hold the hounds back as they pulled against their restraints. The horses were restless and the riders anxious for the horn to blow a second time. Lydie discreetly moved her mount to the edge of the pack and so far, George and Mr. Marland were so involved in entertaining and preparing for the hunt that they seemed unaware of her location.

When the horn finally blew, all chaos broke loose. I got a glimpse of Lydie heading toward the Red Bud Creek Bridge as I struggled to keep up with the pack and keep the Marlands in sight. Fortunately, George and E.W. stayed in the same general proximity to each other as they rode hard in pursuit of the hounds. I tried to keep them in sight while staying as far away as possible, which was a challenge with my limited riding ability. As best I could, I also tried to stay between the hunters and the bridge. I feared the fox would either be caught quickly or worse, lead the hunt toward the bridge.

Lydie had experienced the confusion and unpredictability these hunts could produce before. Fortunately, the fox was clever, extending the hunt longer than I expected and was leading the group away from the bridge location. Things seemed to be going Lydie's way until I spotted something that did not look right. In the distance, a car was careening over the hills, driving toward the main hunting party.

For a brief moment, I did not comprehend the significance, then immediately I bolted toward the bridge. I rode as hard as I had ever ridden. Lydie had once told me Mr. Marland had hired men to watch Walt, but I had always been suspicious of this tale and had discounted it as one of her paranoid fantasies. Seeing the strange man driving toward Mr. Marland made me wonder, however. I felt Lydie had to be warned of this unusual intrusion of the foxhunt. I rode hard for fifteen minutes before spotting Lydie and Walt standing next to the Red Bud Creek Bridge.

I shouted as loud as I could, "They're coming…I think."

Lydie and Walt looked into each other's eyes.

"Walt you've got to get out of here!" I admonished.

Lydie had thought of all contingencies. Walt had secured a horse somehow for the trip out. Without hesitation, he leaped onto the horse and galloped back toward town. As I dismounted, Lydie was obviously distressed. She had been crying and was emotionally shaken. Even in this state, she was able to maintain her composer to complete the deception.

"Quick," she said. "Ride with me."

With that, she mounted her horse and galloped hard for a quarter of a mile to a low place in the creek. Without hesitation, she jumped the short expanse and then leaped from her horse landing hard on the ground!

In shock, I dismounted, crossed the creek on foot, and ran to her aid. She was crying but was obviously not hurt.

"He's been drafted," she cried.

"What?" I asked not expecting this type of conversation from a woman who had just tumbled from a horse.

"Walt's been drafted into the army," she exclaimed.

"I didn't know," I assured. My shock could have said that without words.

"I know. He said he hadn't told anyone. He said he didn't want me to find out from anybody but him."

"When?" I asked.

"He leaves next week," she explained. "I begged him not to go. I told him I would run away with him. We could go to Mexico or somewhere, but he said he had to go. He said it was his duty."

I had known Lydie for nearly six years and had seen her in many situations, but had never seen her as shaken as she was this day.

In moments, the thundering of approaching horses headed our way. It seems Lydie was the fox this day. Her cleverness had kept the secret meeting with Walt from George and E.W. Marland. Sure enough, there was a spy who had seen the two lovers together and found Mr. Marland to make the report. If not for Walt's quick retreat and Lydie's faked injury, they would have certainly been found out. Lydie's real tears and distress added to the illusion.

"Lydie are you all right?" asked a concerned E.W. Marland.

"I think so," she replied with tears still streaming down her face.

"What are you doing so far out?" he gently asked.

"Charlie and I thought we saw a hound come this way and I guess we got lost," she coolly replied bringing me square into the plot.

"I told that security guy it couldn't have been Johnson," George interjected. "I bet he's been shipped off by now."

Lydie shot me a quick glance, but maintained her ruse. It was obvious to her that Walt had not been the only person in town to know about his draft status.

"Not now," Mr. Marland scolded.

Mr. Marland seemed genuinely more concerned for her well-being than Walt's location at that moment. That meant there would be no inquisition this day. He ordered a car to take Lydie back to the house after she convinced him that she did not need a trip to the doctor's office.

I hurried back to town as soon as I could to get more details from Walt. Many boys from Kay County would be drafted for the Great War in Europe that America was preparing to fight. I was not eighteen yet so I was off the hook, but Walt was headed off to be a soldier.

Walt confirmed that he would be leaving in six days for training. We promised to write and I promised to keep an eye on Lydie. Walt seemed to sense that the distance of the war might accomplish what E.W. Marland had not been able to do, separate him from Lydie.

CHAPTER 25

▼

Walt was the first young man from our town to go to war. As he prepared to board the train to begin this perilous journey, he and I stood alone at the same train station where we had witnessed so many happenings in Ponca City. We talked about nothing in particular, but there was a tenseness in our conversation as neither one of us knew exactly the proper protocol for this type of situation. Walt had once said the station was like a gateway to the world and now he stood poised to step through that gate.

"You be careful over there," I warned.

"You don't have to worry about me," Walt replied as his eyes searched the surrounding crowd.

"I don't know why you have to go. This is not our war," I argued.

"It's not our war, but sometimes you have to join the fight. You can't let a bully get away with being a bully or they'll go bully someone else," he reasoned in a matter of fact tone.

"I still think George…" Walt stopped me before I could say I thought the Marlands had something to do with him being drafted.

"It don't matter. I need to go. I need to get outta here," he sighed.

I stood in awkward silence, not knowing what to say.

"Do you think she'll come?" Walt asked as he nervously bit his lower lip.

I had delivered the time and date of Walt's departure to Lydie the night before. "If it's within her power she'll be here Walt, but she doesn't always have the final say in her life."

Walt began to grin showing his big smile and said, "You don't understand Charlie, Lydie is one determined woman."

At that moment, I became aware of clamoring behind me. The conductor was calling all aboard at the same instant Lydie Marland slid to a stop in Mr. Marland's prized Duisenberg at the end of the platform. She had waited until George and Mr. Marland had gone to the polo grounds then stole it.

"Walt!" she screamed as Walt stood on the steps of the train. She ran dodging passengers and baggage with reckless abandon then threw her arms around Walt as he lifted her several inches off the ground.

"Don't go," she pleaded.

"I gotta go," he replied with a compassionate smile.

"You be careful," she demanded.

"Charlie's already told me to do that," Walt informed her as he winked at me.

Lydie whipped around to catch a glance at me then turned to Walt and said, "You be careful for me."

Walt grinned even more, "I will...for you. I will be back for you," he assured.

"I'll be waiting," Lydie assured.

"I'll hold you to that," Walt replied.

Lydie became more serious and said, "Walt, I don't know why you have to go halfway around the world to fight people you don't even know."

"We've been over this," he calmly affirmed.

"I know," Lydie pouted, "but it's not your responsibility to try to fix everything in the world. There's not one thing you can do that will change that war so be careful and don't be a hero."

"You never know what one Oklahoma boy can do," Walt teased. "A hero might look pretty good to some of those French girls."

"Don't you be a hero and don't you even look at any French girls," Lydie scolded.

"I won't be looking at anything but that North Star, because I know you'll be walking in the night and looking at it too."

Lydie blushed and said, "I guess you know me pretty well. You look at that star every night and know I'm thinking of you."

"That's a deal," Walt assured.

"Here take this," she demanded as she handed him a photograph of herself.

Walt looked at the picture of Lydie for a moment then said caringly, "This is a bit better than the North Star, I'll look at this every night too."

The conductor called for everyone to board the train again.

"I love you Walt Johnson," Lydie declared.

Walt smiled and gave her one last hug before saying, "And you know I love you too."

With that, the conductor forced Walt onto the train that steamed out of town in a few minutes more.

Lydie had been bold to come see Walt off in front of the whole station and she had been able to keep her composure for Walt. She broke down, however, and pleaded with me to assure her that Walt would be all right as soon as the train was out of sight. I told her that if anyone could take care of himself it would be Walt. As much as I could, I assured her with stories about his tenacity and abilities to overcome difficulties. I do not know if Lydie was convinced, but I was leaving the station with an apprehension like I had never known before. I honestly wondered to myself if we would ever see Walt again. I felt like I was losing a part of myself when my good friend Walt Johnson left for Europe. I could only imagine the emptiness Lydie felt.

CHAPTER 26

▼

By the late spring of 1917, all America was preparing for war in Europe. The Miller brothers had secured a lucrative contract to supply horses for the army and Zack Miller even secured a commission as a Major in the army. George Marland also volunteered and was made an officer with Zack. No one ever knew if George or even Mr. Marland had anything to do with Walt being drafted, but it probably made no difference. Kay County was a patriotic place and many were volunteering without being drafted. For a guy like Walt, the army was maybe the best way out of poverty and economic plight. Although Walt could not stand the thought of leaving his Lydie, he was ready for a change of pace and a chance to see the world.

I found myself reading the daily papers more diligently than I had ever done before trying to piece together the theater of war and what role my friend would play in it. I tried to write once a week to keep him up to date with our world and possibly cheer him up. Lydie, I found out, was writing everyday, although it sometimes took her several days to find an excuse to get by the post office to mail her letters.

Walt was one of the first Americans off the boat and found himself used as a replacement in the French army stationed close to Paris. He did not think much of the French. He found them to be defeatist and cynical. In later letters, he did admit they had been fighting a long time and that life in the trenches could bring anyone down. I shared most of my letters with Lydie. Occasionally Walt enclosed a private letter for Lydie that he wished to be delivered without Mr. Marland's knowledge. Walt wrote more letters to Lydie then she received, which led both of them to believe someone in the Marland household intercepted much of their correspondence.

One letter, however, was so disturbing that I did not dare share it with Lydie, but it showed the grim realities of Walt's war situation.

Charlie,

I'm in the trenches now. Nights are dark, wet and stormy. It's cold and I shiver all the time. I hear a lot of French cursing, but don't understand it. The trenches go for miles. Stray bullets hit all around. The trench is six to seven feet deep so we are fairly safe from rifle fire.

The French soldiers have a strange look in their eyes. It's like they're looking a mile away, staring into nowhere. It's creepy, almost like their bodies are empty.

We're close to a place called Dead Cow Corner. Bullets crackle through what's left of the trees with mud everywhere. I think I'll never be clean again. What I wouldn't give for a dip in the Arkansas River on a hot summer day. That would be heaven.

We're a few hundred yards away from the Germans. There's a continual hiss of bullets overhead. We fire in return just to let them know we're here. It keeps patrols out of no man's land. They fire high so most bullets go over our heads. They say many men get killed behind the trenches, but I've been on the front line since I arrived. It's risky moving anywhere.

Sleeping in the trenches is terrible. The dugouts are small, damp, cold and overrun with rats. Once I left England, I've practically slept in my clothes and I'm filthy. I lay down between a waterproof sheet and overcoat and snatch as much sleep as I can. God knows I'm tired all the time. One night the order to "stand to" came and we had to be ready and awake all night long. I found myself wishing those attacks would come so we could get a half decent sleep.

Our rations include tea, bread, hard biscuits, and bacon most days. There's also as much rotten cabbage as you can eat. I hate the stuff. I'd love to have some of your mom's okra and tomatoes with some thin jelly. Rations increase when we're going into action. The rumor has it we're getting extra rations tonight.

The sky is grey and everything looks dead. Something nasty hangs in the air. The bombardment is terrible and never stops. Overhead the sky roars like one of our thunderstorms only much more evil. The air trembles like a giant drum beating, and the ground shakes and heaves beneath us. Could anything live in that no man's land? I don't consider myself brave but I'm ready to fight and end this insanity.

I've seen terrible things here. Things I cannot describe. Do whatever you can to stay out of this place. It is a hell on earth. Tell Lydie I look at her picture everyday. Thoughts of her keep me strong.

Your Friend,

Walt Johnson

I always told Lydie about the parts of the letters Walt sent to me about her, but I saw no sense in troubling her with many of the more graphic parts of his letters. Mr. Marland still had his parties and gentleman still showed up to call on Lydie, but she no longer flirted with any of the boys. The parties had become a duty with her, something that was part of the job description as designated hostess of the Grand Mansion.

While Zack Miller and George Marland were doing important supply work in England for the army Walt was in the trenches. The news had not been good. Russia was out of the war and the German army was mounting a huge offensive, driving within 30 miles of Paris. The Germans hoped to win the war before Pershing's American Expeditionary Force could take the field.

Walt had written about a fight he was in at a place called Chateau-Thierry near the Marne River close to Paris. About the only detail he had given was that he was in a fight and had been wounded slightly, but not to worry. The newspapers had revealed a more colorful story a few weeks before.

The Headlines screamed, "Local Boy Hero!" The local newspaper picked up a story off the Associated Press wire about an important battle close to Paris. The German's had broken through one line and were pressing the last line of defense, supported by strong machine gun positions. Allied reinforcements were mustered but the situation was desperate. The paper said, "The battle turned when Private Walter Johnson, of Ponca City, Oklahoma mounted a supply pony with six of his fellow French soldiers and charged the flanking machine gun position." The story said four French soldiers were killed in the charge, but Walt and two others continued the attack. It said Walt's horse was shot out from under him, but the three were able to secure the position and rain fire on the German lines until the machine gun overheated and jammed. The three soldiers then used their small arms to hold off a counter attack until the Allied counter offensive swept the field. All three soldiers, including Walt, had been awarded a medal from the French Army. The article said Walt had been slightly injured and was recuperating in a Paris hospital.

The whole town was a buzz with the news. I stashed a copy of the paper in my jacket and headed to the Grand Mansion. I would rarely go to the mansion, primarily to avoid suspicion about my role as liaison between Lydie and Walt. This was big news, however, and I just had to talk to Lydie. Lydie was out riding with Mr. Marland, but I left a message. About three hours later, she came by the golf course and we went for a walk in the Grand Gardens.

"Did you hear," I asked excitedly.

"Yes," Lydie replied with a grin of satisfaction.

"Walt's a hero. The whole town is talking about it," I continued.

"I'm angry," she replied with not much sincerity. "He told me he would be careful and look at him now."

"It doesn't surprise me," I added.

"Do you remember..." we both began to say in unison, and then stopped to laugh at interrupting each other.

"I was going to say, if you remembered the time he tackled Craigan?" Lydie asked.

"That's exactly what I was thinking of. I can just imagine Walt charging head long into the whole German army and stunning them with his audacity."

We both reminisced about the experience then Lydie asked, "Seriously do you think he's all right?"

"The papers said he was only slightly injured. I check the casualty list every day and I haven't seen anything. I'm sure he's okay and if he is in a hospital, he'll be safe. I'm sure Walt would say, 'don't worry,'" I assured.

"He always says 'don't worry,'" Lydie complained. "But worry is all that I do."

"We've got to think the best." I added.

"You're right, we've got to think the best. That's what Walt would do, that's what he would want," Lydie surmised.

We walked a little further then Lydie asked, "How is Elizabeth? She never comes around to see me anymore."

I smiled blushingly, "I think Elizabeth is doing fine. I see her at least twice a week at church and sometimes on the weekends. I've even learned to sing."

"That's right they don't use music or anything in that church do they?" Lydie observed. "I always thought you two would be perfect. Have you discussed the future?"

Elizabeth and I had actually talked about the future a lot. My father was not a millionaire, but he had done very well at Marland Oil and was planning to send me to the University of Oklahoma in the fall. Elizabeth and I were not engaged, but we had talked about our future life together.

Before I could answer Lydie's question, however, she revealed, "Walt and I are engaged."

"What?!" was my stunned reply.

"Well there's no ring or anything, but that day at Red Bud Creek Bridge, the day of the foxhunt, we promised each other that we would be married, no matter what," she said wistfully as if this revelation was a big burden off her mind.

"Does Mr. Marland know?" I asked suspecting the answer.

"Heaven's no," she admitted. "Things have actually been going better at home. Since I have quit all my flirting, Mr. Marland is much less suspicious. I will tell him, but mother has been sick and I don't want to burden him now."

I listened intently.

"I think Walt and Mr. Marland will someday be great friends. They are so much alike," she observed.

Virginia Marland had noticed this same characteristic and I was even beginning to see the similarities. I could definitely see Mr. Marland charging the German Army.

"Do you think he'll come home now," Lydie asked wishfully.

"I guess it's possible. He is a hero. They might send him back to recruit or sell bonds or something," I said.

"I do hope so. I miss him so much," she said with a tone of unmistakable sincerity.

We talked a little more, caught up on some of the gossip from the old gang. I learned George was eager to get in the fight, but for the time being was safe in England. Mr. Marland's oil business was still booming and making more money than even he could spend. He was developing a national reputation for his lavish lifestyle and as an art collector. I left the garden a little before dark and Lydie headed back to her room inside the Grand Mansion where she would listen to "Till We Meet Again" and "I'm Chasing Rainbows" on her phonograph over and over again.

Walt Johnson could never catch a break. The army did not send him home to recruit or sell bonds. Instead, Walt seemed to be in the middle of every fight from the Marne River through the Ardennes forest to the Argonne and he was promoted to sergeant by the end of the war.

The war years at home went by painfully slow. American troops were attacked with poison gas. Walt missed that. Russia was out of the war, but created The Red Army. American warplanes were now over Europe and the Red Baron had been killed. The Flu Epidemic was killing more Americans than the war and over 1,000,000 American soldiers ended up in the fight in Europe, including George Marland and Zack Miller. The Armistice happened on Monday, November 11, 1918 and the world celebrated the end to what Walt had called, "insanity". Lydie celebrated the fact that her Walt was safe and coming home.

CHAPTER 27

▼

I waited on the platform of the train station as I had the day Walt left. This time, however, I was not alone. The whole town seemed to have come to see its hero, Walt Johnson, step safely off the train. A marching band, local elected officials, and most of the prominent people in the county including Joe Miller came for the celebration. E.W. Marland was conspicuously absent and had schemed for days to get Lydie out of town, but to no avail.

Walt Johnson left town as an unknown draftee. He arrived back in town wearing a Purple Heart, a Distinguished Service Cross, and a French medal called the "Croix de Guerre" or the Grand Cross. A multitude of important people came to meet Walt Johnson that day, but he was only looking for Lydie.

After nearly two years, Walt stepped off the train to see his Lydie had been true to her word and was waiting for him. Lydie pushed through the crowd desperate to touch and feel the man she had only been able to think about since the day he left. As she and Walt came face to face, the two stood motionless for a brief second before embracing in a tearful reunion hug. They would not get much more time together this afternoon as the crowd pushed hard to get a glimpse of the boy they had sent to war who proved to be a man. The newspapers wanted their story, the politicians wanted their pictures, and even the radio station was there to chronicle the event.

Walt and Lydie's secret engagement was still a secret to everyone in town except me. I did not even tell Elizabeth for fear of the apocalypse that would surely come if word slipped out to George or E.W. Marland.

The relationship between Lydie and Mr. Marland had actually improved during Walt's absence. Like most people, Lydie almost always called him Mr. Marland and never father. They participated in various sporting activities together and Mr. Marland had come to depend on Lydie to entertain his many guests at the Grand Mansion. Mr. Marland still did not think Walt Johnson worthy of Lydie, but he did not seem to think anyone was good enough for her. Mr. Marland had ceased having the two followed by his "secret police" but Lydie was subtle and secretive in her relationship with Walt nonetheless.

Although Mr. Marland had not expressly forbidden Lydie from seeing Walt in casual settings, Walt was still not welcomed at the Grand Mansion. Mr. Marland did not "blacklist" Walt from any jobs, but their former bickering had made Walt a less than desirable job applicant in a county where one third of the people worked for Marland Oil. Even with his new title of hero, Walt had to look for work. It is unsure whether E.W. Marland would have given Walt a job if he had asked, but both men were proud, stubborn, and driven to be right. Virginia Marland and even Lydie had seen their similar personalities. Walt never asked for a job and Mr. Marland never offered.

For a man wanting to make good money in Kay County without the endorsement of E.W. Marland there was only one option, the Craigan Oil Exploration Company. While Mr. Marland was building a vast oil empire including, exploration, production, refining, and even distribution, Daniel Craigan barely managed to survive with only occasional successes.

Craigan's luck was about to change, however. Walt Johnson started out as an underpaid hand on one of Craigan's wells but soon advanced to foreman. Craigan was notorious for poor wages and unsafe conditions in a chronically hazardous environment, but he soon learned he had to keep his new star satisfied. The boy who had once taken Craigan to the ground was now a man making him a lot of money. It seemed everything Walt touched turned to black gold. Walt was smart and energetic. Craigan started drilling one gusher after another even with the most used up and antiquated equipment.

The Craigan Oil Company would never be a serious competitor to Marland Oil, but Walt Johnson was making a name for himself inside and outside of Ponca City. He had a reputation for having good instincts, common sense, and a way of working with people to get the best out of them.

Walt moved into the three-room house I had lived in as a boy soon after he began making money. This seemed fitting since in many ways it represented the only home he had known as a child. He could have afforded a nicer house, but Walt was saving money like a miser. Walt got job offers from several outfits located in Bartlesville and Tulsa, but stayed with Craigan and thus stayed in Ponca City and close to Lydie Marland.

Walt saw Lydie when he could but spent most of his time working and building his reputation. E.W. Marland took Lydie on extended trips to New York City and even Europe to separate her from Walt. It did not matter. Lydie was clever and resourceful in keeping in contact with Walt without Mr. Marland knowing. One thing was for sure, people were starting to take notice of Walt Johnson and soon E.W. Marland would be forced to take notice too.

I saw Walt often when Lydie was away. We talked about old times, his war experiences, and even his future dreams. He was ambitious, but all Walt's efforts were focused on Lydie and making enough money to someday provide for her.

Fortunately, Walt and Lydie were able to communicate with each other well enough that I no longer had to be the liaison between them. Walt and Lydie were inconspicuous in their social encounters. Few people knew of their relationship and even fewer suspected they might someday marry. Although they both talked about their future life together, I wondered if Mr. Marland would ever let that happen.

I had no such obstacles in my life during these years. I was able to go to college in Norman and complete law school with ample financial support from my family. After attending a two-week tent meeting with Elizabeth Cassidy during a summer break, I was baptized. Six months later Elizabeth and I were married. Lydie always said we would be a perfect couple and she was right. Walt would come for supper sometimes after we were married and even went to church with us. He was a strong bass singer and even learned to read shape notes. Walt was never as regular in church as Elizabeth and I, but he went often enough to keep the preacher from visiting him.

Lydie even came to church with him once. It caused quite a stir in the congregation. It would have caused even a bigger stir if E.W. or even Virginia Marland had found out. The two sat together. Walt held her hymnbook and they discreetly held hands during the sermon. Elizabeth told me it was sweet.

By 1922, E.W. Marland lived a lifestyle that could only be dreamed of in fairytales. The decade was known as the roaring twenties and the good times roared loudly in Ponca City. E.W. Marland was one of the wealthiest men in the nation. He may well have been the wealthiest man west of the Mississippi. E.W. Marland certainly lived the most lavishly. He had a fortune of over $100,000,000 and his oil company produced ten percent of all the oil in the world.

Virginia Marland was more sedate in her lifestyle and had experienced ill health, which kept her bedfast many months. Lydie assumed more and more responsibility for the Marland's busy social calendar. She was well prepared, having attended some of the finest private schools in the country. Lydie had an astute appreciation of fine art, music, and even performing arts, but still preferred the outdoor sports of swimming, polo matches, and the foxhunts.

Parties at the Grand Mansion were frequent and extravagant. These lavish celebrations featured the best food, entertainment, and company. Everyone coveted invitations to these events. On a warm April night, Walt Johnson finally invited himself to the party. The secret romance would reveal itself like a bolt of lightening in a clear dark sky. Few would ever forget.

CHAPTER 28

▼

The Marland's eight-acre garden had three huge tents erected in case a rainstorm dared interrupt the party. Outdoor lights strung high in the trees gave the grounds a surreal yet festive atmosphere. The night was warm, but the Marlands sported plenty of drink, plenty of food, and plenty of ice.

Lydie had long past being the debutante and focus of attention at these soirées. She now had the role as primary hostess. Lydie dutifully prepared all the details of the gala scheduled to happen that evening, giving no indication of the storm that was to come.

The most eager people came a little before dusk when the white-coated waiters outnumbered the partygoers. These impatient guests were conspicuous because they always wandered aimlessly when first arriving, gawking at the opulent surroundings. Before long, these more mundane guests would break up into small groups and await the arrival of the more prominent invitees. As the crowd grew, these smaller groups began to merge into larger more boisterous gatherings.

The band on the west patio included a piano, bass, saxophone, trumpet, clarinet, trombone, and drums. They played fast and with rhythm. As the party swung into high gear, the roar of the crowd nearly drowned out the jazz music.

The walk from Grand Avenue to the front door of the Grand Mansion was nearly a quarter of mile up a slight incline on a serpentine and graveled walkway. Hedges, small trees, and flowering plants were organized into sculpted mazes, but the approach from the street was fairly straight toward the west patio.

The hush started inconspicuously at first. No one near the house took any notice at all. The muted whispers grew with every step Walt Johnson made toward the front door of the Grand Mansion. By the time he passed the fountain closest to the house, the quiet had grown until you could hear the gravel crunching under his boots. Everybody knew who Walt Johnson was and nervously anticipated the tempest his arrival at the Marland's home would cause. Someone had gone to get Mr. Marland, who had yet to make an appearance in the gardens. By the time Walt reached the west portico, E.W. Marland stood defiantly at the top of the steps, leering down at the young intruder.

"What do you want son?" E.W. Marland asked in his most intimidating tone.

The crowded party of people stood in silence as if they were in a theater. Everyone strained to hear the drama that was unfolding, anxious and unbelieving of this strange showdown.

"I've come to see you, sir," was the direct answer. "Would you like to talk here, or in your study?"

"I don't see that you have any business in my house or even at this party for that matter, so I guess you can say what you will then kindly leave."

Walt looked to the ground for a second then slowly raised his eyes to look E.W. Marland in the eye and with a little grin said, "I've come to ask your permission to marry Lydie."

You could tell by the expression on Mr. Marland's face, this statement had caught him completely unaware. By the time he could respond, Lydie had made her way off the front porch to stand by Walt's side.

"That's...preposterous. What...What makes you think she has any interest?" Mr. Marland asked, struggling for words, which was a rare occurrence for him.

The silence seemed to last for an eternity as the scene playing out on the Marland's front porch riveted the whole party. Lydie moved closer to Walt and took his hand.

"It's true Mr. Marland," Lydie confessed breaking the tense quietness. "I do love him. We've been secretly engaged since before the war."

Mr. Marland was too stunned for words. He could not believe what he thought to be a harmless infatuation had maligned into this. Lydie had been secretly engaged for a couple of years and he was completely oblivious to the situation. E.W. Marland who was always in control, always knew what cards he had to play, and was prepared for every contingency, looked like a boxer who had been dazed. His bewilderment made him look as if he might physically stagger.

After a few seconds Walt added, "I've saved over $4,000. That may not be much to you Mr. Marland, but it will get us a comfortable start. Phillips is buying out Craigan and I'm moving to Bartlesville after I finish this last well. I won't go without Lydie...if she'll have me."

As Walt and Lydie looked at each other, the multitude of partygoers could tell what Lydie's answer would be.

"I'll be back at five o'clock tomorrow afternoon for an answer," Walt concluded sensing that Mr. Marland was not going to be able to answer him this evening.

E.W. Marland could not muster a response. Walt turned and squeezed Lydie's hand as he gave her a kiss on the cheek, which she did not resist. He then turned and walked down the gravel path with the same bravado with which he had entered. Someone had the good sense to start the band playing a lively tune, which seemed to distract the crowd, but E.W. Marland just stood at the top of the steps looking at Lydie. After a few seconds more, Lydie could not bare the silence and quickly exited to her room. She had packing to do.

CHAPTER 29

Walt came by my house a little after ten o'clock that evening. Elizabeth was expecting our first child and was already in bed. Walt took off his fedora hat as we sat out on the front porch and he began telling me about the events of the evening.

"Marland was speechless, I think," Walt said with a sly smile. "I told Lydie I would come by. She wanted to elope, but I didn't think that would be right. I still think Mr. Marland's a good guy and I wanted to give him a chance to do the right thing."

"He must have come undone," I added.

"Not really," Walt revealed. "I think he was surprised. I guess Lydie and I have been pretty good at keeping this thing a secret. You're pretty good at keeping secrets too."

"Well, I am an attorney," I smiled.

"Good, I may need one someday," Walt chided.

"Seriously, what do you think is going to happen?" I asked.

"I really don't know. Lydie's coming with me. That I do know. We've talked about this for years and again last night. I have no idea what E.W. will do. George will do whatever E.W. does. I hope he gives us his blessing, but I don't see that happening."

"Yeah, I have a hard time seeing Mr. Marland giving in to an ultimatum," I surmised.

"You should have seen Lydie tonight," Walt continued. "She came down and stood with me in front of Marland and everyone. I'm telling you, that girl's got some guts."

I had never noticed Lydie being that courageous, but Walt Johnson did seem to have a powerful effect on her.

"We'll be married in two days," Walt boasted. "Two days and I'll finally have a little family of my own, just like you got Charlie."

I had always been blessed with a good family life and I could not help but be excited for Walt and Lydie. Walt never knew his father, but I knew he would be a great dad, if given the chance.

"So, are you going to work for Frank Phillips?" I asked.

"For a while anyway. Everyone I talk to says he's a good guy. He's kinda like Marland I hear. He stepped into that mess in the Osage Reservation and helped some people."

Walt thought a moment and continued, "The oil business has been good to me and I seem to be good at it, but you know what I'd like to do?"

"What?" I asked.

"I wish I could go back to school like you did Charlie. Get an education and teach."

"Really," I replied. I had just finished law school and did not see the glamour in going back to school.

"I had to drop out, but if I could that's what I would do."

"Why don't you?" I asked.

"Oh, that's a pipe-dream. I'm good at what I do and making good money. I never dreamed when I was a kid I could make this kind of money. Lydie and me will be just fine."

As I thought about his last statement, I felt I had to ask, "Do you worry about Lydie...I mean worry about keeping her in the same financial standards she's used to?"

Walt frowned a bit and raised his eyebrow to say, "Thought about that a lot the last couple of years. Lydie and I have talked about it a bunch too. You probably don't know much about Lydie and George before they came here?"

"No, not really," I answered.

"Lydie's told me a little. She doesn't like to talk much about her days in Flourtown. It was different from her life here. She hasn't always been rich you know. She told me about it that night you two came to my place at the Norwood. I was so embarrassed, but she told me her neighborhood growing up was no better," Walt confided.

He looked up at the stars in the sky, took a deep breath then said, "Sometimes money costs too much, Charlie. I think Lydie will like living a more ordinary life...somewhere in between you know. She doesn't really like the attention as much as you might think. When you own a lot of stuff, a lot of stuff owns you. Lydie feels trapped sometimes."

I began to realize Walt knew Lydie and the details of her life in a much more intimate way than I did. They had obviously been spending their time in some serious conversations. I do not think until that night I realized how deep their connection was.

Walt and I talked a little longer about a variety of subjects not related to his showdown with Mr. Marland. He had been reading some quotes from Ralph Waldo Emerson and a book by James Allen. Walt loved to read and discuss various thoughts and philosophies about life. I had attended college and been around great thinkers, but Walt Johnson was one of the most insightful people I had ever met.

Walt was always interested in improving himself. He had survived and overcome a difficult childhood to find security and success in life. Walt seemed to be searching for something more, however. Walt wanted his life to have some higher significance. He wanted to make a difference. It is probably why he was so successful at working with people. Whatever he was searching for, Walt Johnson was sure he could find it with Lydie by his side. His one goal, his one passion, his one desire was to have Lydie as his wife and make her happy. Walt was now so close he could taste it.

"You want to sleep on the couch tonight?" I asked as the hour grew late. I could not help but think this would possibly be the last opportunity for the bachelor Walt to talk and visit late into the night.

"Naw," he replied. "I'm heading out to that well sight. We're about done and Craigan wants to see if we can finish this one before Phillips takes over. I think we'll have it done by morning."

Walt flipped his hat back on his head and stepped to his truck parked in the drive.

"Good luck tomorrow," I told him, as I thought about his potential confrontation with Mr. Marland.

"Thanks, I think it will be okay," Walt replied. "Charlie, I don't think I'll ever be able to thank you enough for all your help."

"What do you mean?" I asked, figuring he meant my help with Lydie all these years.

"I mean you're like a brother to me," he said in a serious tone. Walt hesitated a moment then said, "You're like the only family I got. What I mean is, it would mean a lot to me…and Lydie, if you'd be my best man."

"Sure," I agreed.

Walt walked back over to the porch where I was standing and said, "We've had some great adventures, you and I. You need to know I wouldn't be the same person I am today without you and I've always depended on you like a brother. A person's as small as their fears, or as big as their greatest aspiration. You always helped me dream big and believe in myself Charlie and that's a lot to do for any person."

With that bit of Walt Johnson philosophy, he stepped back to his truck and drove into the dark night. Lightening flashed in the western sky and a warm wind blew the fragrance of honeysuckle through the front porch. I have never since met a man as comfortable with who he was and where his life was going as Walt Johnson was that night. I went to bed with a feeling of joy, knowing Walt and Lydie would be happy together.

CHAPTER 30

▼

Mr. Marland left early the next morning, much earlier than normal. He had business to attend to, meetings to make, and he had to think about his options with Lydie. As for Lydie, she awoke with the intentions of speaking to Mr. Marland to work out a suitable compromise. She was always a practical girl.

The day had been clear and she had been organizing her things and her thoughts. She thought once she heard thunder, but a look outside revealed nothing but clear blue skies. In the early afternoon, she was taking a late lunch when a car screeched into the drive toward the garage. It was not a car she recognized. Mr. Marland was still out and George had gone to the stables to ride. Leroy Finchem, the sheriff and a friend of E.W. Marland, exited the passenger side of the car in a hurry.

The sheriff asked assertively, "Lydie, is Mr. Marland around?"

"No Mr. Finchem. I haven't seen him all day. Is everything all right?" she asked.

"There's been an accident at Mr. Craigan's new well. You probably heard the explosion," he informed.

Lydie's heart sunk. She now scanned the horizon to the west and could see a billow of black smoke in the distance.

"We're going to need some of Marland Oil's equipment. I was hoping to catch your father," Finchem continued.

Lydie feared to ask, but knew she must, "Was anyone hurt?"

"One killed....and one hurt real bad," the sheriff replied.

Lydie dropped the glass of tea she was holding. It shattered on the marble floor, but she did not notice.

Leroy Finchem knew he had bad news. He did not make her ask. "Walt Johnson has been hurt real bad."

Lydie breathed again. Hurt was bad but hurt meant alive. Without thinking, she scampered down the steps and started running down the gravel drive towards town and towards the hospital. Sheriff Finchem was able to stop her and get her in the car for the drive to the hospital.

They arrived to crowded confusion at the hospital. It seems Walt was out on the well sight welding some of Craigan's old equipment back together. One of the inexperienced roughnecks turned a valve releasing gas that ignited with a fiery explosion. The roughneck died instantly, but Walt had survived somehow. He had been wearing a welder's hood and some protective gear, but the news was not good. Walt Johnson was burned over ninety percent of his body.

Lydie rushed in and after locating the operating room, headed straight in to see her Walt. The men at the door blocked her. She broke free then three men had to restrain her as she strained to get in, screaming the whole time, "I've got to see my Walt. I have to know he's okay."

Sheriff Finchem was finally able to calm her enough to explain the situation. "Lydie," he said, "Walt is burned pretty bad. Believe me, you don't want to see him now and he doesn't want you to see him right now, at least not like he is. The doctors are doing all they can but you have got to stay out of their way, if Walt is to have any chance."

Lydie was still sobbing but more in control now as she nodded in agreement. Mr. Marland arrived twenty minutes later. After briefly checking with Lydie and assuring her things would be all right, E.W. Marland took charge. He immediately got an update from Finchem and made some phone calls to have his personal train ready to go to Tulsa. He was determined to take Walt to the best hospital in the state at his expense.

It took the local doctors some time to convince Mr. Marland that Walt was much too seriously injured to make such a trip. With a few more phone calls, Mr. Marland had the train rolling to Tulsa bringing three of the best doctors in the state immediately to Ponca City.

Bad news traveled fast in a town the size of Ponca City. As soon as I heard that Walt was involved in an accident, I hurried to the hospital. I was there shortly after the train left the station to pick up the doctors from Tulsa. The doctors would not let me see Walt at the time, so I sat silently next to Lydie as she stared purposelessly into the wall across from her. After a frenzy of activity by Mr. Marland, he took the other seat beside Lydie. In some of the best salesmanship I had ever seen him do, he proceeded to calm and reassure Lydie that all was being done that could be done. The rivalry and games were over for Mr. Marland. I was convinced he was totally focused on getting Walt all the help he could muster. It reminded me of the times Mr. Marland had come to our rescue as kids and I somehow felt things would be okay.

After the doctors had stabilized Walt as best they could and given him as much pain medication as they dared, they allowed the family to see him. For Walt that was Lydie and I. As I braced for the worst I was somewhat optimistic to see him. His body was completely covered, but his face was nearly untouched. He had been wearing a welding helmet that protected the front part of his head. It was probably the only thing that saved his life.

He was not very alert, but he recognized Lydie. You could see in his face that he wanted to reach out and touch her, but his arms and body were completely wrapped. Lydie walked over to touch his cheek. He tried to talk, but Lydie put her finger to his lips to quiet him. For now, it was enough to see her Walt and to think he might be all right.

The doctors from Tulsa arrived about midnight. They spent about an hour with Walt then went to see Mr. Marland. It appeared E.W. was negotiating and arguing with the doctors. They just looked at him, however, shaking their heads. After a few moments in the still of the early morning night, E.W. Marland painfully walked over to the seat where Lydie was and said, "The doctors…they…well they say there's no hope. They don't see how he's survived this long. His skin…the skin is too damaged. I'm so sorry Lydie…I'm so sorry for everything."

Lydie cried into Mr. Marland's shoulder and said, "They don't know Walt…I know he'll be all right." She kept crying, "They just don't know Walt."

"I know. He's a fighter," Mr. Marland acknowledged with a grim and sober look on his face that Lydie could not see. "He always has been. I've retained the doctors to stay here as long as it takes, but you've got to be strong Lydie."

He then turned to me and said, "Can you stay here with her Charles?"

I nodded.

"You two can stay here. I'm going home for some sleep. I'll make some more calls in the morning. I know a guy in Chicago at a hospital there," he assured.

Walt had been to war and seen unspeakable horrors. He probably knew from experience he had little chance. Walt refused much of his pain medication and was able to hold brief conversations. You could see the pain in his face, but he would somehow conjure up the strength to hide it from Lydie. You could sense the hopelessness in his eyes, but he kept hope alive as long as he could. He kept alive for Lydie.

Lydie Marland spent the next three days at the hospital sleeping only occasionally in the hospital's waiting room. Mr. Marland had exhorted her to go home for rest, but she was in one of her defiant moods and E.W. did not challenge her this time. As much as possible she stayed by Walt's side. Talking softly to him, reassuring him things would be all right, and telling him repeatedly, "I love you Walt."

Walt Johnson died at nine o'clock on a Saturday morning on April 19. To this day, I cannot think of him without shedding a tear in my heart.

CHAPTER 31

▼

The new church building on Grand Avenue could not hold the thousands that wished to pay their respects to Walt Johnson. Although Walt had no family, he had many friends. The blonde-headed kid who was always on the verge of trouble, who grew up with the wrong kind of family, and who never seemed to catch a break, had grown into the kind of man all could respect.

Lydie wore black and she would wear black for a long time. I realized later, a part of Lydie died that day too. I sat by Lydie and tried to encourage her, but she was too distraught to have a meaningful dialogue. She talked and she listened, but you could feel no connection. Lydie looked straight ahead as if she were looking far away, while looking at nothing at all.

Walt wrote during the war about French soldiers with a strange, far away look in their eyes. He wrote, "It's like they're looking a mile away, staring into nowhere...it's almost like their bodies are empty." I felt Lydie had that same shell-shocked, empty appearance.

Mr. Marland was there with Virginia who was in a wheelchair for one of her few public outings. George came to give his respects and I felt confident Walt would have been glad to see him there. Daniel Craigan even made it into the church building without the roof caving in.

The minister spoke kind words of Walt's hope, his good nature, and his faith. He said some people are too good to live in this world for long and that the goodness of Walt would stay with all of us. Walt would forever be frozen in time, a young man full of hope and promise.

I was asked to say a few words and tried. I wanted desperately to share what I really felt for Walt Johnson, to describe the kind of friend he had been to me. I wanted to tell the town about his good humor, his optimism, and his courage, but all I could do was choke-up.

The congregation sang, *Whispering Hope*. The tune was Walt's favorite and the words would from that day on always make me think of him.

> *Soft as the voice of an angel,*
> *Dim be the region afar,*
> *Hope with a gentle persuasion*
> *Whispers her comforting wind.*
> *Wait till the darkness is over.*
> *Wait till the tempest is done,*
> *Hope for the sunshine tomorrow*
> *Watch for the breaking of day.*

After the services, people gave their personal reflections and remembrances of Walt Johnson. Even the two old adversaries, E.W. Marland and Daniel Craigan, suspended their feud for a day.

"He was a fine boy," Daniel Craigan stated.

"He was that," E.W. Marland agreed. "I wish I had got to know him better. I just couldn't see him for more than that boy I had known so long ago."

"He had changed. If he had lived, he might have out done the both of us," Craigan continued.

"He made you a lot of money," Marland noted.

"He did. Thank goodness that Philips deal is signed. Frank didn't want my company. It's worthless to him. He wanted that kid."

E.W. Marland nodded. Even in this time of mourning, he regretted the fact that he had been so blind to an opportunity. E.W. had had enough socializing with Craigan and tactfully excused himself.

"Marland," Craigan added. "I'm leaving tomorrow, but I've got some advice for you."

E.W. Marland stopped to listen skeptically.

"You've always worried about me. I'm not as bad a guy as you think. I'm telling you this because of the boy. He always respected you...he always wanted to be like you."

E.W. felt somehow small and naïve for not realizing this.

"I'm leaving town so you don't have to worry about me anymore, but you got rats in your own cupboard and you need to watch yourself."

E.W. Marland did not know what to make of this strange advice. He would have liked to question Craigan further, but knew Craigan would say no more.

E.W. Marland bought a burial plot for Walt Johnson to lay in rest adjacent to his own family plot. For the first time in E.W. Marland's life, he felt as if he were not in control. He had a feeling he was not accustomed to, a feeling of guilt.

A few months later Elizabeth and I had a beautiful blonde haired, blue-eyed son. We named him Walter Johnson McDonagh. We love him very much.

PART III

▼

CHAPTER 32

▼

It took a long time for me to get over the death of Walt Johnson. I was struck by how quickly everyone else seemed to get on with their lives after his death. The oil field was a dangerous place where men risked life and limb on a daily basis. People were hardened to the personal tragedies that happened routinely in this harsh environment. It should not have been a surprise when others took this loss in stride, but Walt Johnson had been my friend.

Lydie did not get over the tragedy quickly either. I am not sure she ever really did. I missed seeing the spirited girl of twelve who had blossomed into the poised and enchanting young woman she had become. Lydie disappeared into the confines of the Grand Mansion and no one saw her for weeks. I actually called on Lydie a couple of times, but on each occasion, I was given a polite excuse by the staff as to why she was not available.

E.W. did not have time to reflect on the misfortunes of the past. Walt used to say, "Tomorrow happens today," and E.W. Marland was certainly building his empire of tomorrow. It seemed as if he could do no wrong when it came to business dealings. Pride comes before the fall, however, and the storm clouds of destruction were gathering, although they were still invisible to E.W. Marland.

E.W. Marland believed that a vision for the future required a clear vision of today. He prided himself on being able to see the current reality, to make intelligent decisions to positively influence the future. A strange dynamic, however, was emerging that even he did not perceive. Virginia Marland was a woman of superior intelligence and quiet wisdom. Through the building of the Marland empire, it was she that provided the controlling force to E.W. Marland's drive and ambition. Though calm and unassuming, she was the perfect compliment to his boisterous style. Virginia had been battling cancer the past few years and felt she had won, but her health steadily declined. Mr. Marland went to every expense for her wellbeing, even installing air conditioning in her suite at the Grand Mansion.

By 1923, Virginia was more or less an invalid, lacking the strength to guide her ambitious husband. For his part, E.W. Marland did not have much time to devote to a convalescing wife. He had an empire to build and dreams to achieve. He made Virginia as comfortable as possible, got her the best care available, and continued with his relentless work of building Marland Oil. Some criticized his inattention to Virginia during this time, but Marland Oil was a very demanding mistress.

E.W. Marland often seemed a contradiction of character. While he sometimes seemed callous and uncaring in personal relationships, he was generous to the extreme with friends, charities, and even employees. He supported the Boy Scouts, Girl Scouts, Young Men's Christian Association, Young Women's Christian Association and many other local community causes. He gave $100,000 to build a building to house the American Legion Post and the Masonic Lodge. He also founded the American Legion Orphan's Home shortly after Walt Johnson's death.

Mr. Marland constructed an up-to-date hospital for Ponca City and paid for the construction of the high school athletic field and grandstands. E.W. Marland's name and financial contribution could also be found on the new stadium and student union at the University of Oklahoma.

Mr. Marland was generous to the extreme with his employees in the form of bonuses, benefits, and time-off. He had told my mother great economic prosperity would come with the oil fields and it seemed everyone associated with Marland prospered. In a time when local labor was often used and abused, E.W. Marland was a progressive leader in developing an empowered workforce.

E.W. Marland was a perpetual promoter and innovator of his business. He was no longer a regional petroleum producer; he was continental with holdings from Canada to Mexico from the Atlantic to the Pacific. His optimistic outlook knew no boundaries so he often struggled with curbing his outgoing expenses to meet his considerable income.

E.W. showed a good deal of geological common sense in his exploration for oil in the early years of Marland Oil. He supplemented that by hiring the best engineers and geologists he could find. E.W. Marland was the first to experiment with seismic reflection exploration. He was a groundbreaking entrepreneur, willing to try new ideas. Besides controlling one tenth of the world's oil production, he had recruited and developed a talented pool of loyal employees. He built an extraordinary research and development department that was the envy of the whole industry. He was the undisputed king of Ponca City.

The popularity of the automobile, the conversion from coal to petroleum for industry, even the advent of plastics in consumer life did not escape Marland's opportunistic eye. He was a man of extraordinary talents placed at a historic window of opportunity in an emerging industry. E.W. Marland was close to stepping through that window to develop a legacy that would change the world.

E.W. Marland could visualize the big picture, but he struggled to see the small details happening close to him. He failed to perceive some of the internal dynamics of his industry and his own company. These small details foreshadowed changes destined to overwhelm him. Having a vision for the future requires a clear vision of the current reality. E.W. Marland's aspirations for greatness blinded him to some real dangers facing his empire.

Joe Miller continued to be a friend E.W. Marland could count on for ideas and energy. The 101 Ranch was still an important enterprise in Kay County, but oil was the economic driving force now. The ranch was beginning to see storm clouds of change affecting its own future. A flood swept away the bridge over the Salt Fork River, cutting the Ranch off from Ponca City for a while. Besides the loss to livestock and crops, the flood cost the Ranch tourism that year. The Wild West Show was still in tact, but times were changing. The show had been stranded in Europe for a while during the war and putting on big outdoor shows was expensive. Motion pictures were becoming the entertainment of choice in America and although the Millers tried to attract moviemakers to the Ranch, most stayed in California.

Things got worse when the Federal government filed a suit in Oklahoma City to get 3,000 acres of the ranch taken away from the Millers. The government claimed the land had been acquired from the Ponca Indians by fraud. The Millers never much liked the government anyway. The Millers tried any kind of attraction they could to lure the tourist dollar. Besides the ostrich herd and the bear, they added a herd of elephants and an eleven-foot alligator. The times were changing and the end of the 101 Ranch had begun.

The train station was still where commerce happened. Walt had said, "The station is a gateway to the world." People no longer came in masses to see the 101 Ranch, but they still came for the business of oil. Jack Pierpont Morgan, Jr., was the most prominent American financier of his day. The son of J. P. Morgan Sr., he was as big to the world of finance as E.W. Marland was to the oil industry. His father had made a fortune in the panic of 1907 at the expense of E.W., but J.P. Morgan Jr. had made serious money of his own during the Great War in Europe.

Morgan requested a meeting and E.W. Marland made sure the meeting was in Ponca City.

Randle Haman, Marland's Chief Financial Officer, had struggled to keep pace with E.W. Marland's explosive growth. Without E.W.'s knowledge, Haman had sold huge quantities of stock to investors in Morgan's bank. The investments were lucrative enough to warrant J.P. Morgan's personal attention. He arrived by chauffeured limousine to the Grand Mansion to meet the man behind Marland Oil.

E.W. Marland had set up tea in the west sunroom, looking ever bit the part of an English gentleman. Lydie was there employing all the charm that she had acquired through aptitude and training. She was the official hostess of the Grand Mansion and every detail was in order. After brief introductions, the meeting started with E.W., J.P. Morgan Jr., and Randle Haman.

"What can I do for you, Mr. Morgan?" inquired E.W.

"Lovely place you have here. I've never seen such a garden," Morgan replied. E.W. fought back the swelling pride the compliment brought. He was shrewd enough to know J.P. Morgan did not come all this way to talk about flowers.

"I've come," Morgan continued, "to talk to you about your company."

Marland listened intently. He knew Morgan wanted to talk about Marland Oil. That was obvious. E.W. was interested in determining *why* Morgan was so interested. E.W. had a deep distrust of outsiders and Morgan was the prototype outsider to him. He had always felt Morgan's father had swindled his first company away in the Panic of 1907. E.W. was determined that history would not repeat itself.

Morgan continued, "We've got several partners in the bank invested in your company."

"They're doing well then," E.W. curtly responded.

"Yes, quite well. We're looking at your past growth and your growth potential and it looks very promising."

E.W. nodded in agreement.

"The refining operations have turned into cash cows," Randle Haman added.

"Yes," Morgan agreed. "It seems that everything Mr. Marland touches turns into a cash cow." He said with a slightly artificial laugh.

Mr. Marland smiled for a moment then said, "I appreciate the flattery and admiration for my company, but I'm still left wondering. What the devil do you want?" Marland's pleasant tone had evolved into a more stern and demanding tone.

"This industry is about to explode with growth. Energy will be as big a business as railroads and timber at sometime in this country's future. Bigger. It may well be the biggest industry in the world someday," Morgan proclaimed.

E.W. Marland would never trust J.P. Morgan, but he had to admire his vision and foresight of the future. E.W. would agree with the banker's assessment about the future of the petroleum industry.

J.P. Morgan Jr. straightened in his chair, "You have built a tremendous company. The plant assets, the equipment, the personnel, the expertise…everything is top shelf, but you need capital to take advantage of this tremendous infrastructure that you have created."

E.W. pondered the proposition. It was true. He knew it as well as Morgan. Marland Oil did need capital. It needed pipelines to the markets back east. It needed refineries. It needed more retail outlets. The sky was the limit, but all this investment would take dollars, more than E.W. wanted to scrimp out of his general operations.

"What are you talking about?" E.W. asked cautiously feigning naivety.

"We want to be your banker, your only banker, that simple," Morgan affirmed.

"What kind of collateral…what kind of strings will be attached," E.W. asked.

"As far as collateral, your company assets and holding look sufficient. I don't see any reason to leverage any of your personal assets. As far as 'strings', there are none. We want you to run the company as before. You've been making money, make more money."

E.W. was still suspicious, but J.P. Morgan had come at a perfect time. Marland Oil was growing, but needed capital. Morgan's backing could mean that E.W. could accomplish in years what might take decades if Marland Oil had to absorb the growth through revenues from the company.

"I'll have my people look at it," E.W. affirmed.

"I think this could make both of us a lot of money," Morgan teased.

"We'll look into it."

Morgan left and probably knew the answer. E.W. Marland did not trust outsiders and certainly did not trust Morgan, but a chance to accelerate growth and still be in charge was an alluring prospect. He would talk things over with his trusted advisor Randle Haman, but E.W. knew Morgan was his new banker.

CHAPTER 33

▼

Time passed and I was getting on with living life. Elizabeth was busy making a home out of our house by putting all the little details together that only she could appreciate. I was a fledgling new lawyer with a shingle hung in an office window close to the courthouse and hungry enough to take almost any case. Our Walt was a teething toddler. I could not wait to get home every evening to play with him and marvel at his daily development.

After a hard day at the office, helping Elizabeth with the supper dishes, and playing with little Walt, I would often excuse myself for a brisk walk about town. I had no route in particular, but often strolled towards the golf course, which would take me around the perimeter of the gardens at the Grand Mansion.

The gardens were in splendid form. Even in the darkening dusk you could tell the azaleas were in bloom, smell the fragrance of roses in the air, and see that the Red Bud trees would soon be at the peak of their springtime glory. Admiring the tranquility of the place, I walked quickly without breaking stride when I heard my name spoken timidly from the shadows.

"Charlie?" came a soft, surprised voice from a dark corner.

I stopped momentarily trying to determine the exact location of inquiry.

"Over here," the unmistakable voice of Lydie Marland announced.

Lydie appeared from the shadows wearing a gown that looked as if it belonged in one of the Marland parties, but it was apparent that no special events were happening this evening.

"Lydie!" I exclaimed both surprised and excited to see her. "It's so good to see you."

"It's good to see you too," she replied looking around as if to see if we were alone.

"I came by a couple of times to see you. I haven't seen you in ages."

"I….I've been doing….things. It's been so hectic around here," she said apologetically. "What on earth are you doing here?"

"I'm just out on a walk. I needed a little fresh air. I walk a lot in the evenings after Walt…" I hesitated realizing the name of my son might be awkward in this conversation with Lydie. "My son…he's nearly one now, goes to bed."

Lydie did react to the mention of the name, but quickly regained her composure. "Yes Walt," she said as if relishing the opportunity to say that name. "How is he? He must be such a beautiful baby…I'm so sorry I haven't been to see him. Is Elizabeth all right?" she began to ramble then realized she was asking questions without getting any answers.

"We're all fine," I assured. "It's really good to see you. What have you been doing?"

"I've made several trips, been keeping busy here of course. Do you have a few minutes?" she asked.

"Sure," I replied. "What do you need?"

"Come walk around the garden with me. It's been so long since we've walked in the garden."

I agreed and stepped into the Marland Garden for the first time since Walt Johnson's death. Lydie and I had often walked in her garden when I was shuttling messages between her and Walt. The garden was expansive, with several secluded areas ideal for discreet meetings.

"I love the garden," she began. "I particularly like it this time of the evening. It's so cool."

"It's kind of dark," I added.

"Yes," she admitted, "but it's so peaceful. No one to bother me…no one to spy on me."

"How's George?" I asked.

"George is fine," she assured. "He's always playing polo or throwing the football or some such nonsense. Mr. Marland is always encouraging him to go to the office more to learn the business, but I'm afraid George is too content playing his games."

Lydie spoke in a strange listless manner. She was pleasant and seemed glad to have the company, but her thoughts seemed to be somewhere else. I so much wanted to ask her about Walt, to ask if she was really all right, but she seemed so fragile this night that I dared not bring up the subject.

"How's Mrs. Marland?" I asked.

Lydie became even more melancholy and said, "Not well. I'm so worried about her. She sleeps most of the time and looks so frail. Mr. Marland will try anything to help, but she gets so frustrated that he has business to do all the time."

"How's Mr. Marland?" I asked desperately trying to maintain the conversation.

Lydie perked up slightly and said, "Oh, he's been so busy. He's away tonight, but I expect him back tomorrow. He's been running crews down in the Gulf coast and spending a lot of time down there. We're going on a trip next week. I'll be gone for several months."

"Really, where to Lydie?"

"We're going to Italy for vacation, but we're going to Germany first. There's a geologist there that Mr. Marland wants to meet. He's some kind of expert on seismic exploration."

"What on earth is seismic exploration?" I asked.

"It's some kind of new science where they send vibrations into the ground to record the echo to tell what lies beneath. Mr. Marland thinks it will revolutionize oil exploration. That's what he wants to try in the Gulf."

I nodded as if I were interested.

Lydie became a little more animated as if she had an inspiration and said, "You should come to work for Marland Oil. You would love it Charlie. Mr. Marland can always use a smart lawyer, especially one local that he can trust. He would love to see you work for him. He was a lawyer himself, you know"

I smiled appreciatively then said, "Maybe someday, but right now I want to focus on my law practice."

My father had done very well as an executive at Marland Oil and had often made the same career suggestion to me, but for the time being my energies were devoted to building my own law practice.

"Charlie, always your own man. I respect that," she observed. "It's so good to see you. I've missed you so much. I miss everyone so much…you know our old gang."

I nodded expecting the conversation to evolve like most conversations between old friends; reminiscing about the past, exaggerating the nostalgia of days gone by, and remembering old comrades. Lydie caught me off guard by totally changing the tone of the conversation.

"I'm so lonely, Charlie. I feel so alone."

I did not know exactly how to reply.

"I haven't been that busy. I just don't go to town. I don't really go anywhere. I entertain the people coming here, but I feel empty when they're here. George…he knows and tries to help and be the big brother…you know how George is. Mr. Marland does his best to keep me entertained and busy. I try to be brave. I try to face people, but it's so hard and the longer I stay away the harder it has become."

I listened somewhat dismayed at the distress coming from my friend's voice.

"I feel people are always looking at me, expecting something from me. It's like I'm the center of all this attention, but still all alone. That's why I come to the garden in the evening, to be alone and be lonely. I guess I'm a self-fulfilling prophecy. I'm being silly now. You came for a nice walk, not to hear all my problems."

"No Lydie, it's okay. I think it helps to share what you're feeling. I find it good to talk. Elizabeth and I have worried about you. It's like you've disappeared. I think you need to get out and see your old friends."

She smiled as if to agree. "You have Elizabeth. I knew from the first night you two would be together."

"How did you know?"

"It might have been personality, or even your temperaments, but I think it was the way you looked at her. It was like there was a whole world going on, but all you wanted to see was her."

I smiled remembering that first encounter at the Grand Mansion. "Yes, I did probably look at her a little much while I was dancing with you, but you set me up good. 'You should ask her to dance' I bet you got a laugh from that."

Lydie actually laughed a little and said, "I did, but I couldn't believe how long it took you to ask her. I had to be rude to one of my guests, just so I could see the look on your face."

For an instant, I could see the old Lydie. Her smile was back as was her playful laugh. I continued that lighthearted conversation by confessing, "I used to have a huge crush on you, you know."

She smiled and said, "I know. You probably don't know that I had a little crush on you too."

This was a shock to me.

"Really?" was my surprised reply.

She laughed a little more then said with a slight giggle, "That night in the cemetery. I grabbed your arm and held it tight."

I nodded in remembrance, "You were scared that night."

"I wasn't that scared," she said a little sarcastically.

I pretended to be offended.

Lydie hesitated a moment as if in fond remembrance and said, "That's the night Walt knocked Craigan down." Her tone changed to a more sullen one as she said, "I think that might have been the night I began to fall for Walt."

I paid careful attention to her, thinking in some way this conversation was helpful to Lydie.

"Twelve year old girls are so impetuous with their infatuations," she said somewhat apologetically. She looked off in a distance as if looking at something that really could not be seen and stated, "Walt used to look at me like you looked at Elizabeth that night, as if I were the only person in the world. I always felt safe with Walt. I don't feel right since he's gone. People must think so badly of me the way I've handled this mess."

I became a little braver in the conversation and tried to console her by saying, "You were the only person in the world for Walt. He and I talked a lot when he couldn't be with you. I wish you knew how much respect he had for you. I dare say there was not a waking minute of Walt's life that you were not on his mind."

Lydie put her hand up to her lips and began to tremble. I feared she would break down, but she quickly regained her composure as we arrived at the front gate. She then said, "You were right Charlie. It is good to talk about things…even the painful things. I haven't talked to anyone about Walt since he's been gone. After that night when he came for me it hasn't been a subject we talk about here. People have said some terrible things about Mr. Marland. I overheard one of the gossips suggesting he caused the accident. You must know he did everything he could for Walt in the end."

I nodded in agreement, somewhat surprised at the accusation.

"You've got to believe me Charlie, I wouldn't stay for a minute if I thought that could be true. But you hear those things in town and you wonder what people must be thinking. What they must be thinking of me. I can't help but feel guilty for no reason at all. I've just stayed away."

I felt Lydie needed some reassurance so I said, "I'm confident, no one in their right mind thinks E.W. Marland had anything to do with that accident. It was just an accident. Craigan was always cutting corners; it was just a bad day."

"Thanks Charlie, I could always count on you," she said softly. "I should have never introduced you to Elizabeth, I think you and I might have been an interesting pair," she said in jest.

"No we're both too analytical," I laughed. "We would have talked every issue in the world to death."

She smiled and I felt for the first time that evening that Lydie might be okay. As she stood at the gate ready to see me walk away, I felt compelled to say something so I reached for her hand and said, "Lydie, Walt's gone. He loved you very much and I'm confident you still love him, but he wouldn't want to see you this way, hiding in the shadows, afraid, and alone. You've got to move on. You've got to live your life. Believe me when I say Walt would have wanted it that way. You go on this trip of yours….enjoy life, fall in love, get your heart broke if necessary, but live for today. That's the best you can do for Walt."

She looked down like a little girl being scolded then said with a smile, "Thanks Charlie, I'll try."

Lydie reached up to give me a kiss on the cheek and big hug.

I walked silently back to a routine life, with a loving wife and baby boy. In a few days, Lydie left for Italy searching desperately to find some renaissance for her soul.

CHAPTER 34

▼

My house was within walking distance of my office. Dad had given Elizabeth and me one of his old cars, but I preferred the walk most days. The car was good and sturdy, but I only drove on rainy days or when going out of town. There was no need to leave the car at home, Elizabeth did not drive, but I always liked to walk. It gave me time to clear my head and think.

The old gang had gone our separate ways. Lydie was off in Italy. Perry McGee was working in a hardware store in Shawnee, Oklahoma. Bobby Williams was still in town working for Marland Oil, though he traveled more than he was in town. Floyd Wills, was teaching high school. Raeford was still playing music, but alcohol had taken its toll on him and he already looked fifty.

All our old adventures were just romanticized memories. I had found a new distraction, however, on my morning walks to the office. My path took me by the train station where people still came and went. I walked by our old tree to see a new generation of "the gang" surrounding it. This group of barefooted boys could be seen most any day hustling tips like Walt and I had done years before. The generations had changed, but a group of boys had hung around the train station so long that they seemed natural there. They were woven into the fabric of it like a character on one of the Marland's tapestries.

It is a timeless mystery why adults who have made such a grand endeavor of messing up the world are so doubtful of the merits of youth. It seems each aging generation is determined to treat the next with a certain amount of suspicion and contempt. Ponca City was no different and a number of good citizens had complained and tried to get the "delinquents" off the street. Some went so far as to try to pass an ordinance banning the boys from public places like the train station.

Common sense prevailed and the boys still occupied the fringes of the "gateway to the world."

For my part, I found the boys to be an entertaining distraction. I looked forward to seeing their daily antics and taking those times to remember my own youth. Two boys caught my interest to the point that I developed a friendship with them. Tim Wilson and Ron McKeever were the modern ringleaders of the gang, much as Walt and I had been in our day. I often stopped to visit briefly with the boys, asking what kind of troubles they were having that day. I shared stories of E.W. Marland and the old stories from the train station. I would manufacture odd jobs so they could earn a nickel. Elizabeth, baby Walt, and I even took them on an excursion to the 101 Ranch, like E.W. Marland had done for me. The conversations were always casual, but I had become one of their good guys.

I found the practice of law fit my demeanor well. Added to the training received in school, I discovered an aptitude for dealing with conflict and helping people through their problems. It was comforting to know we had a court of law where people's points of view could be examined by facts and evidence. I made my share of enemies, as any good attorney will do when helping people discover their opinions are not necessarily the truth, but for the most part was building a solid reputation in the community.

Confusing opinion with truth, I was beginning to believe, was the cause of many of the conflicts and troubles in the world. E.W. Marland had the opinion that Walt Johnson was not worthy of his adopted daughter, which blinded him to Walt's inherent abilities and the similarities between the two men. I began to believe more and more in being open to the possibilities with people and determined in my own mind to think the best of them whenever possible.

One of the benefits of working downtown was my close proximity to Marland Oil and my dad's office. We had lunch often. Sometimes in the fancy dining room at the Arcade Hotel, but more often at a little place called Kelly's Sandwich Shop. We ordered the "Pargen" burger nearly three times a week. The Pargen burger was a patty of ground beef mixed with sausage, served on a hard rye bun, with a thick slice of tomato, and a sweet relish sauce. I sat down with Dad on a muggy spring day and noticed a change in his demeanor.

"How's it going Dad?" I asked as he entered the sandwich shop. "I went ahead and put our order in." I knew what Dad would want, so I ordered his Pargen burger and a Coca Cola.

"Good," he replied looking around at the crowded booths and the people waiting for open seating. "Look's like we barely beat the rush."

"I think the weather has people wanting burgers."

We continued the customary small talk typical between a father and son. I found out Mom had not been feeling well lately. Dad got caught up about the exploits of his only grandson. We talked about the weather and an assortment of local politics with varied levels of importance and interest. I began to notice Dad was changing. He was an unassuming man who had been one of the first employees at Marland Oil. He was attentive, smart, and did the right things to be valuable in the business world. He had started out as a production foreman, but was now an executive with the company working in the distribution part of the business.

Dad looked tired this noontime. For the first time I perceived a slight tremble in his hand and that look in his eye that comes with age. My dad was not really old. He was not in bad health. It was just the first time I had noticed that my dad was not the strong young adult I had known as a child. It occurred to me that I had become my dad in many ways.

"How are things at work?" I asked sensing a little more stress in the lines of his forehead than usual.

"Same old things, too much to do and too little time," he answered.

E.W. Marland was possibly the best employer in the nation to work for. He provided a health benefit plan. He also paid eye and dental bills for employees. Mr. Marland had even built 400 homes for his production employees when he thought local builders were taking advantage of them. He allowed time off for family emergencies, and provided generous bonuses to his employees. The atmosphere, however, was always hectic, busy, and growing.

"Been working long hours again?" I asked.

Dad nodded, "We're trying to get the land rights secured to run the pipeline E.W. wants to operate between here and New York. We've got most of it worked out, but there are always the details."

"How's Mr. Marland?" I asked.

"Fine I guess. I haven't seen much of him lately. Got a couple of telegraphs from him though. I think he'll be back from Italy next week."

I had forgotten the Marlands were out of town. It had been several months since my walk with Lydie in the garden. My daily routines had nearly erased her from my consciousness.

"E.W.'s not around the office that much anyway," Dad continued. "He's got that private train so he goes wherever he wants. You know we're exploring down in the Gulf of Mexico?"

I nodded. It seems that Lydie, Dad, or someone had told me about that.

"We're getting awfully spread out. I got crews working from Mexico to Canada and E.W. is determined to run them from here."

"I guess business is good then?" I asked.

"It's insane. We keep hiring more people, finding more oil, and selling more product, but there never seems to be a let up. It's really been busy since Morgan's people arrived," Dad commented.

"Who's Morgan?" I asked not really in the loop of the Marland Oil business.

"J.P. Morgan Jr.?" Dad acted as if he could not believe I had to ask. "He's only the biggest banker in the world."

"I thought E.W. Marland had plenty of money. What's he need with a banker?" I noted.

"E.W. makes a lot of money, but he can sure spend a lot too. We're still growing. The investments in equipment and leases will definitely pay off, but even E.W. needs a little seed corn. 'You can't sell corn from an empty crib,' he always says."

I listened with lukewarm interest to the financial dealings of Marland Oil. I had my own financial interest. Fifty dollars a month rent for a place on Main Street and thirty-three dollars a week to a middle-aged bookkeeper who kept closer tabs on me than my mother had.

"We're bringing in a lot of new people," Dad continued. "I used to know everyone coming through the door, but not now. I doubt E.W. could call half of us by name. Haman's brought in a bunch of suits to work up front. College boys like you. Smart boys from Yale and Harvard, but they don't know beans about the oil business. Half of 'em wouldn't know what a derrick looked like if it fell on 'em," Dad lamented.

"George's friends," I asked, knowing he had been a Yale man.

"Some I guess. He's always got a bunch riding those ponies on the polo field. Most of these boys work in Haman's accounting area though. They think Haman's the boss sometimes the way they're always polishing his shoes. They'll learn different when E.W. learns their names," he said with a grin of satisfaction.

The end of lunch was always a predictable routine. I would grab the check and try to buy Dad's lunch then he would use any means possible to get it away from me. It was always good entertainment. He would always seem to get the check, even if he had to turn the table over getting it. On one occasion, he had caused a commotion getting hold of the check only to find he did not have his wallet on him. I got to buy that day.

As we left the sandwich shop, he waddled back toward Marland Oil and I hurried back for a one o'clock appointment. There were dark, blue clouds building in the west. You could tell a spring storm was brewing. I braced for the tempest to come. Others should have been watching the clouds forming that day.

CHAPTER 35

▼

Elizabeth and I were not wealthy, but we were comfortable. The law practice was going well and we were prudent with our finances. Walt toddled around the house and we were impressed with every step, sure that he was the most extraordinary child ever born. Walt, however, was going to have some competition soon. Elizabeth was expecting our second child in May. Her "nine month virus" was barely noticeable, but I teased her about keeping a newspaper handy anyway. Elizabeth's aunt had birthed eight children. The aunt used to tell the story about keeping a newspaper to hide her condition when visitors would come to the house. She used to quip, "Of course, I kept a newspaper over me most the time."

I was in the back room reviewing some case files when someone knocked on the door.

"Better get the newspaper," I yelled as Elizabeth went to attend to the door.

In a few moments, I heard Elizabeth squeal, "Lydie!"

I immediately put my files away and got up to move to the front room. Standing in the front door gently hugging my wife was Lydie Marland. She wore a cream yellow dress fashionably cut showing leg to her knees and a hint of collarbone. She had graduated from the Gibson girl look to the free spirited 20's style. The fashion suited her athletic body type and she looked stunning.

"Charlie!" she exclaimed as she saw me enter the room. She left Elizabeth's side to come and give me a big hug. "It's good to see you."

"How are you doing, Lydie?" I asked.

"I'm doing well. We arrived back last night and I just had to see you guys," she said with a big grin.

About that time, Walt came staggering around the corner and into the room.

Lydie shrieked a little and said, "This is who I really came to see," as she moved across the room to pick up Walt. He squirmed out of her grasp and stumbled away from the stranger.

"He's so big and so cute," she said in a little bit of baby's voice.

"Sit down Lydie," Elizabeth suggested.

Lydie positioned herself in the chair in the corner of the front room.

"Would you like some lemonade?" Elizabeth asked, "I was just fixing some for Charlie."

This was a surprise. I was unaware Elizabeth had been planning to make lemonade.

"Yes please," Lydie answered.

Elizabeth walked across the room and in her mothering way picked up Walt, carried him across the room, and coaxed, "Come here Walter, let's sit on Lydie's lap." Elizabeth had seen Lydie's failed attempt to pick up Walt. She gently set him on her lap and encouraged, "There Walt, how do you like Lydie's lap?"

Lydie sat stiffly, obviously not accustom to holding a small child. Walt was obedient to his mother and seemed to be enjoying his new perch.

"He's so adorable," Lydie admired.

I took a seat at the end of the sofa opposite Lydie. Elizabeth disappeared into the kitchen when it became apparent Walt was content in his new spot. Lydie touched and poked at him like you would a little doll.

"What do you think?" I asked.

Lydie smiled and said, "He's so perfect."

"Thank-you," I said in a satisfied tone.

Lydie kept her eye on little Walt and kept touching, squeezing, and admiring him. Lydie's own motherly instincts were taking hold as she became more comfortable by the second about holding him.

"It's a surprise to see you," I said.

"I'm sorry it's been so long since I've come to visit," Lydie apologized.

It occurred to me this was probably the first time Lydie had seen Walt and it was possibly the first time for her to visit our home.

"It's good to have you now," I confirmed. "You look great."

Lydie had more of her youthful swagger than when I had seen her last. She was tanned and smiling. She looked as if she had been spending a considerable amount of time outdoors. It was difficult to describe the subtle differences in her appearance, but she looked radiant….and happy.

"Thank-you," she acknowledged in a perky tone. "I feel great Charlie."

"I'm glad to hear it," I replied thinking of our last meeting in the garden.

Lydie then stood up with Walt to move across the room to sit by me on the sofa. In a softer tone, almost a whisper, she leaned in and said, "Thanks for your advice that night in the garden Charlie. It's just what I needed then."

I felt a little embarrassed, but replied, "Sometimes we just need an encouraging word."

Lydie sat back up straight and said in a normal, more matter of fact tone, "Elizabeth looks beautiful."

"Yes, she does," I said looking back over my shoulder to see her squeezing lemonade in the kitchen.

It was obvious Elizabeth had stretched the truth when she had said she was fixing me lemonade. Perhaps she wanted to give Lydie and me some time to talk. She knew we had been friends and that we had both been close to Walt. She made brief eye contact with me then continued to bang away in the kitchen trying to get the lemons squeezed as fast as possible.

"It looks like you're feeding her well," Lydie said with a sly smile.

It took me a moment to get her comment then I blushed and said, "Yes, we're expecting again in May."

Women must have some kind of sixth sense about these things. Elizabeth did not look like she was expecting to me, but women always seem to know.

"That's perfect. I hope it's a girl. That would make you the perfect family. One boy and one girl…that would be the perfect family for the perfect couple."

About that time, Elizabeth reappeared with a tray full of lemonade. Walt by this point had tired of sitting on Lydie's lap so I carried him to an area were he could play unhindered.

"He's just adorable Elizabeth," Lydie commented again. "I love his little nose and his blonde hair."

"Thank you," Elizabeth said with a tone of satisfaction of Lydie's unabashed approval of her son.

We all took a taste of our lemonade and the conversation ground to an awkward silence. Elizabeth did not seem to want to engage in much conversation this afternoon and appeared distracted. I was also struggling for conversation. Elizabeth and Lydie had been acquaintances and Lydie and I had been friends, but as a couple, we did not have that much interaction with her. Lydie had not been seen around town since Walt's death and many had not noticed that she had gone on an extended trip. The trip, I finally remembered.

"How was your trip?" I hurriedly said eager to break the awkward silence.

"It was grand. I loved Europe. Everything is so old and stately. Everything here is new and kind of shoddy looking by comparison," Lydie explained.

"Where exactly did you go?" I asked.

"We went to Germany for some business. Mr. Marland wanted to meet a man doing seismic research. A very depressing place right now, I was glad to leave. Then we went to Rome. Rome was a beautiful city. We saw the coliseum ruins and the Vatican. I was glad to get out of Rome also. The people were so high strung. We then went to Florence in Tuscany," she said with a little more excitement in her voice. "I loved Florence the art, the architecture, and the culture. It's just so romantic."

Lydie continued on with her detailed description, "We went to Milan to shop, but decided to return to Florence. We stayed in the Davanzati Palace…a real palace. It was a wonderful time. So much to see and you meet the most interesting people in Florence," she said with a sly gleam.

Lydie continued for sometime with descriptions of what she had seen and done on her European vacation.

Elizabeth interrupted the monologue with, "When are you going to take me to Florence, Charlie?" Elizabeth, of course, knew such a trip was not likely in our near future.

"Maybe Kansas City…or Newkirk," I replied. Both women laughed.

"You really do need to take her sometime, Charlie. Everyone should see Florence. Going to Florence is always a good idea," Lydie added.

"It will give us something to look forward to," I assured looking at Elizabeth sitting in the chair across the room.

"I'll have to say," added Lydie, "that I did miss Ponca City. It seems hard to imagine. Although the Tuscany landscape is breathtaking, I missed Ponca City. I got dreadfully homesick, but Florence is a great place to think and recharge."

It then seemed as if Lydie remembered something she wished to say and rushed to say it before it left her mind.

"I almost forgot why I came over," she said.

I had thought she had come to visit and see Walt, but it appeared she had another motive.

"Mr. Marland is throwing a huge European Ball a week from this Saturday. There will be people from all over, but I would really like you both to come. I don't know about Walt. I don't think he would be well entertained, but he is such a lovely child. Maybe you could find a sitter."

I assured Lydie that would be possible and then she produced a rather formal looking invitation with our names on it.

We said our good-byes and I reaffirmed once more how good it was to have her at the house. Lydie promised to come again then drove away in her chauffeured car.

I began helping Elizabeth collect the lemonade glasses and said, "It was good to see Lydie looking so well. I think the trip did her some good."

"Yes it did," Elizabeth agreed. "She was like the old Lydie. I wonder who she met in Florence."

"Met?" I questioned.

"Yes, she seems as if she's gotten over Walt and that usually means a woman has her eye on another," Elizabeth mused.

"Another. You women and your theories," I concluded.

"Yes, our theories," Elizabeth whispered.

I went back to work not knowing that my dear sweet Elizabeth was wondering if Lydie's new flame was me.

CHAPTER 36

▼

My mother always relished an opportunity to keep Walt so Elizabeth and I had our baby sitter. I wore an old tuxedo that for the most part still fit. Elizabeth had to shop and fairly well exhausted the options in Ponca City before finding a dress to suit her.

I had not been to a Marland party for years. The house shined on the hilltop like a beacon. Lights strung throughout a large portion of the gardens, gave the whole place a surreal glow. People were already assembling and settling into their various sub-groups. Marland parties were always lavish, appointed with the finest foods, drink, and entertainment. Some parties were smaller than others, but this was undoubtedly one of the largest gatherings.

Elizabeth had wished to drive, but I feared parking would be a problem so we walked from our house. I was right. Expensive cars were parked in the adjacent field and in the surrounding neighborhoods nearly to downtown. We stumbled on to Ron and Tim, who were trying to peak through the hedges to get a glimpse of the event. After a few words with the two boys, we headed into the party.

It was a pleasant evening. With such a crowd, many people had congregated in the garden and the large terrace adjacent to the house. As we approached the steps, Lydie enthusiastically greeted us.

"You made it!" she exclaimed.

"Everything is beautiful," Elizabeth politely observed.

"I don't think I've ever seen this many people here before Lydie," I added.

"Everyone in the state is here I think, I don't know the half of them," Lydie said.

After guiding us to the refreshment area, Lydie disappeared into her crowded gathering to assume her duties as hostess. There seemed to be a crowd of boisterous partygoers everywhere you turned. Elizabeth and I were fashionably dressed for our station in life, but were obviously on the lower rung of this social ladder.

It was easy to sort the Oklahoma natives from those transported from the east. Besides the accent, the locals all seemed to have a deeper tan. It may have been because so many of us had an Indian heritage or maybe we were just outside more, but the distinction was obvious. Lydie was tanned from her recent trip and in every way looked like one of the Ponca City natives.

I had to smile a little every time Lydie came into my view that evening. She was the Lydie of old, in command of every detail of the gathering and flirting with all the young bachelors. She was poised and looked content, which added to her attractiveness.

There were possibly more senators and representatives here than in the state house in Oklahoma City. Important people were to be seen everywhere. Mayor McFadden entertained a group of what appeared to be oilmen. Joe and George Miller were leading a group of rowdy characters with a collection of attractive young ladies that were not necessarily their wives.

Randle Haman was presiding over a large group of men dressed in fashionably tailored suits who had an air of superiority. Some of these men were surely the ones Dad had told me about at our lunch meeting. Mr. Haman was clearly in charge of this assembly and they seemed to hang on his every word. Even these privileged sons of the blue bloods of American society had to be impressed with this gathering.

A smaller group of athletic young men surrounded George Marland, probably from his polo group. They were completely surrounded by a host of attractive young ladies vying for attention. Unfortunately for the girls, it seemed the young men were more interested in talking about their sports.

Appearing from the upstairs living area was E.W. Marland. He seemed to be timeless in his appearance. In many ways, he looked as he did in those first years when he took me to the 101 Ranch. The people in the crowded house began to hush in waves as they recognized the host had arrived. Not everyone at the gathering could fit into the Grand Mansion, but all inside were focused on E.W. Marland.

On each side of the hanging staircase were mysterious, new pictures covered in plain canvas wrappings. Mr. Marland stepped towards one of the pictures and announced, "Welcome to the Marland home."

The whole party applauded the opulent feast that had been offered them this evening.

"By the looks of things we've about outgrown the Grand Mansion."

There was a smattering of laughter from the crowd.

"I've just returned from an extended vacation in Italy and have brought a few of its treasures back to Ponca City," he proclaimed.

Several of the wait staff moved to unveil five magnificent pieces of art that Mr. Marland had purchased on his recent trip. There was one painting still covered by canvas. A general stirring had begun among the crowd as they admired the art treasures presented before them.

"But as I look around," he continued, "I find no walls suitable for their hanging and not enough room to accommodate my many friends and associates, so tonight I have invited you here to make an important announcement."

The crowd grew silent with some trepidation. There was always an unspoken fear in Ponca City that Marland might move his residence from the community, which would have disastrous effects on the cultural enhancements and quality of life in the city. Even worse, there was the dread in a city, where one third of the population worked for Marland Oil that the company might move to another location.

E.W. Marland had the full attention of those within earshot of him and said, "While I was in Florence, I was privileged to stay in the beautiful Palazzo Davanzati. It is a magnificent palace that is of inspiring beauty. Tonight I would like to announce that this grand palace will be reborn in even more splendor in Ponca City."

There was a low hum of conversation at this announcement as Mr. Marland continued, "Master architect John Forsyth has been retained for this project. We are going to be bringing the finest artists in the world here for its construction."

The low hum had grown into a buss of speculation, as the individual groups whispering among themselves requiring Mr. Marland to increase the volume of his speech.

"I would like to introduce Mr. Forsyth and the 'Palace on the Prairie.'" Mr. Marland continued.

Mr. Forsyth was a dapperly dressed, slightly built man standing by the last unmasked picture. Mr. Forsyth removed the covering to expose a detailed architectural drawing of an immense, three-story, brown stoned château and artist's rendition of the surrounding grounds. There was a collective sigh of admiration, which grew into enthusiastic applause at the grand vision of E.W. Marland. E.W. stood at the head of the stairs, slightly above the rest of the crowd and looked every bit like a king. He was, in fact, the unofficial king of Ponca City, at least for that night.

Word quickly spread to those outside who were not able to hear Marland's announcement and people politely pushed and jockeyed for position to get a better look of the detailed drawings. What had been an energetic gathering turned into a full-blown celebration as the band began to play and people began a myriad of conversations about one topic, the Palace on the Prairie. It was hard to tell if people were more impressed with the scale of the project or relieved to know that Marland was making a long-term investment in the community. The new home was magnificent in every way and would easily eclipse the Grand Mansion in size, artistry, and grandeur.

Elizabeth and I mingled with the people we saw. Neither one of us excelled at being the life of the party, but we were handling ourselves adequately. As I moved about the room, I was suddenly tapped gingerly on the shoulder. It was Lydie.

"Charlie, they're playing a waltz. Could you dance with me for old time sake?" she asked.

In the glory days of the Grand Mansion parties, I routinely was paired with Lydie to block more aggressive suitors.

I hesitated slightly then said, "I don't really dance anymore Lydie."

"Don't be silly," she replied.

"Honestly, I don't think I remember how," I tried to humorously reason.

"Oh please Charlie," she pleaded. "There's really no one else I want to dance with tonight. Elizabeth won't mind. You two might not have ever met if we hadn't been dance partners."

Elizabeth looked a little uncomfortable but put on a cheerful voice and said, "Go ahead Charlie. I can use a good laugh."

Lydie and I began our waltz. I had not been lying. It had been years since I had waltzed and it took several steps to regain any kind of rhythm. After I became confident that I would not fall or step on Lydie, we engaged in small talk on a variety of topics of no real merit or importance. For the moment, Lydie seemed to be happy with life and happy to be back in her home of Ponca City.

At the end of the waltz, the band began a more jazzy number and I was glad to retire to the sidelines for the evening. As I located Elizabeth, another hand landed on my shoulder to turn me around. It was none other than E.W. Marland.

I was taken aback to be shoulder to shoulder with the host of the evening when so many more prominent social prospects were in the room.

"Charles, my first friend in Ponca City," E.W. cheerfully proclaimed. "It looks as if you are doing well and it's good to see your wife Elizabeth too," he said as he acknowledged Elizabeth's presence.

Elizabeth curtsied slightly with a smile. After a moment of pleasantries, Elizabeth excused herself and walked over to hold a conversation with Lydie. The two women slipped off to a more secluded area leaving Mr. Marland and I in conversation. I first thought he would quickly dismiss himself and move on to other guests, but he seemed eager to engage in conversation with me this evening.

"How's the law practice going?" he asked.

"Very well," I replied.

"You know, I went to law school and practiced law for a few years," he noted.

"Yes," I said, "I remember Lydie telling me about that."

"You know I always thought you would be a part of Marland Oil like your father," he said.

"Marland Oil has certainly been good to Dad. If he had his way, I would be there, but I love practicing law and having my own practice."

"You've got to do what you're passionate about Charlie. I've always said that," Mr. Marland confessed with a more fatherly tone.

"I've been up on the balcony," he said pointing at the railed landing at the top of the huge staircase. "I like watching things from up there. You can see everything from the balcony. It gives you perspective. Like I saw old George Miller was getting a little free with his hands. His wife wouldn't like that," he said with a laugh, "she's not here."

"I noticed my George is standing on the sidelines when there are ample young ladies wanting to dance. Haman and his group are doing who knows what, but they look a little too serious for a party. I also noticed you and Lydie dancing together."

I nodded slightly in acknowledgement that we had been dancing.

"For you, all you could see was a small part of the dance floor. Lydie just ahead of you, the couple on either side maybe, but I could see the whole thing. It's good to step back sometimes and evaluate all that is going on with some perspective."

I did not really know where Mr. Marland was going with the conversation, but was still impressed that he would take the effort to spend so much of his time with me.

"It was good to see you and Lydie together again," he continued. "She looks happy doesn't she?"

"Yes. I think your trip did her much good."

Mr. Marland seemed to be satisfied with that comment and said, "I got to spend a lot of time with Lydie in Italy. She told me about the conversation you had with her in the garden before we left. I wanted you to know I think it made a big impact, Charles."

My eyes widened a little in surprise as I said, "Really. We just talked." I was hesitant to bring up the parts of the conversation regarding Walt to Mr. Marland.

"All I know is she was sulking around and there didn't seem to be anything to cheer her up. But since that trip just look at her."

We both searched the room for Lydie but she was out of sight.

"I just wanted to say thank-you and good luck on that law practice. You keep doing the things you're passionate about and you'll do okay," he assured with a smile.

I searched the room for Elizabeth and noticed she was not in sight either. I was unaware that she and Lydie were having a conversation of their own.

CHAPTER 37

▼

"Lydie, is there somewhere we could speak?" Elizabeth asked in an almost urgent tone, "In private."

"Sure," Lydie answered.

Lydie led them to a small downstairs parlor that was secluded from the increasingly jovial crowd.

"It's a wonderful party, isn't it?" Lydie cheerfully asked as they entered the room.

"Yes," was Elizabeth's curt reply.

Lydie proceeded with the typical small talk until Elizabeth interrupted with, "I've noticed a change in you since you've come back to Ponca City."

"Really," Lydie said casually, "I hope it's for the good."

"I'm not sure," Elizabeth said solemnly.

Lydie immediately picked up on this more serious tone and asked, "Is anything wrong Elizabeth?"

Elizabeth hesitated for a moment then said, "I know Walt Johnson's death had an affect on you. The whole town knew it too. I know how long it took Charlie to recover and I suspect you took it hard also."

Lydie's joyous demeanor seemed to vanish like the morning dew on a hot August day. She stood in silence, listening more attentively to Elizabeth.

Elizabeth avoided direct eye contact as she shifted her weight nervously from one foot to the other and said meekly, "It's been my experience that a woman who has lost a man can only be satisfied when she has found a new love. Since you've been back you are playful, cheerful, and flirty."

"I think the trip to Florence has…" Lydie was interrupted before she could say anymore.

Elizabeth was eager to speak her mind without interruption and continued, "You have come to my house for the first time ever. You seem to be a different person around Charlie and I know he has liked you for a long time. You danced cozily with my husband in front of everyone this evening and I have to know. Are you in love with my husband?"

There was a tense silence as Elizabeth unloaded the accusation that had been haunting her the past week. Lydie was completely surprised at the bluntness of Elizabeth's question. Lydie looked away and stood in stone silence looking into the far corner of the room staring at something that was not there.

"Let's sit down," Lydie suggested perhaps thinking the change in posture would defuse the confrontational tone.

Elizabeth sat rigidly on the end of the sofa staring coldly at Lydie. After a deep breath Lydie said, "When Walt died, I think a part of me died with him. I spent weeks that turned into months that turned into two years where I just struggled to move each day. I struggled to find a reason to go on and was literally pining away. Your Charlie…and I emphasize your Charlie, was the one person that was able to get me going again, who explained to me that I had to move on."

Elizabeth hung on every word as Lydie continued. "You asked me if I love your husband and as I think about it I would honestly have to say yes, but I love him as a dear friend. He only has eyes for you Elizabeth. Charlie has helped me through several difficult times. I think you more than anyone understand his ability to listen and analyze things in a way that makes sense out of nonsense."

Elizabeth had to agree with Lydie that Charlie did have a unique ability to see things for what they were and explain them in commonsense terms

"The thing I love best about Charlie," Lydie continued, "is that he is dependable and honest. If he were ever to betray you, I first of all would not believe it possible, and secondly, he would lose all that makes him attractive."

There was an awkward silence and Elizabeth pondered this confession.

"Charlie and I are friends. I don't have many people I can trust. In retrospect, I suppose it was a bad idea for me to dance with your husband tonight, but I've danced with him a hundred times. I was dancing with him the night he asked me to introduce you two…."

Lydie hesitated a moment as if she had just realized something horrible then said, "Oh my, I must have put you and Charlie in such an awkward way. I am sorry. I know Charlie could have no special feelings for me. It's so difficult for me to have friends, especially male friends, my own age. It seems sometimes like everyone I know is older. I am so sorry."

Lydie was looking pitifully at the floor when Elizabeth broke the awkward silence by confessing, "You must think I'm quite paranoid."

"No. I think you are lucky to have found the love of your life and I understand completely your desire to protect him. I've told Charlie many times you two are the perfect couple and now you have dear Walt."

Lydie's brow rose as if in deep thought as she continued, "I must be more discreet in the future. I probably need to stay completely away."

Elizabeth sat silently for a moment staring at the floor before confessing, "I think I may need to apologize also. I have no basis for such an accusation really. It's just my own insecurity. I trust Charlie and I know you two are special friends. I know Charlie…"

"There they are," I announced intruding into the small parlor unaware of the scope or content of the conversation until Elizabeth revealed it to me later.

"I've been looking everywhere for you Elizabeth," I said.

Both women looked sheepishly at each other. It was obvious to Elizabeth that Lydie had been right. I did only have eyes for her.

Lydie broke the uncomfortable silence by announcing, "Elizabeth was just asking about my transformation since returning from Europe."

Elizabeth had a look of quiet panic on her face, fearful Lydie was destined to betray her insecurities.

"I was telling her that I found a passion in Florence," Lydie explained turning on the excitement and energy in her voice as if truly inspired, "this great house that Mr. Marland wants to build. It is going to be like no other house on this continent I believe. I had such a grand time in Florence that I do want to bring a bit of it back home. A person needs something to be passionate about I think."

Elizabeth, relieved at Lydie's explanation added, "Yes, I would be excited too. I can't wait to see it. Maybe you'll have Charlie and me over sometime."

"Absolutely," Lydie assured. "We're building a huge pool outdoors; maybe Walt will be old enough to learn to swim by then."

Elizabeth stepped toward Lydie and gave her a hug then said, "Lydie come see us anytime…I mean that."

Lydie smiled sweetly and nodded.

"Elizabeth, we need to think about leaving before it gets too late," I suggested.

"Yes, you're right. Grandma McDonagh is probably ready for a break by now," Elizabeth confirmed.

As we prepared to exit the huge party, Elizabeth took Lydie by the hand and again said, "Do come by anytime Lydie, if for no other reason than to hold Walt."

"I will," Lydie assured.

As Elizabeth and I walked back to our modest home, we talked about the grandeur of the night's party, the possibility of the new Marland home, and some potential clients I was able to meet. There was lightning in the western skies as dark, ominous clouds boiled in the sky. It reminded me of the night at Sacred Heart cemetery. We hurried home to buckle down for the storm that was sure to come in the night.

As we approached our front door Elizabeth said, "It was good to see Lydie happy tonight. It was good to see she will have something to keep her busy."

CHAPTER 38

▼

Construction started on E.W. Marland's Palace on the Prairie with a scope and scale reminiscent of one of his great refineries. A seven-room cottage, called the Artist Studio, was constructed immediately to house various artisans and craftsmen employed to work on the project. The estate was located on a piece of property close to where Mr. Marland had conducted many of his famous foxhunts.

The details of the mansion consumed much of E.W. Marland's time and most of Lydie's. It would be several months before I would see her again. Marland Oil was still growing at a record pace and Mr. Marland was still pushing to get the details worked out for the pipeline to the east. My dad would periodically complain that the bureaucracy of the expanding corporation was becoming more of a barrier to getting things done. He had expressed frustration several times about getting timely support form Randle Haman to complete important contracts.

The oil industry as a whole was experiencing a strange time. Before, producers scrambled to find the oil and get it out of the ground to meet the ever-growing demand. Oil barons like E.W. Marland, Frank Phillips, Robert Kerr, Erle Halliburton, and others were so successful at producing the black gold that prices plunged from fifteen cents a gallon in 1920 to around twelve cents a gallon by 1926. Still Marland produced and pushed to get his pipelines built.

Besides the construction of the new home, E.W. was spending heavily on seismic research, which he believed would revolutionize the exploration industry. Marland had been supporting Dr. John Karcher and Dr. Irving Perrine, former University of Oklahoma professors, in their research on seismic reflection exploration. Karcher, however, had left the oil exploration business for a government job by 1925.

In all the fuss and chaotic growth of the Marland empire, Virginia Marland was almost a forgotten part of E.W.'s past success. Her health had steadily declined during the past several years. Virginia stayed inside her suite in the Grand Mansion for most of those years and was seldom seen with Mr. Marland during that time. She died June 7, 1926 before the first walls were constructed for the Palace on the Prairie. The official cause of death was pneumonia, but she had never fully recovered from her battle with cancer.

Every business in Ponca City closed the day of the funeral out of respect for this great citizen of the city. Over 1,500 people attended the public portion of the funeral and it took three trucks to carry all the flowers to the Mausoleum. Mrs. Marland had been a kind soul to many of the children of Ponca City and she remained to many the epitome of a lady. She was laid to rest only twenty steps from Walt Johnson. It somehow felt comforting, to me, knowing she was resting in peace so close to one of her favorite boys.

For the rest of the Marlands there was little time to mourn. E.W. had a business to run, Lydie was spending countless hours guiding the artisans through their task to make sure every detail was authentic, and even George was hooked up with some special projects at Marland Oil.

One of the first artisans to occupy the new Artist Studio at the Marland estate was Jo Davidson, the famous sculptor. Davidson was commissioned to work on some of the more detailed carvings that were to grace the mansion. He was a distinguished looking gentleman about forty-years-old who had done sculptures of President Wilson, George Bernard Shaw, and a young politician from New York named Franklin Roosevelt.

Lydie worked closely with Davidson for many months, making sure his artistic touch was consistent with the overall project. The two appeared to have a close working relationship. The artist and Lydie were often seen together in town, as he was generous to lend his artistic eye to other aspects of Lydie's project. Davidson's work on the mansion, with his crisp and vigorous style, soon landed him another commission from E.W. Marland. Davidson was asked to sculpt three life-sized statues, one of Mr. Marland, one of George Marland, and one of Lydie. He spent extra time on Lydie's statue making sure, he said, to capture her youthful assurance and feminine allure.

Davidson's effort on the statues was nothing short of outstanding. E.W. Marland's statue had him sitting in a chair wearing a three-piece suit and looking as if he were sitting on a throne. George Marland's sculpture showed him wearing a polo outfit, with knee-high boots, a collared shirt, and sweater. George's hands were placed casually in his pockets and the statue looked as if he were ready to mount a pony for a match.

As outstanding as these two statues looked, they paled in comparison to Lydie's. Jo Davidson obviously had a special relationship with Lydie and he had spent many hours to capture her form. The sculpture showed a sensuous young woman near the pinnacle of her appeal. The statue showed Lydie standing with her hand on her hip wearing a full-length dress, which highlighted her feminine, yet athletic shape. It was a seductive and provocative likeness of a stunningly beautiful woman.

Many marveled at the inspired work Davidson had displayed on Lydie's statue. Some in town wondered if Lydie, herself, had been the inspiration.

CHAPTER 39

▼

With Virginia Marland gone, E.W. Marland's old friend Joe Miller was still an advisor he could trust. Joe Miller had been a true friend and confidant to E.W. Marland since his arrival in Oklahoma. A man like E.W. Marland needed perspectives and ideas he could trust. Joe Miller was a person he depended on and respected.

The 101 Ranch, however, was in a time of change and the change was not positive for the Miller boys. The Wild West Show was still an attraction, but was becoming increasingly expensive to transport and drawing decreasingly fewer audiences. Even the tourist trade at the Ranch had suffered. The automobile, which had been such an asset to the oilmen, meant people had more options in traveling. No longer were they restricted to the great railroad lines to access interesting points across the country. The 101 Ranch had been slow recognizing this trend and was stuck with a location with wide-open beauty and very poor roads. George Miller worked on a project to bring a highway from Kansas through the 101 Ranch into Oklahoma City, but building roads took time.

The 101 Ranch received another major setback when the chief promoter and eldest of the Miller brothers, Joe Miller, died of carbon monoxide poisoning. This was a shocking loss to all of Kay County. Before E.W. Marland had even come to Ponca City, Joe was well established as a solid businessman, rancher, and citizen. Joe was one of the people that had encouraged and supported E.W. during those early years of oil exploration and the two men had become great friends. The 101 Ranch had lost its visionary leader but E.W. Marland had lost a person he could rely on to give him perspective and help him generate ideas. Joe Miller was also one of the few men who could warn E.W. to slow down on things and have him listen.

Joe Miller's reputation as a national celebrity was significant enough for a New York newspaper to eulogize the great showman. The paper wrote, "In an age when land barons and cattle kings are a vanishing breed, the country lost perhaps the biggest. Joe Miller of the famous 101 Ranch in Oklahoma was laid to rest today at the ranch's White House. Its vast acres were filled with real cowboys, entertainers, Indians, Mexicans, and others dependent on the ranch for their livelihoods. It was truly an eclectic group to mourn this great rancher and entertainer."

The government had charged the Millers with taking advantage of the Ponca Indians. Apparently, not all Ponca Indians thought so. They provided Joe with a ceremonial Indian burial fitting for an honorary chief of the tribe.

E.W. Marland had lost two of his best partners, friends, and chief advisors in Virginia Marland and Joe Miller within a year. He still dreamed of making Ponca City a center for oil, commerce, and culture, but unbeknownst to him, this dream would be much harder to reach without these two great influences.

A man with the passion and drive of E.W. Marland desperately needed strong controlling forces in his life to help guide him. Without the guidance of Virginia Marland and Joe Miller, E.W. Marland was like a locomotive running full steam with no one to warn of dangerous curves in the tracks ahead. This dynamic of strong driving forces without strong controlling forces made a train wreck possible if not likely to occur. All of Marland Oil braced for the ride to come.

CHAPTER 40

▼

A few months after Virginia Marland's death, I came home one evening to see an expensive tan convertible parked in front. Not recognizing the car, I proceeded into the house to find Lydie Marland sitting in the front room talking to Elizabeth and holding Walt on her lap.

"There he is," Elizabeth acknowledged in a relieved tone. "Look whose come to see us."

"Hello Lydie, It's a surprise to see you here," I said, "a good surprise of course."

I was taken back to see Lydie. Since construction began on the new Marland home, our paths had only crossed once when I saw Lydie briefly at Mrs. Marland's funeral. Besides being caught unaware by her being in the front room of our home, I was pleasantly surprised at her appearance. I had feared Lydie might be experiencing the same type of melancholy she had demonstrated after Walt's death. Instead, she seemed energetic and full of life. She looked wonderfully fit. It appeared the task of overseeing the details of the construction on the new Marland home had kept her constructively occupied.

"I just wanted to come by and see this little guy," Lydie said looking at Walt on her lap.

"Lydie's invited us out to see the progress on the new house," Elizabeth interjected.

"Yes," Lydie confirmed, "you will not believe it Charlie."

"I've been watching the work from the road," I said.

"If you can come this Saturday, I'll give the McDonagh family the grand tour."

Elizabeth and I agreed that Saturday would be a great day for a family outing and we arranged to meet Lydie at the house. After a little more small talk, Lydie excused herself, gave Walt one last pat on the head, and left in her car. As soon as she turned the corner, Elizabeth started scrutinizing the visit.

"Don't you think that's a little strange?" Elizabeth asked.

"What," I asked, "us going to see the new home?"

"Not that," Elizabeth replied. "I mean her coming here."

"I don't know, I guess I really hadn't thought about it," I responded.

Elizabeth looked down the driveway from our front porch like she expected to see some revelation then said, "Maybe I'm being silly. It's just been all these months we haven't seen Lydie and she just shows up and we're invited for a private tour. There's something odd about her these days."

"Maybe, but that's just Lydie," I explained. "She gets focused on a project like that house she's been involved with and she becomes obsessive. I'm sure she's just got to a point where she wanted to show off her work."

"But to us?" Elizabeth asked.

"I'm not sure Lydie really has that many friends around here anymore…you know people her own age," I added.

"Hmmm," was Elizabeth's coy response.

"Do you not want to go Saturday?" I inquired.

"No not at all," Elizabeth was quick to respond, "I'm looking forward to it."

"I think it will be fun," I stated. "And didn't Lydie look happy. I think this house has been good therapy for her."

"You may be right," Elizabeth said. "We'll see Saturday. I can't wait to see it."

Elizabeth's intuition told her something was up with Lydie. She did not know what, but felt there was something more than the house that had Lydie glowing. What Elizabeth thought and did not say was that this was the first time Lydie had been to visit since their heart to heart conversation the night the Palace of the Prairie project was announced. Elizabeth did not really fear Lydie was after her Charlie anymore, but she was determined in her own mind to be cautious and observant when her family went to see the new Marland Mansion.

CHAPTER 41

▼

Elizabeth, Walt, and I arrived Saturday morning to receive the grand tour of the new Marland Mansion. The main entrance included imposing stone pillars and a massive wrought iron gate that greeted us nearly a quarter of a mile from the front door of the home. A long gravel road led to the porte-cochere, which was a roofed structure covering the driveway to provide shelter while entering or leaving a vehicle at the main entrance of the house. The grounds were already immaculate as workers attended to every detail.

The mansion contained over 40,000 square feet of space on four levels. It had 55 rooms, including 10 bedrooms, 12 bathrooms, 7 fireplaces, and 3 kitchens. Large brown stones, accented with detailed carvings, covered the exterior along with a red clay roof. The whole estate looked like a castle from the outside.

Lydie was detained by some contractors who had questions, which gave me an opportunity to explore the exterior of the property. About 100 yards west of the main house was the Artist Studio where Jo Davidson stayed. It would have been a fine home in one of the neighborhoods around town, but looked like a modest dwelling in this setting.

Five lakes surrounded the east side of the property dotted with small islands. Each island had a landscaping theme, which made a striking display. Also located on the east side of the house was a gargantuan size swimming pool. Shaped like a three leaf clover, it was over 100 yards in any direction.

As I moved to the north side of the property, I discovered a picturesque vista. This north vista featured grass walkways, framed with knee-high hedges and a variety of exotic flowers. At the end of the scenic landscape was a semi-circle rock wall that separated the grounds from a larger lake called Lake Whitemarsh.

Lake Whitemarsh was named for one of Mr. Marland's yachts. It included an adjacent boathouse and rowing boats some 200 yards from the main house. E.W. Marland was always a generous man and allowed people in the community to enjoy his grounds and his lakes, including the row boats from the boathouse.

I later learned from Lydie that the boathouse connected to the main house by a "secret" tunnel. The secret, however, was not too well kept since it was one of the first things she boasted about on the tour. All types of hidden passageways filled the house adding to its intrigue. It even included a hidden room behind one of the kitchens where E.W. and his friends could play cards, free from the worries of prohibition.

I observed Lydie giggling with a handsome, middle-aged man in front of the Artist Studio. She was leaning toward him looking at some type of drawing. When she saw us, Lydie waved for us to come over.

"Charlie and Elizabeth," Lydie greeted. "I would like to introduce you to Jo Davidson."

"Nice to meet you," I said as we shook hands.

"Jo is a sculptor," Lydie explained.

"I try," the dapper man said with a pleasant laugh.

"He's done a lot of the carving for the Mansion we'll be seeing today," Lydie continued.

"And don't forget the special project," Jo Davidson added.

"What special project?" I felt compelled to ask.

"Why the statue of Lydie," he answered. "It is one of my best works, carved from the finest French limestone. This statue is as beautiful as the lady herself."

"Jo," Lydie responded as she blushed at the compliment. "Charlie and Elizabeth know me too well to be impressed."

"How did you get her to pose," I asked, not wanting to miss an opportunity to tease Lydie.

"My approach to my subjects is very simple. I never have them pose. We just talked about everything in the world. Lydie is a great study in American womanhood," Jo continued. "Mr. Marland wanted it placed in the north vista so he can see it every morning at breakfast."

A blushing Lydie interrupted, "I know they will be anxious for the unveiling Jo, but we really need to get going."

"Some other time," the artist assured.

"Nice to meet you," I said as Lydie led us away from the Artist Studio and towards the main house.

"He seems to be an energetic fellow," I told Lydie.

"He has energy all right," she said with a smile as we continued walking. "These artists all have a passion about them…when they decide they want to."

We entered through two large oak doors into the Palace on the Prairie, the new Marland Mansion. Lydie began a detailed tour through the interior of the home. The furnishings for the most part, were still arriving, but it appeared most of the interior work was nearing completion. As impressive as the outside of this palace appeared, the interior was pure artistry.

The front door opened into a large foyer, with a carved, built-in cabinet making the area look like a fine hotel lobby. Intricate carvings and painted ceilings amazed the eye. Everywhere one looked creativity, imagination, and beauty were on display. A large, double stairway led to the gallery level. The ceilings of the stairway were treated with an exquisite Chinoiserie attached to a high vaulted ceiling, trimmed in gold. This was impressive until you entered the gallery level, which included a grand ballroom and several other larger open areas, obviously designed for large social gatherings.

Crowned gold leaf patterns decorated the high ceilings of the ballroom, which gave the area a definite European air. Waterford crystal chandeliers with wrought iron bases hung high from chains over the patterned marble floor. Large windows stretching from the floor to the ceiling gave adequate light during the day, but I could only imagine the elegant evening light these grand fixtures would produce. Several long halls Lydie called loggias filled the house. Each hallway was richly adorned and had places for the many Marland art treasures to be displayed.

A dining room, which Lydie said would comfortably serve 20, looked to be slightly larger than our entire home. Exquisitely carved oak walls adorned the dining room. Lydie explained that Mr. Marland received special permission from the royal family in England to cut this magnificent wood from a forest there.

A serving kitchen was adjacent to the formal dining room. On the other side of the kitchen was a small octagonal dining room. Colorful plaster relief, painted in warm yellow gave the room a cozy feel. Two French doors opened to a small balcony giving a full view of the north vista where Jo Davidson indicated the statue of Lydie would be located.

Outside this small private dining room was a hallway leading to a private staircase and an elevator. The elevator was lined in buffalo leather and was protected by a brass gate. It serviced all three floors, including the more private upstairs rooms. Obviously, Mr. Marland had considered his late wife's needs in the design of his palace.

Lydie apologized that the upstairs, where the family living quarters were located, were still under construction. She did slip us into Mr. Marland's bathroom, which was nearly the size of a small house. It featured a new invention called a sauna and a shower with nine spigots to shoot water from every direction.

The tour ended downstairs in a large open area Lydie called the inner lodge. The whole area had the look of an English hunting lodge. The ceiling featured hand painted, oak beams showing the history of Kay County including ancient Indian tribes, the plains Indians, the railroad development, the ranching life, and oil derricks. The paintings even depicted a picture of the mansion, which was appropriate since it was becoming a part of Ponca City history. Reddish, clay tile covered the floor.

"This is my favorite room Lydie," I commented.

"It's one of my favorites too," Lydie cheerfully replied.

"I love the painting on the ceiling," I continued.

Lydie smiled broadly and said, "That was an accident."

"What do you mean?" I asked.

"Mr. Forsyth originally planned this room to have a plain wood beam ceiling. Vincent Margilotti, the Italian mural artist that created many of the ceilings in the house, saw this room and wanted it to tell a story. He offered to paint it for Mr. Marland for free, if he could design it himself. I guess he felt inspired. One of his associates spent six weeks at the Smithsonian researching the history of this region. This is what they designed," Lydie explained as she pointed to the ceiling.

A kitchen was attached to a huge serving buffet and the room was large enough to seat hundreds of people. The inner lodge opened into another large atrium area, which then opened into the swimming pool.

The swimming pool, Lydie explained, was one of the focal points for the whole house. An abandoned stone quarry used as a crusher depot by the Santa Fe Railroad determined the location of the mansion. The excavations for the quarry were used to construct a magnificent swimming pool that was completed before the house was even begun. The pool's T-shape was Olympic size in all directions. It connected to the inner lodge and many Marland visitors would enter the house through the pool area.

The house had an artistic quality everywhere you looked. Although the furnishings were not yet placed the architecture was magnificent. From the polished marble and wood floors decorated with expensive Persian rugs to the intricately designed ceilings, one could see the sense of care and planning that went into the construction. The large house featured small details everywhere, including carvings of angels, dragons, and even some of Mr. Marland's hunting dogs. The details in the home uniquely reflected E.W. Marland's vision and interest.

"What do you think?" Lydie asked at the end of the tour.

It was hard to describe how impressive the whole structure was. Elizabeth simply said, "Magnificent."

I echoed the sentiment by saying, "Extraordinary."

Lydie beamed in our appreciation.

"The outside of the house is so impressive Lydie, but it pales in comparison to the inside. It's like being in an art museum," I said.

Lydie answered with a near giddiness and said, "I think we quite captured the spirit of Florence in it, but like I said, this is my favorite space."

She guided her hand around the inner lodge, which featured so much of the local flavor and said with flair, "I think this is where Florence meets Ponca City."

Elizabeth and I lavished more praises on the beauty of the place. You could tell Lydie was taking great pride in all the effort that had gone into the project. She never talked about the price or cost of the home, but I had heard in town it was into the millions.

As we prepared to exit the inner lodge and return to our more ordinary abode Lydie said, "Mr. Marland is having a big foxhunt here in a few months. He would love for you to come Charlie. We're going to be serving breakfast in this area. It would be a good opportunity for you to meet new clients," she tempted.

I looked at Elizabeth and did not perceive that she would mind, so I gladly accepted the invitation and looked forward to my next trip to the great house.

When Lydie was out of earshot Elizabeth leaned into me as we walked and observed, "You can tell Lydie has fallen in love with this house."

"I can't blame her," I said.

"I personally wouldn't want to have to clean it," Elizabeth said jestingly. "It was good to see Lydie so happy, wasn't it?"

I agreed with a nod.

"It is a true palace," Elizabeth continued, "and she is definitely its princess."

"She does seem to be a part of the place, doesn't she?" I added.

"Yes, and how about that Mr. Davidson?" Elizabeth added.

"He seemed very artistic," I admitted. "It looks like Lydie has had fun working with him."

"I think he might be just the medicine Lydie has needed," Elizabeth concluded.

Elizabeth's intuition still told her that something was up with Lydie, but she could see why Lydie was so enamored with the place. It truly was a dream house and it seemed Lydie was living the dream.

CHAPTER 42

▼

The McDonagh law practice was growing, and I valued my time enough to take the car to work most days. Occasionally, however, I would pick a glorious sun filled day and walk to work. I always did like walking. It gave me exercise, kept me fit, and gave me time to think. The walks to work also allowed me to see my two favorite delinquents, Ron and Tim.

One of the days I had picked to walk turned out to be a particularly long day with several surprise appointments and interruptions. I was walking hurriedly around dusk to get home before dark when a panicked voice of a young boy yelled, "Mr. McDonagh! Mr. McDonagh!"

I spun around to see that Ron McKeever was yelling my name. He and Tim Wilson were running as if a stampede were after them.

"Mr. McDonagh you've got to help us," pleaded Ron.

I could imagine a host of potential disasters the two could have caused, but knew I had to calm them down before I was to get any useful information.

"Settle down boys and tell me what's up," I instructed.

"There's some men gonna hurt Mr. Marland," they claimed.

"What?" I replied dubiously.

"He's right Mr. McDonagh. We heard 'em," Tim affirmed.

"Slow down and tell me exactly what you heard," I requested, "one at a time."

I was dubious any real peril could be imminent to E.W. Marland but felt it would be good entertainment to hear the boys out.

Ron began, "These men came on the train this afternoon. They's saying they're gonna get Mr. Marland's company."

"What?" I replied still confused by their concern for Mr. Marland's safety. "Tell me exactly what they said."

Ron thought for a moment, but before he could respond Tim said, "They said 'I think we can take over Marland's company next week with the board.'"

"Yip, that's what they said," Ron affirmed.

My interest was a little more peaked, but I asked, "What did these men look like?"

"There was about six of them. Tall and wearin' nice black suits and carrying big black cases," Ron related as he seemed to be the calmer of the two boys.

"Black suits like I wear sometimes?" I asked.

"Yip," Tim replied.

"They's dressed just like that Mr. Haman," Ron added. "He was with 'em"

Tim nodded in agreement and the two boys commanded my full attention. Dad had been relaying some strange information about happenings at Marland Oil and most of them involved Randle Haman.

I digested this intelligence for a moment then said, "Why are you afraid for Mr. Marland's safety?"

Ron bullied ahead with his answer, "They said they were gonna git him with a board."

"Yip, they's gonna hit him with a board," Tim affirmed.

The two boys had heard much more than they knew. I certainly did not think the men were going to hit Mr. Marland in the head with a board, but I did know the Marland board of directors met in the morning. I had to see Mr. Marland tonight.

I hastily said goodbye to Ron and Tim assuring them everything would be all right. I walked and nearly ran home, quickly kissed Elizabeth while explaining I had some business needing my attention this evening. I drove over to Mom and Dad's house to find Dad. Mother explained he had not made it home yet and did not really know where he was. Dad worked late more often than not and there was no telling where he was located in Marland Oil's massive facility.

Unable to find Dad, I decided to go to the Grand Mansion and talk to E.W. Marland myself. I hated to bother him, but felt the information the two boys had shared with me would be vital intelligence for him. I pulled up into the long drive at the Grand mansion and hurriedly knocked on the front door. A well-dressed gentleman answered the door. When I asked to see Mr. Marland, he informed me that Mr. Marland was unavailable. I pressed to see if Mr. Marland was unavailable in the house or unavailable at another location, but the faithful house servant would not betray that information.

Frustrated I said, "Is Lydie in...is Miss Marland available?"

"I wouldn't be at liberty to say," the man replied.

In a somewhat frustrated tone I asked, "If I leave a message, would you get it to her as soon as possible? It's an incredibly urgent matter."

The man at the door seemed unimpressed but stoically said, "I will get her the message at the earliest convenience."

I quickly scribbled a note saying I would wait in the garden for twenty minutes. If she could come, I urgently needed to see her. There was thunder in the west and the night air was thick with humidity. All the signs indicated a storm was brewing. In five minutes, Lydie joined me by the gate of the garden. She was dressed in a robe and obviously did not have plans to be out this evening.

"You needed to see me Charlie?" she asked somewhat confused by this intrusion.

I did not have time for detailed description of the situation so I bluntly asked, "Do you know were Mr. Marland is?"

"Yes," she said in a somewhat dubious tone. "Why the interest?"

"I need to see him and I need to see him tonight," I answered.

Lydie looked perplexed at my insistence. She contemplated the dilemma then replied, "He's not in tonight and he won't be available until tomorrow, Charlie."

"Lydie, I have some important information about Marland Oil," I insisted.

"Surely it can wait until the morning," Lydie surmised seeming relieved that I was there on business instead of a personal matter.

"I don't think so. I have information that leads me to believe Randle Haman is going to try something at the Marland Oil board meeting tomorrow.

Using Randle Haman's name definitely got Lydie's attention. She looked around the garden a few seconds debating whether it would be prudent to share the information then timidly replied, "He's at the Arcade Hotel this evening. I think he's playing cards."

"Thanks," I said and started toward the car.

"Wait," Lydie pleaded. "Mr. Marland doesn't like to be interrupted, especially when he's playing poker."

I turned to her and said, "Believe me Lydie this is a matter of grave importance to Marland Oil, he will want to hear what I have to say..."

Lydie cut my explanation off and nodded her head saying, "I know, but wait just a minute and let me get dressed. You won't be able to get in without causing a commotion."

Like a young doe in the woods, Lydie trotted into the house and returned in a remarkably short time dressed and ready to go. We drove to the Arcade Hotel and I explained as best I could what the boy's story possibly meant. We arrived at the hotel in a matter of minutes and rushed into the lobby.

Mr. Wiker was at the front desk and his eyebrow rose a bit at the sight of Lydie and me.

"Are they in 211?" Lydie asked.

"Yes, but they won't want to be disturbed," Mr. Wiker reminded.

E.W. Marland, Bill McFadden, George Miller, Lewis Wentz, and others often had all-night poker games where they got together to share the latest gossip, play for high stakes, and get away from everyone else.

Lydie did not break stride as she bounded up the lobby staircase. We were face to face with the door of suite 211 before she stopped. Lydie knocked gingerly on the door.

A loud gruff voice from inside said, "Who is it?"

This voice was followed by a slightly more obstinate voice saying, "Go away!"

It sounded as if there was a commotion inside the room.

Lydie chose to respond to the first voice and said, "It's Lydie...Lydie Marland."

The commotion quieted and you could here the rustling of chairs on the wooden floor. In a few seconds, the door slowly opened. Plumes of tobacco smoke bellowed from the open door, which framed the profile of E.W. Marland.

"What in the devil are you doing here Lydie?" Mr. Marland asked in a somewhat perturbed tone.

His demeanor did not seem to improve when he noticed me in the hall with Lydie.

"Charles needs to see you," Lydie informed.

"Why? You know I don't like to be disturbed on my card night," Mr. Marland scowled.

This card night was obviously a ritual of which the Marland family was well aware. I began to understand Lydie's reluctance to interrupt.

"It's about Marland Oil and if Charlie thinks it's urgent I think you should listen," she scolded.

This was the most assertive I had ever witnessed Lydie or anyone else, except for Daniel Craigan, speak to Mr. Marland.

I was not prepared for his response. Instead of using his considerable force of presence to put her in her place, he actually softened his tone and said, "Perhaps you're right Lydie."

Mr. Marland excused himself from the group and took us to a secluded part of the hotel's dining room. I explained my conversation with the two boys and what they had overheard. I did not know much about the details of Marland Oil politics, but I was well versed on corporate law and had pieced some things together from Dad. Mr. Marland listened with grave concern.

J.P. Morgan was his banker, but Morgan himself had been buying up more and more of the company's stock. In the beginning, Morgan had let E.W. Marland call all the shots. Marland was the king of the company that bore his name, but as time went on Morgan, through his bankers, had systematically gotten more and more control of the board of directors.

They had been able to filibuster many of Mr. Marland's initiatives, including the expansion of the pipeline delivery system and the seismic research. They had become more and more intrusive in how Mr. Marland spent money and conducted business.

Lydie dropped the bombshell by saying, "They said Haman was with them."

E.W. Marland had a reputation as a fearless and tenacious card player that never blinked at a bluff, but you could see E.W. Marland's countenance falter at this revelation.

He thought for a moment then said defiantly, "It will be okay, I still think I have enough votes, but I'll need to get on the phone. Charlie would you mind escorting Lydie home? I'm getting my staff together and I think we'll be working through the night."

I agreed and headed for the door, not wanting to be in Mr. Marland's way.

"And Charlie, my good friend," Mr. Marland said as I pulled the door open for Lydie to exit, "you may have saved my company."

CHAPTER 43

▼

The information I shared with Mr. Marland may not have saved the company, but it provided E.W. Marland with a reprieve. The board meeting lasted from ten o'clock in the morning until the early morning hours of the next day. E.W. Marland went 28 straight hours without sleep to defend his beloved company.

All prior Marland Oil board meetings had been rubber stamp affairs where E.W. Marland would announce his bold plans for the future. This meeting was contentious and confrontational. Morgan controlled almost 50% of the voting stock and E.W. had barely been able to scrape up enough votes to keep Morgan from taking over completely. If not for some careless talk in front of two young boys, Morgan might have succeeded.

The fight was not without its cost for E.W. Marland. To stay as chairman of the board, he had to agree to cancel the pipeline projects. Morgan and Haman had been secretly blocking this venture for months, fearing the price of oil was on a permanent decline. Research and development dollars were also cut over E.W.'s fervent pleas that the seismic research was an investment in the future. E.W. Marland's personal spending was another issue of debate. The board put more separation between his personal finances and those of Marland Oil.

There was a turnover in management personnel over the next several weeks as the two sides wrestled for control of the giant corporation. E.W. got his pound of flesh when he could. He fired Randle Haman immediately after the meeting. Any satisfaction was short-lived, however, as Morgan hired Haman with a lucrative contract with his bank. Randle Haman had done his job.

Rumors went through the town like wildfire during the fight. The local employees supported E.W. Marland and he made himself more visible around town than he had been in several years. He was fighting a corporate takeover by any means at his disposal, including public relations. E.W. Marland had a gift for communicating and influencing other people. He was putting all of his charms to work for this fight.

I was in the office one morning when a messenger dropped off a note from Mr. Marland. It was an invitation to lunch at the Arcade Hotel. I was puzzled by the invitation. Mr. Marland had a host of legal representatives and I could think of no reason for the meeting. Nonetheless, I replied that I would be happy to meet him for lunch.

Upon entering the lobby of the Arcade Hotel, I noticed more activity than I had in a number of years. It appeared that E.W. Marland had temporarily expanded the headquarters of Marland Oil, from his office building to the Arcade Hotel. Invitations had been sent out to many stockholders who traveled to Ponca City to get a firsthand account of the company's operations. E.W., himself, was meeting many of these investors as they arrived in town at the Arcade Hotel. In the dining room sat E.W. Marland at his special table tucked into a cozy back corner.

"Charles, glad you could make it," he greeted as he stood up to shake hands.

"Thank you for the invitation," I replied.

"I've already ordered lunch, I hope steak is all right with you," he said in a pleasant tone.

"That sounds great."

"I'm a little pressed for time so I thought I would get them started. I'm sure they can change the order," he offered.

"No that will be fine," I assured.

"You're probably wondering why I asked you here," he began.

"I'm guessing it's not just for lunch," I answered.

Mr. Marland laughed a little and said, "I sometimes forget you're an attorney now. Time is money isn't it?"

I smiled politely and nodded in agreement.

"I wanted to thank you for the information you brought to me the other night. Your sharp ears and thinking really saved me from being totally ambushed," he said in a serious tone.

"Well, I thought it was information you needed to have," I sheepishly replied.

"You thought well. You always have been an intelligent boy. You have a good head for the law. I expect you will do well."

"Thank you," I said as I gloated with pride at the compliment from such a successful man.

"Haman. I should have known," he said as he shook his head. "You know I was roommates with Randle back at Michigan."

"No, I didn't know that," I said.

"Yes, he was a rascal back then, but he was my friend. I thought he still was," Mr. Marland said shaking his head slightly.

"I guess people can surprise you," I said.

"People will always surprise you," Mr. Marland stated. "For better or worse I suppose."

I had known Mr. Marland since I was a boy. This, however, was the first time I had ever talked to him when I felt like I was an adult. He seemed to simply want to talk this day and I still did not know the real purpose of our conversation.

"I remember my senior year at Michigan," Mr. Marland continued. "We played cards every chance we could. We played a lot of Black Lady, some people call it Hearts. I was always a good card player. I always took more chances than Randle would. Playing cards was a nice diversion from those tedious law books. I like the simplicity and strategy of the game. Knowing what you have and making an educated guess at what the other players are holding. Playing cards requires some luck, but it's more about reading other people and out thinking them."

"One night we played Black Lady until late in the night. Randle had brought this dull-witted underclassman with him. I shot the moon on the last hand and beat Randle by 5 points, but he wanted a rematch. Randle wanted to play one hand of stud poker. If he won, he wanted me to take a weekend trip with him to Holland, Michigan to meet some girl and if I won, he was going to do my laundry for a month."

This conversation was not anything like I was expecting. E.W. Marland was telling me a personal story and I was beginning to feel like one of his gang.

He continued his story by saying, "I agreed. This kid he had brought fell out of his chair. While I was distracted, Randle switched decks and I lost."

"He cheated you?" I asked thinking I had revealed something of Randle Haman's character.

Mr. Marland laughed a little and explained, "He did, but we were both pulling stunts like that. I was used to being Randle's partner in his little romances. This kid he had brought to the card game had a sister. His family was in the furniture business in Grand Rapids. Randle always liked pretty girls, especially if he thought they might have money. This girl had a cousin and Randle needed me to go to keep the cousin company while he stalked the pretty one."

Mr. Marland's tone changed gradually from lighthearted story telling to a more serious tone.

"Ironically," he continued. "Randle tired of his girl after the first night and I fell for the cousin. Her name was Greta Vanhoosen. She was a few years older than I was, but she was the most beautiful thing I had ever seen. Randle had rudely ignored the girl he had gone to see, but I kept in contact with Greta for many months."

"She was the first girl I loved. She was twenty-two and I was only nineteen," he said with a little laugh. "It would have never worked out. She came from a nice family. They were Dutch Reformed and I was Catholic. I wrote Greta every week and was sure we could work things out," he said shaking his head.

About that time, our food arrived. E.W. had ordered us both big steaks with all the trimmings. He chitchatted with the waitress a little. E.W. was friendly with almost everyone he met, no matter his or her station in life.

I was enjoying this casual conversation with Mr. Marland and wanted to know the rest of his story so I asked, "What happened to the girl?"

Mr. Marland stopped chewing for a moment and seemed to wince slightly as he continued, "Her family didn't think much of my friend Randle. I guess they were smarter than me about that. I don't know all the details, but I'm afraid Randle might have caused a scandal with Greta's cousin. Greta and I were in love though. She was all I could think about. We did what we could to stay together, but she died in an accident. Her family didn't approve of our relationship so she would sneak off sometimes to see me in Ann Arbor. The train derailed and she...she didn't survive. I've always felt the family thought I was responsible and I guess I would have to say I've always felt a little responsible myself."

Mr. Marland stopped talking for a moment and took a long sip of his ice tea. I sat awkwardly not knowing what to say, but immediately realized the similarity between Mr. Marland's youthful situation and Walt Johnson's.

"If I had just abided by the family's wishes or had the courage to take Greta away, she might be with us today," he said as he scratched the back of his head behind his ear. "It took me years to get over Greta. I didn't marry Virginia until I was nearly thirty. Virginia was a wonderful woman, perfect for me."

He took another long drink of ice tea as I nodded in agreement of his assessment of Mrs. Marland as his wife.

"I didn't ask you here to bore you with the details of my life. I wanted to thank you again for the information about Randle Haman. Sometimes you don't see things clearly, Charles. I should have seen what Randle was doing, but was a little too trusting. I just didn't pay enough attention to what was happening. I also wanted to thank you for all you've done for Lydie the past few years. I know she took the death of that Johnson kid hard and I think you've been a real friend to her."

I was somewhat surprised by this sudden change in subject matter and struggled to respond by saying, "Lydie's always been a great friend to me."

"She respects you and that's important. How do you think she's doing?" he asked.

"I don't know if anyone ever gets over a loss like that. It seems to me like it's a part of you gone forever, but Lydie seems to being doing fine. She's strong. I think that the trip to Florence and this project you've got her working on has taken her mind off a lot of things," I reasoned.

"Yes, Florence is a beautiful city," he said as he looked to be recollecting. "Lydie's a special girl and I do want to see her happy."

"She showed us the mansion the other day and it is truly amazing," I added.

"Lydie's done a great job. I consider it her house as much as mine," he said with a grin.

We finished our meal and I thanked Mr. Marland for the lunch. He thanked me again while giving me a hearty handshake. Mr. Marland obviously had other business to attend to, but as he left he turned to say one last thing.

"Charles, I'm having a foxhunt in a couple of weeks to kind of show off Lydie's mansion. I would like you to be there. There won't be a lot people Lydie's age and I'm sure she would love to have you there," he invited.

"I'm not much on a horse, Mr. Marland, but I would love to come," I said knowing Lydie had already invited me.

He laughed a little at my candor but said, "Great."

E.W. Marland exited the dining room to take command of the lobby area. He had people to see and deals to make. I walked back to the office looking forward to my second Marland foxhunt.

CHAPTER 44

▼

The spring foxhunt was a pleasant distraction for E.W. Marland from the distasteful battle for control of his company. This hunt included all the familiar ambience of past hunts. Men and women were fashionably dressed in English attire and the hounds were howling for the hunt. E.W. was mounted on his favorite horse, Tom James. Mr. Marland was dressed in knee high shiny boots, a colorful wool jacket, and his trademark fedora hat.

Lydie was on a tall dark horse wearing a red jacket cinched tight at the waist showing her slender figure. She wore a smaller version of a fedora hat matching Mr. Marland's. Lydie was glowing that day as she rode her horse named Rosenbar. She looked beautiful and in control of her world. I spotted her several times and noted how contented she looked; later wishing I had enjoyed her luminous joy and happiness that day with more attention. Little did I know it would be one of the last times to see her as the energetic and optimistic girl I had known for the past sixteen years.

Today was a special day for the traditional foxhunt. It was the first time for E.W. Marland to entertain in his new house. The house was nearly finished with only a few details and furnishings left to complete the project. The guests of the hunt were allowed to get a sneak peak before it was scheduled to officially be occupied in the fall. The hunters enjoyed a feast for breakfast and then everyone was instructed to assemble. The battles and stress of Marland Oil were forgotten for today. Everybody's attention focused on the hunt.

I was an average rider at best, but did enjoy the outdoors. I had no delusions of catching the fox or even keeping up with the hounds. It was just a nice day to be part of the festivities. The horn sounded and the hunt began. I rode at a leisurely pace, keeping the main group within sight for the most part. The steady trot of my mount, however, was soon interrupted. Lydie, who was a superior rider compared to me, galloped beside my horse and grabbed the reins stopping the animal.

"Come chase me," she challenged playfully.

Lydie galloped away from the furor of the hunt. I kept up as best I could, but she was toying with me until she slowed down. I had been so intent on staying on my horse that I had not realized Lydie had led me to the bridge over Red Bud Creek. Lydie jumped off her horse, laughing heartily at my limited riding abilities.

"How can someone live in Oklahoma all their life and ride as poorly as you?" she teased.

I grinned and said, "Some of us find a car more comfortable." I dismounted from the horse and asked in a more serious tone, "What are we doing here Lydie?"

"This has always been one of my favorite places," she said. "I've traveled the world and seen many great places, but I always find this place…familiar."

I listened, still not knowing her intentions.

She hesitated changing her tone of voice, "You and Walt brought George and me here on our very first day in Ponca City. Do you remember Charlie?"

"Sure," I said, "this has always been one of my favorite places too."

She looked around as if examining every detail and wistfully said, "This is where Walt asked me to marry him."

I looked at her not really knowing what to say.

"As a lawyer you have something called client attorney privilege don't you?" she asked.

"Yes. If a client tells me something I am ethically obliged to keep that information confidential," I replied like I had hundreds of times in my office.

Lydie reached into her coat pocket, handed me a twenty-dollar bill, and asked, "Will twenty dollars buy me client attorney privilege."

I declined the payment but with concern asked, "Lydie what's wrong? Are you in some kind of trouble?"

She laughed insincerely and repeated to herself, "Am I in trouble?"

Lydie walked around in small circles as if searching for a way to start a topic she did not know how to breech.

"Charlie," she said suddenly, "I'm getting married."

Shock was not an adequate adjective to describe my surprise. I just looked at her in disbelief for a moment, finally wondering if she were teasing me. Elizabeth always had her suspicions that Lydie was seeing someone, but if Lydie was seeing anyone, it had been a secret to me. As an attorney, my mind filled with a host of issues a woman of her wealth might need to consider. As a friend, I went through a fairly short list of men I thought might be the lucky groom.

I finally determined that it must be someone far away or even someone she met while in Europe. I even wondered if she had developed a relationship with one of the many artisans that had come to work on the new palace. Jo Davidson and John Forsyth had spent a lot of time in town and with Lydie, but I had never seen her with anyone socially.

She looked uncomfortably at me, cocked her head a little, and said, "You're surprised I see."

"I...I am...I had no idea Lydie," I stammered for words, "That's great, I had no idea you were even seeing anyone."

She smiled slyly and said, "I don't think anyone does."

I was still confused and her coyness was not enlightening the situation much for me. The only thing I could think to ask was, "What does George and Mr. Marland think?"

She turned away and took a few steps before replying, "George doesn't know. No one knows but you and Mr. Marland."

I still was ignorant of the bombshell she had yet to deliver.

"You can't tell anyone. You can't even tell Elizabeth. You will promise won't you?" she begged.

I nodded in agreement.

She vacillated a second longer then said. "Charlie, I'm marrying Mr. Marland."

If I was shocked before, I had no idea how to describe the feeling of disequilibrium I felt with this revelation. I stood in stoic silence just looking at her.

"You can't tell anyone Charlie," she pleaded. "I took such a risk telling you, but I had to talk to someone. You're always so easy to talk to."

I still could not respond. She had asked me not to tell anyone but I was too flabbergasted to say a word at the present.

"Charlie," she asked and then pleaded, "please don't...please don't look at me that way Charlie."

I had no consciousness of my look or demeanor. I was numb to any outside perception.

"I can't bear it," she pleaded as she stepped toward me. "I expect it from everyone else, but not you. Please...it's too much."

"How Lydie?" I was finally able to ask. "He's your father."

Lydie responded quickly as if she had rehearsed this answer for a political debate, "He's not really my father Charlie. You know that."

My expression must have still been skeptical as she said, "I was the niece of Mrs. Marland. I'm no blood relation to Mr. Marland. You know Charlie...You know better than anyone that he never really treated me like a daughter."

I was still letting the information sink in trying to find the right words to say.

"But he is old enough to be your father and you are Lydie Marland...you are legally his daughter," I argued.

"He's only 52. I'm 28. Lot's of 28-year-old women would marry a handsome millionaire of his charms and you know that he seems much younger than that."

I did not think it appropriate to agree, but I suppose my body language was softening as Lydie seemed to be turning the conversation into more of a sales presentation instead of a debate.

"I'm 28 years old Charlie and I have no one. You have Elizabeth. You have Walt. I have nobody. I want a family I can call my own before I'm too old."

She turned away again as if to regain her composure then said with her back to me, "I've never talked to my friends in Ponca City about my life in Flourtown before coming here. We were poor for sure, but there were other things, bad situations back there that....that are better forgotten. I have always felt safe with Mr. Marland. I need to feel safe. I need to feel like I belong to someone."

I felt that she might break down emotionally. Lydie was not in the habit of losing control of her emotions, but she was struggling to fight back the tears now.

"Lydie, this will cause a stir you know," I observed, beginning to soften to Lydie's situation.

"I know. People are such gossips but..." she paused momentarily, "he needs me."

After a few more seconds she added, "And I need him."

I still was struggling to draft the words that needed to be said, but I did want to be supportive of my friend.

"I need you Charlie...I need you to tell me things are going to be all right. I really have no one else to speak to. If I can do this thing, I need you to believe in me," she said subconsciously biting on her lower lip.

"Do you love him?" I asked.

She turned away from me again and walked randomly for a few steps before saying, "I respect him...I think I love him Charlie. I don't see I will ever have the infatuation I felt for Walt with anyone, but yes I love him and I feel as close to him as any man I've met since."

She continued this monologue as if convincing herself, "That's why I came here to tell you. I knew if I could convince you here in this place….in this place where I sense so strongly my feeling for Walt….that my love for Ernest must be genuine."

It was the first time I had ever heard Lydie call Mr. Marland by any name other than "Mr. Marland." It also occurred to me that with Lydie's sweetness and feminine charms, it was easy to overlook her intelligence and reasoning abilities. Lydie did very few things without purpose. She had calculated this meeting and this place for sometime. She had orchestrated this time with me to test herself to the possibility of this most unlikely union.

"I think this will be a practical solution to my happiness and I feel I can make Mr. Marland happy too. He desperately needs someone since Aunt Virginia passed," she continued. "You know him Charlie…you know how charming and kind he can be. I feel we will be a happy couple. I think I can be a good partner for him. You need to know that he has always been proper toward me and I respect him very much."

I could not disagree with Lydie's appraisal of Mr. Marland. He did seem young and full of energy for his age. He was as likable a person as I had ever known and he was generous to his friends almost to a fault.

"How will you do it? I mean will you have a big wedding?" I asked.

"Heavens no," Lydie exclaimed. "Mr. Marland would never want so much publicity. We are leaving in a couple of weeks to go to Flourtown to have the adoption annulled, then we will be married there…by a justice of the peace I assume."

It seemed strange to think of the many grand balls and parties that had been given for Lydie in her debutante years. I remembered the many suitors who had pursued Lydie at those parties. It seemed strange that she would be married with so little fanfare. I had always envisioned a big wedding and a citywide celebration for Lydie's wedding day, but then again I could never have imagined events as extraordinary as what she presented to me this afternoon.

I thought for a moment while she waited for some response. She had laid out her case. She had bore her soul to a friend and now it was in my court to judge. I felt inadequate to give an opinion in this matter, but sensed her level of extreme anxiety. What she was proposing had the distinct possibility of alienating her from a large portion of her acquaintances. As I thought about and contemplated her proposal, I could not help but admire Lydie's courage. She had been coura- geous when she was willing to marry Walt Johnson without Mr. Marland's approval and she was possibly showing more audacity now in her desperate bid for happiness.

Lydie was my friend and I determined, no matter the barriers, that I would support her as best I could. I had no idea if it was the right thing to do, but I believed then and believe now that people are responsible for their choices and this had been Lydie's choice.

"Lydie, I'm happy for you," I said as I gave her a hug around the neck. "I've seen such a change in you…such vibrancy since you have returned from Florence that I think you must be in love. Elizabeth thought as much the first time she saw you back in Ponca City."

Lydie looked as though the weight of the world was off her shoulders and she smiled slightly for the first time since she had told me her news. She then said, "I know, Elizabeth thought I was in love with you."

I blushed slightly and then made a face as if surprised, though Elizabeth had already shared her silly theories with me.

"Maybe in another time or place Lydie, but I do hope you will be as happy as Elizabeth and me."

"Me to," she sighed. "We need to be getting back. I'll wager the poor fox has been killed or gone forever by now."

We mounted our horses and slowly rode back toward the house. Lydie admonished me to secrecy again before we rejoined the party. In two weeks, Lydie Marland would have an extraordinary day in which she would start the day as Miss. Lydie Marland, be transformed by a judge to Lydie Roberts only to be wed as Mrs. Lydie Marland in the same day. Ponca City, Oklahoma was still the wild, wild west.

CHAPTER 45

▼

E.W. Marland had taken Lydie back to Flourtown, Pennsylvania in his luxurious, private rail car to annul Lydie's adoption. He then married the girl who had served as principal hostess for Marland functions since the chronic illnesses of Virginia Marland. Lydie had been wrong on one detail; the couple did not get married by a justice of the peace, but in the home of Lydie's parents by a priest. I hoped Lydie had made peace with some of the painful memories from her childhood.

The couple took an extended honeymoon in Mr. Marland's private rail car as they traveled to the Hudson Bay of Canada where Mr. Marland had business holdings then across Canada until they ended up in California.

Lydie had been right about the gossip. As soon as the papers announced this most unlikely union, rumors and gossip began to spread like a wild prairie fire. Some of the women were sure they had sensed something going on between the two. Others asserted that Mr. Marland's indifference to Virginia in her last days had been part of a scheme to secure a new bride. The old unspoken rumors of E.W. Marland's whereabouts on the morning of Walt Johnson's death were even rekindled.

It was an awkward situation for me having to feign surprise with my wife Elizabeth, while tactfully trying to defend the newlyweds from some of the more vicious slander circulating around town. Elizabeth had been right though. Lydie did have something in her life besides the Marland Mansion project.

There was a picture of Lydie in one of the papers. She was wearing a dark ankle length dress with healed shoes, a fur coat, and pearls draped around her neck. She looked elegant and she looked happy as she smiled broadly, but I could not help but notice a subtle maturity that saturated her look. I feared the youthful and exuberant Lydie I had known was gone forever.

It appeared the couple had a wonderful trip and enjoyed the sights, the travel, and each other. They slipped back into town secretly, with no fanfare, into Lydie's Palace on the Prairie about two months later. The storm of gossip had relented somewhat while the couple was on honeymoon, but news that the great house was now occupied by the millionaire and his young wife rekindled the fury.

Lydie arrived as mistress of a house few could even imagine. The finished house boasted 55 rooms with several large ballrooms. The house included the finest furnishings and the most modern amenities available. Rumors around town had the house costing over 5.5 million dollars. This in a time when a nice house cost about $7,000 and a loaf of bread was less than a dime. There were literally miles of roses lining the stone walls surrounding the property. A staff of 40 kept the house operating and Mr. Marland hired another 40 men as gardeners to maintain the grounds. Few kings and queens lived in such luxury. The grounds were idyllic in their beauty with five small lakes, sunken gardens, an artificial waterfall, flowering trees, and plants of every kind. The attention to every small detail gave the whole place a dream like quality.

Lydie had arrived back in Ponca City to this dream. She had a loving husband, who was powerful and wealthy. She was mistress to a massive estate. There could not have been anything added to complement this grandiose lifestyle, but like the Oklahoma weather she loved, the winds of change were in the air and the storm clouds of change were gathering.

One of the tragic ironies for E.W. Marland was that in a time when his great oil empire was growing at its fastest rate, it was methodically being taken from him. By the time Lydie and E.W. arrived back in Ponca City, the damage done by Randle Haman and J.P. Morgan Jr. had matured into calamity for Mr. Marland. Morgan's group steadily gained control of the board of directors and made in-roads influencing the executive committee.

Some would say the restrictive policies of Morgan's bank saved the company millions, while E.W. Marland contended they were stifling growth. It did not matter. Morgan's policies had eroded the credibility of Mr. Marland with the stockholders enough that he no longer controlled the company bearing his name.

Elizabeth and I made a social call on the new couple at the new Marland Mansion. Although Elizabeth was less than enthusiastic to go, I felt obligated to welcome Lydie back to town. E.W. was out fighting the battles for Marland Oil that day. Lydie was pleasant and affirmed she had a great honeymoon. Walt tried out the massive swimming pool constructed at the estate. Lydie, who was an excellent swimmer, even gave him a swimming lesson. She was playful and patient with young Walt and I was convinced she was genuinely happy.

While they swam, I admired the grounds and noticed the new addition of the three statues. The one of George Marland stood on the west side of the house facing the boat dock. In the front of the estate was a statue of E.W. Marland sitting in his chair, looking like a king. On the north vista facing the sunken gardens and sitting where the evening shadows would fall, was a stunning likeness of Lydie.

Lydie was glorious in this extravagant setting and she seemed to be content with all aspects of her life, but she was concerned for Mr. Marland's business fight. We sat down beside the large pool for lemonade and to visit.

"Those wolves of Wall Street are bound and determined to ruin Mr. Marland," Lydie explained.

I was sure she borrowed the phrase "wolves of Wall Street" from Mr. Marland.

"These bankers don't know anything about running an oil company. They need to leave well enough alone," she added.

Elizabeth had little interest in the oil business and asked, "How was the honeymoon?"

Lydie glowed a little then said, "It was wonderful. We went to Canada to see the Hudson Bay. It's beautiful. We stayed several nights in the train and I liked that. We were away from everyone and no one could bother us there. Except of course for those annoying telegrams…Mr. Marland would get several of them a day. That was distracting."

Lydie seemed to realize she was rambling so she hesitated to ask, "How were things here?"

This was a difficult question. Since the Marlands had gone, there was precious little gossip to share. I talked a little about the law practice and Elizabeth updated Lydie about Walt and our daughter Lizzy.

"Where did you go from the Hudson Bay?" Elizabeth finally asked, focusing the conversation back on Lydie's trip.

Lydie seemed eager to talk about her honeymoon and answered, "We traveled by rail across Canada. I loved it. It's more vast and vacant than Oklahoma and the weather was so cool and refreshing. We stayed in all the best hotels and were entertained everywhere. I even got Mr. Marland to take me to a picture show. We ate high on the hog everywhere we went. We ended up in California. Mr. Marland had business there. I feel like we saw the whole continent together. He was very sweet the whole time. I was anxious to come home, but hated to end our trip."

Lydie filled in many other details about the trip and the sights she had seen. She never revealed much about the marriage ceremony or her trip back to Flourtown, but it was evident she enjoyed being Mrs. Marland and was enamored by her husband.

Ironically, this would be one of the last times Lydie would entertain friends while living in the great mansion. Things were changing for Lydie, quicker than she could have imagined. She married into the Marland empire at the zenith of its glory, but events were conspiring to change this enchanted life to one more public than she would have liked.

The "wolves of Wall Street" smelled blood and by the end of the year had completely neutered E.W. Marland's role in Marland Oil. J.P. Morgan Jr. and the other bankers feared E.W. Marland would start a new oil company and hire away significant talent and expertise from the corporation. They offered to let him stay on as Chairman of the Board, an honorary position, if he and Lydie would move from Ponca City. By the end of 1928, E.W. Marland defied his adversaries by resigning from Marland Oil and staying in Ponca City.

The world E.W. Marland had built and lived in for the past twenty years seemed to be falling apart. George Marland resigned from Marland Oil when E.W. did and bought into a car dealership. E.W. still had some oil interest and royalty in the area, but was more or less out of the business he had helped pioneer.

February of 1929 was bitterly cold. On one of the famous poker nights at the Arcade Hotel, an ice storm hit. Tree limbs snapped all over town and sounded like pistol shots in the night. George Miller, the younger brother of Joe and the financial brains of the 101 Ranch, decided he needed to get back to assess the damage to the ranch. His car crashed on the icy roads killing him instantly. Zack Miller, the surviving brother, would battle for the survival of the ranch for the next three decades, but without Joe and George Miller the 101 would never come close to its past glories.

Marland Oil became the Continental Oil Company. The distinctive red triangles that had read Marland Oil at gas stations through the region no longer bore the Marland name. E.W. did not leave the company empty handed, but his financial condition was considerably depleted. E.W. fashioned plans to build a new oil company and show the eastern "vultures" how to run an oil company. Lydie did her part as a loyal and supportive wife. Everyone in Ponca City had complete confidence that E.W. Marland would be back, but the storm clouds of events outside his control were working against him.

The stock market crash greatly deflated many of E.W. Marland's remaining assets. He had never been one to horde cash and found himself unable to hold on to some of his promising properties. The Great Depression did not ruin E.W. Marland but it did crush his dream of rebuilding Marland Oil quickly. Although E.W. did not enjoy the large revenues he had experienced in the twenties, he continued to spend as if money were limitless.

A friend approached E.W. to commission his favorite sculpture Jo Davidson to create a large outdoor statue commemorating the vanishing American. Marland's friend had envisioned a gigantic depiction of an Osage or Ponca Indian, possibly a representation of one of the great chiefs. Marland liked the idea, but thought the "Vanishing American" should depict the pioneer woman. He commissioned Jo Davidson to create the sculpture, although he really could not afford it. Lydie even asked my Walt to stand as a model for the sculpture of a pioneer woman guiding a small boy through the prairie.

E.W. spent $200,000 of his own money on the project. In the glory years of Marland Oil this would have been a pittance, but at this time it was a great personal sacrifice. The statue was unveiled in the spring of 1930 with great fanfare and on the 41st anniversary of the Oklahoma Land Run. Will Rogers, a personal friend of E.W. Marland, spoke at the unveiling less than a mile from Marland's Palace on the Prairie. Much to the embarrassment of Mr. Marland, who valued the propriety and decorum of the event, Will Rogers began his speech by saying, "I've come all the way from California to undress a woman." Mr. Marland was not amused, but the rest of the large crowd loved Will Rogers.

In the midst of all the celebration and laughter, I was deeply touched by the unveiling. The boy in the statue did not look much like my Walt, but I could not help but see the strong resemblance to a young Walt Johnson in the sculpture. The Pioneer Woman seemed to me to have a strong similarity of Virginia Marland.

Months after this great gift to the people of Oklahoma, E.W. and Lydie Marland were forced to leave their Palace on the Prairie because they were unable to staff it or pay the utility bills. One of E.W.'s early business partners bought the mansion and gave it back to him to keep the Marlands from losing their home. The great house that Lydie had come back to from her honeymoon, however, was gone forever as their home. The Marlands moved into the Artist Studio on the grounds while the great Marland Mansion was destined to stay unoccupied by the family forever.

E.W. Marland was down, but never out. He was a fighter. No one heard complaining or resignation in his voice, just an assurance that he would be back.

E.W. had lost a fortune before and had that same air of confidence he had demonstrated in those early years in Ponca City. This was a different time, however. Getting in the oil business was much more expensive now and the country was in a depression. People were suffering and E.W. Marland decided he needed to do something about it.

Marland ran for the congressional seat in northern Oklahoma. He was a natural politician and had immense personal popularity. He had been a generous employer, loyal friend, and fair business partner. E.W. was able to keep Lydie from cruel public scrutiny. Despite his unusual marital relationship, Marland won in a landslide. In the fall of 1932, Lydie and E.W. were leaving Ponca City and going to Washington.

CHAPTER 46

▼

Lydie had been right. I was not much of a horseman, but I had found a passion in golf. E.W. Marland introduced the game to Ponca City and I learned the game as a caddy from my teenage years.

These days I particularly enjoyed playing with my dad. It gave us a chance to see each other on a regular basis and we had a friendly competition. I could hit the ball much longer and straighter than he could, but Dad played a perpetual slice that somehow found the fairway on every hole. Dad would chip in from off the green at least once a round and somehow keep the matches interesting.

It was a hot and dry day and I had noticed a change in Dad this day. He seemed relaxed and pleased just enjoying the game. We finished the round and headed to the car to return home. I usually carried my own clubs, but Dad was not able to carry his so I had been hiring Tim and Ron to tote our bags. After giving the boys their tips and inquiring about their latest adventures, I found Dad looking across the parking lot and toward the far away outline of the Marland Mansion.

"What are you looking at Dad?" I inquired thinking he must have spotted a hawk or some far away point of interest.

"I'm just thinking," he replied.

"Be careful, that can be dangerous."

He laughed a little then said, "I was actually looking at the Marland Mansion and remembering how much this town has changed."

I looked in the distance at the site I had become used to seeing and said, "I guess things have changed a lot since you and Mom came here."

"That's for sure. When you were born, this was a wide place in the road…a train station and not much else. Do you remember when I used to cut meat?"

"Sure."

"That was a good life," Dad continued, "but I could never have provided for you boys and your mother like I have without Marland Oil."

I listened, wondering what was on his mind. Dad and I had many conversations, but generally a little less abstract than this one.

"Do you ever hear from Lydie or Mr. Marland?" Dad asked.

"No, not really," I replied.

Dad shook his head casually.

"Why do you ask?" I inquired.

Dad looked into the distance and said, "I was let go this week from the company."

I was taken back. Dad had been with the company from the beginning. Many people had lost their jobs during the Marland fight. The beginning of this nationwide depression was also having an effect, but I always assumed Dad would survive all that.

"Dad, I'm sorry. I had no idea," I tried to comfort him.

"It's okay. It was time for me to go. In fact, I really enjoyed today. It was the first time in a long time that I didn't think a part of me was back at the company. I've done well. I've done real well. Your mother and I have always been able to save more than we've spent. I was guided into some good properties by Mr. Marland that have been profitable. I was able to send all you boys to college. It was time for me to go."

I listened in silence to his reflections.

"I'm worth almost $300,000, Charlie. I don't need to work anymore. When I was your age, I never dreamed that much money was in the world. E.W. Marland told your mother one time that if he found oil it would be good for a lot of people. I didn't really think I would be one of those people."

I was not used to my dad being so introspective. I also had no idea he had accumulated so much net worth. My parents were always frugal and always seemed able to give that little extra help to myself and two brothers, but I was surprised to hear Dad give such a number.

"I know you and Lydie are friends and you bump into her sometimes. Do me a favor. Next time you see E.W. Marland, tell him thank-you for me."

Dad and I loaded up the car and drove back to the house for some of Mom's homemade ice cream. Dad seemed content with his world.

Later that year, I had a client disputing with the government about some land that was once part of the Ponca reservation and I needed to visit the Bureau of Indian Affairs in Washington. Mom agreed to keep Walt and our daughter Lizzy so Elizabeth and I planned a train trip to Washington. We had not gotten out of Ponca City much in the past two years so we decided to make a business vacation out of it. I telegraphed our congressman, E.W. Marland, and secured an appointment to see him. I hoped to see Lydie as well.

The train trip to Washington was a good vacation for Elizabeth and me. The passenger cars were not as busy as they had been before the depression and the travel was relaxing. The economic downturn that started with the stock market crash was having some impact in Ponca City, but as we moved east, I could tell the effects were much more acute.

We passed town after town with businesses shut down and men wandering the streets in worn clothing. It was as if a dark cloud had descended on the glory that had been the twenties. There was a sense of gloom, but when we arrived in Washington, it was nothing but hustle and bustle. Elizabeth and I checked into our room and then I left to make my appointments. The last stop of the day was at the Capital building to see E.W. Marland.

I was curious to see Mr. Marland. I had not really talked to him much since his marriage to Lydie. I wondered if there might be some awkwardness, since Lydie and I had been friends for so long. Mr. Marland's office was in a line of similarly undistinguished offices. The offices were nice, much nicer than I was accustomed to, but they certainly did not meet Mr. Marland's standards. For fifteen minutes or more, I sat in the outer office staring at his secretary, struggling to make small talk while not interrupting her work. I could hear Mr. Marland on the phone carrying on a series of conversations. The dialogue was not common chitchat. E.W. Marland was making deals and talking loud, just like he had done in building Marland Oil.

Any apprehension I might have had about seeing Mr. Marland vanished as he stepped through the door.

"Charles, my friend," he warmly greeted.

"Mr. Marland," I replied as I reached out to shake his hand. After a firm handshake I said, "I hope I'm not bothering you."

"Nonsense," he assured. "Come in and have a seat. It will be good to talk to someone from home instead of these vultures around here. The whole country's falling apart and all these fellows can do is bicker and thump their chest. What can I do for you?"

"Well, that's it Mr. Marland," I somewhat sheepishly replied, "I don't really need anything."

"Come on Charles, everyone needs something…especially in Washington."

I told him a little about the case I was working on and the dispute my client was having with the Bureau of Indian Affairs. He summoned one of his aids and jotted down some notes. Without me even asking he said, "I'll get something done about that."

He asked about people back home, the weather, the local politics, the happenings at the Arcade Hotel, and just about everything imaginable until he finally asked the question that was really on his mind.

"What are you hearing about the company Charles?" he asked in a distinctly more somber tone.

"It hasn't been real good. Mr. Rutherford has been making a lot of cuts. I guess he has to with the depression and all," I answered. Mr. Rutherford was an experienced executive who had been brought in by J.P. Morgan's bank to manage things after E.W. Marland lost control of the company.

"Rutherford's not a bad guy," Mr. Marland admitted. "He's just been put in a bad spot. If Morgan had stayed with banking…."

About that time, the phone rang again and Mr. Marland encouraged me to stay, but said he had to take this call. I could gather from the one-ended conversation that the subject involved a piece of legislation. It appeared the bill had something to do with water rights. After a few minutes of heated discussion, Mr. Marland returned to our conversation.

"There's never a shortage of people telling you what to do around here," he lamented.

"I can imagine," I said.

"What were we talking about?" he asked.

I uncomfortably replied, "Mr. Rutherford."

"Yes. Rutherford's not the problem. He's just been put in a pickle by Morgan. If Morgan had let me develop the seismic technology and build those pipelines, they wouldn't be in this mess. Morgan could never understand the oil business and the investment it takes on the front end."

"They've fired about everybody from the research department," I revealed.

E.W. shook his head in disgust.

"But," I quickly added, "They are building that pipeline to Chicago."

"We should have had that already built," E.W. stated seeming as if the company was still his. "We could have nearly connected with New York City by now."

The phone rang again and Mr. Marland was involved in an even more heated argument after a few profanities he slammed down the phone and said in disgust, "What on earth is the world coming to when I get threatened by my own party leader!"

It was becoming apparent to me that Mr. Marland had all the personality and persuasive abilities needed to be a politician, but he did not have the temperament or aptitude for politics. I could easily see him as a soldier, defying all the odds and fighting to the bitter end, but compromise and letting the other side win occasionally was not in his personality.

"How are your father and mother? They're some of my favorite people. You should have come to work for me Charles like your father."

His last statement put me in a somewhat awkward position. "Mother is doing great. She's keeping the kids for Elizabeth and me this week. Dad is doing great too, but he's not with the oil company anymore."

I always struggled to know what to call Mr. Marland's old company. It was not Marland Oil any more and I did not feel comfortable calling it Continental Oil Company so I usually just called it "the company." Many in Ponca City, including myself, felt E.W. Marland was destined to come back and start a new Marland Oil.

"He left the company?" Mr. Marland said in disbelief. "Did they let him go?" he asked in a stern voice.

I nodded somewhat sheepishly.

Mr. Marland was noticeably shaken by this news. He whispered something under his breath then apologetically said, "I guess I've let a lot of folks down in Ponca City. They've gone after all my old warriors I guess."

I was quick to respond, "No it's not like that at all. Dad's doing fine. It was time for him to go."

I let this sink in for a moment then added, "In fact, Dad gave me instructions to personally thank you Mr. Marland for all you've done for him."

Mr. Marland was unconvinced but I thought Dad might be doing better financially than he.

"Times change, Charles," he said, "and now we have this depression to deal with. These bankers can make the worst kind of mess and expect the government to come in here and fix it all. I would throw them all in jail if it were up to me. Their behavior is treasonous."

It was obvious E.W. Marland had strong feelings about the big eastern bankers. I suspect he challenged and harassed them as a congressman as much as possible.

After a little more small talk Mr. Marland said, "I bet you didn't come to see me at all, did you Charles? I bet you want to know about Lydie."

I had not known how to ask about Lydie. I was still not totally comfortable with the thought of Mr. Marland being Lydie's husband and it somehow seemed ill-mannered to ask another man about his wife.

"How is Lydie?" I asked now that I had permission.

"She's doing great. You know she was born for this political game. People like her as much as they dislike me," he said with a little jest.

"In fact, I told her you were coming to town and we've arranged for you and your wife to have brunch with us tomorrow, if you can work it into your schedule."

Elizabeth and I did not have any specific plans other than sightseeing. I had hoped to see Lydie so accepted the invitation.

The phone rang again and I took the opportunity to excuse myself. The secretary out front had all the directions and information I needed. Obviously, Mr. Marland had intended for us to meet socially.

CHAPTER 47

▼

Elizabeth and I arrived on the front steps of a townhouse in a fashionable neighborhood in Washington about mid morning. It was a glorious sunny morning. The house was red bricked with a large white front door trimmed in brass hardware.

Lydie greeted us both with enthusiastic hugs and invited us inside. There was a full breakfast laid out reminiscent of a micro version of the kind of breakfast Mr. Marland served on his foxhunts. Mr. Marland was waiting for us in the dining room and we commenced with conversation on a variety of subjects.

The Marlands were indeed an odd couple. Lydie looked beautiful, but appeared to be doing as much as possible in her dress and demeanor to look more mature. Mr. Marland, for his part, seemed to be trying the opposite, which was to look younger. His hair was slicked down and it looked as if it might even be colored. As hard as they tried to match each other's age, the gap in their generations was obvious.

After brunch, we continued the conversation a little longer until a messenger arrived for Mr. Marland. E.W. read a telegram then excused himself. Undoubtedly, congressional duty had called.

I had always enjoyed Mr. Marland's company and had great respect for him. This, however, was my first experience as an adult being so intimate with him in a social situation and I was relieved to have him gone.

"Tell all the real news now," Lydie implored as if we were holding back in front of the congressmen.

Elizabeth and I proceeded to reveal all of the town gossip of which we were aware. Lydie left the conversation open several times to see if we would say anything about the attitude the people of Ponca City had towards her. We really did not have much to say. With Lydie out of town and the layoffs at the Continental Oil Company, people in Ponca City were not too interested.

"Mr. Marland has made many enemies here," Lydie informed us. "He has taken on the bankers and they really run everything in the country. I fear he is making powerful enemies."

I tried to guide the conversation away from politics and even Mr. Marland as much as possible to find out how Lydie was doing. She had been busy going to parties and entertaining constituents of Mr. Marland. She assured us that we were not constituents, but friends. She seemed less carefree than the Lydie I was accustomed to, but still seemed happy. You could easily tell Mr. Marland was the center of her life.

After awhile the conversation became more tedious as it often does with old friends. After rehashing the old times we had little left to talk about. Our lives revolved around two kids and a law practice, while Lydie's focal point was Mr. Marland. Elizabeth and I excused ourselves. We invited Lydie to come sightseeing with us tomorrow, but she declined.

After a brief pause, she asked hesitantly, "I'm going out tomorrow…if you…I mean I planned to go alone, but if you would like to see some of Washington, I would love to come along."

Elizabeth and I looked at each other with puzzlement, but were glad to have an experienced guide. I do not know how enthused Lydie was by our invitation, but we scheduled a time to meet her and spent the next two days having her show us the sights of her new town.

CHAPTER 48

▼

Our sightseeing expedition revealed some of Lydie's quirky behavior I had never before noticed. For most of the time Lydie showed us the sights of Washington D.C. including the Washington Monument and the Lincoln Memorial. The size of the buildings and monuments made them look much closer than they were. Lydie walked quickly on her tour to cover the surprisingly long distances. I was accustomed to walking fast but Elizabeth was not. She had to ask Lydie several times to stop or slowdown in order to catch her breath.

Most of the next day was spent at the Smithsonian Institute. Lydie also took us to the construction site of the new Supreme Court Building. The project was little more than a hole in the ground at this time, but Lydie pointed out a drawing of the building on a billboard that showed an impressive structure with a facade that looked similar to the Greek Parthenon. She joked that I might have a law case to argue in the building someday and needed to know its location.

This part of our time with Lydie seemed natural and familiar. She was a gracious hostess and had a broad knowledge of the history and architecture of the city. It reminded me of the meticulous tour she had given us at the Palace on the Prairie back in Ponca City. At other times, however, Lydie appeared distracted and even agitated. Her eyes constantly surveyed any people who happened to be in the area we were visiting. Several times she abruptly stopped her conversation and ushered us away, almost like she was running from somebody. These instances occurred erratically and with no apparent warning.

One time, Lydie mentioned that she was going to Philadelphia for a few days, which was close to her home in Flourtown. While making conversation, I mentioned it would be nice to go with her sometime to see her hometown, which caused her to manufacture an array of irrational reasons why that would be a bad idea. I assured her that I did not really have the time to make the trip, but she continued to give me chaotic rationale about why I should stay away. Lydie had always been secretive about her past in Flourtown. This was certainly odd behavior, but did not distract from her charm and affability. All in all Elizabeth and I had a great time with Lydie while receiving a first class tour of the nation's capital.

On our last day in Washington, I had one final appointment at the Bureau of Indian Affairs before Elizabeth and I headed out in the afternoon on a Pullman car. I woke-up early to organize and pack. Elizabeth had already ordered breakfast and was eager to start the trip back home to see our two children.

We were recapping some of the highlights of our trip when Elizabeth asked, "What did you think of Lydie?"

"She seems happy," I surmised.

"I guess so," Elizabeth replied.

"You don't sound too convinced," I said with a hint of curiosity.

"It's just…she seemed so different to me."

"How so?"

"She well she…" Elizabeth struggled to find the right words.

"She's older," I suggested.

"Well yes," Elizabeth said in a frustrated tone. "The way she's wearing her hair and the costumes she's wearing do make her look more mature."

"We're all getting older I guess."

"It's more than that Charlie," she continued. "She seems so suspicious of everything."

Elizabeth was always perceptive and she often saw small details about people's behavior that I overlooked. Lydie did seem much more conscious of her actions on our two days together. She was pleasant and willing to go everywhere we wanted, but you got the sense she was always looking around as if she felt someone was watching her.

"She is a congressman's wife," I noted. "She's probably worried about a reporter or photographer catching her unprepared."

"You're probably right," Elizabeth conceded with a look of skepticism.

I was less than convinced this was an adequate explanation, but I had meetings to attend if we were going to catch our train back to Ponca City. For her part, Elizabeth seemed satisfied that I had listened to her and not believed her thoughts totally silly.

I arrived early for my meeting at the Bureau of Indians Affairs. Most of my last evening in Washington was spent preparing arguments and devising strategies to best represent my client. That preparation turned out to be unnecessary. The director of the bureau called me into his office to say everything, "had been worked out," and that my client could proceed as planned without any interference from the bureau. He even drafted a memo specifying the details.

Congressman Marland had definitely gotten someone's attention. Since my client received all I hoped for without arguing with a bureaucrat for most of the day, I had time to head back to the capital to see if I could thank Mr. Marland for his effort.

When I arrived, E.W. Marland was leaning on the corner of the desk in the front office drinking coffee with a tall dark fellow who looked strangely familiar. The stranger disappeared discreetly back into the main office, which prevented me from getting a good look at him.

"Charlie," Mr. Marland jovially greeted with a grin. "How'd the meeting go at the bureau?"

I assured Mr. Marland things had gone quite well and thanked him for his efforts.

"Not a problem," he said. "Always glad to help a friend."

"It certainly helped and my client will appreciate your effort," I assured.

"Speaking of friends, I have one of your old friends in my office," Mr. Marland said as he stood up from his perch on the front desk. Mr. Marland laughed a little then led me into his main office.

It only took a few seconds for me to recognize Willie Cry. He was not a close acquaintance, but I had met him at a few community events around Ponca City and he was a distant relative. We greeted each other with a handshake and talked about our impressions of Washington.

I did not have much time to spend at Mr. Marland's office because I had to help Elizabeth pack for the trip home. Willie, I discovered, was traveling back to Ponca City on the same train as Elizabeth and I. We arranged to have supper with him in the dining car that evening and catch up on some of the happenings at the Ponca reservation.

As I was leaving the office, Mr. Marland walked to the front door and said in a soft voice that was almost a whisper, "I enjoyed seeing you Charles. Lydie was on top of the world getting to spend time with you and your wife."

"Really," I responded somewhat surprised. Lydie had certainly been an entertaining guide about town, but I did not have the impression that she was overly entertained.

"Yes," Mr. Marland continued. "I fear she gets somewhat bored with my old crowd and it was good for her to see some people her own age. She doesn't get that many opportunities."

"Elizabeth and I had a great time. Thank you for your hospitality," I replied. "Maybe Elizabeth and I can stop by and see Lydie one more time before we leave."

"That won't be possible," E.W. stated in a matter of fact tone. "She's gone shopping this morning and I suspect she will be sneaking off on the morning train to Philadelphia."

E.W. Marland's tone and body language was somehow disconcerting to me. It was reasonable for a husband to know the general habits of his wife, but for some reason Mr. Marland appeared to know Lydie's whereabouts in a greater detail than I would have suspected. His comment about Lydie "sneaking off" also seemed odd for some reason. I thought nothing more as I bid him a pleasant good-by. I had bags to pack and a train to catch.

CHAPTER 49

▼

I would have liked to have seen Lydie one more time before leaving, but our schedule and her whereabouts did not allow it. As we boarded the train, it began to rain in Washington for our long trip back to Ponca City.

That evening Elizabeth and I met Willie Cry for supper in the dining car. He was immaculately dressed and sported short black hair. In every way, he looked like a well-tanned, handsome businessman and not the stereotyped native the movies had made the Indians out to be. The conversation started out slow and polite. I did not know Willie that well although we were distantly related in some way. The conversation became more interesting, however, as I remembered the day at the 101 Ranch when Mr. Marland brought my mother to see Chief White Eagle.

"Do you remember that day at the ranch when my mother came to the sun dance," I asked.

"Sure," Willie replied. He was relaxed in his conversation as he smoked a big cigar and became more at ease with Elizabeth and myself.

"That was quite a show," I continued, "that sun dance I mean."

Willie laughed a little and said, "You have that right, it was a show. I mean it was really a show. There hadn't been a real sun dance in years."

"Really," I replied. I realized much of the 101 Ranch festivities had been staged for the tourists but was surprised to discover the sun dance we saw was not authentic.

"I actually saw the last real Ponca Sun Dance," Willie confided. "The 'Gizrs Nkemon', as it was known, would begin on the night of the longest day. The fathers believed that was the day the spirits were most with us. The dance would last for days. The young men would dance and smoke and do many other strange things to humble their bodies to the spirits. I was young, but I remember it being a frightening event. The young men would become delirious with excitement and shout in strange languages we did not understand. The elders would then interpret their prophecies."

Mr. Cry's story was captivating. Willie, like so many other Native Americans, had assimilated into the white man's world and now functioned more or less transparently in the new civilization. Some like my mother had married into the white world while some like Willie Cry understood that when change was inevitable the best action is to adapt.

Willie went on to tell us many stories about the traditions and culture of the Ponca Indian. He, like many others, had done well as a result of Mr. Marland's oil field success. Willie Cry, however, was committed to preserving as much of the history, culture, and even the language of the Ponca people as possible. In fact, he had been at the Bureau of Indian Affairs, as I had, to file a claim and get more information about the rights of the Ponca people.

We talked about my mother and her trip that day. Willie doubted she had any real influence with Chief White Eagle, but laughed a little as he talked about how E.W. Marland did not like to leave anything to chance.

"E.W. Marland," he exclaimed with a chuckle, "is always playing *all the angles.*"

I had to nod in agreement with that statement.

"Do you remember that night Marland caught you guys at the hill by Bodark Creek?" Willie asked. "The burial ground?"

Willie Cry did not have to prompt my memory. The events of that night had always been fresh in my consciousness, although the actual facts had possibly been enhanced through the years. Elizabeth's interest perked up considerably when Willie began recalling the events of that night at the burial grounds. She had always heard my romanticized version and was eager for a more objective perspective.

With a big grin Willie Cry related, "Mr. Marland had 'borrowed' a car from Craigan. He knew Craigan would be carousing and would be drunk as a skunk. Mr. Marland wanted to look at the sight without anyone knowing he was interested in that particular place and needed the car's lights. He wasn't worried about White Eagle like you might think, he was afraid of other wildcatters like Craigan who might find the oil first."

Elizabeth listened attentively and I squirmed knowing the rest of the story.

"Then out of nowhere these two kids showed up. This one," pointing a finger at me zestfully, "and that Johnson kid. They scared us to death at first. Once we knew who it was, Mr. Marland and I tried to scare 'em off but they kept coming and we couldn't keep 'em away from that car. Once they saw it, they took off running and nearly knocked Marland down. I was laughing so hard I nearly fell down, but was able to quit before I caught up to you two."

I had relived this story many times, but had never heard this version. In my exaggerated memory, I could remember some strange sounds but had no idea Willie Cry and Mr. Marland had been the source. I also had no idea Mr. Marland had permission to prospect at that spot. He had simply been afraid that we would let someone know where Craigan's car had been.

"And then," Willie continued now beginning to laugh as he talked. "The others down at the camp….the ones too scared to go to the burial grounds, started a fire and nearly burned the whole county down. I had to run down the hill and put it out. That one kid," he commented on Raeford, "was a walking disaster."

We all laughed at the story and I am sure both our versions had been embellished through the years. Willie then spoke in a more serious tone and said, "But you…you and that Johnson kid, you two never backed down. Mr. Marland always liked you two"

This is another perspective I had never known. It occurred to me that Mr. Marland probably saw Walt and me as I now viewed Tim and Ron.

I could not resist adding to the conversation, "I think Mr. Marland got over liking Walt though."

"Maybe," Willie admitted. "I think Marland saw a lot of himself in the kid. He just didn't like him hanging around his daughter. I saw 'em talking that morning at the well when Johnson got…"

Willie Cry stopped talking abruptly. He had said something in the course of an entertaining evening that he wished not to reveal.

"I saw them talk several times and I think Marland actually liked the kid. Everyone else did."

Willie changed the subject by talking about the Ponca traditions and the ancestry of my mother's family. I tried several times to probe more about the meeting between Walt and Marland on the morning of his death, but Willie Cry would say no more. I did not press the point, but was distracted the rest of the evening.

That night I laid in the comfort of my Pullman car. It was raining outside and the train was making a rhythmic cadence that was generally perfect for sleeping.

Sleep did not come easily that evening, however. The careless words of Willie Cry were haunting me.

There had been gossip in town in regards to Mr. Marland and Walt Johnson's feud after Walt's death. Those rumors had resurfaced after Mr. Marland's marriage to Lydie. Mr. Marland had hired security guards at one point and threatened to shoot Walt one time, but no one took that seriously. There had been the scene at the party that night when Walt had trespassed on Mr. Marland's party and defiantly stated that he would be back for Lydie in the morning.

Mr. Marland had not been around his house the morning of the accident. Willie Cry had said Mr. Marland was a man that did not leave things to chance. By my own experience, I knew this to be true. I then remembered the odd comment E.W. Marland had made in his office. He seemed to know Lydie's every move. Almost like, he was spying on her.

My mind began to think the unthinkable. All these rumors and slanders had been circumstantial and not closely connected in my mind. Coincidental happenings that were unrelated, but now it seemed Willie Cry had witnessed the two men meeting the morning of Walt's death. Besides that, Willie had been evasive about this potentially incriminating information involving his friend E.W. Marland.

Could E.W. Marland actually have had something to do with Walt's accident? He certainly knew oil rigs like the back of his hand. Could he have been in love with Lydie the whole time his wife was convalescing? Had E.W. Marland been planning this most unlikely union for years prior? Was Walt Johnson just one more obstacle to overcome by a man used to getting what he wanted? Could Lydie be in danger herself? All these questions filled my mind and I began to think the unthinkable.

The part of me that had known E.W. Marland since I was a child said no to all these wild ideas. Lydie herself had mentioned the rumors and assured me she gave them no merit. I found it hard to believe I was seriously thinking there could be any possibilities to this outrageous hypothesis I had imagined. Sleep would not come easily this night, however, and the questions of the evening would haunt me for sometime to come.

CHAPTER 50

▼

My client was pleased with the outcome of my trip to Washington and my law practice continued to grow despite the tough economic times. I continued to be busy at work and with helping Elizabeth with the kids, but could not get the conversation with Willie Cry out of my head.

When time permitted, I found myself investigating old news clippings or checking court records for the months before and after Walt's accident. I was even bold enough to question the sheriff, although I did my best to be discreet. Having people cognizant that I might suspect a Marland involvement in Walt's death would mean leaving Ponca City forever. He was a United States Congressman, after all.

He would not be our congressional representative for long. On a trip back to Ponca City, E.W. Marland announced on the steps of the Arcade Hotel that he would not be running for re-election for his congressional seat. Instead, E.W. Marland would be running for Governor of the State of Oklahoma!

It seemed implausible for a man married to his own adopted daughter to be governor but this was Oklahoma and the state was accustomed to its characters. The current governor, "Alfalfa" Bill Murray had made national headlines when he tried to restrict the production of the state's oil reserves by using the National Guard. He made even more headlines when he built a free bridge over the Red River going into Texas next to the Texas state owned toll bridge. When the governor of Texas closed the Texas side of the free bridge, Alfalfa Bill called out the National Guard again to make sure his road stayed open. Civil War between the two states was averted, but Alfalfa Bill got his free bridge opened.

The time was right, I had to admit, for a guy with E.W. Marland's vision for the future. The state had missed the brunt of the great depression in 1930, but by 1933, the economic downturn had hit this region hard. Adding to the misery was persistent drought that had some people calling parts of western Oklahoma a "dust bowl." The ferocity of the thunderstorms and twisters was now challenged by a new threat…great choking dust storms.

Elizabeth and I saw the Marlands socially a few times. I appeared to be a common denominator for the generation gap the couple faced at most social events. I tried to think the best of Mr. Marland and not let suspicions affect my attitude, but found it difficult. It was hard to tell if Lydie or Mr. Marland detected any change in my demeanor toward them, but I found myself trying to avoid Mr. Marland as much as possible.

That became easier as the year progressed. Mr. Marland was hitting the campaign trail with the same tenacity with which he had searched for oil. He discreetly left Lydie behind on almost all of these trips. Some in town speculated Lydie was expecting and there would finally be a Marland baby in town.

Lydie and I talked regularly during this time and I felt I knew the real reason. Mr. Marland was a clever politician and realized a wife, who had been his daughter, would be distracting to a campaign. Most of the state did not know about Lydie and Mr. Marland was determined to keep it that way.

Occasionally in my meetings and walks with Lydie, I would inconspicuously pry for any information about Walt and Mr. Marland on that fateful day. Several times I pushed for answers to my own questions to the point that I feared making Lydie uncomfortable. I could never let my yet unproved suspicions known to Lydie or anyone. Elizabeth was even sheltered from these dark premonitions of mine.

My suspicion and intrusion into Lydie's private life were concealed enough that Lydie appeared to still enjoy our walks together. I could determine one thing from these conversations with Lydie. She did love Mr. Marland very much and felt somewhat lost during his absence. He was undoubtedly the focal point of her life and she seemed somewhat fragile when he was away.

At the courthouse, I stumbled across some notes a deputy sheriff made the day after Walt's death at the accident scene. The deputy had made careful observations about the equipment and circumstances. This particular deputy had some oil field experience and provided a wealth of information. There was nothing suspicious in the report, except two pages were missing from a six-page report.

This was just another item that could have been an innocent coincidence, but my suspicions would not be quenched until I had more answers than questions.

Marland could possibly be governor of the state and he was married to one of my dearest friends. I had to know. There was only one person left that might have answers. I was now determined to confront that person. An investigator from Tulsa had located the whereabouts of Daniel Craigan. I had told Elizabeth that I had out-of-town business, but my business was with Craigan in Erie, Pennsylvania.

CHAPTER 51

▼

I was working alone late one evening in the office, trying to catch up on as much work as possible before the Craigan trip. Rain poured down outside as I calculated how long the trip would take. It would require one day getting to Erie, one day to locate Craigan, and one day to get back. I hoped to put an end to these continual intuitions about Walt Johnson's death, which had been haunting me. I wanted to know the truth one way or the other.

As I concluded the evening's task, a slight crunching sound from outside startled me briefly. It was of no real concern, but in a few moments I heard the clatter again and the noise was becoming persistent. The lateness of the evening and the solitude of the situation caused my heart to beat a little faster. The slight noise evolved into steps and the steps outside were now turning the locked door handle of my front door. The door was solid oak, which made me feel somewhat safer, but it provided no access to see who the intruder might be.

I did not want to confront a petty burglar breaking into the office so I shouted, "Who's there?"

After a brief silence I heard, "It's me Charles." The voice was unmistakably E.W. Marland's.

My slight concern about noise outside my door had graduated to full-scale panic. I had been asking questions for several months about the circumstances surrounding Walt's death. Could E.W. have suspicions of this own? Could he be suspicious of me now? One thing was for sure, E.W. Marland was outside my front door and he knew I was here.

The only thing to do would be to open the door and act surprised to see him. If I were nonchalant, as if nothing were wrong, he would go away and I would be gone tomorrow to see Craigan.

I opened the door and said, "Mr. Marland, what a surprise."

The second part of the plan, to send him quickly away, fell apart. Without an invitation, Mr. Marland walked into my small lobby area. He was dripping wet and had a strange look about him. I did my best to remain calm, but was not confident in my success.

"Can we talk?" Marland asked directly, leaving no doubt that we were going to talk.

"Sure, have a seat," I suggested thinking a sitting foe might be easier to escape. He looked around a brief moment then took a chair.

"Charles, when you're in my position you have to be careful. You make decisions that sometimes create powerful enemies."

I listened with trepidation at his tone.

"I'm fairly used to getting what I want and I'm not good at having events outside my control. You need to know I love Lydie," he said. "A man my age has to be careful though. She's a beautiful young woman and could have any number of men. I feel obligated to protect her. I'm taking a terrible chance with her happiness in this governor's race. I fear she will be subjected to more gossip and ridicule than she deserves. Those strong enemies might see Lydie as a tool to use against me. I can't have that happen to her. But I feel strongly that I have an obligation to run…I want to do what I can while I can to help things out."

I tensed up. My stomach folded into knots as I hung on every word he was saying, trying to determine when the hammer might fall.

"People have been talking Charles. People right here in Ponca City. A person in Lydie's situation can be subject to all kinds of unfair gossip and any suspicion of an affair would ruin a couple who are in the public eye like Lydie and me. They tell me that she has been seeing a lot of one person," he said with a steady stare, "and that person is you."

My face must have fallen nearly to the floor as it finally registered in my brain that E.W. was not concerned about the inquiries I had made about Walt's death, he was suspicious of someone possibly trying to seduce his younger wife.

My look of surprise possibly had more effect than my words as I assured him that Lydie and I had always been just friends. He seemed somewhat satisfied. E.W. Marland was a shrewd card player and he knew how to sniff out a bluff and determine a lie. I felt confident he did not see me as any threat after our conversation.

It was the first time I had ever seen this side of E.W. Marland. He was vulnerable, worried, and afraid. I struggled during our conversation to determine what looked strange about E.W. this evening and it was something I had never seen in him before, fear. His devotion, love, and genuine care for Lydie's well-being were also apparent.

Lydie always said I had a gift for listening and being tactful. Mr. Marland and I had a long conversation that evening. I poured a cup of coffee and assured him of Lydie's devotion. I did not get any relief from my suspicions about his involvement in Walt's death, but I found myself feeling empathy for him. It was apparent our conversation was productive in relieving his fears when he became embarrassed at this show of weakness. Mr. Marland left soon after. The next morning I was on a train to see Craigan.

CHAPTER 52

▼

A dreary, wet day greeted my arrival in Erie, Pennsylvania. I caught a taxi from the train station and headed to the address supplied by my informant. The house turned out to be a large estate in an affluent, wooded neighborhood overlooking Lake Erie. I knocked on the door and was greeted by a short girl who spoke in an accent not familiar to me. I asked to see Mr. Craigan and she curtly informed me he was not in. When I pressed for a time when he might arrive, the maid gave me the location of two taverns where Mr. Craigan might be found.

I found him in the first, a dark depressing place called the Hide-A-Way Inn. It was two o'clock in the afternoon and Daniel Craigan was already on his way to getting drunk. I stopped inside the door to survey the surroundings. It was a long narrow place with a bar to my right and a series of booths to the left. The place served burgers and chops, but it looked like beer was the mainstay. There were two younger men at the end closest to the door having an argument of sorts over what seemed to be a matter of no importance. Two more men were toward the back playing pool. At the far end of the bar sat Daniel Craigan.

He had aged much more than I had expected. Craigan had always been so intimidating to me when I was a child. It was always difficult for me to accept that Walt had actually worked for him. Craigan looked thin and frail. He sat on the end stool alone, looking into his half empty glass mug. It was hard to imagine that I had once been afraid of a character, which now looked so feeble and pathetic.

"Mr. Craigan," I introduced.

He looked at me with no recognition and said gruffly, "Do I know you?"

Craigan was not yet drunk, but you could tell he was unsure of his judgments.

"Charles McDonagh," I prompted, "from Ponca City."

He studied me carefully. It had been several years, since I had seen him. We had never really had much interaction with each other.

"Yes," he said hesitantly, "they call you Charlie…Charlie McDonagh."

"Yes," I replied.

"You were friends with Johnson," he queried.

"Yes, we were good friends," I assured. "Could I have a moment of your time?"

Craigan seemed taken back that anyone would actually want to talk to him. "Sure, let's get one of these booths," he suggested.

We moved into a secluded booth and began to talk. We were strangers with no commonality except time spent in Ponca City and our relationship to Walt Johnson. Walt had been my lifelong friend. Craigan had been his boss. It did not take long to exhaust the small talk about folks back in Ponca City. That left us with Walt Johnson.

"Johnson was a smart kid," Craigan attested, "smart and ambitious."

"Yes," I agreed. "I think he would have done well if it hadn't been for the accident."

Craigan was silent for a moment and took another swig of his beer. With a tone of melancholy, he said, "Yeah, the accident."

I took the initiative and began the questioning by asking, "Were you there that morning?"

He nodded then said, "I had already sold the company. We were pushing to get this last well done so we could claim some royalties. We pushed too hard."

"What was Mr. Marland doing there?" I asked taking a chance that Willie Cry's information had been correct.

Craigan straightened in his chair as if surprised by my knowledge. "Marland…I don't really know. I'd been at the sight all night, Johnson came about midnight to relieve me, but I stayed out there to sleep."

I wondered to myself, if Craigan meant "sleep it off" knowing his tendencies to drink too much. I continued to probe and cross-examine, hoping to gain some insight to the unusual meeting between Walt and E.W. Marland when Craigan finally realized my intent.

Craigan gave an insincere laugh and asked, "You think Marland had something to do with Johnson's death?"

This was the first time anyone had been so direct in their questioning of me. Maybe it was our distance from Ponca City, maybe it was the separation of time, or maybe I felt confident in Craigan's dislike of Mr. Marland, but I felt compelled to finally share my suspicions with someone.

"I think…" I stopped myself before actually making an accusation. "I think it's odd that Walt and Mr. Marland had a confrontation the night before then Mr. Marland shows up at well sight that's not his to have another argument the morning of Walt's death."

Craigan looked at me and laughed again, "Marland, he's always at the wrong place at the wrong time."

"So you think maybe he…"

Craigan cut me off and said, "Kid, I don't like Marland and he don't like me. I bet even you can figure that out. Believe me, I would be the last person to help Marland out. He's an arrogant anglophile that thinks he's some kind of nobility. He can find oil like it's a gift from God. I'll grant you that. Johnson had the gift too. In fact, Johnson and Marland were a lot alike, except Johnson was a good Joe. But, Marland's got the worst timing in the world. He didn't know when to sell in 1907 and even though I tried to tell him, he didn't figure out some of his own people were taking his company and giving control to Morgan."

"So you don't think he had anything to do with Walt's accident?" I asked.

"I was there. Johnson and Marland didn't have an argument. They talked, but neither one of 'em shouted or cursed or anything. I don't know what they were talking about, but they shook hands when Marland left and Johnson was in a great mood after that."

"You say it was a friendly conversation?" I asked.

"I wouldn't say friendly, but it was mutual. It wasn't heated."

I pondered this new information for a moment then Craigan said, "Listen kid. It's the oil patch. Accidents happen. This was a bad one, but it was just an accident. I would love to stick this on Marland just to bring him down a notch or two, but Marland liked the kid."

"How do you know that?" I was quick to reply.

"Marland told me," Craigan said.

"When?" I asked.

"At Johnson's funeral," Craigan answered.

Then Craigan nonchalantly added, "Johnson was going to marry his daughter."

This statement by Craigan took me by surprise. I asked, "How do you know that?"

"Johnson told me after Marland left that day at the well," Craigan said. "He told me he wouldn't be leaving for Bartlesville after all that he was staying in Ponca City to get married."

I felt strangely embarrassed about the unfounded suspicions I had been harboring about Mr. Marland and relieved to know the truth at the same time. All these little bits of information, carried by all these different people, were finally beginning to come together in a picture of what really happened. E.W. had not gone out to execute Walt's demise; he had gone to make sure his future son-in-law did not take Lydie away. Craigan would never have covered for E.W. and I finally felt confident my suspicions had been misconstrued.

I had no more interest in reminiscing with Craigan, so I made a convenient excuse and left to catch the evening train out of town. Craigan had been smart in business and had known when to sell to preserve his fortune. Daniel Craigan, however, was a wretched character, with nothing to show for his life's work but his money. E.W. Marland may have been running out of money, but he had friends and respect from the people that knew him. It felt good to be on the train home knowing I could once again feel good about being one of E.W. Marland's friends.

CHAPTER 53

▼

The early 1930's had been relatively good times in Oklahoma. Wheat was the cash crop and even with the soup lines of the eastern United States, people around the world still needed to eat. By the election year of 1934, all had changed. The persistent drought had caused farm after farm to have crop failures. It was a year of extreme hardship, but most people toughed it out. Most people were ready for a positive change and ready to vote for someone like E.W. Marland.

E.W. Marland won in a landslide to become the tenth governor of the state of Oklahoma. The dim economic outlook, the drought, and the general despair made him the perfect choice. He had campaigned tirelessly with a platform of "Poverty must be wiped out" and Lydie had never surfaced as an issue.

The state voted in E.W. Marland because they were hopeful he could turn things around, but they fell in love with Lydie as first lady. She was young, elegant, and beautiful. Lydie was also well schooled and pleasant. She had organized and overseen the many social events held at the Marland homes for the past decade and was well equipped to be the state's hostess. A state newspaper called her "a princess" and she was the closest thing to royalty the governor's mansion had ever seen.

E.W. was a shrewd politician. He knew Lydie would be a distraction in the campaign, but was quick to capitalize on her popularity. The couple often traveled back to Ponca City to open up the "Palace on the Prairie" for foxhunts, polo matches, and grand parties. For a while, it seemed the ghost of glories past had returned for the Marlands.

I did not see much of Lydie in those years, but I did have a chance meeting with her on a visit to Oklahoma City. Lydie was at the downtown library, across from the federal courthouse, giving an award to a high school essay winner. I saw her and then waited for the end of the ceremony to make my way towards the podium.

"Charlie!" was the warm greeting I received from the First Lady.

Lydie hurried to the side of the stage to give me a big hug. Some of the promoters of the event hurried her, but she asked me to meet her at the Skirvin Hotel for coffee that afternoon.

The Skirvin Hotel had a luxurious European atmosphere and was located downtown, about fifteen minutes from the Governor's Mansion. Oklahoma City was experiencing a modest oil boom and was somewhat sheltered from the depression gripping the nation and the western part of the state. The Skirvin Hotel was a 14 story structure featuring a large ballroom called the Venetian Room, an air conditioned coffee shop that would seat 300 patrons, and a luxurious lobby area with floral upholstered furnishings.

Lydie had arranged for us to meet in a corner of the Venetian Room on the top floor, instead of the more public coffee shop. I was anxious to see this new facility I had heard about and was eager to see Lydie. By the time I arrived, Lydie was waiting at a secluded table tucked away in the corner of the huge room.

"What do you think?" Lydie asked,

"This is nice," I replied.

The room featured paneled American walnut, draped with embroidered mohair, brocade, and damask. The Italian renaissance styling was accented with murals depicting Venetian scenes. The floor was specially designed for dances with alternate blocks of red and white oak, polished to a high sheen. The arched ceiling was covered with acoustic tile and Venetian lanterns provided soft lighting. The room was by any standard artistic, but Lydie and I knew it paled in comparison to her Marland Mansion.

"Yes, it's nice, but they have missed the intricacies in the façade," Lydie added.

Lydie had spent years studying Italian architecture and art during the construction of the Marland Mansion, so I agreed.

"Look Charlie, there's a dance floor. *Hal Pratt and his Fourteen Rhythm Kings* are playing tonight. It's fifteen dollars for dinner and all the dancing we could do."

I laughed a little and said, "I don't really dance anymore."

Lydie grinned and playfully added, "WKY radio broadcasts from eleven o'clock until midnight. Dancing with the First Lady could get you a lot of publicity."

"I don't think Mr. Marland needs that kind of publicity," I said jokingly. "How is it being first lady?"

Lydie looked in the air as if searching for the right words then said, "It's much harder than I thought it could be. People are always watching me. It's hard to let my hair down and have any fun. That's why I was so excited to see you. I know I can speak my mind with you."

"You always have in the past."

"How are Elizabeth and the children?" Lydie asked.

"They're great," I boasted. "Walt's in grammar school. He's twelve now and Lizzy will start school next year. I think Elizabeth feels like she's getting part of her life back, but she's busy all the time with school things."

"Twelve years old," Lydie said with a wisp of nostalgia. "That's how old we were when I first met you and your gang."

"They were your gang too," I reminded.

"What a great time twelve-years-old is. It's so simple and so fun. I think that was probably my favorite year," Lydie said with a genuine smile.

"We had fun."

"Did you hear about Daniel Craigan," Lydie asked.

I shuttered still at the very mention of his name.

"No," I replied somewhat sheepishly, given the subject of my last conversation with him.

"He died last month," Lydie informed me. "Some kind of heart failure. One of Mr. Marland's associates told him. Mr. Marland took it kind of hard. He and Mr. Craigan didn't really like each other, but I think it reminded him of those days in the oil field he misses so much."

I was thinking to myself about Walt Johnson's early encounters with Daniel Craigan, but could not bring myself to say anything in front of Lydie.

Lydie was not as timid as she said, "I'll never think of Mr. Craigan without remembering that night Walt took him to the ground."

I laughed a little at the memory. Lydie smiled and I felt for the first time that Lydie was remembering that story without thinking about Walt's death. It had been over twelve years and I felt Lydie's marriage to E.W. Marland may have finally helped her get over her painful loss.

"It is great being twelve," she said again.

"Our gang did have a lot of fun that summer, didn't we?" I added.

"Things get so complicated as we grow older," she said wistfully. "But I guess that's part of the journey of life."

"I know what you mean. I sometimes walk around town and think about all the things I used to do. Of course all the old stories are so exaggerated now, I don't know if they really happened or not."

We both laughed a little and reminisced about some of the old stories and old characters from our youth.

"I guess nostalgia is happening all the time, but we just don't notice. Someday, even this fine hotel may be just a fond memory," I lamented. "I'm finding out my twelve-year-old thinks everything I do is old fashion."

Lydie then became more serious and said, "I wish Mr. Marland and I had children."

I was a little surprised by such a personal statement but said, "You would be a great mother."

"Mr. Marland would be such a wonderful father too," she added.

Lydie seemed to sense she had ventured into an awkward area of conversation so she changed the subject and said, "Mr. Marland has been traveling all over the state. I've gone with him some. I had no idea the state had so much to see."

"I guess you've been busy," I commented.

"There never seems to be enough time, but I've enjoyed the traveling," Lydie shared. "We have a lot of people that are hurting with this depression. It may not seem like it in Oklahoma City or Ponca City, but when you get out in the country, people are worried."

I listened with interest as she compassionately told some of the stories about the challenges people were facing.

"Mr. Marland is working so hard. He really cares about people you know," Lydie reminded me.

Mr. Marland had always been a good people person and was good at listening to their problems. It did not surprise me that he had empathy for people from all walks of life.

"I know he must be doing all he can," I replied.

"I wish we could take a vacation," Lydie lamented. "I wish I could go back with him to Canada for some rest, but you know him. He's not one to leave a job unfinished so I think we'll be in Oklahoma for a while."

I laughed a little remembering how relentless Mr. Marland had been in his early years searching for oil in Ponca City.

"He is tenacious," I observed.

"I did go on a little trip with him last week," Lydie shared. "We went on the train through Shawnee, Seminole, and to McAlester. They have an Italian restaurant in a small town called Krebs."

"I think I've heard of it," I said. "It's Pete's or something like that."

"Pete's Place," Lydie corrected. "It was very good. More southern Italian than the northern Italian food we had in Florence, but very good."

Lydie laughed a little and continued, "They brew a beer down there called Choc beer from an old Choctaw recipe. I think they were a little nervous that the Governor wouldn't appreciate them serving liquor illegally, but Mr. Marland asked them if they had any of that chocolate beer he had heard about. They all had a good laugh and then brought him a mug."

We talked a little more about her trip to southeast Oklahoma and some of the people she had met across the state. Lydie might have felt a little self-conscience about the attention of being First Lady, but I was becoming convinced she was perfectly suited for the role. Then without warning, Lydie abruptly stopped the conversation and focused on a gentleman across the room mopping the floor.

"What is he doing here?" she asked in a worried tone as her eyes moved quickly around the large room. Lydie's countenance changed as she seemed worried and agitated.

The man appeared to be doing routine cleaning and did not appear to even notice us, but Lydie could not keep from looking at him with a strange combination of keeping him in sight while hiding behind my profile.

Sensing her apprehension I said sincerely, "I'll go check."

Lydie nodded nervously then put her hand to her mouth as I rose to cross the room. The man was methodically mopping as I approached and he did not seem to know we were even in the corner of the spacious room. I could quickly determine the man was no threat, but I asked him if he could work somewhere else for a short time. The man shrugged his shoulders and moved to an area out of sight in the kitchen.

"What did he want?" Lydie asked as I pulled my chair back up to the table.

I tactfully replied, "Not anything, he just didn't know any customers were out in the ballroom.

Lydie still squirmed nervously as she looked around and said, "You can never be too careful. People are always watching. They are always out to get us."

I looked around the room and could see no one. I asked somewhat playfully, "Who are 'they'?"

This question seemed to shock Lydie back to a more realistic state and her mood changed almost immediately from dark suspicion to the Lydie I had been visiting with for the past hour.

Lydie laughed at herself a little and said, "I don't always know who 'they' are, but I still fear 'them' I guess."

I looked at her somewhat concerned, but Lydie seemed to be oblivious to this strange mood swing. As quickly as she had become frightened and apprehensive, Lydie appeared to at least put back on the persona of a self-assured woman.

Lydie and I talked a little longer and laughed a little more. It was as if the strange suspicion about the cleaning man never happened. She asked me one more time if I wanted to dance. I could not really tell if she was serious or just teasing me, but I declined just the same. I said good-by and we went our separate ways and to our separate lives.

CHAPTER 54

▼

Lydie graced the governor's mansion in Oklahoma City for four years. She was an energetic and busy first lady. The Marlands traveled all over the state in those years assessing the situation and selling people on his solutions.

E.W. Marland had always believed in the people of Oklahoma and he was eager to make a difference. He loved the attitude of the people and their rugged toughness. Although many people faced harsh economic times, most were working hard to make the best of things.

This rugged toughness was severely tested on April 14, 1935. The day started as a beautiful, sunny Sunday morning. By noon, strong north winds had blown up the biggest dust storm anyone had ever seen. The black cloud stretched one hundred miles wide and the dust billowed two miles in the air. The ominous cloud of dust crashed into everything in its path at over 50 miles per hour. The storm literally turned day into night and many believed the end of the world could not be far away. It would be forever remembered as Black Sunday in most parts of Oklahoma.

E.W. Marland tried to respond to the great difficulties the dust bowl was creating. As governor, he believed people should succeed on their own merits and that they would succeed if given the chance. Running a state government, however, was much different than running Marland Oil. His tendency to give orders and dictate policy worked well in building his company. These same traits, however, had frustrated him in Washington and resurfaced in his personality as governor.

His plan called for major investments in roads, land conservation, and education. The programs he suggested required investment and that meant increased taxation. Just like in Marland Oil, E.W. viewed spending as a necessary investment. His plans met with opposition from many fronts and he was only able to get a fraction of his proposals through the legislature. E.W. Marland was a proud man and this lack of success in getting his political agenda implemented frustrated him.

Although not a farmer, E.W. was particularly distressed at their plight. He told a group of legislators, "These farmers are living on good land but as a result of the drought they have made no crops and no hay or other feed for their stock, have no grain in their bins; and because of failure of fruit and vegetable crops, they have no provisions in their cellars. These farmers are not on relief and do not want to go on relief, but want to work so they may earn enough to feed their families and their livestock."

To E.W., the situation in the state constituted a crisis requiring swift and immediate action. He suggested a plan to hire distressed farmers to build farm ponds and terraces for the future conservation of the water and soil. He was able to get some relief appropriated, but was not able to get the entire plan implemented, which he felt was needed.

The one thing E.W. Marland could still do, however, was find oil. He got the Interstate Oil Compact reauthorized and even drilled a producing well on the south lawn of the state's capital.

For all of E.W.'s frustrations, Lydie shined in her role as first lady. She was compassionate to the many visitors coming to the capital who were facing grave personal financial crisis. Lydie worked tirelessly for a variety of charitable causes in the state and was generous with her time. She was particularly passionate about the children's hospital in Oklahoma City.

As governor, E.W. was annoyed he could not do more to help people get back on their feet. Since governors could only run for one term, E.W. Marland decided he could do more as a Senator so he determined to run for the United States Senate in 1936. E.W. had made plenty of enemies in his first stay in Washington. What E.W. called "the money trust" was not anxious to deal with Senator Marland. They poured money into his opponent's campaign and were barely able to keep him from winning.

Always stubborn and tenacious, E.W. ran for the senate again in 1938. This time the money trust was even more determined. His marriage to Lydie surfaced in this race and many mean rumors were circulated. Losing a second time to what E.W. perceived as the powerful bankers of Wall Street was a bitter setback to a proud man. Beside that, E.W. and Lydie had begun to depend on the salary of the public office to maintain their lifestyle. At the end of E.W. Marland's term of governor, he and Lydie returned to Ponca City.

The people of Ponca City had long looked for the day when Marland Oil would return. George Marland left the company when E.W. resigned and no Marland had been involved in the oil business in a decade, but people now thought this would be the time. J.P. Morgan had worried about E.W. Marland starting a company and hiring away the many loyal former employees of the old Marland Oil. E.W. Marland was back in Ponca City and the glory years were sure to return.

For E.W. Marland, however, the dream was over. His financial condition had continued to decline during the political career and he never really succeeded in living within his means. E.W. was now older and lacked the dogged energy of his former efforts. He tried to maintain an office in the big house, but soon had to give that up and sell his dream palace. He and Lydie were even forced to rent out the Artist Studio they had lived in. John Forsyth, the architect who had designed the entire estate came back to remodel the Chauffeur's Garage into a two bed-room apartment for E.W. and Lydie Marland to live in.

E.W. still had former business partners and influential people come to visit him, but he was no longer the dealmaker. They talked of the old times and things that might have been. E.W. Marland had made a lot of money for many people, but his personal situation was grimmer than anyone knew. E.W. kept his finger in politics and did what he could to promote the state he loved so much.

The 1920's had been the Marland glory years. The 1930's seemed to last for-ever in Oklahoma and for E.W. Marland. The great depression had been slow to reach the southern plains, but it had been longer to leave. Added to that, the state endured what seemed to be a never-ending series of droughts that caused the eco-logical disaster called the dust bowl. To add salt to the wound, John Steinbeck published *The Grapes of Wrath* in 1939. This book was an atrocity to many Okla-homans who saw it as creating an inaccurate stereotype of people down on their luck. Marland was particularly outraged since this work of fiction did nothing to depict the hard work and ability to overcome challenges he had witnessed in the people during this time.

In other years, Marland would have been on the front lines to defend his state from this slander, but E.W. was a broken man by the time 1940 arrived. Finan-cial conditions had deteriorated to the point that his beloved Palace on the Prairie was sold to a religious group called the Carmelite Fathers for a pitiful $66,000 to pay mounting bills.

The cloud of the Great Depression seemed to be lifting for many people. The winds of war were whirling like a great prairie cyclone. The world was changing, but E.W. Marland seemed to be stuck in the shadows of his past grandeur. Many in town quit asking when E.W. would begin to rebuild his oil empire and began to ask if he would ever be able to do it. The answer was coming with the fullness of time and the legacy of E.W. Marland would be as difficult to predict as the ever changing Oklahoma weather.

CHAPTER 55

▼

By the summer of 1941, the economic outlook was brighter in Ponca City. The effects of the Great Depression were softening and the oil business was booming with another great World War brewing. The Germans had turned on the Russians in Europe and the Japanese occupied much of China, but so far, the war had not involved America.

My law practice was growing and keeping me very busy, but I still liked to walk around town when I had the chance. One early fall day I found myself strolling on the old grounds of the Marland Estate. The leaves were still green and boys were playing football. There was a faint hint of coolness in the air signaling the coming change in season.

The garden was wilder and more unkempt than when the Marlands had lived in the big house, but the grounds were still beautiful in their more natural state. I was looking at the statue of Lydie when I heard her distinctive voice calling, "Charlie!"

I was temporarily surprised to hear the voice, which appeared to come from the beautiful statue. It was obvious the sculpture was not talking to me so I surveyed the surrounding ground to determine Lydie's location. She was calling me from the small porch of the Chauffeur's Cottage.

"Over here," she waved.

I walked over to the small cottage and asked enthusiastically, "How's Lydie?"

"I'm fine," she said in a somewhat harried tone. She looked beautiful, but she was slightly rumpled and looked pale as if she had been spending a lot of time inside.

"It's good to see you. I guess you and Mr. Marland are settled in?" I asked. It had been a while since I had seen Lydie and had not really visited with her since the Marland's return to Ponca City.

"Yes, we're doing fine," she quickly assured.

I could tell Lydie had something on her mind as I asked, "Is everything all right?"

She hesitated briefly, somewhat embarrassed that she had appeared so needy and said, "Yes…things are fine…it's just…"

I waited for her request then she whispered in a slightly softer voice, "Charlie would you mind coming in to see Mr. Marland?"

I was a little surprised. E.W. Marland had not been the kind of man you just dropped in to see. He had been one of the world's wealthiest men, a United States Congressman, and Governor of the state.

"Sure," I said.

"He hasn't been feeling well for several months and has been cooped up inside. I think he would really enjoy your company."

"Of course," I said as Lydie guided me to the front door.

"He enjoys company so much and frankly not many people have been by to see him lately," Lydie explained. "I really appreciate it."

The interior of the cottage was nicely furnished, although the scale of the furniture seemed to overpower the small space. Mr. Marland sat in a chair with a plaid blanket over his lap. He was more feeble than I had ever seen him and looked much older than I expected. He was sixty-seven years old, but had never quite looked his age until now.

"Good afternoon Mr. Marland," I greeted.

He looked up and I saw some of the old spark I had known as a child. "Charles," he said in an excited tone as if genuinely glad to see me.

"Look Lydie, it's my first friend in Ponca City," he added.

I had to smile to think he remembered that greeting after all those years.

"I guess I did meet you coming right off the train," I said with a grin.

"You did," he added.

"Lydie, Charles carried my bags to the Arcade Hotel my first day," E.W. Marland stated. Lydie listened politely, but I sensed she had heard these stories before and wanted someone else to carry the conversation with her ailing husband.

"He thought I would give him a nickel, but all I had for him was advice," he added with a cheerful laugh.

"Never miss a chance to make a new friend," I said.

Mr. Marland slapped his knee and touched his chin, "You remember after all these years!"

I smiled as I recalled those first encounters with Mr. Marland. I also remembered that he had actually taught me a lot about life in those experiences.

"But you did take me to the ranch," I reminded.

He hesitated a second as if to remember and said, "We did have a great day at the 101 Ranch, didn't we?"

I nodded in agreement.

"That's the trip I met Joe Miller," E.W. remembered with a little sadness in his voice. "I always liked talking things over with Joe. I liked the way he thought."

"I remember. That's the night you found out I was part Indian," I said.

E.W. looked up with a smile and said, "That was good information to have. You should know by now Charles that I didn't leave very much to chance. I was an old lawyer like you are now. I knew it was better to know the answer to questions before you asked them. Your mother being related to Willie Cry's family was a good connection for me."

I had to smile a little at his candor.

"It's sad to see how the 101 Ranch has declined," E.W. reminisced. "It was a true Oklahoma treasure."

I again nodded in agreement.

E.W. turned to Lydie to speak. It was the first time I had ever noticed how dependent he was on her.

"This kid and Walt Johnson were always into something," E.W. Marland said.

I was surprised to hear E.W. talk so casually about Walt knowing the kind of conflict the two men had over Lydie. Lydie seemed comfortable with the conversation, however, and E.W. continued the story.

"I was coming back from the field one day when that Johnson kid hurled a rock a Craigan's car," E.W. said with a tone indicating he was amused at the action. "I knew Craigan was a hot head so I rode as hard as I could. Before I got there, Craigan had slapped the kid silly. Do you remember?"

I doubt I would ever forget that incident and said, "Of course."

"That Johnson kid would never back down from anything," E.W. stated in a matter of fact tone. "I had to step in between them or I think the kid would have fought him."

This was not exactly how I remembered the story, but it did highlight the tenacity of Walt Johnson accurately. Looking at Lydie, I could tell she was remembering the night a young Walt Johnson squared off with Craigan. There was a small crease in the brow of her forehead and a distinct look of sadness. I still did not know how to talk about my friend Walt Johnson in front of Mr. Marland and Lydie but I said, "We caused a lot of trouble I guess."

"You were just being boys," Mr. Marland assured.

"It was a great place to be a kid," I said.

"Craigan was always in my business," E.W. said in a slightly more serious tone. "I guess I was always worrying too much about him. He tried to warn me about Haman and Morgan you know?"

"No," I said somewhat surprised at this revelation.

"I was always so focused on Craigan and Morgan that I didn't see what Randle Haman was doing right in my own backyard! I thought he was my friend. Emotional thinking will blind you every time," he said with a hint of despondency in his voice.

I nodded in agreement and admired his astute observations.

"Sometimes you get so blinded by the battle you forget the war you're fighting," E.W. lamented with a little more energy and fight in his voice. "I have no regrets though. I've lived well and made plenty of friends. As soon as I get to feeling well, I'm going to get more active about developing some properties around here. This war is coming and it's going to be good for the oil industry."

I listened in quiet awe of E.W. Marland's optimism and seemingly limitless aspirations. It occurred to me that E.W. Marland's true greatness, the ability to pick himself up and start again, was camouflaged during all those years of extravagant wealth and success. For E.W., it had never been about the money, it was about living life. The goal was to build something and do something great.

Marland Oil was not just a company that made money for him, it was a place where new ideas could develop and people could work to make their lives better. The company was a place where he could create and realize his imagination. The magnificent Marland Mansion had not been just a place for him to live and show his accomplishments, it was a work of art. Something he had dreamed of and then put in to reality.

I remember all the things I had admired about E.W. Marland in those early years. He had not really changed. I had changed. E.W. Marland was aging and in ill health but still, he passionately dreamed of what he could accomplish.

Lydie and Virginia Marland had always seen it; Walt Johnson and E.W. Marland were two of a kind. Walt Johnson, however, would be eternally young in my mind because of his unfortunate early death. For all time, Walt would be a handsome, twenty-five year old man full of potential and promise. E.W. Marland was facing advancing years and declining health with as much vigor, enthusiasm, and determination as he could muster. There was something admirable about the man's dignity to me as he courageously faced the reality of his situation.

E.W. Marland could have grumbled about bad luck, been bitter, or pointed to other people for his demise, but that was not his style. He was still dealing with the challenges of today and optimistically looking forward to the future. E.W. Marland was living as best he could for today.

Lydie had asked me to come in to visit E.W. Marland and make him feel better, but as usual, he had been an encouragement to me. E.W. Marland never complained, never made excuses, and rarely blamed others for his misfortunes. He simply made the people around him better.

We talked for a long time about the old times and some thoughts he had on the future. It was a remarkable conversation with a truly amazing man. He thanked me for being Lydie's friend and said he could not get by without his Lydie. I began to understand more than ever Lydie's respect and admiration for this man she had chosen to be her husband.

As I left, Lydie whispered, "Thank you."

It was I, however, that left that small cottage feeling privileged to have known E.W. Marland.

E.W. Marland had come to Ponca City with big dreams and had lived most of those dreams. On October 3, 1941, the dream was over. E.W. Marland died in the arms of his beloved Lydie…of a broken spirit some said. I like to think he had given all that he had to give. For E.W. Marland the dream was over. For Lydie, the nightmare was just beginning.

E.W. Marland was a man most people liked and all respected. He had been a risk taker and innovator. He was the epitome of the oil wildcatter and entrepreneur. E.W. Marland had made and lost a fortune, but he had made numerous fortunes for others. Most people who knew him were the better for it and that is saying a lot for anyone's life.

CHAPTER 56

▼

E.W. Marland's funeral on a grey October day was worthy of his contributions to life. Although his days as a wealthy oil tycoon had long past, E.W. Marland was rich in friends. People came from far and near to pay respect for the man who had done so much to shape the economic fortunes of an industry. The old train station where I first met E.W. Marland bustled with activity as people came from all over the nation to attend the memorial service.

Lydie wore a black dress that was several seasons from fashionable. She trembled during the entire service, obviously shaken by the loss. Lydie had that far away look Walt Johnson had described in the soldiers he had seen in the battlefields of Europe. It was a look of hopelessness, fatigue, and resignation. Her life had centered on E.W. Marland for nearly twenty years, but now she would be alone.

Human beings have extraordinary ability to adapt to their circumstances. Lydie, however, was a victim of economic extremes. She experienced painful poverty as a child, but had been transported to a world of lavish wealth. Years of extravagant living left her poorly prepared to deal with the more common existence now facing her. E.W. Marland had protected and pampered her, but now he was gone leaving Lydie with very little of the former estate and meager resources to maintain even a middle-class existence.

Mr. Marland was laid to rest in the mausoleum next to Virginia. George Marland was now married and lived in Tulsa. I had not seen George in many years, but he seemed to have adjusted well to life without the Marland's extraordinary wealth. Lydie Marland, who had been protected by the Marland men for so many years, now found herself completely on her own.

As monumental as the passing of E.W. Marland had been, Ponca City soon forgot. War in Europe was on everyone's mind. In December, war came to America with the attack on Pearl Harbor. My Walt was nineteen-years-old and was drafted into the army. I still remembered the chilling letters I had received from Walt Johnson and I felt sick in my soul to think my boy might soon face those same horrors.

Forgotten in all the crisis of the world's problems was Lydie. I spoke to her briefly at Mr. Marland's funeral, but she had not been composed enough to carry on a conversation. I stopped by several times to visit, but she was never home. People in town did not know if she was keeping to herself inside the Chauffeur's Cottage or gone on extended trips. People assumed Lydie had more financial means to travel and live the type of life the Marlands enjoyed, but the reality of Lydie's situation was more dire. Memories of her depression after Walt's death concerned me. I began to be anxious about her absence.

Remembering her habit of walking in the evening shadows, I began to take twilight strolls through the old grounds of the Marland estate. The property was still a magnificent sight, but the Fathers did not have the resources to maintain the grounds as Mr. Marland had wanted. The Japanese gardens were overgrown and few could tell the grounds had once been a manicured Eden. The graveled walkways had overgrown with grass, although they were still visible. The boathouse was gone and the magnificent swimming pool filled with dirt.

The statue of George was packed in a crate on the grounds and Mr. Marland's statue still commanded its spot overseeing the front lawn. Conspicuously absent was the likeness of Lydie standing on the northern edge of the garden. While walking, I remembered the grandeur of the old place in the decade of the twenty's and how hopeful all seemed then. My thoughts were never far from my son's absence, but the walks proved to be a nice distraction.

On one evening, I became a little too involved in remembering the past and did not head for home until dusk had turned to darkness. In the bright moonlight, I noticed a strange figure looking to where the hunting grounds used to be. It was unmistakably Lydie. A light breeze swept her hair from her face and in the moonlight, her pale skin gave the appearance of an angel dressed in black. She stared out over the countryside completely unaware of my presence.

I called out to her and she instinctively began to walk hurriedly in the opposite direction.

"Lydie," I called again, "it's Charlie."

She tried to ignore the intrusion, but I could clearly tell it was Lydie. Her graceful way of walking and overall mannerism was unmistakable. She walked a few more steps as if she did not hear me then hesitated and took two more steps before stopping.

She turned around looking dispirited and then forced a slight smile before saying, "Charlie."

As I walked toward her, I was struck by how somber she looked. Lydie had the body type and facial features that physically made her look much younger than she was. She was 41 years old when Mr. Marland passed away, but she could have easily passed for a younger woman in her early thirties. Her mannerisms and demeanor, however, made her appear tired and distant. Lydie's eyes constantly searched the surrounding area as if she expected some stranger to be watching her. Lydie's dark hair was longer than I had seen since she was a girl and was slightly unkempt. She wore an older, black dress that seemed oddly formal for an evening walk. Lydie's face was stoic and she was so pale that the bright moonlight made her seem to glow. I could not tell if she felt put out or happy to see me. Her face was expressionless.

"Lydie," I began, "How are you doing?"

"I'm out for a walk Charlie," she answered listlessly.

"I see. You always did like to walk in the evenings," I said desperate to get some sort of dialogue going.

"Yes. People don't bother me in the evenings," she replied. I felt like maybe I was one of those intrusions, but she quickly recognized her words and added, "It's good to see you Charlie. How's Elizabeth?"

"She's fine. We've come by a couple of times to visit, but you're a hard woman to catch."

"Yes. I suppose I am. I've been so busy," she answered.

I refrained from asking what she could have been doing in that small house to keep busy and instead said, "There never seems to be enough time, does there?"

"How's Walt?" she asked with noticeably more energy in her voice.

"He's at Fort Sill in Lawton," I answered with some obvious concern in my voice. "He's in training to be an artillery observer."

"I've been to Fort Sill," she said. "George and Mr. Marland used to go down there to play on their polo grounds. I'm sorry to hear that he's off to war. War is such a terrible thing. I will pray for him."

"Thank you, we are too."

Lydie began walking a slow, purposeless walk back toward the cottage so I decided to invite myself to accompany her.

"I noticed your statue is missing? Have the Father's moved it?" I asked.

She laughed insincerely and responded, "The Father's found the statue a little too...provocative I think."

"It was a good likeness," I replied trying to lighten the conversation.

"Mr. Marland always liked it. The Father's came and discreetly asked me if I had some place to store it. I guess the monks had no use for such a likeness."

"Where did you store it?" I asked.

"I didn't," she replied. "I paid the gardener five dollars to destroy it and throw it away."

"Destroy it!" I exclaimed.

"I told him to break it, smash the face first," she stoically replied.

"Lydie," I scolded. "That was a work of art. It should have been preserved."

"I saw no point," she said. "The woman in the statue doesn't exist anymore and frankly the image disturbs me."

I sighed slightly, but tried to hide my disappointment. I felt Lydie did not need any judgmental comments from me at this time.

"All my men have left me Charlie," she continued. "My dear Mr. Marland's gone. George has moved away. I have no one Charlie, just memories."

She was silent for a moment as we continued walking at a slow gait.

"I am so alone," she lamented, "I don't think anyone in the world is as alone as I."

"Lydie, I can imagine the loss you are feeling now, but I think you need to talk to somebody. You've got to get on with your life. You're still young, you have so much to give," I reasoned.

"My life might have been different if Mr. Marland and George hadn't screened my romances so carefully. They would interrogate anyone showing the slightest interest in me. I remember that I was infatuated with a young Frenchmen. He was handsome and sophisticated. I think he was a Count or something. We were getting along famously until George gave him the interview. None were good enough for me, now look at me."

"You still have a lot to give," I encouraged.

She smiled slightly then said, "I lived my life and I really don't have many regrets. I loved Walt you know. He was the one they couldn't run away. He was so brave he was so much like Mr. Marland."

The passion in Lydie's voice was a marked contrast from the rest of our conversation.

"Walt stood up to Mr. Marland and Mr. Marland respected him for that. You probably didn't know that Mr. Marland had given me permission to marry Walt after that night in the garden."

"No," I admitted somewhat ashamed of my early suspicions of Mr. Marland's motives.

"He did. Walt and Mr. Marland had the same kind of dreams you know. They dreamed big for themselves and for everyone around them. That kind of optimism is contagious."

I nodded in agreement.

"I learned to love Mr. Marland," she said. "He was so kind to me. I was always so proud of him. I so wish I could have given him children. He did love children you know."

"Yes, he was always good to me when I was a boy," I confirmed.

"Some days I long to let it all go and let other people untangle the messes, but that would be just one more way I failed Mr. Marland and everyone else who ever cared for me. I'm not as brave as people think. Nobody can make it alone and now I'm all alone."

"Lydie, you don't have to be all alone, you've just got to try," I encouraged. "Come by and see Elizabeth and Lizzy. We can play cards or something."

Lydie smiled graciously, almost out of habit, but I sensed that she really was not listening. She was living and breathing, but emotionally she was not there. Lydie walked a little further then said, "I don't know why they treated Mr. Marland like they did. All he wanted was to build jobs and help people, but they wouldn't let him alone. They kept coming back over and over again for their pound of flesh."

Her tone was ominously dark as she said, "And now they'll be getting it from me."

"Who are they?" I asked innocently.

She smiled slightly, "It's good you don't know all that's gone on Charlie. They tried to ruin Mr. Marland in that last election and they used me to do it. You can't imagine the horrible things they said about Mr. Marland...the horrible things they must think about me."

I tried to console her and encourage her as I had done previously, but this was a deeper darker depression than I had known before. I asked her to get out of the house more and asked her to seek some help, but all she did was politely listen. I had no delusions that Lydie was doing any better after our conversation than before.

As we approached the Chauffeur's Cottage where she lived she said, "I just want to be left alone."

Lydie then left me in the yard and disappeared into her tiny cottage to be left alone and to live alone.

CHAPTER 57

▼

For the next ten years, Lydie lived her life as she had said she wished, completely alone. My mother and father both passed on. Walt had made it back from the war and even my little Lizzy was getting married. Life went on in Ponca City, but Lydie seemed to be stuck in a strange time trap.

E.W. Marland had been a gracious host to many and a generous employer to more. J.P. Morgan had feared Marland starting a new company and many residents in Ponca City had longed for the day when he would reestablish his empire. Those who were admirers of E.W. Marland were loyal even after his death. Some of the senior executives who had stayed through the years with the Continental Oil Company had not forgotten E.W.'s role in securing there livelihoods. They took steps to engineer ways to ensure she received a pension on which to live.

Lydie was rarely seen and seldom thought of during this time. She was like a ghost who appeared in the shadows of the evening. Lydie would be seen occasionally moving from flower to flower, like a honeybee. If ever approached, she would vanish in the darkness, to the illusion of safety she had in her small home.

The war was over and prosperity had returned to everyone but Lydie. It seemed everyone but Lydie was getting on with his or her lives. I had few conversations with her during this time. The talks we did have were empty and superficial. Lydie had wanted to be "left alone" and she was succeeding. The feedback from others who knew her, indicated Lydie's depression, paranoia, and quirkiness were deepening. Although her eccentric dress seemed to be stuck in the 1920's, Lydie held on to her youthful appearance even as she moved into her fifties.

It was hard to say if the over-protectiveness of E.W. and George Marland, her experiences in politics, Mr. Marland's distrust of outsides, or just her own inherent nature caused her eccentric behavior. Reports around town indicated she was suspicious of almost everyone and everything.

For some unexplained reason, this all seemed to change in Lydie's 53rd year. Lydie began to be seen around town a little more often. She had even made a stop by the downtown drug store to invest in some more up-to-date cosmetics. It seemed for a while that Lydie might finally be getting on with her life.

Mr. Marland had known that there was rarely an effect without a cause. He had been an astute observer of human nature. Anyone who would have bothered to employ these inductive abilities would deduce that Lydie had someone new in her life.

There was plenty of idle gossip around town. Many thought Lydie was gone on trips much more than she was. The rumor for a while was that she had a special friend she had met in Washington. Others thought it might have been someone from Oklahoma City, maybe from Governor Marland's staff. In fact, Lydie had seldom left her small cottage during the past decade.

Lawrence Simms was a part-time cab driver and sometimes handyman. He had met Lydie while chauffeuring her about town and later talked himself into some extra work around her cottage. He would come around to do odd jobs and she would pay him more than he was worth. Simms was somehow able to break through her shell of suspicions about other people and became her friend.

This friendship had blossomed into a secret romance. Although Simms was nineteen years younger, the unlikely couple would be occasionally seen walking in the old Marland gardens. The two were even seen leaving the movie house after seeing *From Here to Eternity*.

It is hard to tell how long the romance had been going on or even how serious it was, but Simms was able to talk Lydie into giving him $5,000 to buy a farm close to where the old Bar L Ranch was located. It was never clear if the money was an "investment" or a gift, but that amount of money exhausted any savings Lydie had accumulated from her modest pension.

The couple was seen together occasionally over the next several months. I even spotted Lydie once as she shopped in town. We talked briefly, although the subject of her romance never came up. Lydie looked happy and had regained some of the poise of her youth, which had made her so attractive.

This veneer of happiness was to be short lived however. Simms sold the farm for $6,000 and left town. Lydie was frantic and desperate. She tracked him down in Tucson, Arizona and persuaded him to come back for a while, but Lydie had no more fortune to keep his interest.

The whole affair ended badly on the downtown streets of Ponca City. Simms learned there was no more cash and packed his bags for a bus back to Tucson. The rumor-mill later speculated he had a girl there, but no one knew for sure.

Lydie found out he was at the bus station and went to convince him to stay. Simms, however, was determined to leave. She pleaded for him to stay and then begged him to take her with him. When he told Lydie he did not love her and never really had, the whole thing disintegrated into a loud shouting match in downtown Ponca City. Simms ended up heading to Tucson and Lydie was left alone.

This was the situation she had feared most of her adult life. Lydie had been taken advantage of for money. Worst of all, the entire thing happened in public, which in Lydie's mind validated all the bad things she had imagined people thought about her. Who knows if Simms ever really cared for her or if he was just an opportunistic con man? The damage was done and the fragile psyche of Lydie Marland was further scarred.

Lydie looked around to see what she perceived as a multitude of eyes staring at her. She shouted angrily at the crowded bus station and screamed, "What are you people looking at? Why can't you just let me alone?"

After running out of the station crying, she composed herself enough to go to the bank and close her account. She then went to a used car lot and bought an old car, even though she had not driven a car since going to Washington and did not have a driver's license.

Someone at the bank called her brother George who drove immediately from Tulsa. By the time George arrived at the Chauffeur's Cottage, Lydie had the back seat filled with her possessions and was heading out of town. George pleaded for her to settle down, but Lydie was determined to go. After an exchange of words, Lydie yelled at George and said, "Why can't you leave me alone? You never let me live my life! I never want to see you again!"

With that exchange, Lydie drove north out of town and out of George's life forever. George passed away three years later having never seen Lydie again. It would be twenty-two years before Ponce City would again see Lydie.

CHAPTER 58

▼

When Lydie left Ponca City in 1953, she still endured some celebrity status from her days as the gracious first lady of Oklahoma. The *Saturday Evening Post* even ran an article in the 1950s entitled, "*Where is Lydie Marland?*" There were constant and persistent rumors during these years, but no one really knew about Lydie's whereabouts or her life.

Someone had incredibly reported seeing her working as a maid in a hotel in Missouri. Another thought they saw her waiting tables in St. Louis. All of these stories seemed unbelievable to those who had known Lydie from days gone by. Somehow, Lydie managed to pay the taxes on the small piece of the once grand Marland Estate she still owned. Money would come to the courthouse once a year in the form of money orders or even cash. The postmark would always change: Independence, St. Louis, Chicago, Cleveland, Chattanooga, Louisville, New York, and Washington were just some of the places.

Lydie was on the run it appeared, but from what no one knew. I suspected her own ghost and fears. She had been paranoid for years.

Life went on in Ponca City. The town changed and Lydie was forgotten by all but a few. The train station no longer provided passenger service. The local airport and the nearby Interstate Highway were the new gateways to the world. There were remnants and vestiges of the Marland legacy everywhere. The Grand Mansion still stood as well as the great Palace on the Prairie. Many cultural and artistic relics were still enjoyed by the people of the city, including Marland's tribute to the vanishing American in the *Pioneer Woman* statue.

The company Marland had spawned, the Continental Oil Company remained the area's largest employer. Even parts of E.W.'s beloved research and development department were now housed at the facility. All these were evidence of glory days gone by, but E.W. Marland's most precious legacy, Lydie was gone and all but forgotten.

There were still the sporadic reports about Lydie and hearsay from people who claimed to have seen her. One had seen her at a civil rights march; another spotted her at an anti-war rally in the '60's. Someone had seen her serving food at a food kitchen in New York City. No they corrected, she was eating at the food kitchen. All of these reports seemed fabricated until I received a letter from Lydie after 20 years of being away.

Dear Charlie,

I have no one but you now and I'm afraid I haven't been a good friend for a long time. I've tried to write so many times but feel sick and can't concentrate so I trudge through my pitiful life.

I so much want to see Ponca City again, but I'm so conflicted in my feelings about the place. So many good and so many bad memories from one place. I wonder if my little bridge over Red Bud Creek is still there.

My life has been a nightmare since I left, but I fear the ridicule more than the despair of my current situation. I am a humiliating and physical wreck. I fear anyone, especially you, seeing me in such a state so I keep putting off any hope of returning. For years, to make the money last, I've done without basic needs for well-being and appearance. I've done some very distasteful chores to survive and have loathed the prospect of asking for charity.

I feel like I've been watched for these past twenty years. I don't know why they won't leave me alone. Having sneaks and snoops pry into every detail of my life has been too much. They are ignorant, ugly minds that distort truth and exploit the sorrows of my family even blaming me for some deaths. I'm not a missing person. I've spent years trying to evade their surveillance to no avail; I've never succeeded in being left alone.

I so wish to see Ponca City again while knowing it's an impossibility. I'm sorry to dump all this sorrow on you, but I have no one and fear I must leave this place soon.

Lydie Marland

This letter chilled me. I had heard remarkable rumors about Lydie's life for the past 22 years but never really believed things could be so bad for her. The paranoid tone of the letter seemed acute and I greatly feared for her well-being. Lydie had been the victim of economic extremes. The little girl that came from poverty to almost unimaginable wealth—to the life of a princess—now seemed to be living with the worst kind of distress. I wondered how much more acute that living without the security of wealth must be for someone who had lived with so much.

The letter did not have a return address, but it was postmarked in Washington. The Marland estate was coming up for sale and some wanted the city to buy the property to maintain some of its rich history. After consulting with some of the other old-timers in town, a group was formed to locate Lydie and convince her to come home.

She was located living in a cheap hotel in Washington. Arrangements were made to secure her travel back to Oklahoma and one of the local attorneys brought her back to Ponca City. There was no fanfare or celebrations. As her letters indicated, she was not in a good place physically or mentally. The Arcade Hotel had been torn down, but she was put up in the nicest hotel in town until better housing arrangements could be made.

When I saw Lydie, I was emotionally distraught. We had all aged, but she was thin and looked feeble. Her hair was grey, straight, and straggly. Her once athletic posture was bent and stooped. The lines in her face showed a life with little happiness and few reasons to smile. As I got closer, however, I could look into her eyes and see a glimpse of the old Lydie, that warm and energetic young girl I had met at age twelve. I took off my hat and walked toward her.

Lydie stuck out her hand and all I could think to say was, "Don't stick out that hand to me…give me a hug."

We hugged and I wondered how long it had been since someone had hugged her. She cried a little and told me how good it was to see me and how good it was to be back home. It was an emotional reunion to a Ponca City institution.

The Chauffeur's Cottage, which had been the last home of Lydie and E.W., was in need of some repair, so she stayed in the hotel for a few weeks. People were careful to not bother her, but there was genuine excitement knowing Lydie was back in town. In the course of conversation, Lydie found out the city was having an election to try to raise enough sales tax dollars to preserve the old Marland Estate.

In the late summer of that year, Lydie Marland, a person who valued her privacy and solitude more than anything did the extraordinary. She wrote an open letter to the citizens of Ponca City asking them to support the election.

An open letter from Mrs. E.W. Marland
To the citizens of Ponca City:

I hope the people of Ponca City will vote in favor of the proposed 1% sales tax to run for just 2 years, so that the City can buy and own the "Marland Mansion."

I had not wanted to be involved in this matter, or to have anything to say about it, but in the past few weeks I have learned what the alternatives are, to the City owning this property and I do believe that for the City to own it, is the best answer for ensuring the protection and future of a structure that is unique, and also, I feel that it would add to the many unusual and attractive features that make Ponca City the outstanding city of its size, that it is.

I deeply regret that the Church is vacating the property. They have maintained it in dignity, with love and concern and respect for the man who built it. A quiet refuge from the mad, mad, world outside its walls.

My own feelings about the place are naturally emotional and personal, but I would like to say this much, to me it is a place of rare beauty and artistic integrity. A structure that is an expression from mind into substance, of the quality, and strength, and the heart of man.

Signed,

Lydie Marland

E.W. Marland had been a fearless wildcatter, willing to take on any challenge. I doubt even he showed as much courage as Lydie had when she overcame her own fears of public scrutiny to write a letter of support. The sales tax passed. The Marland Mansion was saved and many felt Lydie's letter had made a difference. Within a few months, Lydie was back in her little cottage beside the big house at the once great Marland Estate.

Lydie's eccentric dress and behavior continued, but she finally seemed to be at peace with herself. She would watch local children fish in Lake Whitemarsh behind the Marland Estate, but she would quickly disappear into her small cottage whenever an adult would approach. Lydie particularly enjoyed talking with young boys around the age of twelve and hearing about their adventures. Maybe she was remembering her own first summer in Ponca City.

She developed a few friends in her neighborhood and although she was never again socially active she was interested in other people and thus became interesting to visit with. She would tell the old stories to the younger people of town who probably felt they were the active imagination of an old woman. Little could they imagine the extraordinary life of this seemingly ordinary old woman. She would still take her walks in the cool of the evening. Many times, local groups would rent out the Marland Mansion for special events and Lydie would always politely ask, "Who's in the big house tonight?"

Lydie had always enjoyed the hot summers of Oklahoma. She had loved the outdoors and particularly loved swimming. It was fitting that she should pass from this life to the next on a hot July night in 1987.

Lydie was laid to rest, next to her beloved Mr. Marland in the family's Mausoleum. A memorial service was held in the Inner Lounge of her great Palace on the Prairie where all those magnificent Marland foxhunts had happened.

Elizabeth was gone from me having passed away the previous winter. I went to Lydie's service alone. Walt had moved to Tulsa, but my daughter Lizzy and her family still lived in town. The children visited often and still brought me great joy, but they had their own lives and I lived alone. Being lonely was the hardest thing I had ever known. I cringed when I thought of all those long years Lydie spent alone. As I loitered around the great room after the service looking at pictures of Lydie and remembering the many years I had known her, a gentleman tapped me timidly on the shoulder.

"Mr. McDonagh," he asked.

"Yes," I replied.

"I know you was a friend of Mrs. Marland," he started.

"Yes," I affirmed.

"There's something been bothering me for a long time. I've kept it to myself, cause Mrs. Marland told me too, but now she's gone I think someone should know."

I struggled to think what the man could possibly have to say, what secret he felt compelled to reveal. I thought I knew most of her acquaintances in town, but I had never seen this man.

"What is it?" I curiously asked.

"I'm the one that broke up that statue. I hated doin' it but Mrs. Marland said, 'Break it, smash the face first then throw the pieces in the river,'" he revealed.

"You're the one that destroyed her statue?" I clarified.

I knew exactly the statue of which he spoke, the life-sized version of a twenty something Lydie that had graced the evening shadows of the north vista of the Marland gardens.

The man who obviously was more at ease doing manual labor than talking to a stranger picked up on my interest then said, "Only thing is, I didn't exactly do what Mrs. Marland said."

"What do you mean?" I asked.

"I had to break it up 'cause she was watching. Broke the face first, just like she said, but it was a pretty statue and I didn't wanna just dump it in the river so I buried it."

"You know where Lydie's statue is?" I excitedly asked.

"Within a mile or so, sir. See I broke it up and hauled it down the old road to the river, but the road ain't there anymore. It got washed out then growed over, but that statue is out there."

I thanked the man for telling me his story and exited the great house as the mansion staff was starting to put up the chairs. I walked the grounds and remembered all that was and all that could have been. I went to the spot were Lydie's statue had stood and just stayed for a while. I do not know if it was boredom or trying to find an adventure like I had all those years ago with Walt. I was retired with time on my hands and determined that day to find the statue.

It took nearly four years and I went through several groups of young helpers to find it, but find it we did. People probably thought I was crazy, but some had thought Lydie crazy too. Oddly, the quest for the statue had given me some sense of purpose and now the statue was out of the ground for everyone to see and remember a life and a time well worth remembering.

CHAPTER 59

▼

I finished telling the story of the statue as Lizzy and Mary sat at the kitchen table with our empty coffee cups. Lizzy had heard parts of my stories many times, but I could not remember ever telling the whole tale at one time. It is difficult to know if they believed my entire account, but Mary at least seemed entertained.

Almost every night I come to see the progress on the statue. It was starting to look like the piece of artwork Mr. Marland had commissioned for his gardens all those years ago. For me it was enough to come here each evening to see the statue and remember the people, places, events, and adventures of the grand era when Jo Davidson had carved the elegant likeness of Lydie into the rough stone.

I thought of Lydie during these times. I remembered how easy she had been to talk to when she first came to town. How elegant she had looked at all those extravagant parties. The look of admiration she had when looking at Walt Johnson and later talking about E.W. Marland. I could not think of Lydie long, however, without remembering the shattered aspects of her broken life.

Lydie had been a poor girl thrown into the tempest of events outside her control. She had lived in great wealth but had also endured many hardships. In the end, she died alone. I often wished she could have been suspended in the time when the statue was carved, in a time filled with such hope and such promise of a happy life. I guess in my mind that will be the Lydie I always remember and I hope others will remember as well.

E.W. Marland envisioned a vast oil empire with Oklahoma at its center. He dreamed of his Palace on the Prairie where he would rule as the benevolent monarch providing the best cultural refinements and quality life he could for the people he so respected. His aspirations, however, were smashed like the statue he had commissioned for Lydie by forces outside his control and dynamics he could not see.

He respected the people of this place he had come to call home. E.W. Marland admired their grit and their determination to overcome any hardships. He demonstrated that spirit by his toughness and tenacity in his early years.

E.W. Marland had promised my mother that when he found oil it would be good for a lot of people. Ironically, many did better from his efforts than he did. People like Willie Cry and Bill McFadden prospered in the oil fields men like E.W. Marland helped develop. Anonymous benefactors like my father who did his job, watched his money, and took advantage of opportunities lived wealthy if not extravagant lives. Countless others worked hard, made a good life, and found their piece of the American dream in those oil fields. E.W. Marland touched the lives of thousands of people he had never even met.

Happiness is contentment, but contentment can be a curse to creativity. Life requires balance between contentment and desire. I have lived an average and uneventful life. I provided for my children, had a loving wife, and lived a good life. For me, this ordinary life was balance. E.W. Marland would have never been content with ordinary. He had ambition to build great wealth and do extraordinary things. Although he earned and lost fortunes several times, for him that was balance. Lydie would have been content with an ordinary life with a few friends and a husband to love. Her destiny, however, was to live a life full of economic extremes and tragic heartbreak. Lydie struggled to find a balance between contentment and the grand expectations placed upon her by others. This is perhaps the greatest tragedy of the girl in the statue.

As the pieces of the statue began to be put back together and take form, it came to symbolize to me the true spirit of the kind of people E.W. had admired. People like Walt Johnson who did not care where he came from or what his ancestry was, but instead focused on who he could become. People who accept every adversity and strive against every setback to overcome the obstacles placed in their way with their sweat, grit, and hope for a better tomorrow. People who would put the pieces of their lives back together again and again, just like the pieces to Lydie's broken statue.

Fiction from Fact

The Broken Statue is a story of fiction based on the real life accomplishments of Ernest Whitworth Marland. Most of the story's elements are fictional, but the setting is based on historical places, people, and events from the golden era of the Oklahoma oil boom.

FICTION

Most of the supporting characters, including Charlie, Walt Johnson, the McDonagh family, and the rest of the boyhood gang are fictional as well as any villainous characters like Daniel Craigan, Randle Haman, and Lawrence Simms. Sacred Heart Cemetery and Red Bud Creek Bridge are also fictional places, although such places exist in other parts of Oklahoma. The interpersonal interaction and personalities of the Marland family and other historical figures of the early oil industry are speculation and fiction as well as any motives to their actions and lives.

FACT

Ponca City is a small city in north central Oklahoma where Ernest Whitworth Marland built an oil company that controlled one tenth of the world's petroleum production in the early 1920's. He did marry his adopted daughter Lydie after his wife Virginia's death, served as a United States Congressman, and later as the tenth Governor of the state of Oklahoma. E.W. Marland did have polo matches and foxhunts in Kay County. He also had a business association with the Miller brothers of the 101 Ranch during his early days in Oklahoma.

Lydie Marland was born Lydie Roberts in Flourtown, Pennsylvania in 1900 and was later adopted by Virginia Marland, her aunt and E.W. Marland. Lydie was married to her former uncle for 14 years before he passed away. She lived most of the rest of her life in Ponca City except for an absence of 22 years. Lydie Marland died on the grounds of the Marland Estate at the Chauffeur's Cottage in 1987.

The 101 Ranch was located just south of Ponca City. The ranch hosted one of the biggest and most extravagant Wild West Shows in the world. Joe, George, and Zack Miller built the ranch into an attraction that brought thousands of tourists to the area and many entertainers including the original "Cherokee Kid" or Will Rogers as the rest of the world knew him.

E.W. Marland's oil company he established in Ponca City was later transformed into the Continental Oil Company, which later was known as CONOCO before evolving into the CONOCO/Phillips Oil Company.

Parts of the state of Oklahoma endured a persistent drought during the mid-1930's known as the Dust Bowl. Alfalfa Bill Murray did call out the National Guard to open a free bridge across the Red River and E.W. Marland did drill for and find oil on the south lawn of the Capital during his governorship.

Willie Cry did lease E.W. Marland the rights on his first producing well and Bill McFadden was one of Marland's first investors. The rest of their role in this story is speculation and fiction.

E.W. Marland did commission a statue of the Pioneer Woman, which stands in front of his old estate in Ponca City. Will Rogers did come to Ponca City to dedicate the statue in 1930.

E.W. Marland did build two mansions in Ponca City and the last one was known as the Marland Mansion or the Palace on the Prairie. Within the Marland Mansion are two statues, one of George Marland and one of Lydie. The one of Lydie was indeed destroyed only to be found years later and restored. The statue of E.W. Marland sets in downtown Ponca City. The mansion on Grand Avenue and is available for tours and houses several historical museums. The Marland Mansion is also available for tours and as Lydie Marland herself wrote, "it is a place of rare beauty and artistic integrity. A structure that is an expression from mind into substance, of the quality, and strength, and the heart of man."

978-0-595-41090-3
0-595-41090-1

Printed in the USA
CPSIA information can be obtained
at www.ICGtesting.com
JSHW022034130923
48138JS00001B/45